A Brown Bag Life

By Glenn Anderson

Copyright © 1998 by Glenn Anderson

ISBN 0-7414-1384-1

Published by:

INFINITY
PUBLISHING.COM

519 West Lancaster Avenue
Haverford, PA 19041-1413
Info@buybooksontheweb.com
www.buybooksontheweb.com
Toll-free (877) BUY BOOK
Local Phone (610) 520-2500
Fax (610) 519-0261

Printed in the United States of America

Printed on Recycled Paper

Published January 2004

To Marlene and Mom

Foreword

It seems fitting that I write this foreword, since it was in high school on the Jersey Shore when I met and came to know Glenn Anderson.

We were classmates first . . . and friends shortly thereafter, thanks in part to Glenn's sitting directly in front of me in every course we shared. While good students who were generally no trouble for our teachers, we spent the majority of our time in class paying attention to each other.

When we weren't trying to make each other laugh, we would talk (whisper, really) about one of our shared passions: sports. Usually, that meant the Mets, who, in the late '70s and early '80s, left a lot to be desired as a professional baseball team. But, it made for some great stovepipe discussions, especially during sophomore Geometry on cold February mornings. We'd also delve into my exploits on the soccer field and Glenn's performance on the wrestling mat.

Although short in stature (shorter than me, even), Glenn was earning himself a reputation around Manasquan High School as a smart, tough grappler. He knew the sport, inside and out, and like his approach to just about everything else in life, he addressed it with black-and-white simplicity.

You either won or lost; there was no in-between. You either did it right, or you screwed up. And you either sucked it up, or you wilted under the pressure.

Suffice it to say I liked talking to Glenn. You always knew what you were getting, and you could count on it being, if not politically correct, most colorful and genuine.

That same feeling was evident when we would discuss writing, our other shared passion. From our days as sportswriters for our high school newspaper, to our similar stints on our respective college publications, we always found synergy, and often refuge, in our love of the written word.

Our lives took different paths after that - mine toward marriage, career and conformity, Glenn's toward searching, discovery and independence. But he never lost that passion, neither for the sport he excelled in while an adolescent nor the craft he honed late at night following long days as a blue-collar worker, first in New Jersey and later in Missouri, where he now resides. In fact, it got stronger.

A few years ago, he began writing and sending a few of us back in Jersey a newsletter he created. It's actually a series of essays that shows Glenn's unique talent for seeing the world, in its basest forms, and being able to put those observations down on paper.

Which leads us to this book, Glenn's first. It won't be his last. The knack he has for exploring human nature and experiencing life's ups and downs – and the rare ability he has for sharing it with others through gritty, realistic and affecting prose – guarantee it.

Pete Birle
Westfield, New Jersey
October 2002

Sometimes you just step in it.

That was the sole piece of sagely advice his father doled out to Thomas when he was a young child. And at 19 years old, while driving to the Church of Christ, Thomas McCloskey understood for the first time what the old man was saying.

It was an absolutely gorgeous and perfect day, something even a rich and fat daddy could not buy for his little princess. But the rest of wedding day amenities were, in fact, obtainable with capital, such as a last-minute wedding date at the Church of Christ in posh Covington, New Jersey, as well as the prime reception time at the Covington Yacht Club. Money evidently also bought a son-in-law, and that's when Thomas realized it – sometimes you just step in it.

Thomas McCloskey parked underneath one of the mammoth and ancient black oak trees that lined both sides of the street, about a block away from the church. He killed the ignition to his 1976 El Camino, and as he looked back at the church, his mind began to curiously wander, an innate trait.

He loved that El Camino, busted his ass in area restaurants to pay for that Chevrolet, catering to snobs just like the ones who were sitting stingily upright, shoulder to shoulder, in the church down the street. Thomas remembered bartering with the bartender from whom he bought the car, insisting the fellow would have to replace the eight-track tape deck with a cassette deck. That should be at least a hundred bucks off the price, Thomas told him, trying in vain to get the tag down to nineteen hundred.

"Hey." The soft voice snapped him back to this Saturday morning amongst the tall oaks. "Do you want to go in?"

It wasn't a harsh or demanding question, but one of manners. Of patience. Thomas looked to his right and fixed his gaze on a petite bundle of heaven. He stared politely and in mesmerizing amazement for a couple of moments as his mind wandered again, this time drifting into thoughts of Michelle. With a sudden start and almost unnoticeable shake of his head, he grunted affirmatively.

The two walked down Madison Court, talking extremely courteously like a couple on a first date. But this wasn't a traditional first date, just one after not seeing each other for several months. They had much to talk about, too much for the short stroll

1

down the shaded street, and their conversation ended abruptly as they reached the towering church doors.

Thomas hesitated. Michelle waited patiently for his decision. He had no invitation. He was dressed in faded jeans, wore weathered leather work boots. And the bride despised him. His mind calculated the myriad possibilities the scenario could produce.

He looked once more at Michelle. She stood poised, always ready for the first step. He admired her confidence. Thomas used to feed off that confidence in high school, and he found himself doing it again.

Walk in. Find a place in one of the rear pews. Offer congratulations. Leave. A simple and honorable plan.

Again, his mind began to wander, pondering the consequences of his actions. What-ifs complicated his young life, as perhaps most young lives, sometimes causing brashness and impetuousness, other times causing uncertainty and trepidation. Thomas wanted to work on this. He wanted to work on many things. . . .

"Thomas." Immediately, he returned to Madison Court.

Eleven o'clock sharp. Screw it, he thought, and he pulled on the massive brass handle.

Freshman

TWO

Friday morning after Thanksgiving
November 29, 1991

The telephone rang incessantly in Thomas' dream. He wanted to answer it but lacked the power. Many times he attempted to stretch his arm and grab the phone, but each time he failed. The phone drifted away, and again he tried. Again, he failed.

The ringing mocked his manhood. He couldn't stop a simple ringing. He couldn't find out who wanted to contact him. He could not solve the mystery. For short periods of time, the ringing would stop, allowing Thomas to think he had won. But suddenly, the silence would be shattered with a renewed string of the monotone ring. Again, the mind would snap to attention, but his body remained listless, motionless.

Slowly, Thomas' dream began to switch from blackness to veiled color. Mental images took on clarity. Then Thomas realized he wasn't in a dream. The phone had been ringing, and he had been mired in a deep slumber.

His naked body was tangled in the top sheet and a light blanket, like the way a vine chokes its way through a hedge. Thomas' initial effort was fruitless, actually quite pitiful, as he reached down toward the floor, where the phone lay hidden in a pile of assorted laundry. He succeeded only in tightening the grip the sheet had upon his left arm and torso. Then he felt the pain, low grade at first, but growing steadily.

It took all of his energy to remain motionless, but that slight pounding in his head began to intensify. A rhythmic tapping stayed behind his eyeballs, and Thomas thought the pain would travel no farther. But his Irish luck on this day did not appear.

The tapping turned to thumping, the thumping to pounding, the pounding marching along his scalp, back to his spine and reverberating throughout his soul.

Then the phone began to ring again. Thomas felt nauseous.

He sprang up abruptly, arms flailing violently, legs kicking the entangled foe from his self-tortured body. The receiver flew from its base, bouncing repeatedly against the floor, calling for an answer.

Thomas could hear the muffled voice ask for him continuously as he grasped the porcelain commode, dispensing the unprocessed alcohol from Thanksgiving night's lonely bender.

Thomas Patrick McCloskey sat on the front steps of the ranch house he bought two years before. Only three wooden risers to the small porch, not ideal for playing stoop ball, but he figured he'd give it a shot anyway. One of these days.

He was waiting for Mark Pierce, who had called a half hour earlier, rambling on about some high school wrestling team and Thomas agreeing to help. As a matter of fact, Mark not only called 30 minutes earlier, but also at ten-minute intervals for an hour before Thomas actually got to the phone.

Apparently, after having Thanksgiving dinner at his in-laws' house, Mark had gone on a mission to find Thomas. Normally that would not prove to be a difficult task since Thomas was a regular at the Cornerstone Pub down in Whiting Beach, but the pub was closed on this particular holiday weekend because the owner was attending his brother's funeral, who had succumbed to cirrhosis of the liver three days prior.

So Mark Pierce and an old high school buddy scoured the shore towns looking for Thomas.

They checked the Laurel Hill Bar, the SandSkrit and Murphy's Law, all near Thomas' house in Whiting Beach. At each bar, the pair ran into old friends and acquaintances of both theirs and Thomas', and at each bar the pair had a beer or two for social purposes before heading off to the next pub. "To spread holiday cheer," Mark said to his traveling companion. "It's a good thing I like the liquor, because I certainly never liked any of them."

With a mellow glow about them, Mark and Johnny Callahan headed 15 minutes north toward Evandale, where rumor had it Thomas McCloskey was heading for the evening.

5

After three more establishments and two hours of drinking, they found Thomas in the far corner of the bar of a dimly lit Red Mike's, two hands lightly clasped around a pint of dark beer. His gaze was locked to the sole television of the establishment which aired a rebroadcast of the Australian Rules Football Grand Final, his ear tuned to Stevie Ray Vaughan coming from the grimy juke box. The aura of closing time hung with the stale smoke and the depressingly quiet conversation of the lonely Thanksgiving crowd.

Mark and Johnny felt out of place at Red Mike's, a feeling they didn't get at any of the other drinking establishments that evening. They recognized no one as they entered the bar. Even after they spotted Thomas, Johnny hesitated, for Thomas McCloskey sat stoically, motionless at the end of the bar, entertaining no visitors, inviting no disturbance. His eyes fixed on the violent collisions of the Australian sport.

As the searchers walked past the smattering of regulars who sat along the length of the bar and in the booths along the far wall, they nodded but said nothing. As they reached the elbow of the bar, Mark bid a cheery 'howdy' to Thomas, who had just finished tossing back a shot of murky, dark brown liquid.

Thomas slowly set the shot glass down and belched, holding back some bile which attempted to escape. He dipped his head momentarily, turned halfheartedly to his left and squinted his eyes. The greeting seemed familiar, almost as if it came from another lifetime. It was definitely distant and out of place at Red Mike's. Through his squinted eyes and his intimidating scowl, Thomas first focused on Johnny Callahan's face. Then Mark's.

His body bobbed back and forth, appearing ready to spring to life in an assault on his intruders. Slowly though, the motion in his torso gave way to life in his face. A smile awakened and the eyes softened. Thomas recognized an old comrade.

"Huh, huh, huh, huh, huh, huh," quietly came from Thomas' throat and was a welcome gesture to Mark. Thomas used the laughter to gather his thoughts. Never good with names, the hours spent at Red Mike's that evening and the journeys spent with a variety of demon spirits the past few years robbed any memory recall currently remaining with Thomas. But Mark was an old friend who experienced some long-ago battles with Thomas. Despite the liquor, the memories came flooding forth.

Thomas rose suddenly, causing his bar stool to go crashing to the floor, and he surprised Mark with a long embrace. I guess it has been a long time, Mark thought. The old friends broke from the embrace and Thomas grabbed Mark's hand and held it firmly, eternally.

"Fuckin' Mark," Thomas said, picking out those words he knew he would not slur. He laughed then repeated the words. Smiling and listening to Mark ask the obligatory social pleasantries, Thomas peered with his glassy and steel blue eyes over his friend's shoulder, "And the fuckin' Squirrel. This sure is an odd reunion."

Johnny hated the nickname "Squirrel." It was tagged on him at age 10 because of his curly hair and peculiar mannerisms. At 25, now a Certified Public Accountant with a matching haircut, John Davenport Callahan showed no signs of the jerky mannerisms which gave him his moniker. Nobody called him 'Squirrel' in a dozen odd years. But he wasn't about to correct Tommy McCloskey. Not then. And not now.

Sitting on his stoop, Thomas finished a cigarette as he pieced together the conversation the night before at Red Mike's. The cigarette made him feel queasy, but the crisp autumn air gave him comfort. It was cold, about 35 degrees, yet Thomas wore only a thin, gray sweatshirt, old blue sweatpants crudely cut into shorts, and a pair of construction boots, no socks. He wore a wrestling singlet under the shorts, the shoulder straps pulled down and resting on his hips. Sunglasses blocked the thin rays of the sun, which were trying to muscle through thin cloud cover.

Mark Pierce, he thought. How the hell did he find me? And why the hell did he want to find me? Wrestling was a thing of the past, and so were old friends. Mark had to have known that. Ever since Mark married into money, their friendship began to deteriorate. Mark sought fame and fortune. Thomas sought – well, he couldn't answer that succinctly, but he knew neither fame nor fortune aroused him.

But if Mark needed help and Thomas promised that help, drunk or not, he was obligated to keep his word. Thomas figured he could help get this high school wrestling program started and then bid the sport farewell for a second time.

A pack of red Marlboros sat luringly on the stoop next to him. Thomas hated being bored because that usually meant lighting up. He grabbed the soft pack and knocked a cigarette from the small opening. He had been awake for 20 minutes and this would be his fourth cigarette.

He just finished the last drag and flicked the butt onto the unkempt lawn when a shiny, black Blazer pulled into his driveway. The electric, tinted window buzzed downward and Mark Pierce smiled. "Ready to rumble?"

Nice car. Nice pearly smile. Daddy-in-law must be treating you good. Thomas stared through his sunglasses, took a deep breath and stood up. He immediately felt light-headed and nauseous, and he knew exactly what to do. He leaned over the wrought-iron railing and puked into the dormant azalea bush.

The old man was right. Sometimes you just step in it. And today, it really did stink.

Saint Agnes High School and Church are tucked between modest two-family homes on 10th Avenue in Evandale, some seven blocks away from Red Mike's. Facing the secondary school, it looks like a huge split-level house. To the left, the library is situated behind the grand foyer, guarded by plate-glass windows standing erect from ceiling to ground, appearing like holy war crusaders. Within the foyer, visitors are greeted by the trophy case, its shiny and glittering presence creating an immediate grandeur to the entrance.

The case is of enormous and elegant design, displaying a plethora of academic awards ranging from English to science; club awards such as chess and fencing; and state sanctioned sporting trophies from primarily the two sports of cross country and basketball.

To the right of the library, the edifice rises to magnificent and mysterious heights for its neighborhood. Ten marble steps, a slate platform and eleven more marble steps lead to the recently renovated gymnasium. The old gym, nicknamed "The Phone Booth" because of its quaint environment, suffered a fire a few years back which destroyed the roof and much of the bleacher sections. With a state-of-the-art fire and safety system and additional seating for 200 fans, the new gymnasium held onto the same mystique as the old, packing in hordes of loyal alumni, dedicated parents and students as well as sundry locals, creating deafening sounds that are said to disturb Saturday confessions at the adjacent church.

Up until the fire in 1981, the St. Agnes gym was home to eight small-school parochial state championships for the boys' teams and three for the girls.' In the new era, dubbed A.D. for "After Destruction," the boys added three sectional championship banners, the girls two – one of which was the overall statewide championship, large and small schools included, quite a feat for this tiny private school. The rabid basketball fans flocked to the venerable site every winter to see their beloved Lancers. Thomas wondered how a wrestling team would be received in this milieu. Not very well.

The Lancers. He laughed to himself as Mark and he walked up to the foyer doors. The Lancers had no football squad – unusual for a high school program in the state – so for years the basketball players carried the staff as the hippest and toughest guys in the school. But contemporary high school outsiders knew that the St. Agnes cross country runners were the smartest athletes the school would produce for they could outrun any trouble. That was the joke way back in high school. Could still be, a smile crossing Thomas' face, a low laugh coughing forth.

Back as far as local history speaks, every time St. Agnes basketball players met up with Covington High School kids at the beach or at a weekend party, the Lancers ended up humiliated, skipping away with minor bumps and bruises, and dented prides. That led to the nickname "The Dancing Prancers," a term not recognized then and never uttered in the old or new Phone Booth.

Recalling some of the students he knew who had attended St. Agnes, Thomas laughed again. How the hell was Mark going to find anyone tough enough to make it through one wrestling practice? How was Mark going to find anyone not on the basketball team or in the basket weaving club?

"What's so funny?" Mark asked as the two descended a flight of steps leading to the cafeteria.

"You're in a world of hurt, kiddo. If I realized last night that you meant St. Agnes, I would have talked you out of it instead of you talking me into it."

"It'll be fine," Mark said. "Trust me, Tommy."

Trust me. Thomas never liked that phrase; he thought it was a contradiction in itself. Anyone using it probably couldn't be trusted. It was the first time Mark ever used that phrase with Thomas. And it was the first time Thomas got a queer feeling in his gut about his old friend's intentions.

With winter sport tryouts beginning on the traditional day-after-Thanksgiving, the state mandate, the echo of dribbling basketballs drifted into the serenity of St. Agnes cafeteria, which is situated directly below the north end of the gymnasium.

As Mark and Thomas walked through the swinging doors into the dim cafeteria, the first thing Thomas noticed was six, two-foot square, concrete pillars evenly spaced around the room and decorated with tiled scenes of Christ's walk to Calvary. The next thing he noticed was a man rising from the corner of the cafeteria, moving quickly toward them.

"HeyMarkHowYaDoin'?" He said the greeting so fast, Thomas actually didn't understand. "ThomasMcCloskeyIBelieve. I'veHeardAlotAboutYou."

Maybe it's the hangover, Thomas thought, but he could not understand a thing the man was saying. Playing it safe and keeping the conversation to a minimum, Thomas squeezed out a hello.

"Well, what do you think guys? Do you want to get started?" the man asked, turning away from his two guests as quickly as he approached them. He returned to the table where he was reading a newspaper, neatly and methodically folded the periodical until it appeared freshly printed, grabbed his coat and his hat, turned and said, "Let's go."

Christ, the guy's like a whirling dervish. Thomas eyed him up closely, noting his jerky movements. If he wrestles as quickly as he rambles, Thomas would need to find a way to slow him down. A head butt would work.

The man walked between Mark and Thomas and swiftly moved back toward the swinging doors. Mark began to follow, but Thomas remained motionless.

"Hey Tommy, you coming?"

"Where you heading?" The words were asked in a deliberately slow fashion.

"Oh, we're going over to the community pavilion," the man said. "That's where the mats were delivered."

Thomas breathed deeply. His head was hurting tremendously, and it was about that time to clear some more bile from his stomach. "You're not going to be wrestling here?" he asked calmly, incredulously.

"Oh no, no. The principal determined that there's no room for a wrestling team on the school grounds. The gentleman who

10

has financed the wrestling team has rented space at the community pavilion three hours a day for the next three months. That's where we'll be wrestling."

Thomas still didn't understand a word the man said. "What?"

"We have to go over to the pavilion, over on 21st – off the inlet," Mark said cautiously, knowing that Thomas' patience wasn't worth testing.

"What, are you his fuckin' interpreter?" As soon as the words left Thomas' mouth, he wished he could have had them back. Not a great first impression, but then again, fuck 'em. "Will the kids be there today?" The question was directed at the man.

The 40-year-old man was bewildered. Language that was just displayed was not tolerated in this school – ever. He would not be insulted, and he expressed himself thusly.

The wrestling shoes, tied together by their shoestrings, hung from Thomas' neck, one shoe resting its toe in each armpit. He closed his eyes, took a deep breath and took hold of a wrestling shoe heel with each hand. "Awright. Let's back up. You know my name is Tommy McCloskey. What's yours?"

"I'm Kenneth Lawton, the biology and chemistry teacher."

"Okay Kenneth Lawton. What time are the kids coming.?"

"We had a sign-up sheet passed around this past Wednesday, just two days ago, with a note on the bottom that an announcement would be made on the following Monday regarding practice and times."

"So the kids won't be here today?" Thomas knew this was rhetorical.

"No." Mr. Lawton hesitated for he felt that his message was falling upon deaf ears. "There won't be an announcement until Monday." His speech bore condescending clarity as he enunciated slowly and deliberately for this sloth before him.

Thomas stared, then nodded and turned his attention toward Mark. "Why don't you take Mr. Kenneth Lawton here over to the community pavilion and roll out the mats and then give them a good scrubbing, assuming, of course, you have shit to scrub them with. In the meantime, I'm going to catch a ride home on the train. If you still need my help, call me on Monday with an announcement regarding practice and times."

He turned and headed for the door, shaking his head.

"Wait a second, Tommy," Mark said, pleadingly, somewhat pathetically. "We need to do some planning and get coordinated on this deal. We need to get some work done."

Thomas turned ever so slowly and flashed a terrifying look which startled and intimidated Kenneth Lawton, the biology and chemistry teacher at St. Agnes High School. Mark remembered that look. Thomas used to wear it just before walking out onto the mat for competition. It sent shivers shuddering through Mark's body almost a decade ago, and he felt that quivering sensation shoot from his tailbone into his head on this day. Mark was prepared for the upcoming and inevitable barrage.

"Let me tell you something," Thomas started, more subdued than usual. "The planning you fellows need to do should have been done long before today. Thirty-nine other schools in the Shore Conference are beginning their practices today, half of those going at full speed. Sipping coffee and reading newspapers isn't going to get it done, gentlemen."

Mr. Lawton took offense. "These students at St. Agnes are an extremely intelligent lot," he proclaimed. "When their feet get put to the fire, they will be prepared."

Prepared for what, ultimate humiliation? Thomas Patrick McCloskey was not ready on this particular Friday to have a petty argument of this nature. His brain simply was too tired. "You have no idea what you're getting into." His voice was serene. "If you still want my help, you have it. But only when the kids are here."

He turned and headed out to the railroad station, hoping he remembered to stick his wallet into one of his wrestling shoes.

THREE

Scotty was tired of playing and had completed his business. He had been out playing in the Cambridge neighborhood most of the afternoon and was quite thirsty. So he decided to make his way back through the large estate backyards, running between the shapely hues and over the manicured swards. The barren sycamore branches that towered far above the scotch terrier's head provided a pattern of web-like shadows for the rapidly fading afternoon sun. Scotty was not aware of those shadows, nor was he cognizant of the squirrels gathering supplies for the inevitably bitter Boston winter. It was getting frigid on this November afternoon, and a good meal and a quiet fire would do nicely.

He carefully slipped through the rubber flap at the bottom of the chauffeur's door, remembering quite vividly how he used to knock his head as he jumped over the saddle when he was a pup. Once inside the garage, Scotty stopped and shook any unwanted parasitic hitchhikers from his coat, then trotted past a Chevrolet Suburban, used primarily for hunting trips into New Hampshire; a Ford conversion van, complete with a small television, a bar, and six captain chairs, used for New England Patriot home football games and Boston College soccer games; a black Cadillac stretch limousine used for business excursions; a four-door Lincoln Town Car; and a navy blue Mercedes 450 SL with a white convertible top. The last two being personal vehicles for the man and woman of the house, respectively.

A left and a sharp right brought Scotty into the 20-foot tunnel that connected the garage, built into the side of a knoll, to the basement of the three-story, 10-bedroom, English Tudor mansion. Scotty often rode the elevator up the two flights to the kitchen if Kent, the family chauffeur, was around to push the buttons. But with nobody to help, the famished scotch terrier went to the back staircase at the far corner of the utility room, and ambled up to the kitchen.

Much to the delight and chagrin of Scotty, a soiree of some sort was taking place. That meant Sally would sneak him some tasty morsels of all kinds before taking the platters to the less appreciative guests. That also meant that his plan to curl up in front of the living room fireplace – his favorite spot in the house – was out of the question. A cocktail party full of lawyers, doctors, bankers, politicians and their wives was no place to relax after an exhausting afternoon. Scotty filled up on a variety of hors d'oeuvres before disappearing back down the stairs, presumably to scout out and spend some time with Kent.

Inside the living room, the crystal champagne glasses were raised in honor of friends and family during the Thanksgiving celebration. This particular group – self-proclaimed dignitary – had much to give thanks for but did not quite grasp the concept of giving. Sure, the tax returns were laden with various donations, but "stingy" would best describe that ratio in terms of wealth. Ignorant nevertheless, the glasses were raised for the annual toast on the Friday following Thanksgiving at the Aldrich residence. Giving the invocation for the first time was the eldest Aldrich son, Todd O'Malley Aldrich, who had graduated from Harvard Law School the previous spring, not in superfluous fashion, but all Crimson nonetheless.

Todd O'Malley Aldrich, the baptized middle name derived from his maternal grandfather, had much to celebrate. He was handsome and charismatic. Standing at 6 foot 1, he displayed a magnificent physique at which he worked effortlessly by playing racquetball and golf. After interning as a law clerk in Washington, D.C. for the summer and much of the fall, he was offered a position in the powerful law firm of Smith, Lewis and Bennett, all that despite finishing with modest grades at Harvard. Of course, when your father is a New England shipping magnate and an uncle is a congressman on the Ways and Means Committee, final grades at Harvard don't mean a whole hell of a lot.

What meant most on this evening, though, was the presence of Michelle Jennings. Simply put, Todd Aldrich was still smitten with this beautiful delight. They had been dating for close to three years, and much of his idle time was spent thinking of her. And with the toast bequeathed to him by his father, by design, Todd planned on keeping her in his thoughts forever.

Michelle stood to his left, listening to him ramble on about the relationship between the indigenous peoples and the early settlers of North America. She looked gorgeous and professional. A long black skirt with its slit cut halfway to the middle of the thigh accentuated her athletic legs, which she owed to four years at Boston College as a striker on the soccer team. A white silk blouse with the buttons in the back flowed amiably down a perfect chest. A red Eisenhower jacket magnified the breadth of her shoulders and the slimness of her waist. A mere delight.

"So tonight we give thanks," Todd O'Malley Aldrich said, "not only to the people who gave us this wonderful tradition, but also to the people who we so deeply love." Todd held the glass high aloft in his right hand and lightly brushed back Michelle's shoulder-length black hair with his left. He professed his love for her in front of all the distinguished guests, and lowering the glass directly in front of Michelle's eyes asked for her hand in marriage.

Michelle was dumbfounded. She knew the question would be presented someday, even one day soon. But not this soon. Not in front of all these people. The embarrassment slowly turned to realization, for at the bottom of the glass held by her suitor were a spectra of dazzling and glorious sparkles. Those sparkles drifted forth with every bubble of champagne, shining like colorful stars over the countryside.

Warmth overtook Michelle, but initially she was not as ecstatic as she thought she would be. Todd and she had naturally discussed the probability of marriage, and after three years, the prospect seemed logical. But she seemed more like a sister in the Aldrich family than a bride-to-be. A thousand or more thoughts in a millisecond of time.

She stared at the sparkling and distorted diamonds. Was everybody waiting for an answer? Or had everybody just assumed the answer was yes? Michelle knew what she had to do. She had thought about it before. It was her duty.

She smiled and put her arms around her fiance.

"NO WAY!"

Tamantha Jennings was lying on her bed in the dormitory at Chesterton State when her sister called her about the news. A resident assistant in Dunlow Hall, she came back from an abbreviated holiday break because it was her weekend on the schedule, a 48-hour shift starting at 3 p.m. Friday.

Of course, none of the 250 female residents were at the dorm because of Thanksgiving break, so that was some consolation for Tamantha. A couple of hours after getting back and checking to see if anyone had, in fact, returned for the weekend, Tamantha spread out her books all over the single room on the first floor and began working. She had two term papers due within 10 days and three tests the upcoming week. A 45-minute rotation on each subject would keep her going well past midnight.

The phone rang at 12:30. Tamantha figured it was her mother calling to see if she made it back and was not, in fact, stranded on the Garden State Parkway. "You should get a cellular phone," her mother constantly bugged her. "You never know if your car will run out of gas or if someone is stalking you." Tamantha would always smile at her mother's paranoid reasoning. When she got a full-time teaching job, she'd think about a pocket phone. In the meantime, she wouldn't let the gas tank go below half, and she would keep a can of mace with her in case of stalkers. Appeasement for her mother, not safety for herself.

It was a pleasant surprise to hear Michelle's voice instead. Tamantha had just spoken to her Thursday afternoon when Michelle called home to wish everybody well and to apologize for not being there. The two sisters talked at length, and that usually kept them satisfied for a week.

Books and papers were scattered in all directions when Michelle dropped the bomb. "No Way! No Way!" is all the younger Jennings could muster. Michelle always spoke highly of Todd, but Tamantha never thought it would lead to marriage. It just wasn't meant to be. As storybook as it seemed to move to Boston and marry a member of the old guard, the ending never appeared a happy one to Tamantha. But she feigned her exuberance nonetheless for her older sister's bliss.

"Tammy, it's just so beautiful. It's diamond-shaped with a semi-circle of smaller tear-shaped diamonds on the top and rubies underneath. I didn't know what he was doing holding the glass so close to my nose."

"Did you set a date yet?" asked Tamantha. "Am I invited?"

"Well, we figured that next spring is too soon. Todd thinks that being the new boy in the firm will keep him too busy to think about a marriage so soon. And he doesn't want a marriage in the fall – 'That will interfere with football season,' " Michelle dropped her voice mocking her fiance. "That leaves the spring of

16

'93. But of course, Todd was a little drunk when we discussed this. So this is all tentative. And no, you're not invited."

"Where is he now?"

Flopped face-up and diagonally across the queen-size bed in Michelle's bedroom, Todd snored obnoxiously. The knot of his tie was loosened, but the tail was snaked around his shoulder and stuck underneath him. The blue pinstriped pants of a Brooks Brothers suit were unzipped and the boxer shorts bunched up around the zipper. One wing tip sat on the bureau, the other remained on his left foot.

Someday, he would be married. Someday, he would run for the state senate. Tonight, he would urinate in his $250 Brooks Brothers pants.

Red Mike's was busy for a Sunday night. The long holiday weekend was the unofficial start of the Yuletide in the tri-state area, and all the locals were getting primed for the month-long party, which culminated in the annual Red Mike's "Seeing Red" New Year's Eve party. Thomas didn't like the festivities. He had a great disdain for all holidays, especially Christmas, and he didn't like bubbly people shuffling over to his dark corner to wish him well.

Thomas had a routine for most of the year. On Mondays, he normally would not go out, except for football season when he walked the three blocks to the Laurel Hill Bar. The bartender took book, and although Thomas didn't bet on any of the Sunday games, he would lay a five-timer down on Monday just to get himself out of the house. Through the course of the year, he would break even.

Tuesdays, Wednesdays and Thursdays, without fail, if Thomas went out, he could be found at the Cornerstone Pub. Across the street from the ocean, the Cornerstone was a sports bar with 10 televisions evenly spaced high along the perimeter and two large screens at each end of the bar. From Memorial Day to Labor Day when the college kids and the New York yuppies converged on Whiting Beach for some binge drinking, Thomas headed over to Murphy's Law, where the 30-and-over local crowd frolicked.

Thomas despised crowds and lines, and on the weekends the Cornerstone had both, even in the men's bathroom. Friday and Saturday nights, he headed over to the SandSkrit, about a half mile from the Cornerstone. It was about half the size with twice the amount of snobs, but they were local snobs whom Thomas had known all his life. He wouldn't go to the SandSkrit straight from work all grungy, but instead he would go home, make himself presentable in high expectations of bedding one of the middle-aged beauties. "They're not looking at me for marriage," Thomas would say. "They're looking for someone who won't fall asleep in 15 minutes."

Exclusively, throughout the entire year, Sunday's were spent at Red Mike's. Most of Red Mike's clientele were older drinkers who came in to watch the national news and *Jeopardy* on weekdays, and golf on the weekends. By Sunday night, Thomas usually was back in the corner of the bar, facing the door, eyes fixed on the TV which sat just above it. His eyes undauntedly remained locked on a sporting event, his mind usually elsewhere. If an unwanted visitor would happen through the door, Thomas would wait a few seconds, take a sip of beer, and then head to the bathroom. This was a foolproof, preventative measure to assure his solitude.

Old Man Jack was the one person who sat near Thomas at Red Mike's. A frequent patron of the racetrack, Jack would drool on the tip of his Hemingway cigars, sip his Jack Daniel's on the rocks with a splash of water and study the *Daily Racing Form* and other assorted scratch sheets. Jack and Thomas would strike up conversations on sports, politics and women, sporadically, on Sunday nights.

"Don't you guys ever talk about anything else?" Bobby the bartender would ask, chiding the old man.

Jack would growl back, usually saying "a good game, a good lie and a good lay is all you need in this life. Get me a Jack Daniel's."

On this Sunday evening, with the crowd being so festive in honor of spending another year's end holiday in a dimly lit tavern, Jack and Thomas sat quietly at the short end of the bar, the customary empty stool between them. Jack was studying the Monday's entries for the trotters at Freehold Raceway. Thomas was deep in thought.

He never had a chance to sneak off to the bathroom to avoid Jimmy Zinno, otherwise known as Jimmy the Cut. Slapping Thomas on the back and letting out a thunderous guffaw, Jimmy the Cut sat in the empty chair, not noticing the uninviting stare from Jack and too drunk to interpret the menacing look from Thomas.

"What a coincidence," Jimmy said. "Me and Tony were just talking about you last night."

Thomas took a deep breath to prepare himself for an inevitably long and boring story. Christ, he thought, what the hell would the Zinno brothers be talking about me for, and how could Jimmy possibly remember it 24 hours later. He laughed. "Yeah, what about, Jimmy?"

Jimmy didn't get right to the point. Instead he ordered himself a pint of Killian's, which he spilled a quarter of back onto the bar trying to pick it up, then traveled into a long, laborious history of how Thomas and the Zinno boys met. "We sure did have some fun," he kept saying.

In the middle of Jimmy's left eyebrow, a chunk of hair was missing. On the bridge of his crooked nose was the shape of a horseshoe scar, facing in the unlucky position of open-end down. Two scars were marked on each side of his chin. These all were lasting reminders of how Jimmy got the nickname "the Cut."

The Zinnos had moved with their mother to Whiting Beach from Brooklyn a year after their father died in a car accident back in the early '70s. Being the only Italians in a predominantly Irish area, the Zinnos were subjected to many cruelties. The most vicious was a rumor that Mrs. Zinno, being a single mom before it became fashionable, turned to prostitution to support the family.

Jimmy was 10 at the time and being two years older than his brother Tony, was forced to preserve all family honor. He fought anybody and everybody who dared to speak of this rumor in his or his brother's presence. He was one of the smallest kids in the class, but that merely fueled his tenacity, for he battled until he was sure his opponent would never utter the rumor again.

Jimmy was a big boxing fan, and at the time Vito Antefuermo was a Brooklyn-bred challenger for the middleweight title. Antefuermo had one glaring deficiency, and that was that he was prone to bleeding – excessively at times. Jimmy bled excessively, too, and two nicknames were born. "Vito," which Jimmy preferred. And "Jimmy the Cut," which stuck.

"So last night, Tony comes up to me and he says, 'Guess who I just heard is getting hitched?' And he tells me your old flame Michelle Jennings found some starched shirt up in Boston with tons of money." Jimmy stole a cigarette from Thomas' pack on the bar, lit it, inhaled and blew out a massive plume of smoke, suffocating Thomas even more than he could have imagined.

"I couldn't fuckin' believe it. You know out of all the couples in high school you thought would be together, it woulda been you guys." Jimmy lifted his pint, still talking about Michelle and Thomas as he took a gulp, spilling beer down his chin.

The last time Thomas saw Michelle eight months back, he got the sense that marriage was imminent. But tonight he didn't relish the news, especially by way of the source from which it was coming. He thought about reminding Jimmy of how much he bled when he got slapped in the noggin, but Jimmy was too drunk to learn any lesson.

Thomas changed the subject to the Sunday night game between the Patriots and Packers, then suddenly bid farewell and left.

FOUR

After two fruitless days of wrestling practice at St. Agnes, Mark Pierce decided to put a little more pressure on his old wrestling buddy. Last bell at Covington Elementary is at 2:45, which gave Mark 15 minutes to dismiss the last kids from physical education class, travel north to Evandale, dress for practice and stretch. But the way the first two practices had gone, it didn't matter if he was late today.

Five miles inland from Evandale on County Road 419 sits the Burke Block and Brick Company, which is adjacent to the Burke Sand and Gravel Pit. In 1906, Harold Burke bought the land and started a small brick factory. It was the biggest business in Millersburg then and with his grandsons Harold III and Leonard running the business now, it still is the largest, covering some 80 acres of prime Jersey Shore real estate.

Mark took Chambers Bridge Road from Covington, which angled northwest into the county toward Millersburg. Condominium construction was scattered on the western side of the railroad tracks every mile or so, an indication of the population movement away from the city and down along the shore. After crossing Highway 13, the condominium construction was less frequent, but sprawling estates were springing up in the existing woodland areas. Mark longed for ownership of one of those estates.

The speed limit dropped from 45 mph to 25 on Chambers Bridge Road as Mark entered the business district, which consisted of three blocks of quaint mercantile shops. At the end of town, Chambers Bridge road ceases. With options of left and right, Mark turned right on County Road 419, and two miles north he came to the Burke establishments.

At 3 p.m. in December, the block yard and gravel pits are relatively quiet. Most of the company trucks and respective drivers get hauling deliveries for cinder blocks first thing in the morning and sometimes after lunch, and the truck scale for the pit closes promptly at 3:30. Only a couple of homeowners had pickup trucks loaded down with sand, and nobody seemed busy buying concrete block.

Mark didn't know exactly where Thomas worked, but he felt less intimidated by the appearance of the building proclaiming Burke Block and Bricks than by the building directly behind the scale which read B ke S d it, the windows tinted with dirt and sand, making it virtually impossible to see inward.

Pallets of assorted pavers, blocks and bricks for display lined the outside of the visitor's building. Viewing this as an invitation for consumers, Mark meekly stepped inside, only to find Styrofoam cutaway displays of more pavers, blocks and bricks stacked along the wall and one lonely chair. The cowbell on the door clanked, but for quite a few moments, no one and nothing stirred, not even Mark. Thinking of turning and leaving as timidly as he entered, a sudden shadow appeared in the door frame and a huge, bearded man emerged from a back room. He stood about 6 foot 4, and weighed in excess of 300 pounds. His shoulders blocked out any light from the room behind him, the smoke from the cigarette hanging from his lips disguised the color of his eyes. Mark thought perhaps he would try the gravel pit.

"How can I help you, sir," he said in a deep, coarse but gentle voice.

"I was wondering if Thomas McCloskey was working today."

"McCloskey works every day. Never missed one since he's been here, dopey bastard that he is. I keep telling him that he can't take his sick days once he's dead." The large man laughed at his ingenuity, then added, "But it may be hard to find him at this time of the day, with him putting away all of the equipment."

The burly fellow had no success reaching Thomas on the two-way radios, and finally told Mark to head back to the red brick shanty a couple of hundred yards to the right. That's where the workers congregated at the end of the day.

Six or seven men sat outside the shanty on benches, drinking beer and telling stories. It was extremely mild for early December, the sun was high in the western sky without a cloud in sight. Most of the men were stripped down to their t-shirts. Two men were bare-chested.

"Hey Mac – you got yourself a visitor."

Thomas appeared in the doorway, drying his hands. His flannel shirt was unbuttoned to the waist, revealing a white guinea t-shirt, and his jeans were unbuttoned and unzipped. His co-workers laughed at these common antics. One screamed at him, "Jesus, Mac. We got company. What if it was a girl?"

"That's kinda what I was hopin' for." More laughter and a single proclamation of quittin' time led the company of men to spring to its feet and head for home. Thomas tossed the paper towel he had used to dry his hands into a nearby trash can and busied himself with the chore of buttoning himself up. He knew Mark was there to ask for his help, again, and he felt somewhat flattered. But he also was apathetic to the whole deal. Mark better have a good line of shit, he thought, or else he's on his own. Apathy defeats flattery once again.

"Shouldn't you be at practice?"

"I'm heading over there now. I told Mr. Lawton I'd be a little late."

"Are you addressing him as Mr. Lawton out of respect?" Thomas asked. "Or is this your way of dropping a hint? That he wants to be recognized as the boss, sort of like when you have to address George Bush as Mr. President?"

"I know you don't like him Tommy, but he's not so bad."

"First of all, I wasn't making the point of liking him or not. I'm trying to figure out whether you're kissing his ass or not. Second of all, what's there to like? He's a complete dipshit and I'm not. We have nothing in common, and that doesn't really bother me or affect me, one way or the other. That's my opinion anyway."

Thomas went back inside and asked Mark if he wanted a beer. Mark declined, and Thomas returned with a Natural Lite, setting onto one of the empty benches. "It's the only brand they have in there," he said, changing the subject for a moment. He didn't like the anxiety building up inside of him. The situation he was being dragged into was one he was not accustomed to. He understood wrestling, but he did not know anything about coaching or the politicking Mark was involved with. But he knew Mark had some ulterior motive other than teaching the sport of high school wrestling to a bunch of private school kids. Thomas just wasn't sure what it was. And quite honestly, he didn't care.

Mark had prepared a long hard sell, but he knew that plan was useless. He sat on a bench adjacent to the one Thomas had settled at and looked out into the distance. The shadows of the two gnarled and worn maple trees grew long, touching massive piles of old and new concrete alike. It was quiet for a few moments, except for the wind rearranging a small bed of leaves and a squirrel scurrying up the nearest tree.

"Tommy, the first couple of practices have gone like hell." Mark paused, waiting for a response, but Thomas kept his eyes fixed on the squirrel. "Ken is just there because the school requires an in-house teacher to be present. The diocese was very hesitant in taking on this sport, but the Parents' Club, in particular one father from the club, pushed for the sport and has backed this thing from the start. Not one penny is coming from the school. Everything's coming from the Parents' Club."

Thomas' gaze was fixed on the squirrel. It helped him listen. It helped him think. He remained silent.

" I figured if we can get in there and gain some confidence from the school, we can take over the program next year. Then we can do it the way we want."

Thomas turned toward his old friend. He no longer needed to listen, Mark had divulged his scheme. "What's this 'we shit'?"

"I figured we could build up a powerhouse and challenge. . . ."

"You know Mark, you've been doing an awful lot of figurin,' with the thought of me helping you to the top. You've known me a helluva long time, and you know I hate the spotlight. So why do you insist on trying to sell this spotlight shit and all of this winning shit to me?" He stared at Mark as intently as he stared at the squirrel.

"Listen Tommy," Mark said. "I just thought that maybe you'd be interested in wrestling a little bit, getting back to something you love, instead of sitting on a bar stool, wasting most of your life away."

"Oh, we're switching our gears to the paternalistic mode." Thomas laughed and when Mark began to say something he was told to shut up. Thomas tilted back his head and finished his beer, then tossed it end over end toward the trash can 10 feet away. It was a perfect, high-arcing shot that spilled a drop of liquid out every time the opening faced downward. Thomas watched with pride. By the time the can hit the bottom of the barrel, he had made his decision, almost as if the success of the shot determined Mark's fate.

Thomas stood up abruptly. "Okay, here's the deal. I'll show up tomorrow and Friday. I'll come straight from work, and I'll check out the practices. I don't want to be introduced to the kids, I don't even want to be acknowledged. You and Mr. Kenneth

Lawton do what you can at practice. If I feel I can help, I'll call you Friday night and talk about it."

"And if you don't think you can help?"

"Then you're on your own."

A myriad of Fisher Price toys, two bicycles with training wheels, a dozen tennis balls, a Nerf football, two hockey sticks with a small plastic goal and net, three baseball caps and a hundred or so baseball cards decorated the front lawn of Mark Pierce's Cape Cod in Covington. Two weeks before, Mark's father-in-law had a spotlight installed on the front lawn because nightly arrivals proved to be quite dangerous with the land mines of toys. Mark did not recognize the usual mess as he arrived home studying a piece of paper containing the list of potential wrestlers for the St. Agnes team.

Inside, the scene was not much better. The twins, Taylor and Travis, turned six years old at the beginning of November, and what birthday gifts were not on the front lawn were strewn throughout the living room and dining room. Unconsciously and deftly stepping around games and sporting gear, Daddy slipped into his chair at the dining room table, placing the sheet of paper atop the empty plate. The rest of the table was a mess, food and silverware and condiments everywhere. It appeared that meatloaf complete with tator tots and macaroni and cheese was the complete dinner menu.

As the basement door opened into the kitchen, a rush of delirium escaped. Amanda Pierce closed the door, seemingly callous or immune to the constant racket.

"Is this going to be a normal time for you to come home?" she asked insipidly as she picked up some of the plates from the table.

Mark grunted in acknowledgement, not actually perceiving the question. He was trying, in vain, to decipher a lineup from the list of names in front of him. After most of the table was cleared, he asked of the whereabouts of dinner.

Amanda Pierce didn't like being ignored. As a matter of speaking, being the only child of a corporate president, she did not like anything that did not revolve around her. She hadn't changed much physically or mentally since Mark asked her to date back when she was a freshman in high school and he was a year older. She was tall, almost 5-foot-10, and thin, not weighing more than

115 pounds, with long blonde hair which reached the middle of her back. Most of the time she wore her hair in a French braid, except when she let it out when sitting on the beach.

And she was spoiled rotten. Then. And now.

"Daddy's coming over tonight to take Travis and Taylor out to the ice skating rink," Amanda said, purposefully avoiding the same path of conversation her husband was on. She returned to the kitchen and began working at the sink.

Mark heard "Daddy" but not the rest. "Daddy" always struck out like a siren in the dead of night. She was always referring to her father in some form, and he was always coming over to the house. A long time ago, Mark stopped thinking about the intrusion, right after he was reminded by his wife that the house, his job and everything the children possessed were compliments of her father. Since that day, Mark has just kept his mouth shut about his father-in-law and bode his time.

"I went over to see Tommy McCloskey where he works, today. I think he's going to help out after all."

Hearing that name brought Amanda back into the dining room. Mark had told her that he asked Thomas for his help the week before, but when nothing came of it after the first couple of days of practice, Amanda thought that the issue was closed. She hated Thomas and had no trouble letting her husband know this as often and as vociferously as possible.

Thomas and Mark were best of friends in high school. Their acquaintance dated back to grade school, but once they got to high school and started wrestling, they became extremely close. All four years on the team, they wrestled in back-to-back weight classes. They went to summer wrestling camps together. They worked together and they got into trouble on the weekends together. In fact, the first time Amanda remembered seeing her future husband was at a party where Mark got drunk and challenged three upperclassmen to a fight, only to be taken up on the offer and subsequently bailed out by Thomas.

Amanda liked Thomas at first, with his apple-pie look and his gentlemanly manners. But as she and Mark dated, she grew to despise Thomas. Mark's interest in Amanda took its toll on the mat, and his friend let him know his feelings. "You know, you used to be the quickest guy in the county," Thomas once told him. "But now you're slow, and you don't really give a shit. And because you don't give a shit, half the team doesn't give a shit.

And it's all because of some chick, who you probably won't marry unless you get her pregnant."

Mark had the misguided fortune of telling his young love this message, and she, with her wicked powers of persuasion, created an inevitable chasm between the two friends. The disdain for Thomas McCloskey grew to immense proportions when, during the second semester of Mark's sophomore year in college, she became pregnant during a weekend visit. She was four months pregnant when Thomas showed up at the Church of Christ, uninvited, with a date, and dressed in faded jeans and construction boots.

"I thought Thomas wasn't going to help you?" Amanda Pierce asked of her husband. "You know, you really don't need his help. You know a lot of guys from high school who can help out. Plus, if you just wait until next year, Daddy can get you on as an assistant at Covington. You said Coach Gibbons only has a couple of years left. That's where you want to coach anyway."

Mark was tired of Daddy pulling the strings, but he was too ashamed to talk up or do anything about it, so as usual, he avoided those comments. "Most of the guys from high school either don't have the time, don't want to do it or don't live around here. And all of those guys don't know one-tenth of what Thomas knows about wrestling – combined."

"But he's a drunk. And he's a bum!"

It had been eight years since Mark wrestled competitively, and he didn't recall Covington practices being as chaotic as the ones so far at St. Agnes. If he were to push for the Covington wrestling position in a couple of seasons, he had to prove himself at St. Agnes. And to prove himself there, he needed Thomas McCloskey – desperately.

"I know you don't like Tommy, but right now I can really use him at St. Agnes." Mark took his time to find the right words. It was as if he were a salesman, and every day he had to sell a new line of products to his spoiled wife just for a taste of freedom for himself. "He won't last long. He'll stay long enough until he's knows I'm in control of the team and not Mr. Lawton. Then he'll call it quits."

Finding a good time to retreat from this conversation, Mark got up and headed to the kitchen. Like a machine, a set of words emanated from his mouth different from the words formed in his head. He asked, once again, what was for dinner, and upon opening the stove, uttered, "Mmm, meatloaf."

But in his head he thought, 'Thomas is a good friend, he won't let me sink.' Mark threw a tator tot into his mouth.

FIVE

It was a long and arduous day out at the Burke brickyard and sand pits. At sunrise, it began as a dank and misty morning, with the temperature hovering just below the 40-degree mark. With the forecast calling for clearing skies, it was favorable enough for the bosses to send out the block trucks to the various job sites.

The morning remained cold and damp as Thomas alternated in both yards, moving pallets of bricks to and fro, and mounding up huge piles of sand and stone when he wasn't loading material into a waiting dump truck. Approximately an hour before lunch, the skies opened up, and the Burke plants virtually shut down.

On rain days such as these, when drivers delivering block returned to the yard, they were immediately sent home, and the yard men remained on the clock, getting their hourly wage for some light mechanic work or for cleaning up some of the various shops and buildings. But right after lunch, someone noticed that one of the heavy equipment operators, Willie J. Dunklin, never broke for lunch.

"Aah – he probably forgot his watch again," someone said.

"Either that or he fell asleep out behind the sand pits again."

Thomas grabbed a walkie-talkie and headed for a pickup truck just outside the mechanic shop. "Nope. I'll bet that the dopey bastard is stuck in the mud someplace."

Willie J. had been separating piles of crushed concrete and asphalt back behind both yards near Willever Creek, when his front-end loader bogged down in the swollen waters. The back end of the machine was precariously perched just above the creek. The bucket of the machine was curled forward with the blade dug into the muddied earth, keeping the machine from going any farther down the 12-foot hill into the creek. The metal machine looked like a troubled rock climber holding on for dear life.

Afraid to move, Willie J. had been sitting in the cab of the machine, wishing that the damn radio would have been fixed three weeks ago like he asked. The windows were all steamed up, and the dog-eared Penthouse magazine was no longer entertaining. When he heard the sound of the pickup truck, he wiped clear a window.

"Anybody but you," Willie J. called out. "Call in and get someone who won't call the newspaper photographers."

Good to his word, Thomas showed up at the Evandale Community pavilion, at 3:55, a bit later than planned because of the Willie J. Dunklin debacle. Once a center for social events ranging from beauty contests to symphonies, the building rarely was used anymore. On Saturdays in the wintertime, boys and girls in the third, fourth and fifth grades played organized basketball, and on the first Saturday night of every month year-round, a square dance club hung streamers from the rafters and barked out unfamiliar sounds to the New Jersey neighborhoods. In the humid summers, the unairconditioned building would open its French doors, making it quite uncertain whether you were in the North or the South.

Other than those events, the building stood neglected, especially the external upkeep. Roof shingles were missing due to the high winds blowing in from the inlet during the oft turbulent winter months. Decades worth of layered paint was chipping in large thick chunks from the soffits, and the glazing around the small, rectangular window panes was drying, curling and falling onto the sandy lawn.

St. Agnes received clearance to use the municipal building because of a local realtor, who also happened to be on the St. Agnes' Parents' Club, who also happened to have a sophomore at the high school who was, not so coincidentally, signed up for the wrestling squad.

The sole purpose that Greg Connelly had for starting this wrestling program was so his son, Liam, could toughen up. Liam was an only child and spent much of his youth tagging along with his mother on several traveling adventures, shopping sprees and high society engagements. Wanting to get some balance in his son's life, Mr. Connelly pulled some strings, tossed around a few dollars and reeled in some outstanding favors. The result was a wrestling program which had no substantial ties to the school's athletic department. It had no experienced coaches. It had no scheduled home matches. And it lacked any organization.

Due to the chaos, only the two students who were sitting against the wall next to the rear entrance into the dance floor/gymnasium noticed Thomas. With mud caked onto his jeans and construction boots, his hair matted down from the constant afternoon rains and clothes wet and musty, he did not look like a typical St. Agnes' father.

"Maybe we should get back to practice," one boy said to the other, and they got up and walked to the middle of the floor, mumbling about not wanting to end up on the back of a milk carton.

Thomas eyed up the boys. "Not wrestling material," he retorted aloud. He searched for the whereabouts of Mark and Mr. Lawton, and found them each in the midst of two separate clusters of students. He looked to his right and found a folding chair leaning against the wall. Opening it, he set it in the corner and sat down, quietly observing the festivities.

Mr. Lawton had a group of 15 kids alternating exercises between jumping jacks, sit-ups and push-ups. It was a sad sight to behold. While a few of the students kept up with the boy Mr. Lawton had chosen as the leader, most lagged behind, while others simply could not complete a single push-up and floundered in a prostrate position.

Despite the chaotic clamor of the separate groups, Thomas listened for Mr. Lawton's voice. "Okay, now lead them in push-ups, Timothy," he said. And Timothy would drop sharply from his final jumping jack position to push-up position.

"Ready, set, go – one, two, three. . . ." When Timothy reached seven, two other boys were at a five count, and the others were just flopping to the floor, finding their ways to their bellies, and when Timothy finished his directed set of 20, a few of the remaining 12 boys managed to squeak out four or five push-ups in the permissible girl-style, with both the knees and feet in contact with the floor.

Thomas closed his eyes and shook his head. When he opened his eyes, he changed his gaze to Mark, who was with a group of boys on the three sections of wrestling mats, trying to teach them an array of moves.

Some children lay on the side of the mat, exhausted from the teachings of the new sport. At the far corner of the mats, a few of the younger boys were practicing drop kicks, a professional wrestling move not legal in scholastic wrestling. Others were involved in a game of pile-on-the-rabbit.

At present, Mark was in the corner of the mat closest to Thomas, attempting to teach a cross-face cradle to two larger boys. An advanced and complicated move, the boy executing the maneuver finally got frustrated and tried to rush through the cradle, straining to remember all he was recently taught while still attempting to perform flawlessly. But at the halfway point, when the man on top is to bring his opponent's nose to his knee, a blood-curdling cry brought all activity to an end.

"My back, my back, my back, my back," the young man screamed at first, then switched to moans and sniffles. "Awww, haw, haw – my back, my baaaack." He rolled around holding the small of his back on the right side. "Haw, Haw, Haw – it hurts."

The entire contingency of students and the two coaches stood over their fallen comrade, wondering if he would ever be the same again. The truth be told, he would be whole once again but would never attend another wrestling practice.

"What shall we do?" Mr. Lawton asked Mark. "Should we call an ambulance? Or maybe call a doctor?"

Mark looked at his watch. It was 4:15. "Well, we've been here since three – maybe we should call it a day and continue tomorrow."

Mr. Lawton thought that this idea was fabulous. Immediately, he blew the whistle which he had purchased at the Five and Dime the day before. It had an obnoxious, high-pitched shrill that could send dogs running, foaming through the streets. Since all of the students were already gathered on the mat to check on the severity of the injury, the use of the whistle was utterly needless, but it did disperse the crowd instantaneously to retrieve books and coats from various corners of the room . In moments, the students were shuffling through the rear entrance, looking inquisitively and deprecatingly at Thomas.

By 4:20, all that was left in the pavilion were the two coaches, Thomas, and the lingering howl of an injured athlete.

Thomas looked around the building, trying to decide of its worthiness as a wrestling room. It was certainly large enough. A regulation size basketball court ran east and west, leaving about ten feet out of bounds along each side line. There were no bleachers, only portable benches and folding chairs, which left plenty of room for running without rolling up the mats. And a stage at the far end of the room could serve any number of purposes, perhaps a makeshift locker room or a platform for the captains to lead the team in calisthenics. This place – Thomas thought – has possibilities.

Then his attention focused on the two "coaches." These poor kids don't have the physical or mental capacity – especially the fortitude – to compete in this sport, and they have these two nitwits leading them into battle. One of the guys at the Burke yard would tell them, "You two could fall in a barrel full of tits and come up sucking your thumb." Thomas laughed. Ain't it the truth, he thought.

Mark and Mr. Lawton did not notice Thomas at first. They had been congratulating themselves on a successful four days of practice while they picked up various sporting accessories such as the jump ropes, traffic cones, a basketball, hand grips and a barbell with two 17.4 pound concrete weights from Sears. All of the items were stored in a box, except for the weights and basketball, and then placed in a closet on the stage. This done, Mark only needed to retrieve the mop and bucket, which happened to be against a wall next to Thomas.

"Hey, how long have you been here?" Mark asked cheerfully, as he bounced his way over toward Thomas.

Thomas looked around but could not find a clock. "Oh, about 20 or 30 minutes," he estimated.

"Well, what do you think? Why didn't you come over and check out the practice up close?"

Hearing the voices and turning to see Thomas, Mr. Lawton felt it was necessary to be polite, and he was somewhat interested, if not ready to admit it, "in the troglodyte's opinion." This was a phrase he had come to use in describing Thomas, although never in his presence.

Thomas and Mr. Lawton nodded and exchanged pleasantries with one another. Answering Mark's second question first, Thomas said, "We had a little accident at work, and I got a little wet and muddy, and you don't need this shit near the mat."

Mr. Lawton sighed at the limited vocabulary Thomas seemingly possessed.

"Awful," Thomas said in response to the first question.

33

"What's awful?" Mark asked, confoundedly.

"Your practice. It sucked."

"Well, we had to cut it down today because one of the kids got injured, but otherwise we have been going straight to five or five-thirty."

"Other than the injury, have the rest of the practices been the same?"

"Pretty much," Mark said. "Mr. Lawton takes different groups during the afternoon and does some cals, and I go over a bunch of moves and then I let the kids wrestle around."

"And other than the injury, the practices have been the same, only longer?"

"More or less, identical. Would you agree Mr. Lawton?"

"Identical," the biology teacher added reassuringly.

Thomas liked that the two coaches agreed. "Well then, your practices suck."

Flustered, Mr. Lawton lashed out. "Are you going to continue to profanely criticize the practices or will you be a bit more constructive?"

"Alright," Thomas said calmly. "First of all, as a coach you have to keep your head about you at all times, which means not getting all pissed off at some criticism."

"Could you watch your language, Mr. McCloskey?"

"Next, learn how to fuckin' curse a little bit. Teen-age wrestlers respect and expect that from their coach." Thomas wanted to tell Kenneth Lawton, biology teacher, to just go the fuck home, but the biology teacher was the acting ring master and he had the bull whip. Problem was that he didn't know how to use it.

"This isn't gym class," Thomas continued, directing the instructions to Mark, trying to spark some memory. "This is wrestling practice. It requires discipline and structure. I don't know when your first match is, but the way things are going, you won't only get embarrassed, but someone's going to get seriously injured. You need to map out a plan. Get the kids used to having the same practice every day. Day in. Day out. Teach the basics and teach them again. A cross-face cradle is not the way to go on the third day of practice."

"It's the fourth day," Mark said.

Thomas knew his participation was a mistake. Obviously, Mr. Lawton had never competed in an organized sport in his life, and the only exercise he probably got as a child was chasing around frogs for the purpose of dissection. Or masturbation as an exercise. And Mark simply became a fuckin' simpleton since he married his little princess. He wanted to express these thoughts to the two coaches, but he thought better of it. Suddenly, he felt like having a beer.

"I'm heading on over to Red Mike's for a beer," Thomas said. "If either one of you wants to pick my brain, I'll be at the end of the bar."

And with that, he left, leaving Mark and Mr. Lawton speechless, wondering what to do at the specter of being totally humiliated in their coaching debut.

"It's fuckin' useless Mark. Your biology and chemistry teacher is more concerned with having a title and being in charge. And all you're doing is screwing around with the kids, acting like an adolescent yourself – passing time and bucking for the Covington job."

Mark acted astonished. "What are you talking about? I'm not going after any coaching position at Covington."

Thomas switched his view from the television above the front door at Red Mike's to the irises in Mark's eyes. His shoulders remained square to the bar as only his head pivoted to the left. The glare was intense. It was vintage Tommy McCloskey, and Mark knew that bullshitting him was useless.

"All right," Mark began, "this is a perfect opportunity for me to get an angle on succeeding Gibbons. But Coach Johnson won't stay around either. He'll pack it in when Gibbons packs it in, and I figured you'd head on over and take Johnson's assistant position and then we can make Covington a state powerhouse."

Motioning to the bartender, Thomas needed to take a few moments before exploding and another few moments to think. Why did he actually like Mark? Why did he feel like he had to help Mark? Most adult decisions Mark had made since the two met were against everything Thomas believed in. Nothing Mark did was on the up and up. Nothing he accomplished was done without help.

Thomas ordered another shot and beer chaser. Other than those essential core character differences, he liked Mark, and Mark didn't have any close friends since he started to get serious with Amanda. Despite not seeing each other but every couple of years, Mark considered Thomas his closest friend.

"Listen Mark. The way your practices are going over at St. Agnes, you're going to be so embarrassed after a couple of matches, you won't ever want to coach again. Hell, you'll probably want to enter the witness protection program."

Thomas' own wit caused him to chuckle aloud. He tossed back the shot of Jack Daniel's and took a swig of beer. Mark remained silent, although not at all amused at the slight. Perhaps starting up a wrestling program wasn't as easy as he thought, and for the first time he thought of abandoning the project.

"See, that's where you're wrong, Mark. You started something here, and now it's time to nut up and see it through. Your goal is to get some experience at St. Agnes and jump over to Covington. Now I told you I'd help you get this program started, but you're getting ahead of yourself when you start talking about me and Covington. Let's work on this abortion of a team first."

"So, in other words, you'd still come over to Covington if the position were offered?"

"Mark, all I want to do in this lifetime is eat a good steak, drink some cold beer, bed some beautiful women and die an early but painless death. Covington's part of your plans, not mine."

Thomas' commentary saddened Mark because of its candor. At one time, it appeared as if Thomas was on his way to fame, if not a little fortune. But a few years back, Thomas' hopes vanished and were instantly replaced with apathy. Nobody knew the exact reason, although there were speculations – a lack of success or an injury in the college ranks, alcohol, drugs, or perhaps the unlikely scenario of a lost love. No one knew for sure because Thomas never let anyone in that close.

But something did happen, and every so often, the old Thomas emerged and gave glimpses of renewed hope. Mark sensed it sitting at Red Mike's, listening to his old comrade speak of values.

Another beer and more silence followed. Thomas needed the breaks from conversations to set up his next block of thoughts. Although he was quick to add an opinion, he was careful in what he said when laying out plans or making promises. Once said, there was no retracting or welshing on those already tendered.

"Listen. I don't hate your biology teacher, but he has no business on a wrestling mat. But the school says he's the boss, and he's the type of guy that loves a title. And he's the type of guy that's gonna act out his title. So maybe after this team of his gets whupped a couple of times, he may be more receptive with me helping out. In the meantime, you have to take more control of those practices."

Mark liked the tone in his friend's voice. It sounded strong and confident. He believed Thomas could figure out a way to make this work.

Thomas grabbed a handful of cocktail napkins and asked the bartender for a pen. He wrote "one" in the top corner and began writing and talking. The team needs to stretch for 10 minutes and then run for 30 minutes. Then do some calisthenics for 45 minutes. And he rattled off old exercises from Covington practices which Mark nodded in remembrance.

It was on to the second cocktail napkin and a list of basic moves which needed to be taught and drilled every day. "The double-leg takedown and the stand-up are the keys," Thomas said. "It's like blocking and running the ball in football. Without ball control and time management, you're not going to the Super Bowl. Without the takedown and the stand-up, you're going nowhere in wrestling."

No flashy moves. Keep it simple. Thomas stuck to these themes and repeated them like mantras. He went on to the third cocktail napkin, and a fourth, a fifth, scribbling and talking and lecturing the entire time.

Mark said nothing but an occasional "two beers." He soaked up the information like he was in kindergarten learning the alphabet. With the interjected years, he had not recalled wrestling practice being like this back in high school, and now, as Thomas spoke, vivid memories of the daily agony resurfaced. The practices were grueling and unforgiving, but by the end of a match and by the end of the season, the gratification was tremendous.

Mark remembered what it was like to call himself a wrestler.

It was 7 o'clock when Thomas stopped talking. "That'll take you through a couple of weeks. When's your first match and who's it against?"

"It's December 21st. Against Blakemore Prep." Thomas' face contorted with the mention of Blakemore. "We figured we could have a cut sheet up by Tuesday, and then we can get real serious."

Thomas shook his head. "No, you get real serious tomorrow, and you never have any cuts in wrestling. Kids will cut themselves. Others will get hurt. Some weeks you'll be lucky if you can field the 13 weight classes." A long deep breath followed. "Blakemore isn't the toughest school in the Shore Conference, but they know how to win. It's not the school you want to start your program with."

"We'll be fine," Mark said as he stood and looked at his watch. "I gotta get going. What time will you get home tomorrow night?" Thomas shrugged.

Mark said he'd get in touch with him, somehow, and update him on the team's progress.

Thomas' renewed interest in wrestling had piqued while he scribbled some notes on the napkins. But the adrenalin soon subsided, and he was left feeling subdued and hungry.

He had hoped that a handful of napkins could quell his thirst for the sport, but now he doubted it.

He also hoped a good steak and three eggs could satisfy his appetite. A quick trip to the grocery store could quell his hunger.

That now seemed doubtful, too.

SIX

Something as important as announcing an engagement to your mother should not be done over the phone, so Michelle decided to fly from Boston to Newark, where her little sister would pick her up, and they would make the 45-minute drive south to Evandale.

Mom was everything to the girls, and the only thing, because their father died suddenly of a massive heart attack nine years earlier. He had worked for the town of Evandale, mainly on the street department, jack-hammering and asphalting, in the same town where the family thrived. He was the crew chief at age 35 and well-respected by his men. Two years after receiving his promotion, while having coffee and a cigarette during an afternoon break, he began hacking severely. He told the men in his crew to leave him alone and, as he was coughing, he yanked from his neck the Celtic cross he received for Father's Day a few years prior, held it tightly in his hand, leaned back and died.

For the next eight years, Marie Jennings worked as a secretary, using her income and the money from her husband's life insurance policy to raise her family and send her girls to college. So whenever Michelle or Tamantha had news to share with their mother, despite the distances college and careers may have created, they tried to repay her by telling the news to her in person.

It was not the type of reaction Michelle was expecting from her mother. Mom always showed great affection toward Todd, but when Michelle told her mother of their intentions, her mother smiled and hugged her tightly, yet the smile was not as radiant as usual.

"Well, I'm so happy for you," Mrs. Jennings said. "I'm sure your father had something to do with the arrangement. He was always looking out for both of his girls."

When Michelle heard the mention of her father, tears welled up in her eyes. She had not thought consciously about her father since Todd had proposed, until now. Dad had been dead for nearly a decade, the pain resurfacing whenever his memory was recalled, and Michelle hurt more now than ever before. She would have to choose another male family member to walk her down the aisle, but that was of little matter. She simply would not be escorted by her father.

"Dad didn't have anything to do with it," Michelle said, laughing, trying to hide any tears. Her father used to tell her that big boys don't cry and big girls should only do it when they need money to pay the bills. "Dad would not have picked anyone with blue blood like Todd. 'Pick someone with callouses who hides his money in his boot. . . .' " Michelle's voice stopped abruptly. Mom knew who her husband would have picked as a suitor for her eldest daughter, but memories of lost loves are best saved for cold winter nights in front of glowing fireplaces, alone, perhaps with a cold bottle of wine.

"Like Tommy McCloskey," Tamantha said.

"Tamantha Catherine," her mother scolded. "Hasn't that college taught you any couth, or a semblance of sophistication, for that matter?"

"Mom, I just said what everybody was thinking. College has taught me honesty and communication, if nothing else. Todd's rich and he's a wonderful guy, but Tommy always had a great ass."

Michelle threw a crumpled napkin at her sister while her mother admonished her for the use of such vile language, especially at the dinner table. "And what were you doing looking at my boyfriend's ass?" Michelle screamed. "You were too young to be thinking about guys' butts!"

"Girls mature much more quickly than guys do. At 13, guys want to learn how to kiss. Girls want to look at their sister's dates' butts."

"And how many of my dates' butts have you stared at?"

"All of them, but none were as tight as Tommy's." With her last statement, Tamantha put both hands out in front of her, palms down and fingers stretched, and mimicked squeezing motions. The sisters had a hearty laugh, before both were cautioned for behavior not becoming of ladies.

"Hey mom, do you have any champagne handy," Tamantha asked only to receive a glaring look from her mother. "Come on, Michelle. Let's go get some champagne and some strawberries – and some chocolate. Yeah, we can melt up some chocolate and dip the strawberries and toast Todd with his flabby butt. Let's get two bottles of champagne for that butt. One for each flabby cheek."

"Tammy," another admonishment from her mother was inevitable. "You cannot drive back to school after drinking that much!"

"Mom, I think we should get three bottles and crash on the living room floor. And I think you should call in sick tomorrow."

After a session at Red Mike's of having a few drinks, Thomas frequently liked to go grocery shopping at Kinnerson's, only a few blocks away. He especially liked walking to Kinnerson's in the dead of winter when the streets were deserted and the nights were bitter.

Thomas stuck his hands in his jeans and curled his shoulders in tight to his body. The wind was blowing at his back, in from the east, pushing him unexpectedly with each gust and, feeling a draft sneak past the nape of his neck, he turned up his jacket collar, reveling in his solitude.

Times were not so depressing, he thought. Sure, every once in a while he got down on himself for abandoning college – more so the education than the wrestling – but without any form of a scholarship, he had no real money. He always contemplated borrowing money from the government or from a bank, but he wasn't much on owing anything to anybody. So he came home and worked just like his father had worked, as did his grandfathers.

And within those conflicting thoughts, the feelings of depression would ebb and flow. He loved working with his body, getting up early and busting it for the Burkes, out in the somewhat rural Millersburg, experiencing the humidity of summertime and the blistering frost of wintertime. He arrived at work at 7:00 every day, ready to work, and left every day at 3:30, occasionally called upon to work overtime. In a way, he was his own boss, calling his own shots, not owing anything to anybody and not being owed anything in return, ready to move on if necessary.

Sometimes, when he sits at the end of the bar at Red Mike's, he gets to thinking too much. Things sure could have been different. Things still could be different. There's a lot of life out there, and he always thought that someday he would go out and conquer bits and pieces of the vastness of unknown adventures. When the first beer of the evening is ordered, Thomas has talked himself into waking up in the morning and changing the world. Sure, in the morning he'll be more enthusiastic, more productive, more reverent. In the morning, life will be different.

Instead of getting off the bar stool and going home to work on his plan, Thomas would order another beer, followed by another, complimented by a shot of whiskey. By the time Thomas got home, he had decided that the world would have to wait for the coming-out of Mr. Thomas McCloskey. Tonight, he would reason, it's time to get some rest so he could move some brick around in the morning.

It would be on those particular evenings, while lying alone in bed listening to the faint sound of music playing on the radio, that Thomas would feel most sorry for himself. His parents were gone. His brother was off on his own adventures. And he had no one to share in love. He prayed for sleep on those nights. And he prayed not to remember his dreams.

Kinnerson's was the only store open on the strip mall near the railroad tracks, its light shining like a beacon for wayward souls. Almost unconsciously, Thomas would make his way from Red Mike's to Kinnerson's. The six-block walk to the Ma and Pa store, the time spent in the aisles deciding on his culinary delight and the walk back to his truck were enough to sober him up. If, by chance, he didn't feel up to the task of driving back to Whiting Beach, Thomas would curl up in the cab of his 1972 Ford-100, lock the doors and fall asleep. Winter or summer, it didn't matter, for Thomas did not want to take his chances with some overachieving cop.

The first push cart Thomas grabbed when he reached Kinnerson's had an uneven and wobbly, left-front wheel. He tested a second, which met his liking, and headed inside. Without fail, these shopping excursions would lead to no more than seven or eight items, requiring only a hand basket. But Thomas refused to use one, "I feel like I'm Little Red Riding Hood." Plus, he liked to lean on the cart just in case the warm air put him to sleep in the wintertime or the air conditioning render him unconscious in summer.

The produce aisle never had much appeal to Thomas except for maybe kidnapping a grape or two. But he felt obligated to start every grocery trip through this aisle for posterity. He thought about getting some lettuce for a salad once, but thought better of it when he recalled having a salad at the Cornerstone Pub only a few days before.

Up one aisle and down the next, Thomas was never in any hurry to rush through Kinnerson's or Sendl, the grocery store in Whiting Beach. This is what he did with his spare time. He explored. Slowly. If not a grocery store, then perhaps a mall, or maybe the downtown stores of a small seaside village. He was not in a hurry to get anyplace, for he really had nowhere to go.

Occasionally, Thomas would stray from his usual grocery list and just toss something into the cart that caught his fancy. Sometimes it would be Pop Tarts – Concord grape or cherry – other times it would be a pack of Oreos. The things he never got to eat when he wrestled competitively. Or maybe he would grab some white clam sauce to have with linguine at some future time. It was always prudent, Thomas thought, to have some foodstuffs stashed away in the corner of the cupboards just in case. Just in case.

But tonight, his cart remained empty. The news Jimmy the Cut recently delivered to him was depressing. Oh, sure, Thomas knew it was coming someday, and he knew he would rue the day, but in the back of every man's mind. . . . Thomas dismissed the thought. He realized it was mere melancholy. Michelle and he were not meant to be. She was traveling the high road, and he chose to pull over and take a nap. He smiled. Most often he was too serious, and it made him feel good when he mocked himself.

Aisle four. Canned fruit – nah. Condiments – nah. Peanut Butter, Jelly – mmmm. Aisle five and heading toward the meat department. Yes, toilet tissue. And soap. And light bulbs – can't read in the dark. Now what kind of steak? A London Broil. A nice, juicy, London Broil – blood red, sliced diagonally, with some creamy corn served over white bread. YES. Now where's the Giant's corn?

And as he turned back toward the produce section, his blue-collar culinary specialty of steak and corn was erased immediately from his mind. Walking no more than eight paces away, coming in his direction, with champagne and Chilean strawberries laden in their arms, were the sisters Jennings.

When two people are so close during the nurturing teenage years and then lose touch in the few years following, it's remarkable how time suddenly stands still in an encounter such as this. Michelle and Tommy's eyes locked. The memories rushed forward, engulfing each of them in a montage of fond moments, of those innocent times where everything was magical. Learning the alphabet as a school child, learning to ride a bike without training wheels, and learning love as a young adult.

Michelle rewound to moonlit times on the beach, where they would sit by the Fisherman's Beach jetty, skimming clam shells across the calm ocean until they shattered into the granite rocks. She thought about the times she would call his house late on a Saturday night, mere hours after they had just seen each other, asking Tommy for a Coke, just so she could kiss him one more time. And Tommy would oblige, quietly sitting on her front steps, waiting for her to sneak out the front door so he could kiss her one final time before drifting off into dreams.

Ah, she was always there, Thomas thought. No matter where the wrestling match venue, she was always there. His young nerves would nearly overcome him moments before he stepped onto a mat to do battle, but she was always there. Sometimes alone, sometimes with a friend or with her little sister, Michelle sat in the bleachers, apart from the bulk of the crowd. He would scout her out, and not wanting to let his damsel be disappointed, he would shake off the nerves and decimate his opponent. She was his power. She was his inspiration. She was success.

"Congratulations," Thomas broke the silence with the only word he thought could avoid an awkward dialogue.

She was shocked. How did he know, but quickly she remembered what small towns were like. This was not Boston. She reciprocated in demure fashion.

"Thank you, Tommy. It's very thoughtful of you."

"Yeah, I just ran into Jimmy Zinno awhile ago and he felt that the news be best coming from him." Thomas looked at his London Broil. It wasn't looking as good as it was a few minutes before. "Isn't it customary at this point for me to ask to see the ring?"

Michelle commented that she didn't know if was a custom for an old boyfriend to inquire about the ring, but that Tommy never really did conform to any customs.

"Well now, Michelle," Tommy started as he took her left hand ever so gently into his right, "if'n someday I needs to go a'courtin,' it'd be nice to know whats I should bring."

Tamantha smiled. Tommy always found a way to express himself. And that sense of humor, it always made Michelle laugh. If only Tamantha could scheme to get these two back together. There's still a chance, the younger Jennings thought. There's still a chance.

Noticing the smile and wanting to keep up the positive facade, Thomas turned his attention briefly to Tamantha. "Ahh, and this must be the lovely Tamantha Jennings, with two bottles of Korbel clutched close to her breast because it happens to be her debutante ball, perhaps?" Thomas surrendered Michelle's betrothed hand and with a theatrical and courtly gesture, bowed in Tamantha's direction.

"Hello Tommy. Could you turn around so I can check. . . ." A nudge with the hip let Tammy know that was as far as that sentence was going to go.

She certainly has grown up. "Hello Tammy," he said. "You have gone from cute to beautiful in a short period of time."

"Excuse me, Mr. McCloskey. I don't think you should be telling my little sister such things. Can't you see she's just a little girl."

"Well, since you're off the list of bachelorettes, naturally I can't pass such a comment your way."

Thomas was doing his best in keeping the conversation light. But he knew it wouldn't last. He knew that these encounters with Michelle would end with a sense of sorrow, and the quicker he could get to the good-byes without reminiscing, the better off they both were. At least, the better off he was.

"Actually, you do look beautiful Michelle, and I'm sure you're happy with your upcoming nuptials. It does, though, look as if you have some serious plans, and I don't want to keep you from them."

He stole a quick look deep into her eyes. "Again, congratulations."

Suddenly, Michelle felt very sad. Tommy had never cut a conversation between them to such a short length. This really felt like his last good-bye. The unnatural flow caught her by surprise.

"Ah. Yes," she said, looking at him, then at her sister. Michelle had lost her place. "Um, yes, we're on our way to look for some baking chocolate for the, um, strawberries."

"Baking chocolate, yes," Thomas said. "Always a hard product to find. I wanted to have some in my house, but I never had any luck in finding it."

They both knew it was time to go. Congratulations, Thomas said. Thank you. And their eyes met. Until we meet again, m'lady. He wished, right then, that they would never meet again.

Thomas headed his cart back toward the dreaded produce aisle. Michelle walked aimlessly in the opposite direction. Tamantha turned and stole a glimpse of the gentleman's posterior.

He stood for a moment in that first aisle. He wasn't hungry. He wasn't thirsty. He just wasn't.

And he didn't want to bump into her on the way out of the store, either. Thomas McCloskey left his cart in the produce aisle and quietly left Kinnerson's grocery store in downtown Evandale.

SEVEN

It was a circus atmosphere outside Blakemore Preparatory. If the wrestling fans entering the gymnasium did not know any better, they would have thought it was the middle of summer.

Some of the local kids who attended Blakemore were buzzing all around with their friends from Normandy Township. Despite the temperature hovering around 35 degrees, some of the surf rats were clad in long Hawaiian-type summer shorts, skateboarding on makeshift portable ramps strategically placed on the outdoor basketball courts. Mixed among the long-boarders on the court were a half dozen guys deftly tossing two Frisbees around, interacting with a couple of the more talented skaters. As one would fly up and across one of the half moon ramps, a Frisbee would come flying behind his head. Unbelievably, in some sort of mid flip, the skater would grab the disc and, on the way back down the ramp, toss it off in another direction. On the sidewalk in front of the school, hackey-sackers were hacking while grade school girls were drawing with chalk on the sidewalk, announcing the future success of Blakemore while ridiculing the "Purple Prancers."

Thomas parked a little more than a block away, just outside a small bungalow with Blakemore wrestling banners hanging from the porch rafters. He could hear the commotion as he got out of his truck, and it brought back memories. He lit a cigarette and thought of his senior year when Covington crossed the inlet bridge to face the highly favored Blakemore Pirates. The adrenalin started to pump on this night just as it did six years earlier. Christ, he thought, I'm not even a participant and the blood is bubbling.

The kids outside Blakemore didn't notice Thomas as he walked past them and headed into the gym. "Two dollars and fifty cents. Match starts at 7:30" – the sign hung above the caged window where an elderly gentleman was taking the money.

"Actually, we should only charge a buck because it's going to be a quick one tonight," the man said confidently. Thomas smiled. He didn't look like the typical St. Agnes fan, so he decided not to tell the man to go screw himself. Plus, how could you get mad at the truth.

It was five minutes past seven, and the gym was already half full. This was the time when junior varsity and freshmen matches took place, but Thomas figured that the St. Agnes brain trust didn't plan on an undercard. The lone mat stood in the middle of the basketball court with a couple of preschoolers trying their best to act like their older brothers, rolling around like madmen. Some fans stood around talking politely, but most just sat in the bleachers, quietly waiting. It was an unusually serene sight for a dual match, especially for the opening of the regular season.

It wasn't hard for Thomas to figure out which bench belonged to the home squad and which belonged to St. Agnes. Just inside the main entrance were 12 chairs at the basketball court's endline, set up directly below where the basketball backboard normally would hang, currently in its retracted position. The chairs were split evenly, six to the right of the three-second lane, six to the left. There was nothing at or around the bench except a Blakemore water container and a musty, gray 4x8 practice mat behind the chairs. This is where the St. Agnes wrestlers would sit.

Across the mat at the other basketball baseline and in front of the boys' locker room was the Blakemore bench, 16 chairs split evenly just like at the visitors' bench. Starting from the left side – from the spectators' vantage point – the first 13 chairs had a black and gold towel folded perfectly over the top, each towel embroidered with a number corresponding to a weight class. The first towel, 103. The last, HWT. A pair of black and gold 4x8 practice mats were behind the bench, and two orange water containers, with Blakemore emblazoned on the sides with black magic marker, sat on opposite sides of the bench. Each water jug had a stack of paper cups, each stack of cups had a first aid kit as companion. And four jump ropes hung from hooks on the rear wall.

Thomas thought about going home, but something made him stay. He knew the Lancers were going to walk the gauntlet tonight, and he wasn't one for gloating. It was the impending embarrassment for the kids that made him find a spot to the right of the visitors' bench, in the very back row of the bleachers.

A referee emerged from the girls' locker room at about a quarter past the hour and headed straight across the gym to the boys' locker room where he would give instructions to the Blakemore squad. Moments later, the St. Agnes Lancers appeared.

They strolled forth, looking bewildered, holding their headgears in their hands. Led by a dark-haired middleweight, the crew looked like Christians walking into the lions' den. They milled around for a few moments, finally settling into the chairs on the bench. No warm-ups for this bunch. No stretching. Nothing.

Suddenly out of its locker room sprinted the home team. As Thomas sat and watched Blakemore work in precise order, a skinny little kid with wide, bony shoulders cautiously stepped up the bleachers. With hands stuck in his pockets, he stood down one row from Thomas and a bit off to the right, wondering if his presence would be objectionable. Thomas did notice but chose to ignore, so the kid sat down.

"Excuse me – sir?" The politeness immediately grabbed Thomas' attention "Weren't you at St. Agnes practice a couple of weeks ago?"

Thomas glanced down to measure up the youngster. He was young, seemingly too young for high school, maybe 13, with a face full of pimples. His hair was black and greasy, unwashed for a few days. As Thomas looked more closely, he spotted dandruff on the tips of hair and across his shoulders and the nape of the neck. The boy was 5 feet tall, maybe longer, and weighed about 120 pounds. Thomas refocused on the match.

"Yes. I was at the community center for one of the wrestling practices."

The youngster looked at the mat just as Thomas did. Sensing another question, Thomas remained quiet.

"Did you wrestle?"

"Yes, I did. I wrestled at Covington High School with one of your coaches."

"Actually, he's not my coach. I'm only in eighth grade."

This last statement caught Thomas' full attention. He's not eligible for the high school team, yet he was at practice. Maybe Mark had a genuine interest in the Lancers' program, and like any other sport, the younger they start, the more prepared that athlete will be for the high school level.

When Mark and Thomas were in high school, Covington did not have any elementary or recreational wrestling program. An

49

announcement was made in freshman homeroom that any boy wishing to wrestle needed to fill out a parent permission slip, get an in-house physical and show up for practice – the day after Thanksgiving. About 40 kids showed up that first day of freshman practice in 1979. Only six of those remained on the last team practice of their senior year.

Now Covington has a recreational program sponsored by the town. Still early in the developmental stages, the feeder program is experiencing growing pains, but at least kindergartners are rolling around, headlocking each other. By the time those kids reach high school, they'll be light years from where Thomas began. And district teams like Blakemore not only have recreational programs, but they also have elementary programs for the seventh and eighth grades that compete against other schools in the southern county.

"So, if you're in the eighth grade, why were you at practice? Do you have an older brother on the team?"

"No, I have two older sisters, and they both go to Covington," the boy said. "I go to St. Agnes elementary. Me and another kid heard about the wrestling team and decided to show up. Mr. Lawton won't let us wrestle for insurance purposes, he says. But Mr. Pierce lets us hang around, and he teaches us some moves once in a while."

Whoa! Mark is breaking a couple of rules despite Mr. Lawton. That's the first bit of good news Thomas has heard since the St. Agnes camp broke.

"What's your name?"

"I'm Tony Kingery and my friend is Michael Masterelli."

The Blakemore wrestlers finished their warmup and mechanically lined up directly in front of their chairs with their respective weight classes printed on the towels. They stood stiffly, hands clasped behind their backs, as the public address announcer, a rotund, balding father of the 145 pounder, welcomed the burgeoning crowd to the first match of the 1991 season.

Mark Pierce was scrambling to get the motley St. Agnes crew lined up across from their opponents. He was trying to explain in several separate conversations what the Lehigh Introductions were. In frustration, Mark snapped at his wrestlers, trying in vain for the crowd not to hear. "For crying out loud, just stand in front of a chair."

With their headgear in hand, the wrestlers randomly stood in front of the chairs. Chris Ranklin looked like the loser in musical chairs, the 130 pounder realizing that there were only 12 chairs, so he wandered around until Kenneth Lawton put his arm lovingly around him. They stood in the middle of the team, where the gap was left between the chairs.

"For St. Agnes, in its inaugural season, wrestling at 103 pounds, freshman Mark Cella." Then the portly public address announcer dropped his voice and bellowed. "And wrestling at 103 pounds for the Blakemore Pirates, District 41 runner-up, SENIOR – STACEY PAULSEN."

The crowd went berserk as Paulsen sprinted out to the center of the mat, bouncing like a prize fighter, the cuffs on his over-sized nylon warm-up pants rolled up three times, the hood on his jacket pulled far over his forehead, barely leaving a line of sight for his dark, penetrating eyes.

Mark Pierce was frantically trying to find the young 103 pounder for St. Agnes, calling out, "Who's wrestling at 103? Who's wrestling at 103?" When the coach realized that he was searching for Mark Cella, he tried to yell above the applause of the crowd. "Mark, go out and shake his hand."

With the electric atmosphere causing confusion and embarrassment among the St. Agnes bench, even Mark Pierce forgot the identities of his wrestlers, so he scanned the faces of the terrified St. Agnes line-up, calling out, "Mark, Mark, MARK!"

Every time he heard the name Mark, the 103-pound wrestler thought someone was calling for his coach. Finally, Mark Pierce and Mark Cella came face to face, the coach crouching down, placing his hands on his knees.

"Well, what do you say there champ," he said quietly but sardonically. "You wanna go out and shake the guy's hand?"

Mesmerized by the entire atmosphere, Mark Cella tentatively moved forward, shuffling the 10 feet from the bench to the edge of the mat, stumbling over the two-inch lip as he neared his opponent. He felt like it took him five minutes to reach Stacey Paulsen. When he got there, he offered his hand to the district silver medalist. Paulsen never grabbed the freshman's right hand, he merely slapped it and sprinted back to his teammates, sidestepping down the length of the contingence, smacking the faced-up palms of his teammates.

Mark Cella stood frozen. Mark Pierce called out his name a couple of times, but the freshman didn't hear. Some Blakemore high school juniors and seniors gathered up and to the left of the home team's bench began chanting – dork, dork, dork. Mark Cella did not hear.

Later, in the locker room, the St. Agnes 103 pounder claimed he did not remember the remainder of the Lehigh Introductions, or the national anthem, or the coin flip. The next moment he could recall was lying on his back, staring skyward at the glaring lights high above in the Blakemore gymnasium.

Stacey Paulsen pinned Mark Cella in 11 seconds. The New Jersey state record is 8 seconds.

A complete shut out in wrestling with the 13 weight classes would be 78-0. Blakemore posted a 75-0 victory on the opening night of the 1991 season, the only match not to end up in a pin was at 119 pounds, where Liam Connelly lost 7-1, barely avoiding a major-decision loss which – at an eight-point differential – would have cost St. Agnes four team points instead of the minimum three.

At first, Greg Connelly was ecstatic about his son's favorable performance, but as the night wore on, the elder Connelly failed to see any positive outcomes of this rout.

Thomas watched the crowd file past the St. Agnes wrestlers, who were instructed to graciously shake hands with the Blakemore wrestlers. The outclassed Lancers showed tremendous grace in the loss while Blakemore failed to display any in victory. Mark Pierce attempted a conversation with the Blakemore head coach Ricky Tadesco, but Tadesco offered the obligatory handshake and disappeared.

With Mark Piece left standing quite alone in the center circle, Greg Connelly swooped in like a vulture on a carcass. The tirade began immediately.

"I don't know what you expected, Greg, but you can't buy a championship in this sport," Mark said calmly, trying not to show his embarrassment. "Everyone involved in this program is still learning their roles. Things'll get better."

"Well they can't get fucking worse," an aggravated Mr. Connelly whispered. "A match is supposed to be six minutes long, right? I didn't check, but I don't think your entire team wrestled more than 10 minutes tonight, and my son wrestled six of those."

Standing a few feet away and listening to this exchange, Liam Connelly raised his arms, each forefinger pointedly proclaiming his No. 1 status. He smiled and walked around with his arms raised, chanting, "Spar-ta-cus. Spar-ta-cus," to everyone yet no one in particular.

Greg Connelly continued with his verbal barbs, then he turned and stormed from the gym, Liam trailing, not sharing the same temperament as his father. "Spar-ta-cus."

Thomas rose from his bleacher seat and slowly stepped down toward the court. He was hoping Mark would see him, because he now knew he was urgently needed. Thomas did not want to openly offer his services but wanted to make himself accessible and, if asked, he had decided it was time to immerse himself in this program. Something inherent was making him want to contribute.

But if Mark Pierce did not approach him on this night, Thomas would never help the St. Agnes Lancers. With the varsity team and the remainder of the wrestling Lancers in the locker room listening to Mr. Lawton "dissect" the loss, Mark was left to clean up the carnage and speak with the rest of the parents. Headgear, paper cups, warm-up tops, warm-up bottoms, even a pair of wrestling shoes littered the area where the Lancers just ephemerally camped.

Thomas stopped at the end of the chairs, some 15 feet from a bent and spent Mark Pierce.

"You shouldn't pick up any of their shit," Thomas said.

The assistant coach sighed. What, he queried, another imbecilic parent with more advice. Without standing upright, he looked over to the end of the bench. Ready for another onslaught, he was glad to see the face of an ally.

"Ohh, it's alright. It was a hard night for these guys." Mark stopped. "Pretty embarrassing, huh?"

"It wasn't good. But it will only make them stronger. But so will the little things, like making them responsible for their own gear."

"They were humiliated out there, Tommy. The least I can do is help them clean up."

"I disagree. The least you can do is stop acting like their parents and pampering them. These kids have to learn to wipe their own ass, and you're not helping them."

Mark sat down, folding a pair of warm-ups. He was perplexed. Much of what he and Tommy had outlined a couple of weeks back at Red Mike's never transpired. Afternoon practices were useless. By the time the kids strolled over from the high school and got dressed for practice, it was nearly 3:30. by the time they stretched and finished farting around it was past 4. Then some of the parents come straight from work and picked up their kids just after 5. If it wasn't one distraction, it was another.

"Once one kid leaves, the rest start to belly-ache. So practice is pretty much shot. The most dedicated kid I have is an eighth grader."

"If that's Tony Kingery, then I've met him."

"That's pretty pitiful, isn't it?" At that moment, Mark was contemplating quitting. "I don't suppose you could coach on a full-time basis?"

Thomas did not hesitate. This was a time for decisiveness. For leadership. "I can do it."

"There's no money for a second assistant," Mark added quickly, then he mentioned other variables. "You'd have to do it strictly on a voluntary basis, and if you were to get injured, the school's medical coverage couldn't help you. And you'd have to get fingerprinted for a criminal background check."

Typical of Mark. Spell out the rules of the game up front so he could not put himself in any potential trouble. And he would never offer any money for any services rendered. He was getting good at going along for the ride ever since he got married. But Thomas didn't care about Mark. It was the kids. It was the sport.

"I'll see you at 3:30."

EIGHT

By the time 4 o'clock rolled around on Thursday, only eight St. Agnes wrestlers were present at the Evandale Community Pavilion on 21st Avenue.

"Okay, I guess this is everybody today." Kenneth Lawton began practice as he customarily did. Whatever, Thomas thought. Let him have his fun, then let's get him the hell out of the way.

"Well, we had a tough go of it last night, but that's to be expected. On the bright side, many parents congratulated me last night, and all of the St. Agnes faculty came to my room to offer a hearty well done, and I even had a newspaper call me today."

This was an amazing display to Thomas. When in conversation, this man could not be understood. His words converged and overrun one another. But put him in front of a bunch of students and his eloquence is exemplary.Truly amazing. For the next five minutes, Thomas kept a count of how many times the science teacher said me, my, I or myself. Fifty-seven.

Finally, after the children were sufficiently rested from their long walk from the high school and from changing into their practice clothes, Kenneth Lawton yielded the floor to Mark.

Thomas had arrived promptly at 3:30, cutting a deal with the Burkes to start work 10 minutes earlier so he could leave early. As soon as he got to the pavilion, Thomas grabbed Mark for an oral outline for the beginning of practice. Mark told him that the biology teacher had gotten into the habit of droning on at the start, then Mark would speak for a couple of minutes, outlining the day's events which he had jotted down on an index card.

"Well, let Mr. Kenneth Lawton have his little chat-time today. But eventually that's out," Thomas said. "I doubt he would have a history teacher coming into his room to teach chemistry, so he shouldn't be up in front of a wrestling room trying to explain something he doesn't understand. When it's your turn to talk, keep it short and then introduce me."

Mr. Lawton deferred to Mark and he, in turn, introduced Thomas as a new, full-time assistant coach. "He'll be volunteering to help us along." Thomas had asked Mark that he be identified only as a former teammate of Mark's at Covington, and nothing else. No accolades from high school. No talk of college. And that's exactly what Mark did.

"Well, I had a plan for today, but with only eight guys, we'll have to scrap that," Thomas said. "Of you guys, how many wrestled last night?" Three raised their hands.

Turning to Mark, Thomas asked about the number of wrestlers on the entire roster. Twenty-five.

"Okay," Thomas counted on his fingers, feigning ineptness at mathematics. "That's 17 teammates who are absent. For every teammate not here, I want one minute of jogging around the perimeter of the room, and that is in addition to the 30 minutes which will now be our daily run. Then, for every teammate missing, each boy here owes 30 seconds of spinning. So after the run, pair up and get on the mat. And when you've done those two drills, for every teammate missing, you owe 17 suicides."

Thomas paused for effect, letting his words penetrate their adolescent brains, already burdened with thoughts other than the ones being directed at them. As the volunteer coach looked at the eight faces, he recognized only Tony Kingery.

"Are any of you boys here satisfied with a 75-0 ass-whupping like the one last night?" Mr. Lawton cleared his throat when he heard the profanity. Thomas ignored the science teacher.

"Well, I wouldn't be either. Now this team can't win with eight guys at practice. Tomorrow, with 25 guys in practice, we can start chipping away at the 75-point deficit. And by chance, if any of you boys here today fail to show up tomorrow, today's penalty will be repeated tomorrow by the remainder of this group." Thomas paused again. "Any questions?"

"What about the other 17?" a terrified freshman asked.

"You worry about yourselves. Tomorrow, we'll deal with them. Any other questions?"

The same freshman raised his hand again. "What is spinning and what are suicides?"

Thomas looked at Mark, who shrugged, then he addressed the freshman. "Those drills are something that 39 other teams in this conference are familiar with." Thomas didn't want any more questions. "The clock starts when the last man is running."

As they ran, Thomas spoke to them. He told them about winning, about life, about winning and then about life again. He explained that wrestling was not just a sport, but an attitude. And when, some day, each wrestler eventually hangs up his shoes, whether it's after one practice or after a decade of practices, he'll be part of a group of comrades that is unique in the sporting world.

"I will give you this same speech every day or maybe just once a week. But I guarantee that you will know it by heart, and you'll be able to mock me in the hallowed hallways of St. Agnes as you shuffle from one class to the next. Every single day, I'll talk and explain and cajole and plead. And if every day only one percent of what I say sinks in – well, that's more knowledge than you boys had yesterday. At times you will be sick of my shit, but I promise that you will be better prepared than you were last night."

Tony Kingery had been leading the pack for the 12 minutes it had been running. For some inexplicable reason, maybe to regain the power he had suddenly lost, Mr. Lawton told Thomas that Tony shan't be practicing. "He's only in eighth grade," Kenneth Lawton said. "And I wish you would stop with the profanity." The teacher felt better.

Thomas simply nodded. "Tony Kingery – come here, please." Over came Tony, still jogging in place. "Mr. Lawton has something to tell you."

Kenneth Lawton was surprised that Thomas chose not to tell the student himself but instead passed the issue over to the teacher. After a deep breath, though, Kenneth Lawton accepted the responsibility. He was, after all, still the head coach.

"You're welcome to stay, but you'll have to sit on the sidelines," Mr. Lawton said, after explaining the school policy to the youngster.

Tony thought things would be different once he saw Thomas McCloskey at his first practice. Discouraged and on the brink of tears, Tony looked at Thomas but received no sympathy. Then he walked to the side of the mats, sat down on the floor and untied his white, Converse Chuck Taylor high-top sneakers.

"One more down," Thomas announced to the seven wrestlers laboring around the basketball court. "Now you have 48 minutes, 18 spins and 18 suicides."

Mr. Lawton immediately began to object vehemently, but Thomas spun and whispered into Kenneth Lawton's ear. "If you want someone seriously hurt on that fuckin' wrestling mat this year, then you just keep coddling these boys. Otherwise, you gotta trust me so we can turn these boys into the damn wrestlers they have to be."

Oh, how Thomas desperately wanted Liam Connelly at Friday's practice. The team needed a leader, and if Liam was up to this wrestling challenge, then maybe St. Agnes could start moving forward.

Thomas thought about it all day as he worked at the gravel pit, operating a front-end loader, filling tandem dump trucks until their bodies sank to the metal leaves on the chassis. He liked the repetitiveness of operating machinery on a day like this with abstract thoughts wandering through his head. He was able to think more deeply, concentrate on wrestling while he got paid to work.

So, he thought. He thought of what to say to the team, and to Liam. He decided what shouldn't be said. If by chance, Liam chose to oppose Thomas, then the "volunteer" coach prepared himself with the proper retorts.

Thomas yearned to remember his experiences in high school, especially with a younger Coach Gibbons. Gibbons knew exactly what buttons to push with most of his wrestlers, getting the most out of some of the more uncoordinated athletes in high school. Quite often, his antics would fail and a wrestler would quit, but Coach Gibbons simply would say "this sport is the survival of the fittest, and evidently he didn't fit."

The adrenalin began to pump as Thomas drove from Millersburg to Evandale. His muscles flexed, goose bumps rose along his shins and up along the extremities. He parked in the lot of the community pavilion, and when he got out of the truck, he felt he was walking into a district championship back in his high school wrestling days.

He felt alive.

What greeted Thomas, though, was not exactly what he had expected. Twenty-four students were, in fact, suited up, stretching out lazily as they did every day. Mike Masterelli sat in a chair completing overdue homework. A twenty-sixth sat alongside the mat, suited up for practice, white Converse laced up, ever-hoping. But the two full-time coaches stood at the entrance to the multi-purpose room with a gentleman, a gentleman Thomas did not recognize.

The gentleman greeted Thomas, tipping off that he was more important than Mark or Kenneth Lawton. "I'm Terry Broughton, St. Agnes' athletic director," he said. "I was wondering if we could have a few words prior to practice?"

This was a bit too formal to be a 'Welcome Aboard' chat, so Thomas' guard went up immediately. "You want to chat between the two of us, or is this to be a group chat?" Thomas liked to be firm, show a little intelligence, maybe some jousting in situations such as these. He didn't like to be judged by his appearance, and most people took him for a sewer rat, muddied and ready to fight. It was ironic because, more often than not, that was the essence of his attitude. Muddied. Ready for a fight.

"I thought perhaps just you and I could talk," Terry Broughton said.

"Actually," Thomas voice deepened. "I'd prefer the forum."

The decorum and eloquence impressed Terry Broughton. The picture painted by Mr. Lawton was not accurate. A troglodyte this man was not.

"Very well," Mr. Broughton said. "But perhaps if we move from the doorway, we could get a little more privacy."

The foursome walked 20 feet down the hallway to an ancient picture window overlooking the Evandale Inlet. Some seagulls were dive-bombing off an area of the marina, preying on an early dinner. Terry Broughton stood with his back to the window, Mark and Mr. Lawton taking up positions alongside the athletic director. Thomas looked out the window at the seagulls, calmly ready for the attack. Concentrate on the birds. He repeated that in his mind. You love the ocean, the sand, the seagulls, sandpipers, starfish. Concentrate on the beauty, and you won't get so ugly.

Terry Broughton started, and as he did, Thomas began a silent count to 10. His mother used to tell him to make that count every time he started to feel the anger build. "You have a terrible temper," she would tell him. "You need a diversion, because if you let your anger get the best of you, you will always lose."

After just moments of the preamble to the lecture, Thomas had enough. "Listen. Five more minutes of teachings by Mr. Pierce and Mr. Lawton will not prepare these students for anything but failure. They'll fail tomorrow. They'll fail for the rest of the season, and then they won't return for the next season. That will be the ultimate failure – to quit because they've been humiliated. Once teenagers learn how to quit, they'll be doing it for the rest of their lives."

"And how do you know so much about teenagers, or for that matter, students in general?" Mr. Lawton asked. He was quickly quieted by Broughton, but Thomas chose to answer.

"Because I was one of those teenagers – impetuous, volatile, righteous, all-knowing, arrogant, shy, scared, brave – basically just schizophrenic – and I remember what it was like to wrestle and to fail and to continue after failing. I don't have a gift to teach biology Mr. Lawton, and I wouldn't want you to masquerade any longer as a wrestling coach."

This statement was not meant to be hurtful, and Thomas was actually attempting to pass a compliment on to Kenneth Lawton, but his final words deeply wounded the teacher. "I never asked to be coach," the teacher said. "The principal came to me and asked for my assistance."

"Mr. Lawton, there's nobody asking you to abdicate your position. You don't know a damn thing about wrestling, but that doesn't mean you have to abandon your authority. Act as a leader. Do what you can do best for this team. If that means unlocking the door, then unlock the door. If it means washing the mats, then do it. Be a statistician. A trainer. A cheerleader. But for Chrissake, don't pretend. Don't try to teach something that could get the kids hurt."

Upon hearing the profanity, Mr. Lawton glanced toward the athletic director. Lawton wanted immediate action, but there was only silence.

"I think this is my fault," Mark said. "I asked Tommy at Thanksgiving if he could help out, and Tommy said yes." The future flashed bleakly before Mark's eyes. "Tommy exaggerates when he talks of being so difficult in high school. He actually was a model student at Covington. It wasn't until afterwards that he became such a pain in the ass." Mark shot a smug look at Thomas. The words made Broughton smile. Thomas realized now the ultimate selfishness of Mark's intentions.

"Tommy knows more about wrestling than anybody else I know. He was a champion in high school, he went to one of the best wrestling colleges in the nation, and if it weren't for...."

Mark went too far for Thomas' liking. He interrupted and cut right to negotiations. "Listen Mr. Broughton, I'm no friggin' idiot here. I was asked to help, and I said alright, because I'm good to my word. All you have to do is ask me not to show up anymore, and I'll feel like I haven't betrayed Mark nor have I betrayed my word. I'll tell you what, I got the knowledge, the fire and the fortitude to teach these kids how to win. The problem that many people like Mr. Connelly are going to have is lack of patience. They want to win now, tomorrow at the latest. But the foundation for this program was built improperly, and it's not going to be rectified by tomorrow." Broughton and McCloskey's eyes met in a mutual understanding. "You give me a chance, you'll see results. It may not be wins, but you'll notice a change in the kids."

The four men returned to the wrestling room. Terry Broughton took a seat near the door as Thomas walked in a beeline to Liam Connelly and invited him to the stage out of earshot of all who remained. Mark Pierce and Kenneth Lawton stumbled over their words, trying to remember the best way to begin practice, nervously aware of the athletic director's presence.

The St. Agnes Lancers sluggishly stood and slowly began their 30-minute run, a marathon of an exercise in their estimation – even without the penalties. They turned cautiously to catch a glimpse of the event on the stage.

At the rear corner of the stage, where an actor would be directed to 'enter stage right,' Thomas positioned himself so he faced the runners. He knew his face would remain peaceful while Liam's face would contort as only an adolescent's face could.

"I understand that your father was the brain behind this project."

"Yeah." The junior's body language let Thomas know that perhaps the coach should be talking to the father. Thomas shook his head – me and this kid ain't gonna get along, he thought.

"Why weren't you at practice yesterday?"

Liam shrugged.

"That's not good enough. I want some kind of verbal answer. And I prefer the truth."

Liam's face contorted. "I did awright at Blakemore. Why show up at practice until some of these other dorks can put up a challenge?"

"Oh, that's a great attitude Liam. By losing, you think the team has actually won. So you strut around Blakemore and act like an insurgent slave who was eventually killed. You better watch it or some bad ass out there is gonna stuff your shit. You're not good enough yet to act like an all-world."

Liam shifted in place, wore some apathetic emotions but said nothing. He was intelligent enough to keep his mouth shut, and Thomas liked this.

"Now I need to put a challenge to you. Not because your father is the person who backed this team, but because you're an upperclassman and the one wrestler with the personality – and I hope guts – to take charge."

Liam stopped shifting and began to listen more intently.

"No more Spartacus antics. No finger pointing. No talking. This team needs a leader who leads by example. On time, everyday, suited up and ready to go. Wrestle hard and beat up everyone in the surrounding weight classes. That's the only way your teammates will get better. Then I'll bump you up three or four classes in practice so you can get some stiffer competition. The only way this team is going to get better is if it has someone to take the lead. Right now, the only way I see it, that someone has to be you. Do you think you can do that?"

Liam liked being asked instead of being expected to participate. He felt like a man, like a warrior with a challenge. He couldn't possibly decline. Liam nodded and Thomas offered his hand.

Thomas jumped from the stage. "C'mon guys. Pick up the pace. We gotta be able to go six hard minutes against Flat River. Pick up the pace. Six hard minutes. Pick up the pace. . . ."

NINE

Thomas couldn't remember the last time he was in bed on a Friday night before 10 o'clock. Sure, there were the dismal nights in the wintertime when a cold or the flu would dictate the curfew, and there were the occasions when a divorcee would take Thomas home from the SandSkrit. But those nights did not include much sleeping.

Lying there in bed, Thomas could not sleep. He just stared at a black ceiling, trying at first to fall off with absolutely no sound, then with some music, and then back to silence. His thoughts were on Saturday's dual match and how he would be judged now that he was taking partial responsibility for the team's performance. So he thought, anyway. He thought about how he could improve this St. Agnes team, yet the team had not even been given the opportunity to display improvement.

Thomas awoke around 5:30, having dozed off a half hour before midnight. He hastily got dressed – some jeans, construction boots, t-shirt underneath a long-sleeved flannel. Standing on the front stoop, he surveyed the weather situation. With the sun not due on the scene for another hour, the sky still was dark, but there were no stars, and there was enough light combination from the exiting moon and the arriving sun to notice a heavy cloud cover.

The stillness irked Thomas. He rarely listened to advanced forecasts, only needing the morning report to dress appropriately. No radio reports were needed for this Saturday morning, and, incidentally, all reports underestimated the storm system circling off the North Atlantic.

A slight breeze warmed Thomas' face as he walked to his truck. It was much too warm for a light December rain. Being the land-loving mariner that he was, Thomas could smell a Nor'easter. But it was still a ways off, and the 11 a.m. wrestling match could start and finish before any heavy rains would arrive.

A nice 16-ounce cup of 7-Eleven coffee, the *New York Daily News* and a cigarette were a perfect trio as Thomas sat in his truck listening to the morning news. Nothing interesting in the thin Saturday edition of the *Daily News*. There was a murder in Washington Heights, involving a jealous Latino. The Knicks lost. The Rangers lost. The rest of the area teams didn't play. And Thomas didn't really care about any of it.

His mind kept going over the details of the morning's match against Flat River. In the back of his mind, Thomas dreamt of an upset, but he knew that dream wouldn't come to fruition for a couple of years. Flat River was in a rebuilding process after a decade of tremendous success, but even with the coaching changes and a lean season or two, Flat River was a larger, more dangerous and vicious school, comprised of a mosaic of students: rich kids shared classrooms with Section 8 kids; Hispanics strongly dominated the enrollment recently; whites and blacks still figuring prominently in percentages. And the toughest of all these groups were corralled for the wrestling team.

Always keeping a set of loose goals in his mind, Thomas knew the Lancers needed to take a giant step forward. That meant cutting the points allowed from 75 into the high 50s, and putting some points on the board – 10 would be a godsend.

He wanted to wrestle; stripped down, he could make 189 pounds. One-Hundred and eighty-nine pounds. The number made him laugh. He was so embarrassed about it. At 5 foot 10, he didn't look fat to his friends, but he sure felt huge. Just several winters before, he was starting as a freshman in college at 157. If he wrestled today, he figured that some hot-blooded Hispanic from Flat River would probably make him cry. He decided it would be better to keep his coaching to a mental capacity only.

The St. Agnes team was due at the high school cafeteria at 9:30. A 25-minute ride north to Flat River would get them to the high school at the top of the hour, then weigh-ins, some junior varsity matches and then the varsity contest.

By the time Thomas showered and cleaned himself up, the sky was a deep gray, but not yet ominous enough to postpone the 11 o'clock match. The marquis conference matches which would start at 1 p.m. could be in jeopardy. Certainly, the rare weekend night matches were dubiously perched.

It was going to be a harsh day, both inside and outside the Flat River gym.

It had been raining for six hours by the time Thomas started to make his way home. The last three hours a deluge.

The rain had stopped completely at 4 o'clock, so Thomas decided to give up his chair at SandSkrit – where he had stopped in for an atmosphere fix, ordering two Sprites and three cups of coffee. There was not a soul around to claim his seat, though. The National Weather Service warnings that this storm system could carry winds up to 60 mph scared away all the regulars from the Whiting Beach bar, as well as the Christmas patrons for the local businesses. Only Thomas and his thoughts of wrestling remained on the abandoned shore streets.

Walking slowly underneath the blackened sky, Thomas tried to retrace every move from the morning's match. Results were not far off from his prediction, but Thomas didn't like how they got there.

Once again, Mark and Mr. Lawton didn't talk to the opposing coach to set up any possible freshman or j.v. exhibition matches. So Flat River only had 15 wrestlers suit up for varsity at the match. The rest of the Flat River squad had an early practice, getting a better challenge from itself than it could from St. Agnes. This scenario caused Thomas to proclaim that all the kids need stiff competition, teaching alone would not work. "It would be as if you guys were taught everything about sex but were never allowed to put it to use," he said to the two coaches. Bad example, Thomas caught himself shaking his head immediately after speaking. One guy had been married to an ice princess for most of his adult life and the other was probably still a virgin.

The sun peeked through the clouds and shone brightly for the short time Thomas spent at the Sendl Grocery Store. The day was actually turning into a beautiful winter's day down at the Shore, so Thomas decided to grab a cup of coffee and head back to Evandale to stand on the boardwalk and watch the surf.

About six or seven surfers were sitting on their boards, bobbing up and down over the large swells and whitecaps. Once in a while, a black figure would smoothly paddle until he caught a wave, then he would stand, only the flesh of his exposed face visible. Most often, though, the surfers would let the larger waves go by for these were much too turbulent and much too powerful for the average East Coast surfer to catch.

With the thought of the wrestling match still rolling through his mind and the sight of the surfers, Thomas did not recognize the clouds reforming, despite having a clear head from a health night the previous evening.

Slowly, the wind picked up, smacking Thomas on the left side of his face. Then large raindrops began to fall, followed by smaller drops in a more steady flow, finally a downpour. This Nor'easter sure was showing itself to be a late-season hurricane.

Thomas looked to the sky and noticed the motion of the clouds. Hell, when the sun broke out, they were in the eye. Never mind now. The winds weren't doing much damage, and Thomas decided that if the surf rats could stand a little rain, so could he.

Moments later, as the deluge continued, one by one the surfers emerged from the raging Atlantic. They carried their boards to their jeeps and small pick-up trucks, quickly wriggling free from their wet suits, wrapping towels around their naked bodies.

Standing on the Evandale boardwalk, Thomas felt alone. The month-long excitement from the wrestling may be able to produce solace for the long run, but deep down, he was feeling empty. He longed for companionship, but had not met anyone since Michelle Jennings. That is, not anyone he'd want to spend more than three hours with. Thomas never really noticed the stiffening winds and the stinging rain.

Drenched, testicles squeezed tightly by their sac, Thomas decided to head back home. It was no use standing starkly alone on the winter's boardwalk feeling sorry for what he did not have. He slid across the vinyl bench seat in his truck, fogging up the windows moments after closing the door.

The defrost normally was quick to react in the winter, but the steam from Thomas' body kept a constant film on all the windows, making driving treacherous. Radio reports updated the severity of the storm, noting that the system was stalling and that the wind and rain was expected through Sunday afternoon.

Police detours along the oceanfront forced Thomas to drive inland a few blocks. The ocean, with its high tide, was also being pulled by a full moon, and it went crashing past sections of the Galway boardwalk, creating a new but temporary beach on Ocean Avenue.

The effects of the constant rains and wind were starting to become apparent. Large limbs were down in front yards and in streets. The intersection of Cladda and Fourth was blocked completely by a sugar maple and with it 200 feet of electrical and telephone wire lay on the ground.

Thomas went around the block and came back to Fourth Avenue, where, two blocks farther along, a bronze Toyota Celica was stopped, hazards on, its bumper no more than six inches from a felled locust. The driver's door was open but no one was around.

Thomas pulled to the side and put on his hazards. He looked in and all about the Celica but saw nothing. Rain was pouring onto the driver's seat, so Thomas shut the door. "Hello!" He looked around at the neighborhood houses, but not a light was on. "Hello!"

From one of the back yards a young lady came running. She was crying and asking Thomas for help.

Her wet hair hung wildly over her eyes and back over her shoulders, and at first Thomas did not recognize her. "The tree (sob) came down (sob) and I (sob) wanted to see (sob) if my hood got damaged. (Long sob). So I got out (sob) and that's when (sob) Samson ran out of (sob) the car."

"It's alright. It's alright," Thomas said as he took hold of her. "He'll be alright." The voice seemed familiar to the young lady, so much so that she immediately stopped crying. She suddenly felt reassured and when she pushed back to speak once again, she recognized her sister's ex-boyfriend.

"Now I thought that was you, Tammy," he said, brushing the straggling strands of hair from her forehead and tucking those behind her ears. "Why don't we get these vehicles out from the middle of the road and go looking for your Samson."

After moving the car and the truck, Thomas said he had an idea. He pointed out that the front of Doc Clayton's garage had a two-bay carport. Instead of searching for the cat through the soggy lawns and sticky bushes, spooking the little guy even further, they could sit underneath the carport, call out his name and look ever so intently.

"When you're moving, your eyesight bounces around," Thomas said, trying to sell his idea. "But if you remain perfectly still and move only your head and eyes, you can see a mouse move. And if you can see that mouse move, Samson should be close by."

Tammy smiled. She was content with the explanation, and grateful for the company. Thomas fetched two of the larger logs from Doc Clayton's wood pile on the south side of his garage and set them on end on the concrete underneath the carport. "Now, which way could he be?" Tammy indicated either north or west. Each took up a position and began to call intermittently.

"Tammy, I won't leave until Samson comes back. He's just a little scared right now, but he'll come to your voice eventually." In the grayness, Thomas didn't see Tammy's smile.

The wind howled and, at times, the rain descended sideways. They would both call the cat's name, Thomas allowing Tammy to call more often. Then they would sit in total silence. For 40 minutes, Tommy and Tammy peered into the dusk of that late Saturday afternoon, keenly observing any movement other than wind-blown flora, and oblivious to the fact that no other cars had ventured down this street.

"He's probably underneath a bush or a tree," Thomas said, breaking the silence. He called out.

"I don't know what to do. I can't leave him out here. He's my friend." The emotion which had been absent during the silence returned to her voice. She thought about the predicament if it were she that were lost in a foreign land, cold and wet and alone. Would anyone search for her? Tears rolled down her cheeks, but it was getting too dark and was much too wet for Thomas to notice.

The rain tapered off to a drizzle. Thomas told her to keep calling, that he would stay with her all night. "In fact, I can stay here while you get home real quick, get dried up and get some food and warm coffee. I'll stand lookout."

Tammy was ready to go when she thought she heard Samson's meow. "Shh." She called quietly through the light rain and the descending darkness. "Samson" Another apparent timid meow. "Samson."

Thomas spotted two glowing green eyes in the blackness off to their right, about 15 feet away along the side of Doc Clayton's garage. Whispering so not to startle the creature, Thomas told Tammy what he saw. Tammy slowly walked to the edge of the garage. "Psswsswss. Psswsswss." Hunching over, she extended her hand. "Samson." The two companions were reunited that easily.

Thomas opened the driver's door to the Celica, Tammy got in, put Samson on the passenger seat, and quickly shut the door. Lowering the window but a few inches, Tammy thanked Thomas and pledged her undying allegiance.

"How can I ever repay you?" Tammy already had an answer, but she waited to see if it was the same.

"There's no repayment necessary. Someday, when my cat is misplaced, I'll give you a call."

"You hate cats, Tommy."

"Oh, not as much as I used to," he flashed his smile. "You never know. Someday I may settle down, and if I do, my first companion may be a cat. Now please get home and dry up." He turned and walked back to his truck.

While sitting in the darkness, looking for the cat, Thomas attempted to bury his thoughts. As he sat in his truck, the ancient emotions which always had haunted him resurfaced again. Tammy reminded him of Michelle, and he longed for her company.

An uncommon flash of winter lightning brightened the December night, immediately followed by a deafening boom.

You're right. You're right, he said to the heavens. The defrost in his dashboard was working faster, clearing the fog once again from the windshield. He helped along the process by using a old, dirty rag from underneath the seat.

He could see better now.

TEN

By noon on Sunday, only wispy cirrus clouds decorated the exhausted skies. Thomas had risen early to survey the damage but, more importantly, to fetch some coffee and the massively thick newspaper from 7-Eleven. Accompanying the early rise, Thomas watched CBS Sunday Morning on the television, and, in succession, sports and comics and hard news were read thoroughly. This all-weekend sobriety was not meeting Thomas' initial satisfaction.

The damage he saw was not disastrous but extensive enough to give local municipal crews lucrative overtime hours. Most limbs and trees that blocked streets were dragged into piles or pushed aside with heavy machinery, left for chain-saw crews to cut up, chip and ship. It would not be until late January for all the wood to be disposed of thoroughly.

With a swath of beach separating the ocean from the boardwalk, Evandale was spared any damage to its Ocean Avenue. But Whiting Beach had up to eight inches of sand washed onto its First Street and Galway had sand and large chunks of its boardwalk littering its oceanside avenue.

Under normal operating conditions, Thomas would have slept through much of the storm and all of the initial clean-up on Sunday. After a typical late Saturday night, he would have rolled out of bed on a December Sunday, just in time for the kick off of the early NFL game. The inevitable hangover would dissipate by the end of the second game, giving Thomas time to shower, eat and head north to Red Mike's for the Sunday night game.

By the 1 p.m. kickoff on this football Sunday, Thomas was bored as hell. He searched around the house, perhaps for nothing in particular, maybe sparking some interest in a project or two. Finding nothing, he just sighed and slumped into the recliner.

Two sober weekend nights in a row. Thomas couldn't fathom the last time that had happened, and he had mixed emotions about it. He appreciated getting up early and exploring the weekend world while many of his chums slept. It gave him a sense of accomplishment, some minute piece of additional knowledge of this world that most of his friends would never attain.

Waking up with a clear, thinking mind, however, sure did make matters more complicated.

With more time to kill and with more brain power to utilize, Thomas needed more projects to keep him busy. The more productive he could possibly become, the less simplistic his life would be. It felt like he was selling out. But to whom, he could not answer. Was it the establishment? Or to Mark Pierce? Or to the temperance-of-the-week-movement? To second-hand smoke lobbyists? To the rule-makers and the money-takers?

Thomas decided that if he were to wake up every Sunday morning like he had on this particular morning, he would turn into every asshole he didn't want to become. Being sober on a weekend morning simply sucked.

He came to this revelation during the first 10 minutes of the first game. So Thomas got in his truck and headed to Red Mike's seven hours earlier than his normal Sundays.

The bar was crowded with a male-dominated football audience, mainly middle-aged with bulging midriffs and always trying to speak louder than the adjacent aficionado. Some wives accompanied their husbands, attempting to stave off any trouble their men could get into on the final Sunday before Christmas.

Back in his little corner, Old Man Jack was perusing the race results from Hialeah where he had laid down a significant bet at a simulcast on Saturday. He was sucking angrily on a cigar, creating a cloak of putrid smoke around him. The smoke gave him a buffer of two stools, which he much desired and, if need be, would most certainly demand. Apparently, Goonie Goo Hoo didn't fair too well in the sixth race at Calder.

At first, Jack scowled at the intruder into his space, but when he saw it was Thomas, the menacing look eased amazingly.

"Hey kid," he said, turning his attention back to the sports section, exhaling a cloud of stale smoke. "What brings you in so early?"

"A much-needed beer." Bobby came right over with a pint of Michelob even before speaking to Thomas. "You're clairvoyant, my good man. And here's a tip for ya." With his thumb, Thomas flicked a quarter in the air, which Bobby caught and tossed it higher, end over end.

"Call it," Bobby said.

"Tails."

"Tails it is." And he smacked the quarter on the bar in front of Thomas.

"You feeling lucky today, are you?" Old Man Jack asked, needing a change in his own fortune. "How about you take a look at some of tomorrow's entries at Santa Anita and give your old friend Jack a jump start."

Thomas put the pint to his lips and quickly polished off half of its contents. "Some may consider my change in lifestyle these last couple of weeks lucky," he said. "I'd call it fuckin' annoying."

Jack glanced over his Ben Franklin glasses at his young friend. "I detect a heavy conscience my dear lad. What seems to be troubling you?"

In a second motion, Thomas finished off the pint of Michelob and motioned to Bobby, pointing to both his empty pint and Jack's glass, once filled with Jack Daniel's, now containing melting ice.

"I don't know what direction to head, Jack." Thomas felt comfortable speaking to the old man, who was 40 years his elder. Jack had had some tough times and tough decisions to make along the way, as did a lot of folk, but all in all he seemed happy with his life. If Thomas could be as content as Jack was, sitting in a bar stool at 67 years old alone with his thoughts, he'd take it.

Jack was happy merely because he accepted what life gave him. A beautiful bride from New York and then three, healthy and happy children who reached full growth in less-than-spectacular fashion. An amiable divorce that followed a somewhat listless marriage. A job as a printer that provided a good income and a reasonable retirement fund. The love of a good cigar. The love of good whiskey. The love of the ponies.

As a young man, Jack wanted more out of life, but he had neither the strength nor courage to achieve the fame, fortune and larger family he sought. Sure he had a modest family, but he didn't succeed at it. Now he lived alone in a boarding house on 19th Street in Evandale, close enough so he could stroll down to Main Street and over a few blocks to Red Mike's, where, incidentally, he has, in writing, requested his ashes be kept.

In Thomas, he saw himself but with guts – lots of guts. Thomas wanted to leave more behind than perhaps just a family name. He wanted to leave his mark, but he didn't want to sell that mark. Life was on Thomas' terms.

Now the younger of the two Sunday-afternoon companions was at his crossroads. And he was seeking advice from the one man he confided in, from a man who was better at giving advice to other people than to his own family. Jack, in fact, never had given advice to his three children. He actually thought of them as flourishing horses' asses, primarily because their mother had had so much influence over them, deciding early enough in their development that any personal input would be misconstrued as Jack leading them to failure, leaving the lead horse's ass neighing in discontent. But Thomas was different than his two sons and daughter. Thomas was a thoroughbred, and Jack didn't want to screw this up.

"Well, what's the predicament you're in?"

"Oh, it's not so much a predicament as a matter of life," Thomas said. "Do I keep the cards life has dealt me? Do I just play out the hand? Toss them in? Get new cards?"

"A poker question. I love poker questions." The sarcasm in Jack's voice made Thomas smile.

Jack folded up the newspaper deliberately slow, neatly producing a tight rectangle, and he placed it on the bar. He relit his stogie, which had burned itself out, took a sip of the sour mash and spoke.

"Son, the first thing you gotta learn is that life is not a game of cards. It's not one hand, all or nothing. And if you're going to liken it to poker, then you better be ready to stay awake your whole life, because you can't break the house in one hand. Now let's get away from the analogies. What exactly is on your mind?"

"Actually, it's two things. One is this wrestling program over at St. Agnes, the other is a woman."

"Ahh! Wrestling and women. Interrelated topics, aren't they?"

"Yeah, I guess they are." Thomas tilted his head to one side as he spoke, smiled and then swigged some beer. He liked the way Jack kidded with him when he was seeking advice. The jocularity loosened him up. Thomas, at times, considered Old Man Jack more than just a friend. He considered him a father.

Thomas' own father divorced his mother when Thomas was 10, and moved to the west coast, to Oregon or Washington. His mother said she loved his father, and that's why she let him go so easily, without a fight. "He's a traveler, a dreamer. I thought maybe I could keep him here, but his soul started to wander," she had told Thomas when he got into junior high school. "I would've gone with him, but I couldn't drag two children around the nation without a clue where we were going or what we were doing."

Recognizing the strength and integrity and all those positive words that lend themselves to positive traits, Thomas did confide in his mother, but she would always be mom. He considered her his best friend all through high school, nearly forcing her to be his date for the junior prom. "Next year, I'll go. I promise," she said.

Within months, Patricia McCloskey was diagnosed with breast cancer. Thomas knew she would've kept her promise.

For years following, Thomas mainly kept to himself. He made no close friends in college and went right to work for the Burkes after he dropped out. Most of his friends from high school remained in the area, but the friendships were remote. Then one day, feeling lonely, he struck up a conversation with the old man in the corner of a bar. More often than not, they only spoke to one another on Sunday nights. Once in a while, they'd go to the track. Old Man Jack and Thomas looked forward to those meetings.

Jack dipped the tip of his cigar, already soaked with drool, into his Jack Daniel's, and puffed. "Well, let's get the woman out of the way."

Thomas told him of Michelle Jennings and how she stole his heart and forgot to give it back. "And she just got engaged last month, and since then I ran into her, something that hadn't happened for . . ."exhaustion momentarily flashed across his face ". . . it seems like years. Then I saw her at a stop light. And last night I helped her little sister, who lost her cat in the storm. You know – I hate cats."

"So, your question to me is – would it be moral for you to have sex with a woman who is presently engaged." Jack blew out an enormous smoke ring that traveled in Bobby's direction, a signal to the bartender to spruce up his drink. Bobby didn't notice.

Thomas watched the ring momentarily. "You know you're fuckin' impossible."

"You've been talking to my wife."

"Ex-wife."

"Ahh, very good, young Thomas," Jack said. "The repartee is easy, anyone can do that. It's the speed that people lack. That is a gift you possess."

"So you have no advice on this one, do you?" Frustration was showing.

Jack removed his growing smile. "I'm trying to make you laugh, Tommy. That's the point. You can't take life too seriously. If you do, then some day you're old and ready to die and you realize you've never really laughed. Don't get bogged down any more with the thought of this woman. Did you know I love Jack Daniel's?" Old Man Jack raised his empty glass, hoping Bobby would see.

Yes.

"Did you know I love going to the track?"

Yes.

"Did you know I desperately loved my wife?"

Yes.

"And when I was younger, desperately loved a lovely Polish girl?"

No.

"I did," Jack admitted his confession, his eyes no longer following the movements of Bobby the bartender, instead locking on the amber drink in Thomas' pint. The old man's thoughts began to drift backwards.

"I've loved many things in this lifetime. All were different kinds of love. And none of them are for sale. I don't know how much you loved this girl, but she's engaged now. Just chalk up these meetings as what they are – chance meetings. And cherish the love that you once felt. Now go out and find another love. One that's deeper or more passionate or more physical, definitely more physical if possible."

Old Man Jack and Thomas sat looking at the football game. Mickey Pazienza was screaming from another corner, "The friggin' game is fixed. Look at these friggin' calls that friggin' ref is making. This friggin' game is friggin' fixed."

Jack heard Mickey and wondered if the ignoramus had a point to ponder. But Thomas stared blankly at the television. He stared so he could erase Michelle from his mind – having loved and lost is better than . . . .

Concluding that, in fact, Mickey had no point to ponder and was in fact a friggin' idiot, Jack returned to the conversation. "What about this wrestling?"

"That's another fuckin' passionate love of mine that keeps resurfacing, but that one I'm not done with yet."

ELEVEN

Michelle Jennings stared at the Christmas tree, the warm glow of the mixed colors making her feel like a child again. Sitting on the floor against the couch, snuggled in toasty flannels, her knees brought in tight to her breast, Michelle sipped her madras as she hugged the present in her lap. Oh, how she adored Christmas.

"You shouldn't have bought anything expensive," she said as she cautiously untied the bow and gently untaped the bottom of the wrapping paper. "Did you wrap this yourself?" Michelle's question held skepticism.

A sweater and a cashmere scarf that she held high so she could capture some of the scarce light from the candles on the coffee table. "I can't see all of the colors." So up she popped and off to the bathroom, where she yelled back that it was beautiful.

"I got it from Saks in the city. But don't be too flattered. I went bargain hunting before Thanksgiving."

Michelle reappeared wearing the sweater and scarf. "Well?"

"I already want to borrow it," Tammy said. "I wanted to borrow it ever since I saw it."

Michelle's gift to her sister was a bit more practical, portraying the little sister's personality within her future career. Wrapped was all but the two handles of a soft leather valise. Tamantha, of course, knew immediately what it was, but the contents inside overwhelmed her. A silver-plated stapler, a silver letter opener, a leather binder large enough to plan an entire year's lessons, and a shiny polished silver apple.

Tammy always displayed more emotion than her sister and was brought to tears. "Oh, this is too much. This cost way too much."

"I got all these things before they went on sale, too," Michelle said laughing. "Plus, I put it on Todd's American Express Gold Card."

The two sisters exchanged smaller gifts and idle conversation when Tammy – only as a little sister could do – asked, "So why aren't the two, love-struck fiances spending a romantic Christmas Eve together?" The sarcasm in her voice was not lost on Michelle, who pursued a more tactful route for her answer.

"Todd and I just decided that this would be the last time we could spend Christmas as a part of our own families, so we took the opportunity."

Tammy knew that her sister did not want to spend the rest of her life with Todd Aldrich. It was a life too choreographed. Too choreographed for a Boston wife like Michelle, restrained by a leash, yet her master able to roam wherever and whenever he pleased.

"Isn't that cold-feet feeling supposed to happen closer to the wedding day rather than the engagement date?" Tammy asked, trying like she always did to get Michelle to admit something she wanted to keep private.

"It's not cold feet," Michelle said. "It's just . . . well, it's just. . . ."

"Cold feet."

"No!" Michelle said, emphatically defending her emotions. Tammy knew when to let her older sister speak and when to keep her own mouth shut. Now was such a time.

"It's just that when we finally get married, Todd's going to want me to be with him at all family holidays, if not in Boston, then on some family vacation. And he's going to want me to be with him at all his important social engagements. I fully realize that by marrying him, I'm marrying his job and his image, and I have to maintain that image as his wife." It was a time to refresh her madras.

"Guys are guys – men are men – whatever you want to call them, and they're possessive whether they live in Boston or Brazil or Botswana or Mars. It's just more so up in Boston, and I also realize that. And I certainly realize that this marriage will be my agreement to give him the stamp to call the shots in our marriage."

You don't mind? That was the question that Tammy wanted to ask her sister, but she knew Michelle was currently asking that very question. So Tammy prudently remained quiet, admiring her teacher presents, wondering how to slip Thomas McCloskey's name into the conversation.

"You know – I consider Todd predictable but mysterious," Tammy began, hoping to bait her sister.

"How do you mean?"

"Well, you know he's going to get up every weekday at the same time. You'll hear him in the bathroom, first showering, then tapping his razor against the sink. Then he'll quietly get dressed, putting on the clothes that he meticulously laid out the night before. His belt buckle will chink a bit; the shoelaces of his black wingtips will squeak. Then he'll slip through the bedroom door and you'll hear the latch catch. The front door will open and close because he needs his *New York Times, Wall Street Journal* and *The Boston Globe* – the Globe for sports – of course."

"Of course," Michelle's tone giving tacit agreement.

"To work, back home, a kiss good night. Tuesday's and Friday's you make love because Wednesday and Saturday is golf. He doesn't have to think so hard on those mornings. Football and deer hunting in the fall. Golf and racquetball in the spring, until osteoporosis sets in, and he switches to golf and doubles tennis."

"Okay, that's predictable. Now for the mysterious part." Michelle waited for the other shoe to drop.

"All the rest of the time is a mystery." Tammy got up to get herself another Amstel Light, allowing the dramatic pause for her last statement to be absorbed.

"You ask him about his day. His answer is always curt. You try to get him to elaborate, just to let you into his circle, but his answers are identical, day after day – weeks – months – years. And you wonder what he's been doing all these years because no man can be that boring. Can he?"

"So you're implying that Todd will have a secret life apart from the one he shares with me, which, if I read into the implication further, means an affair?"

Or affairs. But Tammy knew when to stop. She sat down and twisted off the Amstel cap and took a sip, not able to resist to get in one barb. "Maybe it won't be you as his doubles partner." Tammy quickly continued. "Now, on the other hand, I met a man recently who is mysterious – yet predictable. Actually I've known him for some time, he just happened by when Samson temporarily got lost."

Michelle was starting to get suspicious of her sister's motive and the mystery man in the conversation, when she was thrown by the reference to Samson, who was a birthday present to Michelle eight years earlier.

Tammy told her of the rain and wind, which Michelle had heard about on the news. "But then this tree falls down right in the middle of the street, right in front of the car. It actually bounced up and down a couple of times before it came to rest. Limbs were up on the hood and some of the smaller ones were actually rubbing against the windshield. It felt like I was in a car wash! I thought I wrecked the car. I was so nervous and upset that I got out of the car to check out the damage, and Samson darted right out the door."

Michelle got up and walked to the cat, who was resting peacefully on the couch. Gingerly, she picked him up and cradled him against her bosom. "Why did you have him out in that storm?" Michelle kissed his head.

Tammy got up and took the cat from her sister. "Because we had a doctor's appointment." Tammy began to rock Samson. "He had a bellyache and was throwing up for more than a day, so somebody had to take him to the vet."

"Come here, Samson," Michelle said, taking the cat back. "You poor thing."

Samson was now awake from his slumber and he decided he had enough cuddling and baby talk. He jumped down for a bite to eat or a drink of water. Anything.

"And your mystery man?"

"Like I said, he's mysterious but predictable."

"It sounds the same to me." Michelle was about to launch into a litany of the aspects of vocabulary and semantics and how images appear different but, in reality, are the same.

But Tammy, sensing a counter-argument, quickly clarified her position. "He's mysterious, not because you're unsure if he's a dreamer like Walter Mitty, but because you never know what you're going to get with him on any given day."

Like a girl scout telling a scary story at camp, Tamantha pulled in closer to her sister, the candles shimmering off her high cheekbones, her voice hushing itself instinctively. She had Michelle's attention.

"On a wet Monday morning in the fall, he might be as angry as a bear disturbed from his sleep, or if that autumn Monday might be cool and crisp, he could be as gentle as a butterfly venturing into the world."

"The middle of the week could elicit pure excitement from mundane events, maybe because he's looking forward to a movie on television or a concert in the park. Or he could be as solemn or depressed because there's nobody to share his steak dinner with."

"Fridays always makes him happy because that means two adventurous days lie ahead. His adventures could be in the mountains or at the beach or in Central Park – or even better – behind closed doors." Tammy smiled and threw in an almost unnoticeable wink.

"On Sunday night, he's reflective and introverted, because it's like he's reached the end of a book and he wants to understand its message before starting on another novel on Monday morning."

Michelle raised her eyebrows. "It sounds less like mysterious and more like manic."

"That's your problem," Tammy said. "Your education has taught you to evaluate and label a person instead of understanding and enjoying him. To me, when a man embraces every day for what it is, or what it could be, instead of saying . . ." Tammy switched to a mechanical, computerized voice, her hand mimicking a phone held to her ear, " . . . call me anytime. I'm at work 24, 7, 365." Her voice returned to her hush. "And it's not a type of mystery that scares you, or makes you sad. You look forward to the mysteriousness, because it livens up your life. You don't know if you'll get flowers in the middle of March, which, by the way, he undoubtedly picked out himself."

"So, he likes flowers. Sounds less like manic and more like Liberace," Michelle said, trying to annoy her sister. "You see, he's all twisted around with all sorts of personalities trying to become the dominant force. This mystery man is a prime candidate for a state institution, unless he has money. . . ." Michelle's voice trailed off in curiosity.

Ignoring this, Tammy continued. "Maybe a Christmas present in the summer, which he had hid in a closet but completely forgot about."

"Ahh, a squirrel who can't find his nuts." The madrases were beginning to work on Michelle and she snickered at her unintentional double entendre.

"Fine, joke all you want. Deep down, though, you know this is the man you desperately desire."

Sensing the seriousness, Michelle stopped laughing, but kept on a smile, asking of her sister's predictability factor for this mystery man.

"He's going to be there for you every day. Your life is his life, and when he's done doing his manly chores of the day, he turns his undivided attention to the woman he loves. He's predictable because you can count on him day after day – weeks, months and years. Just for you.

"Mysterious yet predictable."

Michelle did not want to speak, because what she wanted to say was "wow - yes." It did sound much more romantic than her impending marriage and subsequent outlined life. It was now her turn to go to the kitchen for a drink and to give the conversation a break. Who could Tammy be speaking of? There was a vague familiarity of the description, but the vodka was keeping the answer from her.

At a loss, Michelle asked her question from the kitchen. "Okay. Will the mystery man, who came to your rescue in the pouring rain, please reveal himself?"

TWELVE

Thomas followed Old Man Jack's advice and forgot about a future with Michelle Jennings. That was easy enough, for every time Thomas would start to vision a house or a yard or a lovely daughter, he would shake his head, quickly erasing such thoughts. Just like clearing the screen of an Etch-A-Sketch, Thomas told himself.

But forgetting about Michelle altogether proved more difficult. A sight, a sound, a flower, a fragrance would spark memories. He would only go into Kinnerson's grocery store if he was coming straight from practice, but would avoid the corner grocery at all costs if he spent an evening at Red Mike's, just in case. And driving back to his house, past the Ice Creamery along Winconcan Way, was the worst. That was where he and Michelle spent many dates, she getting vanilla ice cream with whipped cream and a cherry or butter pecan ice cream with sprinkles, he never changing from chocolate with hot fudge topping.

A night of stiff drinking would bring forth the most memories, so he significantly cut back his nights going to the local gin mills. An implementation of a weeknight rotation so he could make his rounds and see the guys, but he cut out Friday nights at the SandSkrit altogether – the company of a woman currently was not fulfilling.

Saturdays and Sundays were kept on the circuit. Talking to Jack on Sunday afternoons was a type of church for Thomas, and he knew Jack needed it, too. And Saturdays were purely medicinal, for after watching the St. Agnes dual match matinee massacres, Thomas needed something for the pain. And by the time he would get home, many times by foot, by taxi or, in extreme cases in the dead of winter, by thumb, a good spaghetti western would nurse his inebriated state.

Thus the constant in Thomas' life became wrestling. And in that world, oddly enough, the relationship of the St. Agnes coaching staff was not strained where it first appeared. Mr. Kenneth Lawton still did not like Thomas for his abrasiveness and his lack of manners, and they remained cool to one another, at best. The larger chasm was between Mark Pierce and Kenneth Lawton. Matters simply became more vocally heated between those two because every time Mr. Lawton had a difference of belief with Thomas, the argument would be taken up with Mark.

Mark ultimately would lose, for Mr. Lawton would say, ad nauseam, "I'm the head coach and that's the way I prefer it to be done."

In turn, Mark would talk to Thomas who, although not deaf in the reception of any criticism, chose instead to laugh. "Either tell him to go fuck himself or tell him to nut up and talk to me directly."

As the season wore on, it was Mark and Mr. Lawton who would take turns not showing up for practice. Mark said he was so tired of being caught in the middle that he just didn't feel like participating. Most often it was once a week, usually Tuesdays. For two consecutive weeks in late January, he failed to show up twice a week.

"If you don't want to get caught in the middle, then tell Mr. Kenneth Lawton – biology teacher – to nut up and talk to me," Thomas would inevitably say.

"And you'll listen?" Mark felt stupid for asking because he knew the answer.

"No. I'll tell him to go fuck himself."

St. Agnes lost 11 more matches after opening against Blakemore and Flat River, for the most part having success in closing the gap of the team point differential. As fate put it, St. Agnes had one last chance to win in its inaugural season, and that was against Bishop Leary, which was floundering itself, mired with a 1-14 record.

Whereas the Lancers were slowly getting better, improving with certain individuals, Bishop Leary was heading in the opposite direction. In the last match before facing St. Agnes, Bishop Leary's team attitude was deplorable. Boys were quitting, or missing three or four practices a week. Of the thirteen weight classes, Bishop Leary forfeited four in its previous match, and of the remaining nine, only two wrestlers had winning records, one of whom was Pat Davis, a senior 119 pounder. He was 20-2.

84

"I don't understand how he can have 22 matches if Bishop Leary has only 15 dual matches?" the biology teacher asked Mark. "Is there a ruling where he is allowed to wrestle more than one time per match?"

Mark relished these rare situations, when Mr. Lawton would direct a question to Mark with Thomas within earshot.

"Tommy," Mark would say tauntingly, "I believe you can answer his question better than I can."

Thomas would answer the question with laborious detail, purposely bogging down in the minutia, which bored Mr. Lawton. At times during these conversations, the teacher thought that Thomas had finished the explanation and at opportune moments would arise to excuse himself. But at the slightest shift in body weight, Thomas would launch into additional statistics and additional names of wrestlers and teams, all of which Mr. Lawton neither understood nor cared about.

The simple answer to the last proposed question was that most teams in New Jersey – Bishop Leary included – wrestled not only head-to-head matches, but also tournaments, where team scores were tabulated, but individual performances were more highly touted. Most tournaments, exceptions being tri-matches and quadrangular matches, were hosted during Christmas break, either the weekend before the 25th or the vacation following.

Bishop Leary appeared in two such tournaments. The first, on the same day St. Agnes opened with a 75-0 whitewash to Blakemore, was a weak, eight-team tournament. Bishop Leary finished fourth primarily because Pat Davis pinned his way to the gold medal. The second was the more prestigious, two-day, 20-team Oak Hill Classic, in which Bishop Leary finished 12th, with Davis winning four matches by pin, losing in the final against the state runner-up the previous season at 119 pounds, Jamal Stark. The score was 2-1.

Webber Gymnasium had not seen many wrestling crowds in the last decade, but on this first weekend in February, the stands were packed. St. Agnes had been wrestling in front of hostile opposing fans the entire season, but this was the first sellout since wrestling at Blakemore.

The entire Lancer team sat emotionless in the girls' locker room at Bishop Leary, all 13 starters and three reserves. Thomas made it a point to pressure Mark, who in turn would press Kenneth Lawton, to keep all 13 weight classes filled for every match. "If you're going to give up the six points, you might as well let a kid wrestle instead of giving up the forfeit."

This was not Thomas' first line of thinking. His first approach was to get as many freshman and j.v. matches for the inexperienced Lancers as possible, preparing for the next season. Predictably and weekly, Mr. Lawton would not call the opposing coaches – all who assumed that St. Agnes didn't have anything but a varsity team – so only varsity matches were held. The average St. Agnes loss was 52-9.

So instead of having 25 or 30 wrestlers at season's end, the Lancers had 16, the majority wanting nothing more than to close out the season, go home, and play Nintendo. Thomas stood at the entrance of the locker room, watching these 16 wrestlers, wondering, as always, if this was the scene in ancient Rome, just before the Christians were sent to the lions.

"Okay fellas. It has been an interesting and rewarding season," Mr. Lawton said. The biology teacher always held the floor just before he sent his damned wrestlers off to their next annihilation, and most of the time the only person to speak in the locker room. Rarely, Mark Pierce would try a "win one for the Gipper" pep talk, but it would always come off sounding cheesy and rehearsed.

Thomas had not been present in the locker room until two matches prior to Bishop Leary. He knew what to expect, but it still shocked him nonetheless, listening to the uninspiring drivel of Mr. Lawton. This is not the way it should be, Thomas thought. They deserve more of a chance. They need a jolt of adrenalin.

"Now go out there and try like you have all season," Mr. Lawton said, and as always, called the players in to recite the Lord's Prayer.

Our Father, who art in Heaven
Hallowed be thy name
Thy kingdom come
Thy will be done
On earth as it is in Heaven
Give us this day our daily bread
And forgive us our trespasses
As we forgive those who trespass against us
And lead us not into temptation
But deliver us from Evil

Amen.

86

"Any questions? Any comments?" No wrestlers answered, so Mr. Lawton clapped his hands and was ready to say "Let's go then," when from the doorway Thomas spoke out.

"I have a few words," he said. And he slowly stepped to the middle of the locker room, much to the chagrin of Mr. Lawton.

"My mother always used to say, 'You have to crawl before you can walk.' It's a simple enough saying, but she would use it every once in a while to let me know that some things would take some time. And when I started working over at the gravel pit, some of the tougher old-timers would say, 'You gotta pay your dues, kid.' That was their little way of saying you gotta bust your ass before life started to get easy. All season I've been telling you that Rome wasn't built in a day, and I've been telling you that wrestling is a team sport. Well, today it's time for you to learn to crawl, pay your dues and begin to build your Rome – and the only way that's going to happen is to wrestle like a team."

"Now I understand that you guys are young and inexperienced, so it's understandable that you've been more worried about covering your own butts than worrying about your teammates' butts. Now it's time to act like a team. And to act like a team, you have to know your role. Usually a coach will start at the lightweights and work his way to the heavies. But everyone knows who has the marquis match-up today, and that's at 119."

Thomas turned and focused every bit of attention at Liam Connelly. "Alright Liam, it's time to take the lead. Davis is 20-2, and he's a stud. He's going to be a state qualifier. He's the only wrestler on this Bishop Leary team with any talent. Your job is not to lose big."

Liam was shocked to hear a coach concede defeat instead of preparing him for victory. But he remained quiet. Thomas stared at the 119 pounder, hoping he would keep his mouth shut.

"Everyone in this building knows Davis is going to win, barring injury default or disqualification or if you catch him showboating. But that's highly unlikely. Now I have to remind this team, because I don't think it has quite sunk in yet, that each individual match holds a possible six team points." Thomas looked around the room to see if there were any blank looks. Then he returned to addressing Liam. "Your job – and it is any way you can find a way – is to shave off one, two or even three team points. Because the intensity and dedication in which you wrestle with is going to dictate the way the rest of this damned St. Agnes team is going to wrestle."

Liam's and Thomas' eyes locked. Thomas did not budge one whit until he knew Liam understood completely. Thomas nodded. "And that means," he said slowly, "wrestling the six – hardest – fuckin' minutes you have ever wrestled in your young life." Shivers went up Liam's spine. There was nary a sound in the locker room.

Thomas turned on a dime and starting with Mark Cella wrestling at 103 pounds he began a quick rundown of the scouting report he had gathered on Bishop Leary.

"If you keep standing up off the bottom on this kid, you can beat him. If you lie there like a dead fish, he'll deck you, and we can't afford to start off the match down by six."

On to 112, where Thomas expected a decision, worth three team points. Although he singled out Liam for the purpose of not being scared of anyone, including a probable state medalist, Thomas expected him to get pinned. It wasn't so much as the saved points he required from Liam, but the desire. The heart.

Following 119, Thomas told Brien Cauldron that he expected nothing less than a three-point loss from the 125 pounder. "Another situation where a loss could turn out for a victory for the team. This match can go either way, but we can't afford any silly mistakes." Thomas walked up to Brien, who was sitting against the lockers. He bent down and spoke so only the freshman could hear him. "You cannot lose by a fall, a superior decision or even a major decision. I would love to see you win, but I would also love to see you bust your ass and lose by only a decision. Six hard minutes. Understand?" Brien nodded.

Mike Ennis had the benefit of wrestling with Tony Kingery, who had balance and was a natural at the sport, and also got much practice time and attention on the days Mr. Lawton was absent. From Mike, Thomas wanted a major decision. "The team needs those four points."

"Coach," the freshman asked innocently, "What's a major decision?"

Mark answered quickly, knowing that Thomas was in the midst of the motivational speech of the season. A bit more laid back than Mark had actually seen his friend in the locker room back in high school, but still better than anything St. Agnes had witnessed in his rookie year as coach. "That's when you beat your dude from 8 to 11 points," Mark whispered.

"Twelve, 13 or 14 points is a superior," Thomas added, "which is worth five team points and a technical – also worth five team points – is when you're getting your ass beat by 15 points and the ref stops it for mere pity. If you don't know these damn scores, you'd better learn fuckin' fast, or else St. Agnes will be winless – and that's pitiful."

A knock on the door and the gray-haired Bishop Leary athletic director stuck his head in. "Your turn to warm up," he said, directing his statement to Mr. Lawton.

"What time is it now?" Thomas asked. Not being the recipient of the question and not actually a paid coach, the athletic director looked inquisitively at Thomas. He hesitated, then methodically placed his eyeglasses – which had been hanging on a cord around his neck – onto his bony, red Irish nose. "One-thirty."

"We'll be out in three minutes." After the venerable athletic director left, Thomas spun his head back to the team. "Now for Chrissakes guys, you have to get your shit together and beat these pussies. They're hungry as hell and . . . ."

"I will not tolerate this profanity. I insist that you stop." Mr. Lawton's face was flushed.

Thomas shot him a cold look and continued to speak. With his gaze still fixed on Mr. Lawton, he walked to the center of the room.

"It's time to stand up and fight for what you believe in. If you don't believe in this team, then leave now. But each and every one of you stuck it out this far for a reason. And it wasn't to lose." Thomas paused to evaluate the looks of the St. Agnes' wrestlers. He recognized desire, so he continued.

"This is our championship today. This is where we begin to learn how to handle pressure. Someday, this school will be wrestling for a district or a state title, but it can't do it before one team learns how to win a tough match.

"That team must be the one that's here today."

Thomas ran down his expectations for the remaining eight weight classes. That makes 27 points for each team, he said, which in other sporting circles is known as kissing your sister. Everyone laughed except for Mr. Lawton. "That means that somehow – some way – someone has to produce one team point in a win, or save a team point in a loss. That means everybody has to expect to wrestle six hard minutes. Six hard minutes."

The team was loose. Enough with the rah-rah speech. Thomas wanted to have some fun and he thought about beginning the chant, "Toga, Toga." He figured most of the kids were too young to remember the movie, but he could get them to do it. All he had to do was look at Mark. He was childish enough for mimicking. Toga, Toga. Then Mark would begin. Toga, Toga. The upperclassmen. Toga. The sophomores. Toga. The freshmen. Toga. Then Thomas would yell 'Let's go and kick the shit out of this Bishop Leary squad.' And the Lancers would streak from the locker room brimming with desire.

Instead, Thomas called the players to the middle of the room and told them to recite the Lord's Prayer, and this time listen to the words. And they said the words and they listened. When the wrestling team emerged from the girls' locker room, it was ready. For the first time, the Lancers looked like an experienced wrestling team. The mat burns planted on their temples shone like badges of honor. Bruised noses. Drawn cheek bones. Scarred knees. They tossed their headgear to the bench. They sprinted around the perimeter of the mat like an Iowa cyclone.

Thomas never once ventured from behind the bench the entire season. His role, as he was forced to define it, was to remain at the practice mat, passively out of the way, talking to the on-deck wrestler, preparing him mentally for his match. He did not know how long that self-restraint would last.

Pat Davis was by far a superior wrestler and had Liam on his back 30 seconds after the opening whistle. After one period, the Lancer sophomore was down 7-1. And for the first time as a coach, Thomas came to the forefront, stepping in front of the bench, ignoring Mr. Lawton and putting a hand on Mark's shoulder, indicating that he should yield.

"Liam!" The 119-pound wrestler was upset and chose to ignore his teammates and coaches. "Liam!" The referee instructed Liam to choose his position for the second period. "Down! Take down!"

"I'll take neutral," Liam told the ref.

"God damn it," Thomas said, turning his back to the mat and throwing up his arms.

"What? What?" Mark asked.

90

"He's gotta pay attention. The wrestler on the mat has to pay attention." If the crowd didn't hear his first remark, it certainly heard the second. "Davis can school Liam off his feet. Liam's gotta wrestle from the bottom so he can waste time and save energy."

"Can't we call a time out?" Mr. Lawton asked.

"You can't call a time out in wrestling. A ref can halt a match in injury situations, that's it." Thomas was frustrated and he didn't have the patience to be answering Mr. Lawton's questions. Just as Liam stepped up to the line in his offensive stance, Thomas called to him. "After every whistle, every break, you turn and look right here to get directions from one of the coaches. Got it?" Liam acknowledged the coach by breaking eye contact. Then Thomas turned and repeated the direction to the entire St. Agnes roster. "And that goes for everyone. You look to the edge of the mat after every break, and no matter which coach is here, you better well friggin' listen."

Davis caught Liam in a headlock at the 30-second mark of the second period and, for the remaining 1:30, Liam had to fight from getting pinned from the tightest move in the sport. With Davis wrenching the neck and arching all of his weight into Liam, the 119-pound match was certain to be over in moments. First throwing one hip to the ceiling to keep that respective shoulder off the mat, and shifting his weight to keep the other hip and shoulder from relenting, Liam survived for another period – barely.

Although his pre-match directive to Liam in the locker room was a bit of a gambit – attempting to teach the 119 pounder and the rest of the team that there was winning through losing in this sport, Thomas fully expected Davis to pin and collect the six points for Bishop Leary. But when Liam took the contest into the third period, Thomas felt that this could be the individual match where St. Agnes could save some points for a team win.

Thomas was not sympathetic nor forgiving when the horn sounded for that second period. Liam sat on the mat, arms wrapped around his knees, hands clenched and head bowed. The junior's face was beet red. The score was 12-1.

"Hey! Hey! HEY!" Thomas was livid. Liam finally looked over. "You pay attention to this spot when you're out there," Thomas screamed, pointing to the far end of the bench. "When you're out there exhausted, the coach does the thinking for you. And on your back in a headlock for an entire period is what happens when you think you know what you're doing." That's about all Thomas could get in before the ref indicated to Liam that Davis had chosen neutral again, and it was time to start the third period.

"Liam," Thomas called, more calmly, trying to demonstrate the difference between fire and control. Liam glanced over while heading to the middle circle. "Square up your hips and go into a defensive stance." Thomas stood like a middle linebacker waiting for the football to be snapped. He knew Davis was going to come at Liam aggressively and he wanted his 119 pounder to stall a bit, to regain some energy, to waste some time.

After 23 seconds, Liam was warned for stalling. One more stalling call and it would cost him a point. "Go defensive again." This time only 10 seconds elapsed before Liam was hit with another stalling and a penalty point. The score was 13-1 with 1:27 left in the match. "Now I want you to go offensive. Shoot and reshoot if you can."

With this strategy, Thomas wanted to prevent Davis from executing another offensive throw like the headlock, putting Liam on his back again. If Liam lowered his level and shot at Davis' legs, then the Lancer would not expose his back to the mat, and the immediate best Davis could do was counter-attack and gain a two-point takedown. But instead of staying down on the mat, Davis let Liam back to his feet. The score was 15-2.

"Don't let him up. Don't let him up." The entire Bishop Leary bench was screaming to Davis. Another takedown without putting Liam straight to his back would result in a technical fall and only five team points. If Liam ended up on his back directly from a takedown situation, he would have to fight off the pin in order to receive the technical fall loss.

"Do it again. Do it again. Shoot. Keep shooting." Mr. Lawton didn't grasp the urgency of the moment, and he asked Mark why Thomas was so frantic.

"This could be the team point he was looking for. This could mean a team victory."

"But it's so early in the match," Mr. Lawton said. "How can he possibly foresee this point as being the saving grace."

"Because Thomas McCloskey comprehends every nuance of this sport."

The match ended when Davis countered a sloppy and exhausted takedown attempt by Liam. The final score was 17-2. Bishop Leary picked up five team points.

Liam was dejected as he staggered back to the bench. The first person to greet him and the last person Liam thought he wanted to see was Thomas. He was prepared for a verbal thrashing. But Thomas extended a hand, then put one arm around Liam's shoulder and hugged the 119 pounder.

"That's what it's like not to give up. That's the fight that this team needs to see." After his teammates congratulated him – some still were not sure exactly why – Thomas took him to the warm-up area, told him to sit, draped the arms of his sweatshirt around his shoulders, and gave him a water bottle.

After letting Liam regain his wits, Thomas squatted and expressed his pride. "You have to realize that this will be the toughest thing you'll ever do in your life. Trust me on that. Someday, you'll get yourself into a pickle of some sort and you'll remember this match and you'll remember that you didn't quit. And as long as you have this memory, you'll never quit – never again in your life. Good job." And he shook his hand and disappeared, off to prepare another Lancer.

With the dual match progressing somewhat on script, St. Agnes was down four points with 171 pounder, Kevin Reed, closing out a 12-3 major decision, which would tie the score with two matches left.

A freshman was St. Agnes' 189 pounder. A shy, red-headed flabby kid, Chris Ballinger started off the season running with his eyes locked on the ground, throwing up in the bathroom at the community pavilion for the first two weeks of practice. Thomas wanted to remind him of this.

"Remember how you felt at the beginning of the season? How did you feel?"

Chris shrugged.

"You probably felt like a dork. Like a nerd, just like every other kid that first stepped onto the mat, huh? Including myself."

Chris shook his head. Yes.

"Well, I'll tell you what. You ain't no dork. You never have been. Anybody that makes an attempt at this sports has guts – not much in the brain department but definitely guts." Thomas tapped Chris on the head which got a chuckle out of the freshman. "What's your record?"

3-10.

"And those three wins have come in the last four matches haven't they?"

Yes.

"Well, this kid's a freshman who's only wrestled varsity for two, maybe three matches. And there is no doubt in my mind that you'll deck him within a minute. Sabe? Joo know?"

Yes.

"Chris, look right into my eyes." He did. And Thomas knew he was ready. "Good. Now you're on your own. I'm more worried about Chuck."

Chuck Garrison was a sophomore heavyweight who weighed about 230 pounds, distributed evenly around his 5-foot-11 frame. He still wasn't sure how he made it this far in the season. Forced to attend the first two weeks of practice by an irate Terry Broughton, because it seems that Chuck had clandestinely put a piece of chewing gum on a bleacher seat during physical education class and the athletic director was the proud recipient during an unannounced yet common sortie. Since then, every once in a while he would miss practice, hoping that nobody would miss him, and he could quietly retire from this sport he so desperately despised.

Actually, it wasn't the entire sport he hated. He liked to wrestle when he had someone to beat, but that was rare in practice. With the lack of upper weights on the St. Agnes roster, Chuck was grouped with Chris Ballinger and coach Thomas. Once a week, Thomas would cut him a break and send him down with the 160 and 170 pounders, allowing him to work some moves. That was the extent of his fondness for the sport. The calisthenics and running proved to be cruel punishment, and Chuck tried everything to avoid such unnecessary punishment.

Invariably, Thomas would notice Chuck's unexcused absences from practices. "Every team needs a heavyweight and you're our heavyweight, even if it is by default," Thomas constantly told him.

Chuck's presence paid off with a 6-7 record, the six victories compliments of the smaller schools not being able to provide an opponent; the seven defeats all pins.

"I want you to stretch out real good, Chuck," Thomas told the heavyweight prior to his match against Bishop Leary. With Chuck standing, Thomas started at his neck and made him rotate

94

in both directions; then his shoulders; his midsection – touching his toes was a virtual impossibility for Chuck; his hamstrings, calves, then ankles. Then, with Chuck lying on the mat, they went through another series of stretches.

"Now get into a back bridge." And like every day in practice for five minutes, Chuck got into a back bridge. Lying on his back, facing the Webber Gym lights, Chuck raised his torso off of the practice mat by placing the back of his head on the mat and arching his back. Then he raised his posterior off the mat, being supported on the lower half by his heels. Thus the span of his body between his heels and head was arched and suspended in the air like a bridge. In front of his eyes his hands were clasped, clenched tighter and tighter to offset the pain he was feeling in his neck, shoulders and lower back.

"I don't know why I haven't taught you this yet. . . ." Thomas said, knowing full well that he was too busy teaching the proper way to do a push-up or teaching simple moves which gobbled up much of the practice week. Hearing Thomas' voice gave Chuck the excuse to come out of the bridge and lie on the mat. "Get back up there, boy," Thomas said, playfully smacking the heavyweight on his belly. "Now take your elbows and put them on the mat like some of you guys do to cheat during this exercise in practice."

Chuck's head, heels and elbows were in contact with the mat, and nothing else.

"Now, let your butt touch the mat, bend your knees and dig your heels in again."

Knees bent skyward. Heels dug in. Ass penetrating the mat like a ship's anchor. The points of his elbow seemingly nailed into the floor. And his head receiving much of the blood flow. Chuck's shoulders remained suspended in less than thin air.

"I don't care if you're like this for the entire six minutes of the match. But when the ref blows that final whistle – this is how I want you to be. Shoulders – up – off – of – the – mat. *Capisce?*"

Over the public address system, Thomas heard the introductions to the 189-pound match, so he knew they didn't have much time. He had to briefly explain to the freshman the difference between wrestling hard to win and lying on the mat trying not to lose.

"Sometimes there is victory even in defeat," Thomas said. "You are built like a Sherman tank, and when you have the opportunity today, I want you to go at this guy like a you are a tank." Thomas didn't receive the reaction he desired.

"The Sherman was a World War II tank. Are you familiar with World War II?"

Yes.

"General Patton was a tough, old bastard that kept those tanks rolling forward, pushing through France, constantly battering the German lines, tracking onward to help defeat Hitler."

The St. Agnes bench, already more animated than it had ever been before, erupted into a frenzy. Advice of all kinds was being tossed in the direction of Chris Ballinger. The time had come for Thomas and the freshman heavyweight to test their abilities.

A whistle followed by the single slap of the referee's hand to the mat, and St. Agnes had taken a six-point lead, and barring any misconduct penalties, had secured a tie.

The teammates took turns shaking Ballinger's hand and turned to shout encouragement to their anchor. The team stopped jabbering when they saw Thomas still in conversation, dating from the second match of the season when Thomas had invoked the rule that nobody – not intruding parents, friends, j.v. wrestlers, varsity wrestlers or the other two coaches – could interrupt his pre-match sermons.

"Line up," Thomas barked without looking, and the waiting Lancers complied. In two lines, like a gauntlet, the 12 wrestlers and two coaches stood, clapping and cheering. An old wrestling tradition St. Agnes finally had mastered in the last contest of the last match of the season.

Thomas clipped the headgear strap around Chuck Garrison's chins, a practice the coach normally would not do, but he decided the freshman had enough on his mind at the moment. His rose-dotted cheeks were squeezed together by his headgear, his body stuffed into an undersized singlet. Definitely not a fashion show, Thomas thought.

"It's time, kid." Thomas commonly used profanity with some of the wrestlers, trying to spark fire. Some he would actually lightly wrestle with during warm-ups. With Chuck, he simply spoke quietly.

"He's a sophomore. If you fold up, he'll pin you. If you go at him like a Sherman tank, this team will carry you off the mat, that is if they're strong enough to pick you up, kid."

A smile that came to Chuck's face sent shivers throughout Thomas' body. That's what it is all about, and if there's a God in heaven, he'll let Chuck have that same smile in six minutes.

Chuck Garrison rumbled past his teammates and into the inner circle of the wrestling mat and came eye to chin with Bishop Leary's 227-pound heavyweight, Alan Pose.

If one were to pick the favorite, the St. Agnes wrestler actually appeared more confident and better prepared. But Alan Pose was 10-8, seven victories by nature of the forfeit, putting his actual record at 3-8, impressive by the smaller parochial class standards.

The referee directed the wrestlers to shake hands and reminded Chuck to put his foot on the line, which he did not hear the first time, for his entire focus was on his opponent. The whistle blew, a signal to the crowd to go crazy.

Bishop Leary had good, respectable basketball programs with devoted fans, but Webber Gymnasium had not recently been host to the tumultuous atmosphere when Chuck Garrison dove at Alan Pose's waistline, combining the highly technical double-leg takedown with the more gridiron-like double-leg tackle.

"Two" yelled the ref, holding up two fingers of his left hand, indicating control for Chuck, giving him a 2-0 lead. Ten seconds had elapsed.

But Pose quickly stood up on the St. Agnes freshman, and Thomas knew immediately that Chuck could not keep his opponent on the mat for any significant amount of time. By the time the two heavyweights meandered on their feet back to the center of the mat, the score was 2-1 and only 22 seconds had passed.

Wrestling six minutes is one of the toughest feats to ask a conditioned high school athlete to perform, and it is doubly tough for the heavyweights, leaning 200 plus pounds against one another. The two young parochial kids already were breathing heavily at the 35-second mark when Pose, while on his feet, hit a duck under, ended up behind Garrison and tripped him forward for a 3-2 lead.

The crowd went wild. Both benches were wild. The two wrestlers, though, could hear nothing but the heaviness of their breathing. Pose tried a half nelson to turn Garrison to his back, but Chuck cocked his head in the air like a turtle sniffing for water. Then Pose tried a power half nelson, pushing with his forearm on

97

the base of Chuck's neck, making the freshman's nose touch the mat. After much battle, Garrison succumbed and rolled to his back.

Pose could not keep the half nelson tight around the back of Chuck's thick neck, so the Bishop Leary heavyweight had to switch off to a body press. Coach Thomas pulled Coach Mark quickly to him, telling him to get the entire bench to yell – BRIDGE. And it did.

Chuck heard this deafening order above the thunderous noise of the crowd. His heels dug in. His butt anchored itself. His head pushed his chest arching into the air, and with 227 pounds on top of him, Chuck managed to support his bridge with his two fleshy elbows driven into the mat.

Twenty-five seconds remained in the first period. Chuck's bridge was solid, so solid that Pose didn't know what to do. He looked to the Bishop Leary bench where his coach directed his heavyweight to bounce on top of Garrison. And for the rest of the period, Chuck Garrison survived what he believed was equivalent to an earthquake.

Chuck sat on the mat resting yet breathless, while Pose got up and bounced about. The Lancer heavyweight was slick with sweat and his face was beet red, but in his eyes glimmered hope.

Thomas stepped in front of the bench and took up a squatted position 10 feet from the wrestling mat, the closest spot a coach could advance. He was directly in front of Chuck and mouthed the words, 'Like a tank. Like a tank.'

Chuck rose. He was trailing 6-2.

Pose got the initial takedown in the second period, prepared for the lunge from Garrison. But Pose didn't gain good control when the heavyweights hit the mat, so Chuck stood up and wriggled free. The score was 8-3.

Another takedown for Pose, but instead of attempting to turn Garrison to his back with another power half, he tried a cross-face cradle. Bringing Garrison's head to his knee and locking his own hands together to complete the cradle, Pose began to rock backwards to expose Garrison's back to the mat, but the St. Agnes heavyweight was too thick and snapped free from the cradle hold. After a mad scramble, both wrestlers got to their feet. It was 10-4.

The heavyweights needed a breather, so they locked up – ear to ear, arms entwined, trying to gain inside position for a body throw. Neither, though, was looking for a freestyle type of move.

Both were looking to catch their breath. The lack of action caused the ref to whistle both heavyweights for a stalling warning.

The second period ended, 10-4.

Thomas squatted in the same spot and yelled for Chuck's attention. The Lancer heavyweight's battery was extremely low on voltage. This time the coach screamed, "Chuck, right here – Right Here!"

The referee needed a direction from Garrison for which position he was going to take. Thomas told Garrison referee's position top – for two reasons. One – it made the ref set up Pose properly in the down position, giving Chuck more time to rest and more time for last second instructions. Two – by starting in control, it kept Chuck out of immediate danger of getting pinned.

"Keep him down as long as you can. When you get in trouble, just let him get to his feet. Just let him up. Got it?"

Under normal circumstances, Chuck verbally answered yes. But with his hands switching from hips to knees and back to the hips trying to alleviate the pain, the heavyweight was so parched and so tired that he only gave half a nod and blinked his eyes.

"When he gets to his feet – keep him there. Wrestle on your feet for as long as you can. Got it?"

A nod.

"Chuck! It's all up here now," Thomas screamed, pointing to his head. The referee called to the visiting wrestler to assume the top position. Chuck walked sideways, still looking at his coach.

"It's all up here now."

He's as tired as you.

Like a tank.

For a minute and a half of the third period, the wrestlers exchanged escapes and takedowns. The score was 17-7 when the two exhausted wrestlers once again locked up arms, standing on their feet, leaning, breathing and sweating on one another.

Suddenly, with 20 seconds left, Pose swung his hips and tossed Garrison to the mat with a head lock. Unable to get into the back bridge Thomas had taught him prior to the match, Chuck could only prop his right shoulder off the mat with his right elbow.

The ref signalled two points for a takedown and then made the five-second count, giving Pose an additional three back points. The score was 22-7, a technical fall – automatically stopping the match – worth five team points and a St. Agnes victory. But in order for a tech fall to be invoked, the losing wrestler must free himself from the imminent danger of getting pinned. Ten seconds remained, with Chuck Garrison stuck in a head lock.

Moments remained between a 1-13 or 0-13-1 record for the St. Agnes Lancers. Thomas closed his eyes and listened. If the scoreboard horn blew first, followed by the ref's whistle – the Lancers would win. If it is whistle while the ref simultaneously slapped the mat indicating pin, then horn – it's a push. It was that close to the six-minute mark, Thomas had seen it before. What comes first: the ref rewarding a pin or the time running out? Unbearable. Simply unbearable.

It was bedlam in Webber Gymnasium that February afternoon. Kids were screaming. Parents were screaming. Coaches were screaming. And Thomas – well Thomas turned his back, prayed and listened for the results.

Give that kid his smile back. And he listened.

Horn.

Then whistle.

THIRTEEN

Thomas McCloskey avoided all the local taverns the night St. Agnes put a mild shock to the New Jersey wrestling world. That surprised even himself, for after the long season, he felt like he deserved a couple of cold beers. Instead, he found himself on the boardwalk at Whiting Beach, sitting on a bench, his ass on the back support, his boots on the seat, staring into the echoing vastness.

Looking out into the darkness of the mysterious Atlantic, he wondered what surprises lie ahead. What did his future hold? A natural question for anybody at the crossroads, Thomas felt no special need for a divine answer. He just pondered and imagined any developments, and he gauged his possible reactions to the possible events. If - then. If - then. And if - then.

He had decided, win or lose, that this would be his last night as a coach. The promise fulfilled to Mark, his love for the sport – a feeling being challenged by a number of factors this past season – would remain intact. And Old Man Jack set him straight on his other love. It was time to open up his mind and heart, and let someone else in.

The February night was pleasant to Thomas. Cloud cover kept the stars and the moon from revealing their brightness, and the wind was off at other corners, blistering unknown cheeks and watering foreign eyes. The serenity brought Thomas down off his perch atop the bench, to sitting properly. A few moments sitting, then he lay on his back, his knees bent, hands behind his head, his breathing becoming more shallow.

A chill woke him from his slumber. He knew not what time it was, but it felt like he had slept for ages, waking up in the same body but during a different lifetime. The thought of being a modern day Rip Van Winkle held Thomas' imagination until he shook himself from his groginess and got back to his truck, where upon he decided this lifetime was burdensome enough.

Afterwards, Thomas opened up his mind and let his soul soar. He stopped going to the bars during the week, and surprisingly also on Friday nights and Saturday nights. The exercising he had started with the St. Agnes wrestling team continued immediately. He joined a gym that specialized in free weights. He ran three or four times a week on the boardwalks of the local oceanside towns. Only on Sundays would he treat himself to a beer, just so he could sit and chat with Old Man Jack.

Jack liked what he saw. The roundness which had accumulated aside the cheekbones and below the chin began to disappear. The eyes – once too dark, sunken and tired for a young man – brightened and even sparkled in the cavernous atmosphere of Red Mike's.

"How's the love life going, kid," Old Man Jack would ask every weekend. And to his enjoyment, the old codger would get an earful.

Thomas started dating again. And not just dating, but Dating. The first three eligible women Thomas had previously met at the bars and inevitably bedded, separately of course, and in drunken states, of course. Familiarity was familiar, he reasoned simply, so a search for a possible and future Mrs. McCloskey began with a familiar trio. Dinner dates was his plan – good, old fashioned, open-the-passenger-door dinner dates – or so he thought.

Rita he saw one morning while out getting coffee and the newspaper, and she gave him a pleasant hello, which Thomas found encouraging. The next morning, Rita was there again, this time striking up a conversation. On the third consecutive morning, she asked Thomas if he was busy Friday night.

"As a matter of fact, I'm not," Thomas said, shocked at being asked on a date for the first time. Even if he didn't want to go out with Rita, he would have been hard-pressed to come up with an excuse, being caught off guard the way he was. "I was just planning on getting a good Italian dinner."

Thomas picked Rita up at her apartment at eight o'clock – sharp, but she wasn't ready. She served him a white Zinfandel – his first glass ever – which he found revoltingly sweet. He sunk slowly and deeply into her white, leather couch and scanned the room, noticing her black lacquer entertainment center with pictures of her family atop. Their frames were white plastic.

The leather recliner was black. The coffee table with a glass-top interior was white.

The candle sticks were black.

The pots that housed the plants – white.

The frames on the wall – black. The prints – gray.

He couldn't find a splash of any color except in her family pictures atop that black entertainment center. At least the carpet was tan, but that was because she rented.

While Rita was in the bathroom preparing herself for what suddenly Thomas decided would be a dreadfully long evening, he picked up the black remote and turned on the television, just to make sure he didn't have color blindness. He hit mute and watched VH-1, which was airing Don Henley's *Boys of Summer.*

At dinner, Thomas ordered a gin and tonic. He didn't like gin, and this way he could remain sober without seeming temperately boring. Rita started with red wine, before switching to Manhattans. Four drinks in all. She was going to feel it, but Thomas tried not to hypocritically judge.

The evening went fairly well, not too much divulgence on Rita's inner thoughts and dreams, but Thomas did find out toward the end of her last Manhattan that she had been married to a jealous Puerto Rican drug dealer. Thomas looked at his watch. At 10:37, Friday, March 20, 1992, Rita was officially scratched from his black book.

At her apartment door after dinner, Thomas felt obliged to give her a kiss good night. Thomas chalked up the gratuitous kiss for the carnal knowledge the two shared on previous drunken encounters. But he definitely did not want to go inside, and the more Rita pawed and groped at Thomas, the more he found himself freeing his arms as if he were in a wrestling match. Thomas kept thinking, quite a few Manhattans, I can take you, don't push me, I can definitely take you.

"I have an early morning," Thomas thrice said in knightly fashion. "I need my energy," switching, he said jokingly. But he found himself fully engaged in a skirmish. Finally, he freed himself.

"Listen, Rita. You seem to be a black-and-white type of person. So here it is – black and white. I'm sober and if I sleep with you, I'll feel like I'll have to call you back, out of honor and chivalry, that kind of stuff. And, well, with sobriety and honor on the line, I'd rather not call you."

Good night.

Thomas never again saw Rita at morning coffee.

Thomas did sleep with Cathy and Theresa, again – on separate occasions, of course. Both women were a few years older, divorced and friends whom he had met at the SandSkrit. In early April, Thomas brought a dump truck load of gravel to a house in Galway, the house Cathy received in the divorce decree – along with a seven-year-old girl and a four-year-old boy. Cathy commented on how she hadn't seen Thomas "in such a long time" and "how nice it would be to see you again!"

Cathy put a strange accentual twist on the word "see" just before mentioning that her ex-husband would have the children this upcoming weekend. "He lives up in Edgewater," she said, gratuitously, in Thomas' opinion.

"That would be great. I was thinking of getting some Italian dinner Friday night," Thomas found himself saying again. Hell, it worked the first time without causing him to stutter, might as well stick with it.

"Actually, I've been dying to try an Italian recipe I got from Theresa last month. You remember Theresa, don't you?" A mischievous smile grew on Cathy's face, and Thomas found himself accepting yet another invitation to another dinner by a another woman.

Candlelight. A Chardonnay. An alfredo spinach sauce. Frangelica. And sex until the two adults fell asleep from exhaustion in the wee hours of Saturday morning.

Thomas eyes popped open at daybreak. Normally he would simply rise from the bed, dress and tender thanks. But this was different. This had been a date, and chivalry demanded more than leaving a fifty on the dresser.

He slipped from under the covers as best he could, put on his underwear and Levis as he looked out the second floor picture window. Thomas attempted to concentrate on memorizing and bidding a hearty farewell, but the April morning full of sunshine falling about the budding maples and elms in Cathy's front lawn captured his imagination.

Maybe she is the one. She's attractive, intelligent, she's got it together. Okay, so she's got two kids. Almost every other woman Thomas knew was divorced with children. He turned to look at her radiant face. She seemed to be smiling. Perhaps it was a dream she was having. Maybe it was about him. Hmm.

Thomas remained motionless, staring at Cathy, most of her torso under her pastel sailboat sheets. Her right breast was fully exposed, displaying a lovely silver-dollar sized aureole. Her left leg, too, escaped from the sheets. It was tan and athletic.

He decided not to say anything. Let's see what she says. Not being able to locate his shirt at the moment, Thomas sat on the edge of the bed to lace up his shoes.

Cathy awoke and leaned over to run her hand along his back. "I was thinking of switching from gravel in the driveway to brown stone next month. Maybe you could bring by another load." She laughed.

Then again, maybe she's not the one. Or maybe Thomas wasn't the one for her. Or, as Thomas later concluded, she wasn't looking for anyone. Maybe he should be getting the fifty.

Jogging a slow two miles every other day, Thomas was feeling more energetic than he had in a few years. The renewed vigor had the additional effect of Thomas limiting his smoking to no more than 10 cigarettes a day. It was exactly 10 cigarettes a day for the last month because Thomas would count out that number before falling asleep each night.

The older folks walking with their K-Mart sneakers, the young moms with strollers complete with babies bundled up to their noses and the serious marathoners frequenting the boardwalk all became familiar to Thomas. He would nod and sometimes even smile without forcing it as he disappeared down the boardwalk in an opposite direction.

As the weather got nicer, new faces and unfamiliar faces appeared, so Thomas didn't nod as much. But a new and familiar face appeared at the Straptford Avenue walkway, where Thomas regularly began his nightly routine. It was Theresa, exactly two weeks after he spent the night with Cathy.

This time, it was neither an Italian restaurant nor a home-cooked Italian alfredo meal – which Theresa never heard of – but it was Italian.

The night that Theresa "bumped" into Thomas, she invited him over for pizza and a movie. Thomas never did get to see the end of *9 1/2 Weeks*, never did get to finish his second beer. Dating in the '90s was a strange event for Thomas.

After an aerobic hour of sex, Theresa and Thomas fell asleep. Two hours later, about 15 minutes into the new day, Thomas felt a hand down upon his loins, awakening his slumbering being.

Breathless, they fell asleep again, only to awake one more time at sunrise, negotiating a deal to shower.

All of the sordid details were excluded from Thomas' explanation to Old Man Jack, for Thomas was not one to kiss and fully tell. But he left enough of the storyline intact, so Old Man Jack could let his imagination take hold, leaving a smile on his wrinkled, ruddy, pockmarked face.

"After that," Thomas said, "I had normal, old-fashioned dates. You know, like where I did the asking, and nothing more than a peck on the cheek at curfew."

The first date was with Grace Witherspoon, a girl Thomas had a crush on since elementary school. Grace was in medical school at Rutgers and proved to be tremendous company on three dates. "But she couldn't kiss," Thomas said, a look of anguish upon his face. "That's probably why that one never got past the doorstep."

Kelly Newland was the second, who was the same age as Thomas but was a St. Agnes girl. The conversations were long and comical, talking much of Mr. Lawton and the other teachers, also of some of the guys – total dweebs, as Kelly referred to them. But a spark was missing, and after a couple of weeks, the relationship fizzled.

By late June, some four weekends after the New York crowds started to descend upon the New Jersey shore, Thomas was bored with his new, spiceless lifestyle. He had a feeling it wouldn't last, especially if he had to go it alone. Slowly, once a week, the visits with Old Man Jack became twice, then three times a week. The extra time spent at Red Mike's was soon exchanged for time at Murphy's Law and the overcrowded Cornerstone Pub.

Before Thomas got back into flying his circuit, he thought seriously about coaching someplace other than St. Agnes. Covington was out because Mark Pierce had his eye on that, and no matter how much of an imbecile Mark could be, Thomas wasn't much into screwing old friends. He also wasn't into knocking on doors, seeking opportunities like a salesman, so if nobody came to him, he wasn't going to coach.

And why would anybody come anyway? Nobody knew who he was, lurking in anonymity at St. Agnes, and, if they did, nobody would care if he did guide a team to a 1-13 record.

When summer snuck upon Labor Day, Thomas regained half the weight he lost during the previous 10 months, and he was back to smoking a pack-and-a-half a day.

One afternoon in mid-September, at work, while cleaning his hands after taking a leak, one of the guys called in, "Yo Thomas. Got a visitor." The last visitor was Mark, back in December, and Thomas figured to see that pleading mug again.

Instead, it was Coach Gibbons.

"Have you seen the schedule?" his high school coach asked, extending his hand. Coach Gibbons never said hello, but rather asked a question as a greeting, a trait Thomas admired and adapted.

"No. I'm not coaching this year." Thomas purposely left out that both sides in the St. Agnes scenario were noncommittal to his absence. The two men walked into the shanty for privacy, while Thomas finished drying his hands.

"Whose decision was that?" Coach Gibbons liked to get his wrestlers to open up and not hide anything. "Let it all out," was one of his battle cries. He knew something was afoot between Thomas and St. Agnes, otherwise he would not have been at the Burke Gravel Pit.

"Mutual. There's a couple of reasons. I never wanted to get started in the first place, but Pierce kept pushing. . . ."

"You know why?"

"Yeah. He's too easy to peg, Coach. He's after your position. More accurately, Amanda's after it. But she's only good at clawing, not wrestling."

"And the other reason?"

"It's the head coach, a science teacher by the name of Ken Lawton. Actually, it's Kenneth. I don't think he's ever gone by Ken, and that's part of the problem, too. He's too fuckin' uptight."

Quitting time hit. The rest of the Burke crew left, some of the guys ducking their heads into the shanty to say goodbye to the coach, for they remembered him as their gym teacher when he first started at Covington, while others had sons who wrestled for him at one time or another.

"You wanna beer, Coach?"

Sure. Thomas went over to the refrigerator and brought out two Coors Lights. "Not my favorite, but that's all we got right now."

"Light beer is my choice now, anyway," Coach Gibbons said, patting his stomach. "It's this belly of mine that's brought me here. But first back to Lawton."

Thomas scratched his scalp roughly, then squeezed his eyes, his thumb and forefinger pinching inward until they met at the bridge of his nose. He thought of the most direct answer possible. "He's just an asshole."

"That's a good-enough reason."

"Simply," Thomas let the word float for a moment, "he's never wrestled. He doesn't know balance in every sense of the word, he still doesn't knows moves, he doesn't know how to motivate. Actually, he has the opposite effect on the kids. And he's not open to any suggestions."

Thomas saw the look on Coach's face. Gibbons did not have to say it, but he was letting Thomas know that Thomas wasn't the most flexible individual in the world, either.

"Granted. When I hit the mat, I get testy, but I've explained that demeanor to him. But he just doesn't get it. He was sheltered as a kid, just like he's trying to shelter the St. Agnes kids. And you're the one that taught us how to get the thumbs out of our mouths and grow up."

Thomas wrapped up his negative critique. "So he gets to call the shots, and he has no flexibility in his style."

Coach Gibbons had no argument. Thomas knew the sport better than any wrestler he had ever coached. Thomas absorbed any information offered from any expert in the sport, and he came in contact with a variety of coaches from summer camps, high school, club teams and college. But he listened to Gibbons, by far, the most.

"Basically, I already knew this – from watching a couple of your matches last year," Gibbons said. It surprised Thomas that his old coach showed up for a team not on Covington's schedule.

"How'd you find the time?"

"Well, that's why I'm here. And that's why Mark Pierce is coaching at St. Agnes," Coach Gibbons admitted. "I've hinted at the possibility of packing it in, but I haven't told anyone that I've made a decision. George Vickers, though, has had the balls to call me at home in the last year, inquiring about my status. Inquiring was his word, not mine."

George Vickers. Daddy. Amanda's daddy – always pulling strings, trying to manipulate people. Vickers' current and only problem with the Covington wrestling team was Paul Gibbons. No strings were attached to him.

"That's why I'm here. I want you to be the freshmen coach at Covington. This will be my last year. The only other person I've talked to about this – besides my wife – is Coach Johnson, and he said he'd stick it out two more years as head coach, then turn it over to you."

The offer was generous, honorable and shocking. Thomas initially didn't know why Coach Gibbons had appeared at Burke Gravel Pit, but a job offer definitely never entered his mind. To gradually and eventually take over as coach at his alma mater would be a tremendous honor. Strong football and wrestling teams were traditions at Covington, and Thomas could be a part of its future.

"Not this upcoming season but the next," the coach continued his explanation, "the conference, as well as the state, is going to realign, and St. Agnes is joining 'C' division with us. To get a jump on it, the powers-that-be at both schools – which probably includes George Vickers – decided to schedule a January non-conference match this season to start a rivalry."

Coach Gibbons stopped talking because he noticed that Thomas didn't hear the last part. So he waited for the information to sink in before asking.

"What do you think?"

No.

FOURTEEN

Wrestling had once again become a beacon for Thomas, whether or not he wanted to openly admit it, and it illuminated a path in which he could follow. For the first time in his adult life, getting out of bed was not a chore, suddenly it held meaning. Days seemed longer, full of hope and vigor, and all of that stopped because of his own obstinacy.

All he had to do was to say 'yes' to Coach Gibbons. Or he could have picked up the phone and called Mark Pierce. Caught in between personal principles, Thomas chose to revert to being a loner.

And so he sat alone at the Cornerstone Pub on a quiet Saturday evening, just before supper, reading the sports section, oblivious to the employees busily attending to last minute details and preparing an uncommon Saturday buffet.

After two pints of beer, Thomas ordered a grilled chicken sandwich on a kaiser roll with curly fries. After dinner, he had another pint of beer. By this time, he had finished the main section of the paper, the sports, business and entertainment sections, and put a good dent in the crossword puzzle.

It was 6:30 when Thomas noticed the first costume. A bartender was starting the night shift, dressed as a prisoner from a 1930s rock gang. Shit. Thomas remembered the date. "I hate Halloween," he muttered.

When Thomas left his house without his truck 2 ½ hours earlier and a mile away, he had already made the decision that he was going to get tight. A good, old-fashioned, one-bourbon, one-scotch, one-beer type of drunken stupor.

That was his plan. And the bums and vampires and drag queens weren't going to change his mind, so he ordered another pint of beer and a Jack Daniel's shooter. Then another.

Thomas pretty much ignored all of the festivities around him, occasionally catching a glimpse of an interesting costume.

There was a girl with a two-foot square table built around her waist – adorned with an Italian red-checked table cloth, Ruffino wine bottle, wine glasses and pasta in bowls, and she was dressed as a waiter. She arrived early and moved about freely as she socialized, but as the crowd thickened, the table was slapped in a corner, unable to move.

Other than looking around to scan the mobile scenery, Thomas mostly stared blankly at the three televisions in his view: pre-season basketball, hockey and the World Series. Thoughts were racing in and out of his brain, switching liberally from one subject to another. Another beer. Another shot.

Out of the corner of his eye he saw a potato lady, her stuffed torso made up as one large spud. Her shoes were spuds. Her hair was an Afro of beanbag spuds. Her face was brown. A brown shirt. Brown stockings.

Never. Never in a million years would Thomas dress in a costume. Never.

A short time later, he did a triple take. "Now there's the winner." A two-headed Frankenstein. A guy and a gal, standing front to back in one outfit, the guy standing behind the gal. They did have on four shoes, but no one in the bar would notice unless they were doubled over ready to heave.

That costume brought a dim smile to Thomas' face. That was his winner. And he drank to it.

The mixture of whiskey, beer and an unusually crowded autumn Cornerstone Pub was leaving a bitter taste in Thomas' mouth. The time was getting on past 9:30, and he decided it was time to take a lung full of fresh air and bounce his way home. Just as he was picking up his pile of money off of the bar and was calculating a tip, he felt an arm go around his shoulders. Oh no, a friend. Then he got a kiss on the cheek. Worse yet, a female friend, something he desperately wanted to avoid this late into this particular evening.

"Why Thomas Patrick McCloskey, where *is* your costume?"

Before even knowing or caring, Thomas acidly spoke. "You wouldn't catch me wearing a fuckin' costume in a million years." He spoke without turning, eyes fixed on the 10 dollar bill, wondering if this was the legal tender he wanted to leave.

Tamantha knew immediately that Thomas was drunk, but instead of scaring her away, it only made her want to stay, perhaps

111

offering a ride or maybe even an ear. She had never seen Thomas in this state before – drunk or nasty – but she had an idea that since leaving college he wasn't anywhere near the choir boy he was in high school.

"Well, you wouldn't catch me wearing a fuckin' costume in a million years, either."

Now that was an attention getter, and Thomas turned his head slightly and saw Tamantha smiling, wearing a beat up Chesterton State sweatshirt and jeans. "I guess I wouldn't catch you wearing any costume, at that." He meant mask, and he meant it to be a double entendre, meaning that Tamantha would never be two-faced or be caught in a Halloween costume. Either way, he wished he could have thought of something better. "What are you having to drink?"

"Something soft," Tamantha said. "I'm the designated driver for potato head over there." Tamantha pointed to the large brown blob who was currently talking to a Ninja Turtle.

"That would be an interesting combo in the sack," Thomas said, quickly receiving a light-hearted slap on the shoulder from Tamantha. He got the imprisoned bartender's attention and ordered two Cokes.

"You haven't been drinking Cokes all night, have you Mr. McCloskey?" her teaching voice activated.

"No, I haven't, Miss Crabtree." Thomas stepped away from his stool and offered the seat to Tamantha.

"No thank you. You sit. I'd rather stand."

"Please sit. If you don't, you'll ruin my reputation."

Tamantha smiled and sat down just as the bartender brought the two Cokes. She handed one glass to Thomas, then took a hold of hers, bringing it up to her lips with her left hand, holding the red cocktail straw with her right. She looked a lot like her sister, but prettier now with the lighter brown hair, frizzy and shoulder length, naturally beautiful complexion without the aid of make-up, wearing the down-home style jeans and weathered sweatshirt. Michelle once looked like that, except she had long black hair. Now that she's found high society, the hair was short, the make-up thicker and the jeans were at the bottom of a landfill.

Might as well get it out of the way. "How's Michelle?" He wanted to ask quickly, trying to prove he no longer harbored any feelings for her. The quickness of the question sent a different signal to Tamantha. She smiled and sipped, thinking there's still a chance yet.

The Coke was too sweet for Thomas' palate, and he decided that he was actually feeling somewhat sober while pulling off a dazzling conversation. He motioned to the bartender, pushing forward his shot glass and empty glass pint. "Another round?"

"Yeah, but how 'bout some 1600 in the little glass." For Thomas, mentioning the name Michelle was the clincher on the evening. He was going home drunker 'n hell, hopefully escaping before Tammy could detect it, not aware that she already had. He didn't give a shit if Michelle saw him stumbling drunk, but it was something different for the little sister, even if she wasn't so little at 22 years old.

"Cuervo." Tamantha was no little girl any more. "I guess you're planning on walking home?" She sounded like a teacher again.

"You still in college? Do they have a speech class up at Chester that specializes in teaching that voice? You aced it didn't you?"

Thomas tossed back the shot of tequila, choosing to ignore the lime and the vial of salt as he always did. The gold liquid burned his eyes more than his throat as it rolled down his esophagus. His eyes watered, causing him to tilt his head and lean forward, clutching the edge of the bar with both hands.

At first Tammy was hurt by Thomas' snide remark about her voice, but then she felt sorrow. She had known Thomas for such a long time that she was sure that this wasn't his true nature. Thomas liked to laugh and smile, not grieve into a sea of liquor. His head remained tilted forward for a long while. Tamantha wanted to pull him toward her and give him a long hug, but she didn't. She sat quietly within the clamor of the festivities, waiting to see the result the tequila brought upon the young but sullen man.

Thomas had survived much and never complained. Michelle said he spoke of his father, saying he couldn't blame him for wanting to spread his wings. He understood and would tell him so, if ever given the opportunity.

Then his mother died and nobody saw him grieve for the person whom he considered his best friend.

Eyeing up a N.J. State championship his junior year, he was diagnosed with mononucleosis. Too much sustained weight loss; not enough nutrition. He finished the season as district champ and 22-0, then put on 25 pounds of muscle over the summer.

Ranked No. 1 going into the final round of matches at Princeton's Jadwin Gym, Thomas sustained some sort of injury – Tammy couldn't remember what – that kept him from winning the title his senior year.

Then Michelle broke up with him right before they went off to college. He left for South Dakota and Tammy didn't see him again until last year at Kinnerson's grocery store.

Another injury in college, career threatening, but compounded with a broken heart from Michelle and his mom, Thomas came back home.

Then his brother took a job in Florida, and Thomas has been alone for the last five years.

If Michelle could just see how he hurts, she would fall in love with him all over again. Tammy knew her sister still loved him, if they would only get back together.

Thomas pushed his weight back from the bar and stood upright. He had a notion of drinking the beer, but he knew he was done. "Stick a fork in me," he mumbled. He turned and said, "I know this is rude, Tammy, but I gotta go."

And he left.

Sunday morning at 8:30, Thomas opened his eyes and stared at the ceiling. He had that strange feeling he had done something wrong. Something embarrassing. He couldn't trace the events backwards, so he started at noon on Saturday and went forward.

A half day at the gravel pit. Okay.

Home, college football, nap. Okay.

A quick shower, walked to the Cornerstone. Fine, so far.

Beer. Jack Daniel's, newspaper, costumes. All right.

Tammy Jennings. Shit.

Not only did Tammy see him dreadfully drunk at the bar, but snippets of a car stopping when he was halfway home, a ride, and a long talk in the living room. And it all included a vision of Tammy.

All he had to go on was vague remembrances, nothing concrete. He realized his body was underneath the bed's top sheet, and he was stripped down to his boxers. No – it wasn't possible.

A hand slipped beneath the sheet, then under the elastic band of his boxer shorts. His fingers searched about his pubic hair for any evidence. Nothing, and a wave of relief swept through him.

Despite being comfortable and knowing that any movement could cause the onset of a hellacious hangover, Thomas rose to inspect the house. On the end table to the left of the couch was a half glass of Coke, ice melted causing the caramel to be brightened. On the coffee table, four empty bottles of Budweiser, caps stacked neatly on top one another. And on the couch, his jeans and shirt were neatly folded. His socks lying on top. His construction boots placed under the end table to the right of the couch.

Thomas turned, and without the thought of any aspirin, went back to bed.

"What do you mean you've decided his ass isn't his best feature. Tammy, I dated him for three years, and I never saw him naked!"

Tamantha started off their Sunday afternoon conversation with what she thought was the best part – disrobing Thomas and putting him to bed. Then she asked, back-peddling – what do you mean you haven't seen him naked?

And Michelle told her little sister – "not that it's any of your business" – but Thomas and I never slept with one another – "well, not naked. A couple of naps, but . . . you know what I mean." Michelle truncated the explanation, feeling that her sister had more than enough.

Tamantha was taken by surprise. Thomas' feelings for Michelle had nothing to do with physical attraction or sex. It was love, and that was so sweet. Tamantha just happened to mention her sentiments to Michelle.

"Yes, I know Tammy." Michelle wanted to talk less of what happened eight years ago and more of what occurred Saturday night.

Tammy explained that Thomas was rather drunk by the time she said hello at the Cornerstone Pub. "He had a shot of tequila and a seriously pained look came to his face. He looked so depressed. He just looked at me with these sad eyes and apologized and left. Well, I went over to Karen and she told me that she was staying until 12:30, that's when the prizes for best costumes were going to be awarded. So I told her I needed to give Tommy a ride home, but I'd be back before then. I caught up to Tommy a couple of blocks away. He was along the side of Nichols Street. He had his hands in his pockets using the whole sidewalk for a path. I pulled up and told him I wanted to give him a ride home. He said he didn't want one. Do you know how stubborn he is?"

Yes. I know.

"Well, finally, he got in. It was about 10:30 by the time he unlocked his front door. Geez, it took him about five minutes. I wanted to help but he wouldn't let me."

He Is Stubborn.

"He got me a coke, and he got himself a beer. And we talked for about an hour and a half, when I told him I had to go. He had four beers at his house, and he was falling asleep, anyway. So I told him he should go to bed, but he wanted to stay up and find a western movie. I told him he should at least get undressed, and he said 'no funny business,' then he laughed. I got him out of his clothes and left him on the couch with the remote in his hand. I don't think he ever turned the television on."

"And?"

"And what?"

"And what did you talk about?"

Michelle, I think you need to give him a call. He really needs a friend. A friend. Not a psychoanalyst.

Lying on the couch with a t-shirt and sweatpants cut into shorts, Thomas already decided he was going to skip his Sunday chat with Old Man Jack at Red Mike's. He did not emerge from his bedroom until after 2, and when he did, he headed straight to the couch.

He flipped back and forth from the Eagles game on a Philadelphia channel and the Jets on NBC out of New York, but he wasn't really interested in either. His mind was on food, but he wasn't feeling well enough to go out to eat or even to whip something up in the kitchen. Hell, he didn't even feel like getting up to call for pizza delivery.

Just when he felt he had picked the perfect moment to gather enough energy and spring into motion, the phone rang. Kill two birds, he thought, and when he rose he felt violently ill.

"Yeah," he mustered.

"Tommy." It was Cal, a drinking buddy.

"Just a second." He set down the receiver and went to the bathroom to throw up. He returned two minutes later.

"Not feeling so good," Cal said. "Where'd you go last night?"

"Cornerstone. Whaddayawant?"

"Didn't they have their Halloween party. You didn't dress up, did you?"

"I went as a mass murderer. What the fuck do you want."

"Man, you sound like death ...."

Thomas could hear it in his voice and knew that Cal was playing games, so he hung up the phone, and leaned his head upon his arm, which rested against the wall. He knew Cal would call back, and Thomas didn't want to go lie back down on the couch. Cal would let the phone ring forever, just to bust balls.

Thomas answered the phone. "You realize I will be better by tomorrow, Tuesday at the latest, and I will hunt you down." Thomas spoke in his quiet and deliberate voice. "Now Cal, what the fuck do you want?"

"Let's go out and get a beer. A little hair of that animal that bit you. My treat."

"Thanks. But no, Cal."

"C'mon, I can't let you turn into a panzy ass this late in life."

Thomas hung up and went back to the couch. Five minutes later the phone rang again. Thomas contemplated not answering it, but after five rings he sprung from the couch, using all of his remaining energy.

"I will come over to your house and drag you naked through the streets if you call one more fuckin' time!"

"Tommy?"

That was not Cal's voice. It wasn't even a guy's voice. "Oops. Sorry – whoever this is."

"It's Michelle."

For a moment, both didn't know what to say, but Thomas cleared his mind and recalled his guest from the night before. "I guess the normal reaction would be 'what a coincidence,' but I guess it's actually not one?"

"No – it's not. Tammy asked that I call you."

"You got a sweet little sister there that doesn't quite know when the game is over."

"She asked me to call you as a friend, Tommy."

"I'm sure she did. But ever since she was a kid, she's been saying how wonderful it will be when I'm her brother-in-law. And she's still saying it, just not out loud. At least not to you and me."

"Actually," Michelle decided to be as direct with Thomas and tell him everything, something not found in her psychology training, "Tammy made a push on your behalf last Christmas."

Thomas' mind was not enitrely sharp, but he was rather certain that Christmas came after the engagement, but the specifics didn't matter. "How is your fiance anyway?"

"He's good. I called because Tammy was concerned about you."

It was a certain time of a Sunday afternoon which followed a late Saturday night that Thomas neither wished to nor wanted to, and perhaps not able to, explain himself. And this was most certainly to be an explanation that Michelle would continually interrupt and question. Thomas tried to alleviate any concerns the Jennings girls had. "If I told you I'm fine, would you believe me?" Michelle said she wouldn't. "Where are you right now?" Thomas asked. "Will you be there in a couple of hours? Fine. Let me take a shower, grab some food, and we'll talk."

Thomas hung up and forthwith went back to the couch.

As evening passed, Michelle wondered if she would ever hear from Thomas again. She was putting the finishing touches on an assignment in her Master's program, when the phone rang at 10 o'clock.

"Okay," Thomas said. "I'm refreshed and I'm ready to talk. Now the featured dish of the evening is – Is Thomas Okay? But before we get to the main course, let's whet our appetites. Tell me about your fiance. What's his first name?"

Before Michelle knew what she was doing, she was revealing her feelings to Thomas. It was amazing how he had the gift of making her talk about herself, something she did not find particularly appealing. Soon, she was speaking of her doubts whether Todd Aldrich would be a faithful husband – predictable but mysterious. Michelle did not mention the mysterious but predictable part.

"Well, I'm sure you've studied aspects of this nature or you could at least call on some colleagues to help you think it through," Thomas said earnestly. "But even if you love him to death, all of your love won't make a marriage work unless he's willing. And if he's what you think he is – well, spots on a leopard and all that rigamarole." Thomas would much rather pepper a conversation with some expletives for color, but Michelle and Tammy are ladies, and he would feel rather embarrassed. So when he replaced 'shit' with 'rigamarole,' he lost his train of thought, and the conversation momentarily stopped.

Michelle, for an instant, thought Thomas was right. Maybe she was looking at the entire picture of Boston, big house, money, success, children never needing. What she needed to focus on was the love and devotion of a man. She quickly erased those thoughts. Todd would be just fine.

"Okay. We've dabbled in my life. Now it's your turn. And my sister said that I need to be a friend and not an analyst, so let me know when I'm in a gray area, not that I need to tell you that, Thomas."

Thomas thought a lot about life when he was at work, operating machinery, not able to have any conversations with anyone but himself. It was nice to have a sounding board. He began, his world flowing effortlessly.

"You ever been walking down the road or driving along and suddenly, for no apparant reason, you feel like turning? It's like some divine power is giving you a choice. A simple, everyday choice. Sometimes that divine power gives you a choice and a little nudge. Well, I believe that's everybody's life. It's as if we're a Ouija board and these spirits that belong to us are playing – playing in the same sense as guiding. Now, personally I think this is different from predestination because with predestination, people supposedly don't get choices.

"One day this summer I decided to go to the mall. Out of the blue, I just wanted to go to the mall. Haven't gone shopping in a couple of years, but one sunny afternoon when the entire state was at the beach, I go to the mall. I got some jeans that I was in desperate need of, but then, as I was leaving, I passed a bookstore, and prominently displayed was this book about a guy who lost his mother. I bought it, and it made me cry. It was the first time I cried since mom died. And I truly believe it was mom telling me it was alright to cry once in a while."

Thomas sighed almost inaudibly and lit a cigarette, wondering if he should continue this catharsis. "I've felt these choices before, in other circumstances, and I know I'll get more.

Maybe I'll go back to school and get a mechanical engineering degree. Or maybe I'll be driving down the road and a reincarnated Howard Hughes will need a ride. Or maybe I'll just go to pubs and taverns and drink and tell stories until my dying day. Hell, half of Ireland does that and they're a happy lot."

He paused and took a deep breath and screwed his lips about as in deep thought and decided to say what was on his mind.

"Or maybe I'll just fall in love again."

Michelle wanted to comment on his profundity, but the lump in her throat prevented her.

He continued. "Do you know how many billions upon billions upon billions of people have graced this earth? It's hard for me to fathom. I do know that so many in my lifetime have left with a sorrowful soul. Others have left with no soul. If the God above – whoever he or she may be – decided to take my life tomorrow, I would leave happy. Sure, there's more I would like to do, but I would leave happy. My health. My freedom. I can't find myself asking for much more than that."

At first Thomas thought he had lulled Michelle to sleep, for she did not say anything for almost 30 seconds. At last, after she regained in her own mind the purpose to the conversation, she asked, "But Tammy said you looked so lonely. Are you?"

"Sure, I'm lonely at times, but only for companionship. I have my thoughts and my memories and my dreams. As long as I have them, I'll be fine."

"Tommy, I don't think it's healthy for you to be seeking companionship in bars and in liquor."

"You're drifting into analysis, Michelle." Thomas said it as pleasantly as possible. He despised having his brain picked apart by anyone other than himself. "I appreciate your concern, but someday, something's bound to give, and I'll have more choices than I can handle. In the meantime, I'm going to enjoy the life I've been given."

"Are you sure?"

Thomas didn't like the question. "Of course I'm sure. Michelle, I'm heading in the right direction. Don't you worry your pretty little head. I'll be just fine."

The pair finished the conversation and said their goodbyes. When Thomas hung up, he felt confident that things were turning out fine. Up in Boston, Michelle wasn't quite so sure.

Sophomore

FIFTEEN

Unlike the previous year when he was rudely awakened to keep a promise he did not remember, Thomas hung around his house the entire Thanksgiving week. Except for work, trips to the grocery store and time dedicated to exercise, Thomas spent time at home.

Mostly, at night he watched television, but an hour before bedtime he would grab a book. He always wanted to read more, but with the convenience of television and the allure of the bars, Thomas spent almost no time with novels.

Wednesday night he grabbed *Catch 22* from his dusty shelf and dove in. He was glad it caught his interest, for it took his mind from wishing the telephone would ring.

Speaking with Michelle helped Thomas recapture some focus. It wasn't so much what she said. If someday he found choices in front of him, he wanted to be better prepared, more intelligent. So Thomas began to read more than just the sports pages and the comics. Occasionally, he would buy *The New York Times* and look up the words he didn't know. "You can never take away education," Old Man Jack told him.

The phone never rang, and it didn't surprise him, although it did make him feel empty inside. He had made his choice last season when he decided to ignore Mr. Lawton's wishes and do as he pleased. But he felt that he did right and that Mr. Lawton's leisurely gentleman attitude was wrong.

And now he was sitting at home on the Friday morning after Thanksgiving, having his hopes dashed. By midday, he put down his book and headed to the Cornerstone Pub.

The St. Agnes team floundered at the start of its second season, losing to Flat River by 45 points and Bishop Leary by 12 points. Because of this stubbornness, all Thomas could do was monitor the team's results in the newspaper. Slowly, the team regressed and by midseason, the St. Agnes Lancers were 0-8, with the margin of their losses getting wider.

Thomas didn't find the eighth loss insulting, but he was sure Mark was embarrassed. Forfeiting three weight classes, St. Agnes fell to Covington, 59-3, the only win coming from Chris Ballinger, who was still wrestling at 189.

Up to the Covington match, Chris was the only wrestler in the same weight class from the previous season. Some of the students grew, some never returned to the team, and some quit as the season spiraled out of control. Only four wrestlers weighed in for the Covington match who were on varsity last year. Liam Connelly grew two weight classes and was wrestling at 130. Brien Cauldron was at 135. Mike Ennis was at 140 and Ballinger at 189.

Thomas never saw Tony Kingery's name or his friend Mike Masterelli. He could only imagine what decisions were being made by the St. Agnes coaching staff.

It was another uneventful day in a front-end loader at the Burke Sand and Gravel Pit. Thomas loaded tandem dump trucks with blue stone, crushed concrete and fill dirt most of the morning, listening on his headset to Don Imus on the radio – Imus was bitching about President Clinton being a backstabbing fat slob. After that, Thomas shut off the radio and spent time in relative silence, only the roar of the engine's rpm's and the back-up whistle supplying any noise at all.

In the afternoon, Thomas alternated between loading trucks and combining stone and rock piles around the yard. The late January sky was gray and growing dark. Wind was starting to sweep in from the northwest, kicking up small sandstorms around the yard. Snow was on its way.

Days like this never allowed Thomas to contemplate his own life. He usually thought of what it would be like in Colonial America, before mechanization. The winters were cold, miserable and fraught with starvation. The summers hot, long and preoccupied with preparing for the devastating winters. Appreciating how rapidly the world was advancing since the end of the Second World War, Thomas felt comfortable and lucky to be sitting in the heated cab of the front-end loader as the first flurries began to ride on the tails of the wind. When he would end each work day washing his hands in the employees' shanty, he understood that life had indeed been good to him.

Terry Broughton stuck his head in the shanty door and immediately felt terribly out of place. But he thought, this is a place of business, not a prison, so after asking if "a Thomas McCloskey was available," he brought his Rockport soft leather boots, Docker pleated pants, white Arrow shirt, purple and red St. Agnes tie and Stafford tweed jacket – complete with elbow patches – into the room to be scrutinized. Much to his surprise, nobody noticed. Or they just didn't give a shit.

Thomas walked out of the bathroom, tucking in his shirt and zipping his jeans. "Mr. Broughton," he said, nodding, "if you give me a second, I'll be glad to shake your hand." And he went to the sink and poured an unusual amount of liquid soap on his hands, so as to put the athletic director's mind at ease.

"I've been noticing in the paper that the St. Agnes squad isn't doing so well," Thomas said as he lathered up.

"Hey – you the head coach over there?" asked one of the Burke employees, seated in a chair with his feet up on the lunch table, a beer in his hand.

"No. I'm the athletic director."

"Well, you can't be doin' your job that good if you let this damn guy go. You should've seen the fucker wrestle in high school."

"Hey Stitch. I don't think it's polite to go cursin' at a guest without at least offering him a beer," Thomas said.

"Wanna beer?"

No, but thanks.

"Well, can I fuck with him now?" Stitch started laughing as he sprang up and chugged the rest of his beer. "Nice meetin' you. But seriously, you should get this guy to coach. If he can coach half as good as he could fight, you'd have a winner by the end of the season." Stitch ditched his empty aluminum can and left with the rest of the workers, leaving Terry Broughton alone with Thomas.

A look of intrigue drew upon the athletic director's face as the stranger's comments sunk in. It seems most everyone knew about Thomas McCloskey, the wrestler. "Actually, that's why I'm here."

"That doesn't surprise me. Mark use the excuse that he had practice?"

"Mark doesn't know I'm here."

"Then you must be on your own, because I know Mr. Lawton didn't send you."

"No, it wasn't Ken either. As a matter of fact, following the Covington match, Ken asked to be relieved of his coaching position, effective at the end of the year. And my feelings were that after Liam Connelly graduated this season, his father wouldn't be interested in supporting the wrestling team any longer, and St. Agnes would drop the sport."

The logic and the lack of loyalty were not shocking to Thomas. There was never any commitment by the parochial school to properly equip or teach the wrestling program, so it just made sense that the administration should properly finish off the fiasco by teaching the remaining students how to quit. Thomas expressed those feelings to Terry Broughton.

"Coach Gibbons told me that you were a straight-shooting man. He told me not to be offended by your honesty," Terry said. "I am concerned, though, of your conduct in wrestling practice."

Thomas chuckled. Not a ha-ha, "you make me laugh" type of chuckle, but a "you got some set of balls" type of chuckle.

"If my conduct is so friggin' offensive to you, why are you even here? Because I have already made my damn position clear in regard to your wrestling program. If my philosophy can't be – and I won't say embraced – but at least accepted, then you can take your volunteer coaching position and shove it straight up your ass."

"I can see you have no problem demonstrating my point about your questionable conduct," Terry Broughton said, taking a seat up on the lunch table. He was out of his milieu and felt very uncomfortable, but he was trying. His hands wouldn't seem to settle comfortably someplace on his body, his feet not able to implant themselves squarely on the bench seat of the table where he was sitting. He shifted his ass cheeks one way, and moments later, another. "That's why I'm hesitant about offering you the coaching position for the balance of this year and next." Terry Broughton quickly added, "A paid position, of course."

"You can relax, Mr. Broughton." Thomas knew he had the athletic director rattled. Probably a basketball player in high school. Sensing the uneven playing field in his favor, Thomas toned down the attitude and the profane language. "First of all, the money doesn't matter as far as dollar and cents goes. But when two imbeciles view titles and money as measurements of

126

superiority, then there's a problem. And I speak freely here more of Mark than of Mr. Lawton because, despite being the selfish imbecile that he is, Mark is still an old friend of mine. And what I say here is nothing that I haven't said to him in the past.

"Second, and more important, is my selective use of language. It's not ill temperament that sets flying the fucks, the shits, the pisses and the pussies off of this golden tongue of mine. It's a mutual respect of the coach and the wrestler, that they both understand each other. If a coach lets his wrestlers know that he understands and remembers what it's like to be in the trenches, then the coach gets the team's respect. Times are always changing, and some day vulgar language will disappear and then reappear in cycles over the course of time in high school wrestling, and in life in general. Right now, the way kids speak and act, if a coach doesn't speak their language, he's screwed. And that's my philosophy."

The athletic director's interest was piqued, and he unconsciously stopped shifting in his seat and futzing with his hands. He spoke, for the sole reason that after 15 years as a high school administrator, that was how he chided students to continue. "I think I understand. Go on."

Thomas shot Terry Broughton a look, when interpreted, said – I'm not one of your damn students, so just shut up and listen. Thomas liked shooting those facial looks. He had a war chest full of them. Looks saved time and energy.

"Kids sense weakness just as well as any other creature on the food chain. And weakness has no place on a wrestling team. Not weakness of body and not weakness of mind. Estimates vary depending on the coach you speak to, but most coaches put the mental aspect of wrestling anywhere from 75 percent to 90 percent. A couple put it as high as 99 percent, but personally, I think that's bullshit."

"Where do you think it is," Terry Broughton asked, feeling the question was a legitimate one for this interview. He did not receive another menacing look from Thomas.

"That's part of my point. It varies from wrestler to wrestler. Some wrestlers are better off not thinking at all and just going out there, letting their balls hang out. Others need to review the match over and over and over again, constantly picturing scenarios of 'what-ifs' in their heads. Some kids you curse at, others you coddle. And in practice, I feel a coach has to – up to a certain point – toss out some verbal barbs, to let these teen-agers know that you speak their language."

"But they're so impressionable," the athletic director said. "Don't you feel it's detrimental to let them hear a coach speak in such harsh tones?"

"Not as long as they're leveled with. I told them quite a few times last year during practice I was going to curse and piss and moan and spit to get their asses in gear. But I also told them that what I said in practice, stayed there and explained the 'When in Rome' way of thinking.

"Wrestling is not a sport where a coach is deceiving you. There's no room for deception. These kids are wearing these tutu-type uniforms, going out in front of large crowds, half naked in front of mothers and girlfriends, wrestling a stud whose been at this sport since he was five. I am sorry Mr. Broughton, but I can't lie to them. They're going against street-tough kids from Flat River, half of them Hispanics and blacks, and that scares these Anglo-Catholic kids even more, because the newness and the stigma attached to these groups of kids. And they're also scared – and rightfully so – of surprisingly tough, surfer dudes with tattoos down at Blakemore. Tattoos! Sixteen years old and younger, and they have tattoos, while some of the St. Agnes kids still carry superhero lunch boxes to school. It is in this sport, though, that these kids learn for the first time what equality really is. One on one. Same set of rules. Same weight." He paused.

"Now you can either give your predominantly Irish-Catholic kids a rounded education or you can send them to the lions. Shakespeare, calculus, physics by day – then the Dead End Kids for six minutes at night. It's up to you."

The St. Agnes athletic director was impressed, just as Coach Gibbons had predicted. "Well, I must say, that was an interesting philosophical explanation. Coach Gibbons said you were an expensive package wrapped in the Sunday comics. Those were his words, of course."

Thomas smiled. "That sounds like Coach. Where did you run into him?"

"Oh – our meeting wasn't a chance encounter. He made an appointment to see me and left his assistant to run Covington's practice yesterday. So at 3:30 yesterday, he told me he got a call from his principal, who, in turn, had received a call from a very influential person, to notify Coach Gibbons that effective at the end of the scholastic year, Mark Pierce would receive a paid position as an assistant on the Covington wrestling staff. And at that moment, Coach Gibbons said he decided that he was getting too old for the sport, and announced his retirement – effective immediately but not to be announced until June. He said his present assistant coach, a Mr. Danny Johnson, would probably step down as well, leaving Mark Pierce as Covington's head coach for the 1993-94 season.

"Coach Gibbons said he wanted you to succeed him as Covington's coach, but you had too much integrity to step in front of an old comrade – again I'm using his words. He said he purposely used the word comrade because in wrestling, bonds are formed and passed on unlike in other sports, and he doesn't believe that you and Mark Pierce are actually friends, but rather comrades in arms, just like all the other wrestling warriors who beat each other up for four years. And he told me to tell you this, just in case that for some reason you had forgotten.

"So he said you decided to disappear instead of offend. And when he was notified of Mark's appointment, he wanted St. Agnes to get your services. He said that I should sit down and talk to you. Give you a chance, and I'd be sold, he said. Well, I'm sold. The position's yours – if you want it."

Thomas accepted the position, but not before solidifying certain requests. First and foremost, the school needed an in-house assistant coach, not a Mr. Lawton type, but someone who didn't have virgin ears.

"We can work on that. I'm sure there's someone who can put up with you." Terry Broughton was beginning to take a shine to the young upstart coach.

Next was the practice facility. The team needed to be in the school. Too much time was wasted going to the pavilion, which had no showers and no real locker room. The wrestlers needed publicity within St. Agnes, and the best way was to practice at home. A boiler room, an old classroom – or the cafeteria, like all of the other small schools.

"Something could be arranged," Broughton said.

Next, some home matches. In the gym, not in the cafeteria like at Sacred Heart High School. At least four home matches. Some conference.

"Basketball won't like that," Broughton said, "but fair is fair."

Finally, some equipment – some good equipment, not that crap that Mr. Lawton pulled out of a catalog or from a flea market. Compared with other programs, the warm-up sweats are cheesy, but actually those weren't the problem. The team needed head gear that had snaps, not that velcro shit. "I don't know how many times the refs explained to Mr. Lawton that the wrestlers needed to be prepared or else penalty points would be awarded to opposing teams. It was fuckin' embarrassing."

"Is that all?" Mr. Broughton asked unbelievably, hoping that it was. So far, most were minor details, but the principal and the Parents' Club – the entity which ultimately financed the team – needed to be persuaded.

That wasn't all. A scale that was made within the last 10 years, not the ancient pile of scrap metal the school has now. "These kids missed weight half of the time last season because of that scale."

"Is that all?"

Yep. For now.

Terry Broughton saw to it that before the first bell Mr. Lawton would learn of Thomas McCloskey's impending arrival at Friday afternoon's practice. He suspected no repercussions, for the biology teacher was resigned to riding out the last three weeks of the season.

It was Thomas' job, as Broughton saw it, to notify Mark Pierce. After grabbing a Big Mac and a Coke for Thursday's dinner, he drove to Mark's house for a chat.

Not enough snow had fallen from the ominous afternoon skies to call it an accumulation. As a matter of fact, it was barely a dusting. The streets and sidewalks were too warm to allow any flakes to remain.

But the grass had enough snow for Travis and Taylor to whine as to be allowed to play underneath the spotlight in the front yard. When they saw a pick-up truck park in front of the house, they began in earnest to create two snowballs for greeting purposes. All the shenanigans stopped when the twins saw that it was Thomas.

He scowled at them. They sneered back. Spoiled little shits – Thomas said quietly, just audible enough for the twins to hear.

"Mark! It's Thomas," Amanda Pierce bellowed so wherever Mark was hiding, whether it was deep in his basement or high aloft in the attic, he would hear her. Amanda walked back to the kitchen, continued to dry a dinner pan, leaving Thomas on the porch.

Mark came trotting down the stairs and called to Amanda. "What is it? I'm in the middle of grading reports." Amanda yelled back that Thomas McCloskey was on the front porch.

Thomas had taken a seat in one of the Adirondack chairs and was listening to the pleasant exchanges between the couple. "Oh yeah, this is love," Thomas said to himself. He watched the two boys in the front yard poke at and whine to one another. If this is the typical American family, then Thomas wanted no part of it.

"Hey Tommy," Mark said cheerfully. "Come on in."

Thomas was about out of patience for Mark and his life, or lack of a life. Thomas did not like the reception at the door and at that moment forth was never going to set foot in Mark's house again, not as long as he was married to the ice princess.

"Why don't you grab a jacket," Thomas said. "I just wanted your ear for a few minutes." Thomas rose and started down the steps, walking west with the wind to his back. Mark came outside and told the boys to stay in the front yard, that he'd be back in a few minutes. They didn't listen.

Thomas didn't want to offer any gratuitous salutations, so he got right to the point. "I understand that you're jumping to the Covington staff next year."

Mark was amazed. "How did you find out?"

"Actually, someone at work told me. You know how connected some of those old timers are." Thomas neither wanted to lie nor implicate Coach Gibbons nor Terry Broughton, so he left the statement vague. He knew Mark wouldn't pursue for the source of the information. Mark's mind was already churning on how to cover up his end of the Covington coup.

"Yeah, well, I guess I got a little lucky. Next season, I'll be the freshman coach, and after that, if everything works out, I could head the program."

"Mmmm-hmmm." Thomas didn't want to hear the bullshit talk, and the little grunt let Mark know that.

"I will need an assistant coach, and there won't be any Mr. Lawton around. It sure would be great headlines with us paired back up at Covington."

What Thomas wanted to tell him was to shove the Covington job up his ass. But he refrained. "I'm here because I'm planning on coaching at St. Agnes again. With you heading over to Covington, Mr. Lawton – biology teacher extraordinaire – won't be able to make a go of it alone. I could always tone it down for the rest of the year, just so Mr. Lawton doesn't have a heart attack."

"Lawton's not coming back," Mark said. "This season's his last. He made his decision last week after Covington kicked our ass."

Thomas nearly gave up his sources during that last exchange, but discretion took hold. The word was out, but it wasn't exactly common knowledge yet. Now that Mark was privy to the fact that his future position at Covington was no longer a secret, he'd be the one to shoot his mouth off. Thomas was sure of that.

"Well, I'm going to show up tomorrow at the pavilion at the same time as I always did. Terry Broughton said he'd talk to Mr. Lawton before class tomorrow."

"When did you talk to Broughton?" Mark asked, surprised that the two had talked.

"You think I'd just show up uninvited tomorrow and claim a position on the team," Thomas said sarcastically. "I had to clear it with somebody, and I knew Kenneth Lawton wasn't the person. Broughton did voice concerns about my volatile nature, though."

Mark was sold. He accepted the proposed battle lines. Mark and Covington versus Thomas and St. Agnes.

SIXTEEN

He took off early from work, in order to change clothes and greet the few students as they walked into the pavilion's grand ballroom. In his gray cut-off sweat pants, blue t-shirt and ancient white Asics wrestling shoes with white athletic tape holding together the toes and soles, Thomas recognized only a handful of the remaining wrestlers.

Chris Ballinger was the first one to practice and bounced right over to Thomas. "Hey, Coach. How long are you back for?"

Sticking with a safe answer, he said, "Well, it looks like I'm here for the rest of the season."

"Good. 'Cause I really haven't had anybody to wrestle with except for Masterelli, and he just sucks."

Now a sophomore, Chris lost some of the shyness he had the year before. Still not making complete eye contact, at least he would consistently look in the direction of the person he was speaking to.

The next student into the room had to be a freshman because he was no bigger than 4-foot-10 and couldn't weigh much more than 80 pounds.

"Who's that?"

"Oh, that's Jeff LeMone," Chris said. "He's a real rug rat. He's been wrestling in clubs and tournaments since he was in kindergarten. But he's too little to wrestle 103."

The rest of the team straggled in, Tony Kingery the last. A grand total of 13 wrestlers, most of them freshmen. When Tony saw the coach, he, too, ran over with a renewed vigor, asking questions, wanting answers. It was Thomas who was the more curious.

"Why haven't you been wrestling?" Thomas asked. "Are you ineligible or injured? How are your grades?"

My grades are pretty good. I got all B's last quarter," the freshman said. "I'm not wrestling because I'm the same weight as Liam, and the coaches told me that the seniors always start."

"Both coaches told you this?"

"Actually, it was Coach Pierce."

Mark knew better than just to appoint a wrestler to a weight class, or so Thomas thought. Wrestling is the rare sport where a starting line-up is not chosen by the coach but rather by letting two people beat the hell out of one another, the winner going varsity.

Similar to almost all other sports and collective ventures in life, wrestling teams get better when there's competition within. With senior Liam Connelly starting at 130 and junior Brien Cauldron at 135, Tony was stuck behind them. Those two weight classes should be tough for other teams to beat, but with no live competition in practice, mediocrity prevails. And St. Agnes loses.

Terry Broughton stood in the doorway, speaking with Mark Pierce and Kenneth Lawton. Most of the conversation was directed at Mark, who just nodded his head. The three finished up and walked over to Thomas.

"I've explained the situation to both coaches," the athletic director said. "Mr. Pierce has told me that beginning next year he will be coaching at Covington."

Thomas feigned ignorance to the whole matter, keeping up the charade. "Congratulations, Mark."

Mark smiled from ear to ear. "Thank you, Tommy." He would never have any idea.

The athletic director continued. "With Ken stepping down at the end of the year, that leaves a gaping hole at St. Agnes. So the natural offer would be to you, Coach McCloskey, whether you would like to stay on, heading the wrestling staff and keeping the wrestling program intact. Naturally, I've thought in depth about this, and the only answer is to help the kids build upon what they've started. And with Mark going over to the rival next year, some form of continuity is necessary. That's where Mr. Lawton is needed."

During this impromptu and unusual meeting to transfer power, Kenneth Lawton had started to daydream. How nice it would be – he mused – to get home before dark in the wintertime. Fix a cup of tea and retire to his high-back chair, the periodicals and selected novels on the floor to his right, the antique standing lamp from Aunt Audrey to his left. Settle in. Relax. Dose off until hunger woke him at 7 o'clock.

But he was rudely yanked from his thoughts by Thomas. "What does he want now!" were the words formed but never spoken.

This was an olive branch with a string attached. Thomas did not need Kenneth Lawton, biology teacher, as a mole within the St. Agnes hallways – not actually fearing that the teacher would outwardly poison the boys' minds against the wrestling program – but Mr. Lawton could be cold to the program and certainly would not direct any student toward the cafeteria.

"If Mr. Lawton would act as an intermediary, a representative for the program in the school, it would help the boys tremendously," Thomas said, laying down the string. Then giving it a little tug, "Mr. Lawton could be an assistant in charge of discipline, academics, recruiting and all of the minor details that will make a difference. A cross between assistant coach and assistant athletic director."

Terry looked at Thomas, nodding assuredly yet cautiously. This guy is smooth, he thought. Kenneth Lawton, too, was cautious but gobbled up the recognition.

Ignoring Mark, Thomas watched the eyes of Mr. Broughton and Mr. Lawton. Sensing acceptance, "I realize that this program is strapped for funds, if Mr. Lawton approves of the offer, then I'll defer half my salary for his time and efforts."

This guy is real smooth.

"I appreciate the offer and generosity," Kenneth Lawton said. "Let's see how the remainder of the season turns out." A couple of nods and head bobs, no handshakes and the foursome decided to get practice started.

The thin ranks of wrestlers were sitting around, talking, half of them stretching, the others yawning. Mr. Broughton asked for their attention and told them of the future plans of the St. Agnes staff. For Mark's role – he would be moving on. Then the athletic director left the winless team to itself, a bleak future staring it down.

"Well, what do you say we get started?" Mr. Lawton said.

"First, I'd like to make an announcement," Mark said, still grinning like he had indigestion. "The reason I won't be back at St. Agnes next year is because I've accepted an assistant's position at my old school, Covington. Hopefully, we can have great rivalries. Of course, starting next year, I'll be wanting to trounce you guys."

The team didn't smile, moan, burp or fart. The wrestlers just kept stretching in the half-assed manner as they had since the start of the season. What an idiot, Thomas thought. He could have made me look like the bad guy with the remnant of this St. Agnes squad by making it look like he was forced to leave. Obviously, he hadn't talked too much with Amanda about it, because she would have thought of a devious plan. She could have sabotaged the works, crippling the Lancers before her husband ever got paid for day one at Covington.

Once again, Mr. Lawton began practice, and immediately Thomas began working. He walked up to Liam Connelly and told him to check his weight.

"This scale sucks," Liam said as he stripped out of his shorts and ripped t-shirt. "It's always a pound light from the other schools. I have to run after every weigh-in because I'm over."

"That's pretty intelligent, Liam," Thomas said sarcastically. "You know it's a pound off, yet you haven't adjusted that simple tabulation in your mind." Thomas tinkered with the top part of the scale, before balancing. "One-thirty one. Which means you're actually 132 on most of the away scales. Right?"

Yeah.

"Well, I don't expect you to get to 125 for Saturday's match, but I will expect 125 for next Wednesday."

You're crazy!

"Liam. What's your record?"

I dunno.

"C'mon Liam."

"3-5."

"Three and five. A second-year wrestler. A senior who's busted his ass so as not to get humiliated on the mat last year and now you're under .500. How does something like that happen?"

Liam did not answer as he got dressed.

"Now, be straight with me. You been going out with the boys, hitting some of those high school parties, havin' a few beers on Saturday nights. Right?"

Liam thought it best not to answer.

"I'll take that as a yes," Thomas said, trying to figure out a plan he did not have at the moment. "More or less, there's about a month left to your wrestling career, besides hacking around with some of the dorks in a college dorm next year. Do me a favor and help me out." Thomas stopped talking. "I'll tell you what. No more parties for the remainder of the season. You can blame it on me. Tell your buddies that I'm a no-good prick." Thomas hesitated and came up with a scheme that he knew Liam would hate. "As a matter of fact, I think you and I might hang out with one another for the next four weekends."

"No fuckin' way. You're nuts!"

"Watch your language," Thomas methodically instructed, rather pleased to see any type of spark. "Sure, that's what we can do. I'll clear it with your father, and me and you will be the bestest buddies for one entire month."

"It ain't gonna happen."

"I can go to the high school parties with you, as an informal chaperone, but that wouldn't be fun for you guys because then all of the chicks would be flocking to me."

Liam realized that Thomas was busting his chops, so he just waved a hand at him and told him he was fucked up.

"Language," Thomas said in programmable fashion. "I will do it. Trust me. I'll hang out with you if you give me no other choice. This team needs you, Tony and Cauldron in the line-up. It also needs a leader, and that's you. You need to suit up, put on all the sweats and cut to 125 by next Wednesday. If you need an incentive, I'll cut with you. Seven pounds for you. Seven pounds for me. Whaddya say?"

Thomas offered his hand. Liam contemplated for only a moment, then shook it. "It should be seven pounds for me and 10 pounds for you." He tried to sound dejected, but Thomas could sense he was up for the challenge.

"No, uh-uh. Seven pounds for seven pounds. You have better metabolism. Oh, and one last thing."

"What!" Liam tossed his head back in mock disgust.

"Where's all the guys from last year?"

"Mostly just got scared of getting beat up. They were just a bunch of pussies, anyway."

"Actually, I was wondering about Mark Cella and Chuck."

"Cella's just a wuss. He says his parents didn't like driving every night to pick him up. He lives about a half hour away, so he just takes the bus home after school."

What about Garrison?

"He got suspended for coming in drunk to a school dance. He's not allowed to participate in any school activities for the rest of this year. He's worthless."

"Tell both of those guys that I want them at practice tomorrow. I'll give them a ride home. If they don't show up, tell them I'll hunt them down."

All night Thomas lay awake, trying to figure out how to get two wins out of the eight remaining dual matches. Actually with an almost certain loss against North Winfield at 11 a.m on Saturday, he needed two out of seven. Just two wins to top last year's record and give St. Agnes some off-season steam.

If Thomas could get Cella and Garrison back on the team, that would leave just the 171 slot to fill. For most of the season, with rare exceptions, St. Agnes was forfeiting 103, 125, 171 and heavyweight. That's 24 points surrendered even before competition starts. That's too much for any wrestling program to overcome.

Hopefully Cella's weight didn't balloon. Last season, he weighed around 97 pounds, and Garrison couldn't possibly be above 275 pounds – the limit for heavyweights. There would be no chance Garrison could have put on more than 45 pounds of beer and hamburgers.

With Liam cutting to 125 and Tony Kingery sliding into 130, that left Masterelli to claim 171 as the only other open weight class other than heavyweight.

It was a rag-tag, Bad News Bears type of line-up, but it was a full one. And with the first and last weight classes filled, that would give St. Agnes a shot against some of the smaller schools. Hey, a win's a win, no matter how you cut it. And that was the mindset of Thomas Patrick McCloskey.

Of the remaining eight matches, could St. Agnes actually pull out two? Thomas checked the schedule, scribbling on the second half of the season.

*North Winfield	– a 50-point loss
Winfield Heights	– a 30-point loss
*Carlysle Township	– a 30-point loss, if everything goes right
Pope Pius X	– maybe, but not likely
St. Mary's	– maybe

138

*Central	– Its j.v. team could win
St. Peter's	– maybe
*New Welsh	– not likely

* conference match

St. Agnes' only hopes realistically were tied to Pope Pius, St. Mary's, St. Peter's and New Welsh. Thomas would explain his goals in practice on Friday. He would make his goals the priorities of each Lancer wrestler.

At lunch hour on Friday, Thomas shot over to St. Agnes to speak with Terry Broughton. Ten minutes to get there from Millersburg, 10 minutes to talk, 10 minutes back, and that's all the time he had to spare.

Parking around the school at lunch was thin, but Thomas squeezed in next to the dumpster in the parking lot behind the school and on the side of the convent on Ninth Avenue.

Despite being at Broughton's office once before, he had a hard time retracing his steps. Two teachers questioned him, wary to his unusual attire for the private school. Any visitor or worker in the school required a pass, and the teachers assumed Thomas required a pass. "You need to check into the office," he was twice told.

"Mr. Broughton said I could come straight to his office if I had any problems." Thomas lied. He didn't have the time to find the main office and get passes to double back to the athletic director's office. Finally, he found it. He had only half the time he originally allotted for himself, so he told Mr. Broughton he had to be brief.

"I don't see any problem with Marc Cella," Broughton said. "But he will need a doctor's note and six days of practice. That's the school rule."

"I just need him in the line-up as a decoy," Thomas said. "I wouldn't let him wrestle unless he was ready anyway. Six days, huh?" Thomas was hoping the silence would give Broughton the time to reconsider and wave the rule in Cella's case. The athletic director did not. "Well, can we consider Saturday's match and Wednesday's match as practice days? That'll put him in the line-up against Carlysle. They're too tough for him to wrestle against anyway, but it could light a fire under his ass."

Okay. But Garrison is out of the question.

"Wouldn't it be better for Chuck to be active instead of having idle time?"

No chance. He came to a school function drunk. He will not wrestle.

"Alright," Thomas agreed it was a rule that needed to be implemented. "What if he comes to practice and sits his ass in a chair? He won't be wrestling, and he won't be on the street. That way, maybe I can get his mind on next season."

"I'll think about it."

"In the meantime, I need a heavyweight," Thomas said. "This team needs 13 weight classes filled. You got Garrison to wrestle when your ass was stuck to the bleacher. Can you come through again?"

The recollection of being humiliated by a tiny piece of gum and a large adolescent caused Terry Broughton's face to become slightly flushed. "You know, Coach, there are simply not that many big guys in this school. The male total for all four grades this year is down to 191. Thirty-nine are on the freshmen, j.v. and varsity basketball teams, and that's where most of the big kids are."

"Anybody. Anybody over 200 pounds."

SEVENTEEN

Although Thomas was working frantically behind the scenes, he eased himself into his role as future head coach. As he had previously done, Thomas remained behind the bench at North Winfield, prepping the on-deck wrestler. It was fruitless to try and rally the Lancers against a squad such as North Winfield.

The Wildcats were the two-time defending conference champions, and they would eventually share the '92-93 crown with Covington. Thomas was hoping for St. Agnes to score in the double digits.

It didn't happen. North Winfield won 61-6, but Liam and Chris Ballinger squeaked out decisions. And Marc Cella showed up for the match, accepting Thomas' offer to give him a ride home every night after practice. "Sure Marc. I have no love life anyway."

Chuck Garrison was a no-show on Friday and Saturday, and that was disappointing to Thomas. Even though Mr. Broughton hadn't made a decision yet, Thomas thought he would see Chuck one of the two days. His absence was discouraging.

Another small victory came after the match. Thomas convinced Liam to go with him to scout Central, which was hosting a night match against a perennial North Jersey powerhouse. "C'mon. It's your first Saturday night trying to cut weight. Let's go see the match so you won't get tempted. I won't ask again." Thomas emphasized the word ask, letting Liam know the next step was to demand.

Monday's practice would set the schedule for other practices for the rest of the season. If anyone was late, the team ran a minute for every late minute. Late was defined as not being ready for practice. Shirt on, shoes tied, mouth shut. Mr. Lawton and Mark would run the practices as ineptly as they had in the past. Stretching, calisthenics, running some wind sprints. End of practice.

Thomas wanted to change much of that, but since the word got out that Mark was going to Covington, it was as if there was a traitor in the camp. Not as if, Thomas thought, but actually there was a traitor.

During the St. Agnes first season, Thomas instructed Mark to get up in front up the team and run down the plusses and minuses of each match. This he halted for two reasons. One, Mark was an idiot and didn't know how to analyze matches. Two, he did not trust Mark anymore. He felt Mark would intentionally teach incorrect moves, thus he asked Mark to stop teaching moves altogether and concentrate solely on wrestling with the boys.

While practice was in full swing, Thomas would start with the lightweights and, one by one in ascending order, have individual conferences concerning the previous match's performances. Most often he would instruct each wreslter on specific moves that held glaring deficiencies. The method was slow. Thomas would much rather teach one move at a time to the entire team. But in his head, the '93-94 Covington match had already begun, and there would be no sharing of information with the enemy.

Tuesday at lunch, Thomas went back to see Terry Broughton to check on the Lancer heavyweight situation and to ask for a couple of other requests. He parked next to the dumpster. "I should ask for my name to be painted there," he said to himself.

Okay on Chuck Garrison. Thomas can have him present at practice, but he could not suit up.

In the meantime, the athletic director tracked down a 215-pound chess club member who wanted to bolster his resume for college. Anil Nazif really had no idea what scholastic wrestling was about but said, "My father wants me to exercise a little bit more."

The two additional requests Thomas put to Terry could not be denied. The success, or subsequent continuing failure of the St. Agnes program, hinged on these items. Thomas needed to get the Lancers involved in the postseason at the end of the current schedule, and he needed to participate in one preseason Christmas tournament in '93-94.

"I don't know if I can get the Parents' Club to sock in more money in the middle of the season," the athletic director said. "They have a strict budget and don't like to exceed those numbers. And to be quite frank, I don't know if they'd be willing to invest in a team on such tentative grounds."

Thomas did not like the structures of any part of those sentences. He went over and calmly closed the door. "Exactly, what do you mean by 'tentative grounds'? What kind of shit are you trying to sell? You asked me if I would coach next season, then we shook hands. I can understand if I lay an egg next season, then the Parent's Club or the athletic department or the diocese or the friggin' Pope can shut us down. But you set up an agreement. I won't bail out, and I don't expect you to, either."

"That's not what I meant," the athletic director said, not exactly back pedaling, but sidestepping a bit. "The Parents' Club is temperamental. It really doesn't like to be associated with a losing team."

"Ahh. Winning and losing. I forgot. It's not trying to teach these boys how to keep their lunch money from getting stolen while they're waiting for the bus. Fine, if the Parents' Club wants a winner and those tight asses don't have divine faith, then I'll ante up. Just sign us up for the districts this year, and get us into a Christmas tournament next year. Anything but the Oak Hill Classic. I'll foot the bill."

After practice that evening, Thomas drove north to Winfield Heights, where the Garrisons lived. The worst case scenario was that the father didn't like the coach's intrusion and would slam the door in Thomas' face.

The house was small and bungalow-sized with smooth white stone in place of grass in the front yard. A brick house painted white with black shutters, it was the only house on the block with the front porch light on. That was because, sitting on a porch swing, drinking a beer on a freezing January evening was a rather large, bearded man. Seven empty cans sat on the wooden railing, *Ain't Got No Home* playing on a banged up radio that sat crookedly on the floor. The man eyed up Thomas as the 27-year-old coach cautiously approached. The men were separated by 15 years and two rungs on the food chain.

"What can I do for you?" The greeting was not at all friendly. Dressed in thermal overalls, construction boots, flannel shirt and a Franklin Concrete Co. baseball cap, it was quite evident by his posture and demeanor that the fellow did not want company. A strange woman might get a second look, Thomas thought, but not a strange man.

"I'm looking for Chuck Garrison, I'm . . . ." Thomas was interrupted.

"Who the hell are you?" The man did not move.

Thomas did not say anything right away; that's because he wanted to say – if you just shut the fuck up, I'll get to it. So he just eyed up the man, looking for a possible weakness. "Thomas McCloskey. I'm a wrestling coach at St. Agnes."

In an instant the attitude of the large man with the black beard changed. He rose cumbersomely from the swing, causing it to rock to and fro violently. "Shiiit. The wrestling coach," he said smiling. When he stood, his frame blocked the light of the porch. In this eclipse, Thomas could only see the outline of his body. Six-foot-five. Three hundred, twenty five. He had a weakness all right. Right in the crux of his legs.

Thomas needn't worry anymore about the man's gruff greeting. Once Mr. Garrison found out that he was one of the wrestling coaches, he was an instant buddy.

"Now which one are you – the biology teacher or the grade school teacher?" The man was hoping for the latter, although either one would have been okay.

"Neither, I'm a volunteer coach, just helping out. I was just trying to get Chuck to come to practice."

"Hey. You're the one out at the gravel pit. I thought you were done coaching?"

"I was, but I decided to come back for the rest of this year and next," Thomas said, wondering how he knew so much about him. "Next year is the reason why I'm here."

You wanna beer?

Thomas sat on the ledge of the porch railing, trying to figure out when the last time he had a Schaeffer beer. Charles Garrison Sr. sat on the swing, removed his cap and ran his hand through a thinning, greasy, curly, black, widow-peaked hairline and told his story.

Chills went through Thomas, and he couldn't decide if it was the Schaeffer or the cold night air. By the time a second beer took the chill away, Thomas knew enough about the Garrison clan to be considered a distant cousin. Charles was ready to extend brotherhood when Thomas told him of his motives.

"I realize Chuck is suspended from all out-of-school activities for the remainder of the season, but this team really could use him next year. If I can get his head into the sport, his body will follow."

"Like I said, he lives with his mother, I only get the bad news here – bills, report cards, suspension notices," Charles said. "But this here is a bit of good news. It'll get him out of the house, away from his mother. She's really turning him into a pussy. And then he goes from a pussy to a dumb ass and goes out and gets plastered before some school dance, same dumb ass shit I used to pull. And she says, 'Oh, it's nothing. He's just trying to define himself.' Hell, I tried defining myself at that age, now I'm driving a fuckin' mixing truck." The newly cracked Schaeffer was put to Charles Sr.'s mouth and guzzled effortlessly. 'Fuckin' women. Just see what you can do with Chuck. I'll make sure his ass is at Winfield High tomorrow night."

Marc Cella and Anil Nazif rode on the team bus, and Chuck Garrison was waiting with his father in the gym. Sixteen wrestlers walked into the boys' locker room for weigh-ins, eleven were scheduled to wrestle.

Mr. Lawton took pride in filling out the St. Agnes line-up sheet and carrying the clip board. To him, it showed who was in charge. To Thomas, it kept him occupied. But halfway through weigh-ins, Mr. Lawton no longer felt in charge.

"St. Agnes. 125. Varsity." The junior varsity coach for Winfield Heights bellowed every weight class in this manner, standing behind the scale, adjusting the piece of machinery after each pair of boys weighed in.

Forfeit, Mr. Lawton announced.

"No. That's a mistake," Thomas said. "Liam Connelly is 125. Tony Kingery is at 130."

Mr. Kenneth Lawton felt betrayed, but he would hold his composure until they got to the gym. Thomas knew that this maneuver would not sit well with the head coach, but he did it to motivate the team. A little line-up juggling, Thomas later told them in the pre-match talk, will help keep Winfield a bit off balance.

And it would have worked if Thomas could have suited up Marc Cella at 103. Winfield Heights had only one wrestler in that class, and he broke his thumb during Monday's practice. Thomas put diminutive Jeff LeMone on the scale, hoping for an oversight, but little Jeff weighed 79 pounds. The minimum weight for the first two weight classes is 88 pounds, and the opposing coaches knew it. Both teams were forced to forfeit.

Liam, Tony and Brien Cauldron and the sophomore Mike Ennis put on a clinic in the middleweights, picking up 18 out of a possible 24 points. With Chris Ballinger's pin at 189, St. Agnes "put the fear of God," as Thomas phrased it – a saying Mr. Lawton did not care for – into Winfield Heights, losing 30-26.

The exuberance was flowing on the bus ride home. The kids were laughing and joking, and Mark – a big kid himself – was in the rear, wrestling around with Jeff LeMone. Thomas would bring them back to Earth at Thursday's practice, pointing out mistakes that could've helped gain a huge upset.

Everyone was ecstatic, except Mr. Lawton.

"Do you like making a fool of me? Do you revel in the use of chicanery?" he asked of Thomas. "Do you purposely go around breaking your promise, something you claim to hold in such high standards?"

The two coaches had plenty of privacy, separated by five rows of bench seats, the small cluster of wrestlers and Mark packed into the last few rows of the bus. Sitting across the aisle, Mr. Lawton kept his voice low. But Thomas did not.

"And what promise was that," he said at a stern and normal level, that no one could hear but the driver.

"You said I was to retain the position of head coach, then you turn around and humiliate me in front of both teams." The science teacher's voice cracked but remained low.

"Oh, that promise," Thomas said laughing at him. "First of all, I never said promise, so you can drop that word right now. Second, you're still head coach, nothing's changed."

"Isn't the head coach supposed to know his own line-up? Shouldn't he be able to hand in a sheet without being humiliated?"

Obviously, being cordial with Mr. Lawton wasn't the answer. Thomas had attempted that tact a few times during the last two seasons, but the biology teacher would always get in the final word, which he considered a victory. Although when Thomas was forthright and vulgar, Mr. Lawton said little. Thomas considered the latter technique a breakthrough in communication. It was this form of communication Thomas chose in which to confront Mr. Lawton on this bus ride home.

"Every time I've brought a suggestion to your attention in the past, you've nixed it, especially if I had an idea of a kid dropping a few pounds. 'Oh no. That's no good,' you would always say, and I had to live with it because you were head coach. But soon this losing crap won't be a reflection on you, it'll be a reflection on me. And I had no intention of asking you if Liam could drop a weight class. It was Liam's responsibility as a teammate, a wrestler and a man. He's 17 years old. Kids are fighting in uncivil wars around this globe of ours, losing lives, losing limbs, and you're worried about a kid that's gotta lose a few pounds. It'll do him good, and it'll do this team good."

So Thomas, already sitting on the edge of the seat, leaned forward and chose an even more abrupt path. "Now I got a few fuckin' questions for you, Mr. Lawton. Please don't answer until I'm through," he said, his voice suddenly quiet but quivering. "Have you always been a pain in the ass or have you developed this style since you met me? Do you want this team to win or do you want this team to be embarrassed? Do you think that after a record of 1-25 as a head coach that your way is the right way? Do you think that as you pout when situations like this arise, the kids don't notice? And do you think that if the kids see you pout, they'll think it's okay? Who do you think the kids have learned to pout from? Me? You? Mark? Their parents? I know it ain't fuckin' me."

Thomas sat upright for a moment, before he leaned back forward and continued. "You have a fuckin' choice, Mr. Lawton, just like all of us on this bus. You can choose to help me out and whip these private school pussies into a bunch of hungry young men, or you can drag us down with this friggin' bourgeoisie attitude that I would expect from some high society girl. I really don't fuckin' care if what I'm tellin' you hurts, but I've treated you with kid gloves long enough. I've tiptoed around you more than anyone else in this program. Hell, I've tiptoed around you more than anyone else in my life. But that's stopping right here, right now. I'm not here for you. I'm here for the fuckin' kids. And if you have to run to Terry Broughton or whoever the fuck you run to, go ahead, 'cause I won't compromise my position for anyone. No one."

Thomas sat back and breathed slowly in, then out. "I'd be glad to see you in practice tomorrow. But if you're not, so be it."

Thomas leaned his head back and closed his eyes. Kenneth Lawton stared out the window at nothing in particular. The two coaches sat in silence for the rest of the ride home.

Mr. Kenneth Lawton – biology teacher – had the practice mats mopped and ready for a 3:30 start on Thursday.

Carlysle High School was of similar caliber as Winfield Heights, but mistakes and inexperience in the St. Agnes upperweights cost the Lancers.

Marc Cella had his six practices in order to compete, but two were as a spectator at team matches. Four practices were not enough. He was pinned late in the first period.

The teams traded decisions through the rest of the light and middleweights; it was encouraging to Thomas to see seven consecutive matches go the entire six minutes.

Liam and Tony Kingery won a couple of tight matches, but the Lancers trailed 15-12, and Thomas knew they were in trouble. St. Agnes just didn't have the upperweights to compete against some of the larger schools.

Masterelli was pinned in 12 seconds. Ballinger was caught doing an inside switch, which infuriated Thomas, because it sent Ballinger straight to his back. He was pinned 15 seconds later. And even if Anil were cleared, Thomas would not have wrestled him. Carlysle's heavyweight was 275 pounds with a 14-2 record.

In the end, the score did not reflect the effort. 45-12. St. Agnes was 0-11.

"Who wants to practice tomorrow?" Nobody answered, which Thomas viewed as a good sign. "Now I can't make a Sunday practice mandatory, but I'll be at the pavilion at 8 o'clock – sharp. If anybody would like to come, we'll run a light practice until 10. Anil, Marc – it would be really nice to see you there. You guys could use a lot of work."

Thomas didn't like the feeling as he dove back into his coaching position. He didn't like to be perceived as a gung-ho, kiss-ass company man. And he didn't like to be perceived as a Knute Rockne or Vince Lombardi type, the kind of coach who wanted to win at all costs.

But he had to convince himself that he was somewhere in between. He had to be. He would work as hard as he could for the St. Agnes program, as many hours and as many days a week it took. Some of that dedication even could be contributed to his own pride, not wanting to be seen as a second-rate coach. He understood that pride could not be simply taught. Pride had to be constantly displayed.

So with the commitment he made to himself, to the wrestlers and to the school, Thomas read part of a novel and went to bed by 10 o'clock Saturday night. He missed more than half of the season, and it was catch-up time. He hoped a couple of the wrestlers would feel the same way.

Up at 6:30, he was raring to go. A small cup of coffee and the newspaper to read while he waited for a team he feared may not show at all, he got to the pavilion at 7:15. By 7:30 he decided to run a couple of miles.

A few minutes before 8 o'clock, Thomas was trotting along the bulkhead of the marina, a block away from the pavilion. On the front steps he could see the timid winter sun shining down on a group of bodies. As he crossed the boulevard, he recognized the team. Twelve of the 16 wrestlers, including Anil Nazif, Marc Cella and Chuck Garrison, and one coach, a Mr. Kenneth Lawton – biology teacher.

"Morning, Ken," Thomas said, catching his breath. "You forget your keys?"

It was the first time Thomas McCloskey ever referred to or called Mr. Lawton solely by his first name, and the biology teacher felt good. "I went in, but you weren't in there, so I came out to wait for the team," he said. "I thought that since it was a nice morning, it would be good for the boys to get some fresh air."

"Well, I think that's a good idea," Thomas said. "A little cold, fresh air is good for the soul. A five-minute jog along the marina would do us good. Then we go inside and figure out how to win some matches."

Two weeks earlier, Pope Pius X was looming like a certain loss. St. Agnes was giving up 24 points by forfeit, and the remaining nine starters were just plain giving up.

For most of the season, Pope Pius was forfeiting three weight classes – 103, 189 and heavyweight. But against some of the smaller schools, all 13 weight classes were filled. "Which

149

leads me to believe," Thomas addressed the team standing in the bus aisle while en route, "is that these guys in these three weight classes are freshmen. If we can get some points at these spots, we'll win."

The larger picture was more cloudy. Nazif had no concept of the sport, and Thomas had no confidence in that slot. Marc Cella had some experience, but the layoff was costly. Much more abuse and St. Agnes could be without a 103 pounder again. And the biggest problem was that Pope Pius' strength was in the middleweights – mirroring St. Agnes' power.

St. Agnes' sophomore 103 pounder walked from the mat in near tears, just 30 seconds after sprinting to the center of the mat. He walked to the right side of the bench instead of to the middle to accept the obligatory handshakes from Coach Pierce and Coach Lawton. Coach Thomas cut him off.

"Go back there and shake their hands." Marc Cella ignored the remark and tried to slip around him. Thomas reached out and grabbed him by the arm. "I don't give a shit if you win, lose or take a crap in the middle of the mat. But unless you're carried off the mat on a stretcher and you've lost the use of both of your arms, I expect you to shake the coaches' and teammates' hands. It's called sportsmanship, and if you can't be a sport, then you can't wrestle."

"But I suck," Marc said, on the verge of tears. "I lost to a fuckin' freshman."

"First of all, only I can curse outside the practice room. Second, get your ass over there and shake your coaches' hands. We'll continue this conversation on the back mat."

Begrudgingly, Marc walked with sloped shoulders and a lowered head back to the opening in the middle of the bench. The 112-pound match already had started, so coaches Pierce and Lawton were again busy calling out inappropriate moves. The gesture by Marc Cella took them by surprise. They both congratulated him on a good attempt and a gutsy effort, and the 103 pounder slipped through his teammates and flopped down on the practice mat.

Thomas squatted on his haunches like a baseball catcher, waiting for the right words to enter his mind. The sophomore's ego was severely wounded, and the coach feared he may not show up for any more practices. "I don't know if it felt good, but it was supposed to," the coach said as tenderly as he could in the raucous dual match atmosphere.

Marc was confused. "Getting pinned in 30 seconds is supposed to feel good?" His voice had a whine in it which Thomas did not like.

"No. Shaking hands with the coaches is supposed to feel good. It lets you know that no matter what happens on the mat, it's okay. It's only a sport and life goes on. Win or lose, you come back here and reflect on the match. Whining is not part of the deal."

"But he was a freshman. And you needed me to win."

"First of all, I didn't need you to win – we did. This is a team effort. When I stand up and map out strategy, I map it out for all of us – not for me. Second, as far as wrestling experience goes, you're still a freshman yourself. You had a partial learning year last season and a few days this season. You've given the rest of the 103 pounders an 80-yard head start in the 100-yard dash. That's a huge advantage."

Marc's chin was slowly rising and his eyes searching and exploring. The coach's words were encouraging and soothing.

"I know this sucks. I understand," Thomas said. "But would you do me one favor. Promise?"

What.

"No, I really need you to promise."

Okay.

"Promise me that you'll stick it out for the rest of the season, because we need someone at 103 to accept forfeits and to keep a couple of schools from jockeying around their line-ups. Then, after the season, you'll have the entire summer to think about wrestling. Next school year, I'll ask you once, and only once, if you want to wrestle. If you say no, I'll leave you alone. Promise?"

"Okay. Promise."

Thomas knew Marc Cella would never wrestle again after this sophomore season. His mind wasn't constructed to take the punishment and allow him to bounce back. "Intestinal fortitude," Coach Gibbons called it. Thomas' only hope was that Jeff LeMone hit a growing spurt. He needed to gain nine pounds in less than a year.

By the time Thomas returned his attention to the match, Pope Pius was leading 9-3 going into the middleweights. This was not where he wanted to be.

A svelte Liam walked slowly and confidently to the middle of the mat. After numerous attempts at takedowns by both wrestlers, Liam hit a double-leg takedown and snuck in a quick half nelson while his opponent was trying to turn to his stomach. Liam pinned a 14-4 wrestler. The team score was knotted at 9.

Tony Kingery had his hands full with Xhing Lu, who finished second in District 19 last season as a junior and was 16-3 with 13 pins this year. Thomas expected Pope Pius to pick up six team points, but Tony shocked the crowd by wrestling defensively for the first period, only trailing 2-0.

Lu opened the second period with a takedown and two back points with a three-second count, near-side cradle. Lu led 6-0. Tony kept moving, squirming to an escape to cut the lead to 6-1. Then Lu swung and missed at a standing headlock, and Tony was able to duck under the failed attempt, slip behind the talented wrestler and trip him forward.

The period ended 6-3.

Lu was furious. The Pope Pius senior did not expect to go into the third period with a freshman. The fury transformed to frustration, for Tony wrestled defensively and stalled for the entire third period. The final was 8-3, and Tony knew he had achieved victory in defeat.

"Smart wrestling, Tony," Thomas said. "Now see if we can rub some of that onto your teammates."

Brien Cauldron's match could have gone either way. Thomas figured it to be a low-scoring affair, and he was right. Brien escaped in the second period for the only scoring in the match. He rode out the entire third period, neither garnering back points nor stalling calls. He won a rare 1-0 match, knotting the team score at 12.

Mike Ennis had a tough go at 140; the sophomore gave up seven first-period points before getting decked midway through the second. Despite the loss, St. Agnes survived the power of the Pius middleweights, down only six points with six matches left.

Going in, Thomas felt the Lancers needed to win four of the last six to have a chance, and with decisions at 145 pounds and 152 pounds, pins at 160 and at 189, St. Agnes was guaranteed a tie. Out of the 12 points possible at 171 and heavyweight, St. Agnes needed to find a way to save one team point.

Mike Masterelli was not the answer. The freshman couldn't even do a solid push up in practice. In his previous three matches, his average time of departure was 27 seconds, and that included some sympathetic referees.

"He's a warm body," Thomas had told Mr. Lawton. "I'm hoping his presence will inspire other kids in the school. It could be our slogan – if Masterelli can do it, then so can you."

The 171-pound match was over in 48 seconds. "We're getting there. We're getting there," Thomas said, shaking Mike's hand as he left the mat. Mike was all smiles.

Chris Ballinger put a scare into Thomas. The 189 match should have been over in the first period, but the Pope Pius sophomore was fighting gallantly.

"You see what he's trying to do," Thomas said, popping from behind the bench, interrupting his pre-match pep talk with Nazif. "He's trying to save one team point." Thomas walked up and down the bench trying to drill this point into their heads. "If this kid loses by anything less than a pin, Pius could win." Thomas wanted to say that they will win because there was no way Nazif could last six minutes even if he were wrestling alone.

Up 12-5 with less than a minute left, Thomas jumped to the right of the bench to grab Chris Ballinger's attention. Chris had his man flattened out but was unable to open up pinning combinations. The Pope Pius bench was screaming at its 189 pounder to keep his head up. The crowd was screaming for him to keep his head up. With his head up, the Pope Pius sophomore could avoid being pinned with a half nelson.

Chris looked bewildered at Thomas. "Start running a cross-face cradle," Thomas mouthed and pantomimed, knowing that the sound of his voice would only be swallowed by the existing high decibel level. "Switch to a power half. Back to a cross-face cradle. Back and forth. Back and forth."

Chris understood the instructions. A nice, firm cross-face cradle, if that didn't work, then switch to a power half nelson. If that didn't work, then go back to the cross-face cradle until something opened up.

With 25 seconds left, the whistle blew and Thomas starting screaming "No!"

"No! Not now," he yelled. "Don't call stalling now."

Chris was just starting to loosen up his opponent, making him submit to the cross-face cradle. But the ref felt that the bottom man was making no attempt to escape or to wrestle, so he was hit with his second stalling call. The score stood at 13-5, a major decision, which Thomas knew was absolutely no good to St. Agnes.

Thomas stuck his fingers in his mouth, underneath his tongue and sent a shrill whistle that pierced the air. Chris turned and listened for further instructions. "Run and ankle pick. That'll get his weight forward. Then run the hardest spiral breakdown you've ever run – right into a half nelson. Ankle pick – boom – spiral, half nelson." With the break in the action, Chris was able to hear his coach clearly. "Got it? Good." Thomas turned and made a complete lap around the St. Agnes bench.

Chris followed the instructions. Lined up to the left of his opponent, Chris reached across and with his right hand grabbed a right ankle, forcing all of his opponent's weight onto his hands. The St. Agnes 189 pounder then switched to a spiral breakdown, taking his left arm and throwing it underneath his man's left armpit. Chris's right hand released the ankle, went around his opponent's waist to the inside of the right thigh, forcing the leg to jut rearward.

Chris Ballinger got on his toes and with all of his force, ran clockwise in the spiral motion. Within seconds, his opponent was flattened out, and his half nelson was set. With eight seconds left, the match was over.

Exhilaration ran through Chris, Thomas and the rest of the St. Agnes team. Thomas liked the feeling of being in front of the bench, calling the shots. It seemed to him that everything was so clear, so natural. Almost like he was out there wrestling. The ref raised Chris's hand in triumph and he rushed back to the awaiting high fives, handshakes and slaps to his back. Everyone but Nazif congratulated him.

An identical situation greeted Anil as it had greeted Chuck Garrison in St. Agnes' only wrestling victory in the school history the season before. If the chess club member turned heavyweight wrestler could last six minutes, the Lancers would taste victory again.

There was not a snowball's chance in hell, and Thomas knew it. But it was decision time. Does Thomas throw in the towel and explain to Anil that he shouldn't wrestle, he wasn't prepared yet, he could get injured? Or does he send him out and hope for the best?

Fuck it. "We came to wrestle," Thomas told Anil. "You go out there and you give it everything you got. You can beat this guy."

Thomas snapped the head gear strap tightly to the heavyweight's head, pushing Anil's cheeks, making it appear as if he just lost his wisdom teeth.

Anil Nazif was back 15 seconds later, blood trickling from his nose. Thomas smiled and told him he earned a varsity letter.

Thomas McCloskey sometimes regretted the decision to send out inexperienced wrestlers. He would always return to "No guts, no glory," as his excuse. He wondered if this would traumatize these children for the rest of their lives. Then he would tell himself to snap out of it. "For Chrissakes," he would say aloud to himself while in a contemplating session at home. "You're starting to sound like the damn liberal media. Your job is to toughen these kids up – not coddle them."

St. Agnes tied Pope Pius X. The Lancers were 0-11-1.

Anil Nazif would return for more matches and more beatings for two more seasons, thanking Thomas for the opportunity to wrestle as he headed off to Yale, with his sights set on a medical career.

Marc Cella's and Anil Nazif's willingness to wrestle sparked the Lancers to two wins in their next three matches.

St. Mary's had neither a 103 pounder nor a heavyweight, and St. Agnes benefited greatly, making what could have been a close match a relatively easy 37-20 victory.

That was Saturday, and with an unusual Wednesday off day, St. Agnes could gain an extra practice day for its conference match against Central Regional. "We could have 100 extra practices, we still couldn't prepare properly for Central," Thomas said.

The sparse crowd at Central was indicative of the interest in the match. Central's head coach decided to rest many of his starters and still cruised to a 52-20 win. St. Agnes was 1-12-1

Injuries and disciplinary actions had taken its toll on St. Peters' since the mid-season mark, yet their coach, Ben Adams, expected to win a close match against the Lancers.

Marc Cella was pinned in 3:10, and the St. Peter's bench and crowd were confident. Too confident, for St. Agnes rattled off seven straight pins and bolted to a 42-6 lead. St. Peter's won three of the last five matches, but it wasn't enough. St. Agnes was 2-12-1 after the 51-22 win.

One match left in the season, and Thomas was redefining the team's goals.

New Welsh had a .500 season, but was 0-5 in the conference. This was the rally cry Thomas used in practice for the last match of the season.

"Remember last year? We used Bishop Leary to act as our championship match. Well, that was step one," Thomas said. He weaved in and out of the wrestlers sprawled on the mat after a tough calisthenic workout. "New Welsh is step two. It presents a new challenge. Last year we were bad, really bad. This year we're bad, but not so bad. But instead of not being the worst in the entire Shore Conference, now we're shooting for sixth place in the division. Sounds a hell of a lot better, doesn't it?"

The Lancers worked hard in their Thursday and Friday practices, preparing for their second season-ending "championship match." Thomas hoped that St. Agnes could catch a New Welsh team sleeping, wrestling on its heels, wanting to finish out the regular season and start the districts.

He was wrong. New Welsh was ready for them, not wanting to finish last to a second-year team. New Welsh pinned in the first three weight classes before Liam stopped the onrush with a major decision. The score was 18-4.

"It's gut-check time." Thomas had gathered the three remaining middle weights behind the bench. "You guys need to pick up some points and wrestle hard and smart. Don't let this fuckin' team walk all over us."

Tony Kingery responded with a pin, but then Brien Cauldron drew at 135, giving each school two team points. St. Agnes had its hopes dashed when Mike Ennis was pinned in the first period. The Lancers trailed 26-12, with the strong part of New Welsh's line-up coming up.

St. Agnes managed decisions at 152 and 189, getting decked at 145, 160 and 171.With Anil Nazif walking to the mat, St. Agnes trailed 42-18.

"Hey Tommy, you think we should just forfeit heavyweight? I mean there's no use."

The forgotten coach, Mark Pierce, had blended into the background the final two weeks of the season, cloaked more in mystery than advice. Thomas could not understand why he suddenly would want to speak out now. What was up his sleeve?

Actually, he had a point. Nazif was doing nothing but putting himself at risk for injury. He was gaining nothing from competition except getting used to the crowd. "Well, whaddaya think, Anil? Pack it in or wrestle? It's up to you." Thomas kept the tone in his voice as neutral as possible.

"Pack it in? Coach, I'm Pakistani. That means I wrestle. You tell us not to look like pussies. I'm not going to be a pussy."

Twenty-seven seconds later, New Welsh's heavyweight closed out a 48-18 win. Thomas shook Anil's hand and told him he'd never be a pussy.

Thomas could never say that to Mark Pierce.

EIGHTEEN

He could remember the awful feeling of exhaustion after weighing in for the 17th time that season, a Friday night, the preliminary and quarterfinals of the District 41 wrestling championships. It was different from the complete exhaustion after a six-minute match with a formidable opponent, when the lack of energy keeps a wrestler from lifting his arms to accept congratulatory or consoling handshakes from teammates. Different from that six-minute battle in which his legs don't wish to carry the weight of his own body, but the mind and heart imploring to continue. Different from the exhaustion which denies the memory from recalling details of the excruciatingly painful final minute of a match.

The fatigue Thomas Patrick McCloskey experienced that night in 1982 occurred prior to wrestling the first postseason match his junior year. His legs were rubbery, his arms felt like they were attached to anchors, his eyes stung as if salt were in them, his stomach empty and shallow, not wanting any food, wanting to repel any that it already had. But worst of all was his mind. Never before had he wanted to avoid wrestling.

Maybe it was something he ate, or maybe a cold. Thomas wished it wasn't a cold, because a cold made it virtually impossible to cut weight. He had gotten sick one time during midseason his sophomore year, and Coach Gibbons let him wrestle up one weight class before he regained his stamina, thus allowing him to cut weight again.

The districts, though, locked a wrestler into a single weight class. The districts, the regions and the states were the individual portions of the high school wresting world in New Jersey, and if one were fortunate enough to make it to the semifinals of the state championships, that wrestler would have had to make weight an additional seven times and would have competed in 10 or more matches. The sniffles of a little cold might be battled. Anything lingering could lead to strep throat, tonsillitis or worse. It happened thousands of times with devastating results.

Thomas quickly disposed of the thought of a severe ailment. Some juice and aspirin would do the trick. He would skip dinner and would take advantage of the weigh-ins following Friday night's quarterfinal round instead of weighing in on Saturday morning. Fluids and aspirin. He would sweat off the weight during the warm-ups and the match, weigh in, go home and have a steak. The next weigh-ins wouldn't be until the following Wednesday.

Bristol Arias of Bell Harbor was the seventh seed with a 7-14 record, having defeated the 10th seed, 9-2, one hour earlier in the preliminary pigtail match. Thomas had never wrestled Arias but did not expect much trouble. His game plan was to work a solid two periods, wrestle into the third and pick up some team points with a pin. He wanted to work on single leg takedowns, leading with the left foot, showing the competition what he was not going to utilize. Working from the top in referee's position, he wanted to work from the unorthodox right side. From the defensive bottom position, he would work some sit outs, allowing Arias to follow him. That certainly would get off the 1 ½ pounds he had imbibed since weigh-ins.

Standing in the inner circle, waiting for the start of his tournament, Thomas already had his forearms resting on his knees, his hands unnoticeably shaking. He was forced to radically alter his match, sensing that if he allowed Arias to enter the third period, disaster could be at hand. At the one-minute mark, after taking down Arias twice, Thomas threw his right forearm into his opponent's left shoulder, stepped back with his left foot simultaneously, and twisted his hips counterclockwise. Arias found himself on his back in an airtight headlock. 1:07. Pin.

Thomas walked off the mat, determined not to display any signs of fatigue. He grabbed his warm-ups and told Coach Gibbons he wanted to weigh in. He walked into the boys' locker room, draped his hooded sweatshirt over his shoulders, sat on the floor against the lockers in the far corner and fell asleep.

The early weigh-in period for the Saturday morning matches was coming to a close. The heavyweights were preparing for the thunderous finale of the tournament for the Friday quarterfinal matches when Covington Assistant Coach Danny

Johnson came in to check on Thomas. It had been 35 minutes since the end of his match.

Despite the constant flow of competitors and coaches to and from the locker room, Thomas never moved. He slept amidst the victorious whooping calls and the disappointed slamming of lockers.

Coach Johnson kicked Thomas' shoes. "Hey T-Mac. Did you make weight?"

Thomas opened his eyes, not knowing what time it was, not clear of his surroundings. "No. Not yet."

"Well, you better get going. You only have about 10 minutes," Coach Johnson said. He noticed the sluggish movements of the awakening wrestler. "You feeling okay?"

"Yeah Coach. I guess I didn't get enough sleep last night."

By the time Thomas rose, walked to the two scales and stripped, he had but five minutes remaining until the end of the Friday weigh-in period. The scale master tapped the weight until the bar came to a balance. "You're about a pound over. You can try this scale, but it's been weighing an ounce or two heavier all night."

Thomas was too tired to care. "I'll just run a little tonight and make it in the morning, Coach."

When Thomas got home, the first thing he did was check his weight on his home scale. He needed to know exactly what his weight was, for the prospects of losing a pound and of wrestling two high-caliber matches with not much energy to spare was dismal. Thomas went to bed, drinking a half glass of orange juice and taking two aspirins.

While monitoring a strict diet during the season, Thomas could hope to lose a ½ pound during a weeknight and a pound on Sunday nights because he ate more during the weekends, the extra food helping to speed up his metabolism.

When Thomas woke Saturday morning, his body was stiff, his joints ached and his stomach felt hollow. With a burst of energy, he decided to spring into the shower, hoping the hot water would rejuvenate him.

After the shower, he stepped on the scale. He was still ¾-of-a-pound over. Under normal circumstances, that would really piss him off. But on this day, it depressed him. He sat on the commode with his head in his hands, hoping for any type of movement. He barely urinated.

Downstairs, his mother asked him if he had time for breakfast, but Thomas pleasantly declined, instead going to the kitchen drawer. There he found his stash of Bubble Yum and took out three pieces, unwrapped them, popped them into his mouth and began chewing.

"Thomas! Do not tell me you're not eating because you're overweight." Thomas found a paper cup on top of the garbage, straightened it out and began to spit. "How much do you have to lose this time?"

"About a half."

"Thomas, so help me, next year I won't let you lose weight. This is not healthy."

"Okay, Ma." Thomas grabbed his varsity jacket and his gear and walked to school, hoping to make weight in the 10-block walk.

Thomas didn't bother checking weight at Covington for the walk tapped much of his energy, so he just sat and spit into the cup. He had no idea how close – or how far – he actually was to making weight when he eventually stepped onto the scale at Timbrook High.

"Half over," the scale master said.

Coach Gibbons was a little surprised. "Why don't you try the light one?"

"That is the light one." Both Thomas and the scale master said together.

"Don't worry. I'll just go break a sweat and make it."

Most everybody at the district weigh-ins was shocked to see Thomas McCloskey suited up in full warm-ups, running around the two mats in the Timbrook gym. At the time, four other wrestlers were running prior to the 10 a.m. semifinals, but Thomas garnered all of the attention.

"I don't like this," Coach Gibbons said.

"Oh, he'll make it, Paul," Danny Johnson said.

"I know that. But there's something not right with Thomas. A cold or an injury or, God forbid, a girl."

With 10 minutes left to the close of the final weigh-in period, Thomas stripped naked. He toweled off all excess sweat, dried the little hair he had on his head and waited. He wiped the soles of his feet with the palms of his hands – a wrestling superstition more than a productive measure – took a deep breath in, exhaled and stepped gingerly on the very front of the scale's base. The sudden upward movement of the fulcrum caused Thomas to back off before the two scale masters could make a determination.

"That didn't feel like the sweet spot," Thomas said. He wiped his feet again, inhaled, stepped gingerly on the back right part of the base, and exhaled. The balance touched the top, retreated, touched and retreated. By the time it came to a rest, a sliver of light no more than the width of a dime shown through.

"Good."

"Good." Both scale masters agreed.

Coach Gibbons allowed Thomas to dress and gather his gear before he put his arm around his wrestler, guiding him to the idle showers for a quiet conversation.

"Cutting it this close is something I would've expected from the renegade Thomas McCloskey last year," Gibbons said. "So why don't you tell me what's wrong. I'll accept anything but female troubles."

"No," Thomas said quickly. "I haven't had a date with Michelle for a month. That's the last thing on my mind."

"Good. Then it's got to be physical. We can fix physical."

"I don't know. I'm just tired. Drained. It might be nerves, being the favorite and everything."

"Do you feel nervous?"

"No. Not really."

Gibbons thought for a moment. "Well, on Monday, we'll get you into the school nurse and let her check you out." Gibbons wanted to get Thomas to a doctor, but he knew Mrs. McCloskey was on a tight budget, so maybe the school nurse, the ancient Sara Campbell, could help out. "Let's go get some food in you."

"Actually, I just want to lie down on the bleachers and shut my eyes for a while."

Tom Vargas was the fourth seed from Woodrow Wilson whom Thomas had met earlier in the season in a dual match. Vargas was thin and lanky, and he liked to go on the offensive from the first whistle. The style was tailor-made for Thomas, who liked to counter most situations he got into.

In the first match between the two, Thomas built up an 11-0 lead midway through the second period before pinning Vargas with a double-arm bar. But matters didn't progress the same way in the district semifinals. Trouble started early.

Everybody in the building knew Vargas would shoot low to the outside at the opening whistle. Thomas understood this better than anyone. And it didn't matter which ankle Vargas picked because Thomas' sprawl and cross face was quick and powerful.

Vargas shot as expected but was far short of an ankle and Thomas sprawled too far. Both wrestlers ended up on their knees, face to face about an arms length apart. After a quick scrum, Vargas managed a half duck under and fell on top of Thomas for a 2-0 lead.

Thomas remained flat on his belly for a few seconds, a peculiar sight because whenever he made a mistake, he turned into a tornado of energy to regain control. Coach Gibbons stood up and was ready to call for an injury timeout, when Thomas slowly pushed back to his base and hit a reversal to tie the score at 2. He worked several pinning combinations from the top without success, not able to score any more points in the first period.

Gibbons asked Thomas if he wanted to take injury time, but the wrestler shook him off. "It looks like he's drunk," Gibbons said to Coach Johnson. Vargas set up in the down position, Thomas took top. The referee stood directly in front of the pair, held out his hand to signify 'get set,' then simultaneously blew the whistle and snapped his wrist.

Calling on all of his energy, Thomas reached underneath Vargas' chest and pulled his left arm while lifting his right leg – a butcher and a Turk ride in wrestling terms. It wasn't a tight pinning combination, but it was safe. It picked up quick points and it saved energy. Thomas rode it for the entire second period. He led 5-2.

The choice for position in the third period belonged to Thomas, and when he chose top, Gibbons was convinced that something was seriously wrong. "He's chosen down for the last two years. Maybe I should stop this, Danny."

"Tommy's a big boy. He'll let you know if you should stop it."

Thomas worked different breakdowns and a couple of pinning combinations for the first 1:45 of the period. With the Woodrow Wilson coaches screaming for a stalling call for more than a minute, the ref finally succumbed, whistling a warning. Thomas finished the match without any other incidents. The final score was 5-2.

"What's wrong, Tom?" Coach Gibbons asked as Thomas wandered back to the locker room. "Maybe we should think about defaulting for the finals. You've already got your spot in the regions."

"Don't do that, Coach. My goal was to win the district championship. That's all I want right now."

After a quick shower, Thomas and Coach Gibbons went to the cafeteria. Thomas got some chicken noodle soup and water, and the coach got some coffee. Thomas choked down as much as he could.

"I'm really thinking about stopping this," Gibbons said. "If your mother were here, she'd kill the both of us."

"Well, that's why I don't let her come anymore. She saw me getting pinned in an arm bar my freshman year and she thought I broke my neck. She says she's more comfortable when I bring the results home to her." He barely got all the words out. Talking made him tired.

"I'm concerned, Tom," Gibbons said. "I'm going to tell the ref to keep an eye on you in the finals. We'll take injury time if we have to. But if this condition worsens, I'm pulling you."

"Don't Coach. I'll be fine."

Thomas' record stood at 21-0 with 2 ½ hours left until the final round.

With his eyes closed, Thomas stretched on the back warm-up mat. Coach Gibbons told him not to expend any energy before the match, just to keep the warm-ups on and stretch out.

Thomas knew he was sick with some kind of flu or virus, but Coach Johnson got a thermometer from the trainer, and Thomas wasn't running a fever. Anytime the thought of not being 100 percent, Thomas would quickly say aloud, "Suck it up. There's absolutely nothing wrong with you, so suck it up." And he thought about a scene in the movie *The Deer Hunter* where Robert DeNiro was being tortured in a game of Russian Roulette. "That's a problem," he said to himself. "You don't have a problem."

Everyone in the crowd knew that something wasn't exactly right with Thomas McCloskey, especially Tyrone Claremore of Timbrook Township, the host school of the district. Claremore had lost to Thomas twice during the regular season by large margins, a major decision in the first match, a superior in the second, two of the five matches in which Thomas didn't deck his opponent. The Timbrook coaches had closely monitored Thomas in Friday evening's match and during the semifinals on Saturday, and they had Tyrone convinced that he was the favorite. "McCloskey has lost all of his fire. It looks like he's stoned off his ass, moving slow, out of breath. Look at him, he's stoned. You go after him and go fuckin' hard. If you want this fuckin' district crown, you go out and beat his ass."

Covington and Timbrook were battling for second and third place for team standings in the district, which didn't mean a whole hell of a lot but bragging rights. But Timbrook wanted to brag, being the host school and not finishing higher than fifth the previous three seasons, toppling Covington and its mighty McCloskey would be a tremendous end to the season.

So, on the opening whistle, Claremore shot at Thomas – just as Vargas did in the semis – but not with as much success. Thomas sprawled and tried to counter by throwing a cross face with his right forearm and spinning to his left. But Claremore stuck up his arm and blocked. Thomas pushed off and went back to neutral.

As soon as Claremore set up, Thomas lowered his level and shot at the right leg. A rare single-leg takedown attempt, Claremore was caught off guard but still managed a decent sprawl.

Knees and elbows on the mat, arms wrapped around Claremore's right knee, and Claremore's body draped over Thomas' back, the crowd was screaming all kinds of advice, encouragement and obscenities. Predominantly Timbrook High School fans, the prevailing scream was simply, "Kick his ass, Clarence," although there were some knowledgeable fans screaming, "Pressure the head. Pressure the head."

Thomas was content with hanging onto the leg for the meantime. As long as he kept his hands locked together, Claremore couldn't counter and get control for a two-point takedown. The worst case scenario was the referee calling a stalemate, starting the entire neutral position process over again.

While down underneath a groping Claremore, Thomas finally admitted to himself that he was sick and not a little cough, "hkeh, hkeh," type of sick either, but a potential season-ending illness. This could be his last six minutes on the mat his junior year. So he decided to wrestle in spurts, for that was the best he could do.

It was time for spurt number one. Still clutching the knee and his own torso facing the mat, Thomas formed a tripod. Raising his knees off the mat, his two feet became two points of the tripod. The final point was his hands, still clasped together behind his opponent's right hamstring. He shuffled his feet, two giant strides to his right, quickly going from a head to head position to a hip to hip position with Claremore. The quick maneuver threw off Claremore's balance, and Thomas knew he was in good position.

Thomas pulled the knee into his chest and then drove into Claremore's hip, driving the far hip to the mat. Releasing his grip, Thomas reached for a half nelson with his left hand, retained hold of the knee with the right and had Claremore on his back.

Thomas didn't have enough energy to finish the combination, so he just laid on top, finally letting Claremore off of his back with 20 seconds left in the first period. Thomas stood up, conceding the one-point escape. The period ended with the two wrestlers on their feet, the score 5-1.

It was Thomas' choice and he looked to his coach for advice, but Gibbons couldn't sense how he felt. "It's up to you."

If Thomas chose neutral, he could get taken down and lose two points.

If he chose top, he could get reversed and lose two points.

If he chose down, Claremore would have to turn him to his back for any points, and he wasn't about to let that happen.

Nobody Thomas had wrestled all season had been able to keep him down for more than 20 seconds, except for Vargas in the morning match. All Thomas had to do was keep moving and everything would work out fine. So he decided to pick the defensive position.

Thomas stood up for his first move, but with Claremore standing behind him, he was quickly tripped forward and went crashing to the mat with Claremore's entire body weight directly atop of him. After pushing back to his base from his stomach, Thomas tried two consecutive sit outs and then a switch, but none were crisp. He stood twice more, landing back on the mat with tremendous thuds. The lack of energy even kept him from properly bracing for the trips, knocking some of the wind from his lungs.

One minute, 10 seconds had passed and Thomas was beat. He kept his head up but remained virtually motionless in the referee's position. Claremore saw an opening and threw in a leg, entwisting his left leg with Thomas' left leg.

Fine, Thomas thought, this will give me a breather. So he switched from his palms flat on the mat to leaning on his forearms, and kept a wide base with his knees and feet spread apart. Twenty seconds passed, and the whistle blew.

Good. A stalemate, Thomas thought. The call would give him a break without penalizing him in any way. But instead the referee thrust a fist into the air, notifying a warning for stalling against McCloskey.

Gibbons jumped from his seat and went ballistic. "The top man is responsible for action when he's got legs in," Gibbons said. "If Timbrook can't use the move, then he's got to give it up. It's either a stalemate or stalling on Timbrook."

The referee calmly discussed this with the Covington coach, who was more than happy to discuss the philosophical use of the legs in wrestling, anything to give Thomas an extra breather.

Thomas sat on the mat, his arms holding loosely onto his knees. Nearly two periods had passed and he was hardly sweating. The argument ended, and so did the second period. The score remained 5-1, but another stalling call would cost him a point.

Claremore chose the down position for the third period, and after 30 seconds of rolling around on the mat, he finally got to his feet and broke free for a point. A quick low shot to Thomas' left ankle was successful, and with a minute remaining and Claremore in wrestling control, the score was 5-4 in McCloskey's favor.

Thomas couldn't afford that second stalling call, so he remained in motion, content with staying on the bottom. If he stopped moving, either the ref would signal stalling or, even worse, Claremore could now turn a weakened Thomas McCloskey to his back. So Thomas stood and sat and hit his front bridge and did it all again, until it was apparent to the Timbrook coaches that the Covington wrestler would never go to his back – not today.

"Let him go," Timbrook Head Coach Eddie Liddle yelled with 17 seconds left. "Let him up and take him down. Let him up and shoot." With 14 seconds left, the two wrestlers were on their feet, 10 feet from the out-of-bounds line. The score was 6-4.

"Shoot. Shoot. Shoot!" It seemed everyone was yelling. It became the Timbrook gymnasium Saturday mantra. With nine seconds left, Claremore shot. Thomas sprawled. Out of bounds. Seven seconds left. On one knee, Thomas clutched his chest.

"Injury time," Gibbons called to the ref, who drew circles in the air, indicating to the scorer's table to begin injury time. Thomas was allowed two minutes, if needed.

"What the hell is this, Kevin?" Liddle called to the ref. "He's not injured. He's gassed."

Gibbons rose and a great battle was on the horizon, but before the two coaches and the referee could engage, Thomas rose and staggered back to the middle of the mat. "I don't need the time. Let's go."

Liddle then turned his ire toward Claremore. "Take him down and send it to overtime. Take care of this bum in overtime."

Overtime would mean three, one-minute periods, and with the apparent stitch taking residence in most of Thomas' right lung, he knew overtime was not an option. And his mind brought him back to the basics. Of all the information and of all the strategy he soaked up in the last three years, Thomas understood that double-leg takedowns and stand-ups win matches.

Claremore and McCloskey set up in neutral position. Sweat dripped from Claremore's nose, his dark eyes locked on Thomas' blues. Thomas forehead was bone dry, his eyes locked on Claremore's hips.

The whistle blew.

Claremore stepped twice to shorten the distance before his shot – his shot that never came. Just as his hands and hips gave the slightest indication that he was about to lower his level and shoot, Thomas reacted.

The double-leg takedown was textbook. His hips dropped. Right leg stepping between Claremore's legs. Head on Claremore's right hip. Thomas pulled Claremore's leg into his body with his right arm, lifted the other leg with his left, drove against Claremore's hip with his head and his neck.

Takedown. Two seconds. One. Buzzer. Then Whistle.

Thomas was exhausted, but he could rest anywhere on the planet, just not on the center of the mat in the middle of Timbrook's gymnasium. Claremore went to shake Gibbons' hand. Thomas went to Liddle.

"This bum is 22-0," Thomas said.

It was the last match of his junior year. Thomas was diagnosed with mononucleosis.

* * *

Ten years later, Thomas McCloskey was back at Timbrook Regional High School, sitting in the back left corner of room 210, waiting for Mark Pierce to finish writing the St. Agnes entries on the chalkboard, watching cliques of coaches talk about past accomplishments and future goals.

The groups that the coaches congregated in were the blocks of votes they tendered for seeding the current crop of wrestlers. The larger coalitions garnered more favorable seeds. Of course, allied coaches many times would have wrestlers vying for the same seed. That is when the coaches were at their most despicable.

Up to the right of the room sat Eddie Liddle and two assistant coaches from Timbrook. Once a powerful program, Timbrook had fallen on hard times, finishing in the bottom three district spots the last six years. Liddle, now in his mid 50s, was the reason, having been dragged through a messy divorce and dragging the Board of Education through an ugly defamation of character suit. The two incidents were intricately related. All of the bad feelings resulted in funding cuts to the wrestling program in an attempt to force out Liddle, which prompted parents to attack the duplicitous actions of the Board of Education, which, in turn, resulted in harsh times in his home.

The end result was that the Timbrook wrestlers suffered. So did his own kids. Liddle lost custody in the divorce settlement.

With the Timbrook staff sat the two coaches from New Welsh and the two coaches from Carlysle. Drinking partners from early in their coaching days, Liddle and the other two head coaches were diametrically opposed to the contingent sitting to the left, in the middle rows. A web of former wrestlers and coaches, Flat River had a staff of four; Fairview a staff of three; North Winfield had two.

The remaining four schools were spread throughout the room but were close in the voting practices, being as ethical as possible – apathetically neutral at worst – in District 41. Coach Gibbons always came alone – "there's no need to add to this circus;" Blakemore's two coaches had been at their school for 22 years; Jefferson had two young coaches not sure with which side to align; and St. Agnes had Thomas and Mark.

169

Thomas figured that one year Mark would probably love to hobnob with the Flat River crew. There was more opportunity with those coaches.

Thomas kept his ears open as he thumbed through the paperwork Mr. Lawton had left him. Thomas was going to come alone, just to get a feel for the proceedings and prepare for next season, but Mark whined and intervened.

"Why don't you let me represent St. Agnes as the head coach?" Mark asked as if it were his right. "Since I'm heading over to Covington next season and you're not officially part of the staff this season, it would give me good experience."

Whatever.

So Mark got what he wanted, which was fine with Thomas, because he never liked writing on the blackboard. He always made the chalk squeak and his writing always headed north.

At the left on the front chalkboard, the names of the schools were listed, vertically and alphabetically. Along the top were the weight classes: 103, 112, 119, 125, 130, 135, 140, 145 and 152. On the right side of the classroom was another chalkboard, school names similarly written vertically, the weight classes of 160, 171, 189 and HWT written across the top.

Mark was writing St. Agnes' 10 entries, three short of a full line-up. Thomas had spoken to Marc Cella and told him it would be good experience for the sophomore to wrestle in the districts. "It'll prepare you for next year," Thomas said, only to hear 103 pounds of rejection. Thomas would be right about Cella not coming back.

At 171 pounds, there was a mutual agreement between wrestler and coach. Mike Masterelli did not want to compete and Thomas would not let him. "Even if there is a pigtail match – where the tenth seed meets the seventh, and eight meets nine in the preliminaries – you're just not ready." Mike was glad to hear that.

Anil Nazif was prepared to compete but told Thomas, "Because it is for individual status, I would rather not. If this meant more for the team, I would." Thomas understood and told the chess club member that his mere presence was a bonus down the stretch. Anil may not have wrestled at the District 41 tournament, but he cheered for every teammate during every match that weekend.

Mark Pierce took forever to write down the 10 names, misspelling three, getting incorrect records tabulated. He walked back to Thomas to check with him on a couple of points. "Don't even worry about it," Thomas whispered. "The entire squad will get 10th seeds."

Finally, the seeding procedure started. The district manager, hailing from the host school, would ask coaches for a nomination of top seed. If a coach felt his wrestler was worthy of the seed, he would raise a hand. If there was only one nomination, the seed would be declared as uncontested and automatically awarded.

Upon two or more nominations, each head coach would take turns stating the wrestler's best victories, the level of competition, and losses to worthy opponents. After each coach had his say, a vote would be taken, each school allowed one vote. Most votes got the higher seed. Each seed in each weight class went through the nomination procedure.

Thomas sat back, relaxed and watched the proceedings. The political jockeying for positions for seeds was amazing, almost a science. To avoid certain match-ups, some coaches would not nominate their own wrestler for certain seeds. For instance, Liddle wanted to take the 10th seed in the weak 112-pound weight class, giving the ninth to St. Agnes. That way, Liddle would have a better chance of getting to the finals with upsets against the 7th and 2nd seeds. And St. Agnes would have to wrestle the 8th and, with a victory, the top seed. The 112 top seed was 19-2. Number 2 was 12-9.

"Contest that, Mark," Thomas said. "I know it doesn't matter much for team points, but you gotta stick up for your wrestlers."

Mark shook his head and mumbled that there was really not much of a difference.

It took an entire hour to set the seeds for the first three weight classes.

At 125 pounds, the first four seeds fell right into place, the first time it had happened that night. For the fifth seed, Liddle nominated Timbrook's Richie Pilone, who was 11-8. Thomas nudged Mark, who in turn raised his hand for Liam Connelly.

"Any more?" the district manager asked. "Well, St. Agnes, why don't you start it off."

It was the first time Mark got to speak at the meeting. St. Agnes had no entry at 103, got the ninth seed at 112, and an uncontested eighth seed at 119. Mark cleared his throat and began. "Well, you can see, Liam is 10-6. He started out slow. . . ." There was an awkward silence as Mark sifted through the paperwork to find Liam's sheet, then he had to count. "He won seven out of eight, only losing to the kid from Central. He's a senior and he's wrestling real well right now."

The district manager nodded and received a nod from Mark. "Eddie. You want to talk about Richie Pilone?"

"Actually, instead of talking about my kid, I think I'd be better off just saying that I've seen this kid from St. Agnes wrestle. He's wrestled nobody, and, well, basically he's a bum."

The coaches in the front right corner of the room representing Timbrook, New Welsh and Carlysle all laughed, just as they always did when Eddie Liddle flaunted his abrasive humor. Liddle soaked up the laughter and was ready to resume when someone from the back of the room spoke. It was Thomas McCloskey.

"How do you know he's a bum? Where'd you see him wrestle?"

"I saw him at one of the Christmas tournaments, and he really stunk up the joint," Liddle said out of the side of his mouth and over his shoulder. His cronies laughed but not as loudly.

"So you saw him way back at the beginning of the season, and you get to base your argument on that?"

"Sure. I know a bum when I see one."

"You're full of shit." A hush came over the room as Eddie Liddle turned completely around to see who this detractor was. "St. Agnes wasn't in a Christmas tournament. Why don't you try again."

Liddle stared down Thomas. While continuing his glare, he said in an aside to the district manager, "Hey, Tony, I thought only head coaches were supposed to speak."

"Since Mr. Lawton isn't present tonight, I'm assuming head coaching responsibilities," Thomas said.

"What about the other gentleman," the district manager directed with diplomacy, attempting to regain any semblance of decorum with this wrestling crew.

"I was just letting him practice his verbal skills," Thomas said curtly to Tony, the district manager. Thomas returned his attention to Liddle. "You wanna try and remember where you saw Connelly?"

"You know, I'm starting not to like you," Liddle said, his face growing red.

Thomas ignored Liddle and spoke to the entire group. "Besides a tough loss to Slocum from Central, who finished second over in District 19 last year, Connelly's 7-1 with five decks down the stretch. In the second half of the season, he's got wins over North Winfield, Winfield Heights, Carlysle and New Welsh – all of those schools got decent programs." Finishing with the quick recap for the Lancer 125 pounder, Thomas said to Liddle, "You called me a bum 10 years ago, now you're calling a St. Agnes wrestler a bum. Who the fuck are you gonna call a bum next?"

Liddle stared at Thomas trying to figure out who he was while Tony, the district manager, reprimanded Thomas for his inappropriate language.

In the last 10 years, Liddle had called quite a few wrestlers bums, but he had yet been challenged. "Who are you?"

"That would be Tommy McCloskey," Paul Gibbons said proudly.

"One of Gibbons' boys. Now I understand the sharp tongue," Liddle said, switching to alternate attack, much rather bringing the level-headed Paul Gibbons into the fray than staying in an isolated fracas with McCloskey. Gibbons didn't bite. "Didn't you go up to some school in Alaska and flunk out?"

"I missed all the nice folks back home such as yourself," Thomas said, putting an end to that part of Liddle's pronged attack. "Do you have more to add on your 125 pounder or are you sticking with Connelly's a bum? I wanna vote so I can get the hell out of here. I gotta pack for Alaska."

Thomas' continuing attack was not meant to be vindictive. Sure, Thomas did like lashing out and wished Liddle would have crossed the line, but the St. Agnes coach was sending a message to everybody in the room. Thomas didn't like playing games and the entire seeding process was an ego pleaser for most of the coaches present. Thomas almost said, let's just seed the kids – the cream will rise to the top on Saturday. But he didn't.

Liddle made a feeble attempt at making his 125 pounder look like the next coming of Dan Gable. Sensing the end to his presentation, the district manager put the fifth seed to a vote. "We have Connelly with a 10-6 record, and Pilone of Timbrook with an 11-8 record. St. Agnes?"

Seven coaches raised their hands.

For posterity, the district manager asked, "Timbrook?"

The voting block of Timbrook, New Welsh and Carlysle voted for Pilone.

Tony the district manager finished out the 125-pound weight class and promptly moved to 130 pounds. Tony Kingery was 5-2, and Thomas saw no arguments arising, figuring the freshman was deserving of the sixth seed. Thomas had his adrenalin pumping excessively, so he took a break. He leaned over and told Mark Pierce to take over.

When asked which coaches wanted to nominate wrestlers for sixth seed, the district manager indicated St. Agnes. Noting that, Liddle raised his hand for his 3-11 wrestler.

"St. Agnes, tell us about Kingery."

"Tony is 5-2," Mark said, pointing to the record on the chalkboard, "and he didn't start to wrestle until mid. . . ."

"Wait a second," Liddle said, "I thought McCloskey was speaking for St. Agnes."

"Coach." The district manager looked at Thomas. "What about that?"

"Coach Pierce and I each took a list of wrestlers and studied them. This one belongs to Mark."

"Well, this won't be any fun when it's my turn. I was going to call Kingery a bum." Liddle's clan laughed, as well as a couple of the other coaches. Thomas smiled deviously. "In that case, I withdraw," Liddle said.

The seeding meeting continued, bogging down in straightening out the top half of the weight class brackets. St. Agnes received draws from the bottom three slots in the 135, 140, 145, 152 and 160 weight classes.

Next up was 189 and Chris Ballinger.

This season, 189 was packed with upperclassmen, so it wasn't until the sixth seed that the St. Agnes staff had an opportunity to put Ballinger's name up for a vote. Thomas raised his hand, as did Fairview and Timbrook – legitimately this time.

"Let's start with Fairview," the district manager stated.

Peter Capps. 13-9. Third place in the Eagle Classic in December. Senior.

"Alright. Timbrook, how 'bout Weller?"

"Chris Weller. He's 12-7, he finished fourth in District 41 at 160 last year. He lost three of his eight matches because he had the flu, so he never got into a groove. One of the losses was in the first round of the Dover two-day tournament. That's when he first got sick, then he came back and beat the kid later in the season. He's a senior and like I said, he finished fourth at 160 last year."

All right. St. Agnes.

Thomas cleared his throat. "Ballinger – 12-4 on the year and is 7-1 in his last eight matches." Thomas stopped because he knew Liddle had something to say.

"What? Is this a new trend we have to put up with?"

"With all due respect Mr. Spencer, if it's all right with the rest of the coaches, could we just let me and Mr. Pierce conduct our team in this manner. Perhaps the better judgment would be to cut out the other bullshit and shenanigans that's been going on for the past ten years."

Tony Spencer recognized the look from a young Tommy McCloskey's eyes and was not about to find out any more about his current mindset. "Okay," he said without seeking a vote. "Let's finish this up as is."

"Fine. Like I said, Ballinger is 7-1 in his last eight, his only loss to a tough kid from Pope Pius, who finished third in District 20 last year." Thomas' voice suddenly became sardonic. "So, if he was 7-1 in his last eight, that means he was 5-3 in the first eight. But Ballinger didn't have the flu or the sniffles or the clap – he just sucked."

All of the coaches laughed except for Liddle. Even the Fairview and New Welsh coaches laughed.

Ballinger got the sixth seed.

The district tournament itself wasn't half as explosive for Timbrook or St. Agnes. By Saturday morning, Timbrook had three wrestlers still alive in the semifinals. St. Agnes had two.

Liam Connelly trounced the fourth seed on Friday night, 11-2, becoming the first St. Agnes wrestler to ever win a district match. "You made the history books," Thomas said, shaking the hand of the ecstatic senior.

Chris Ballinger was the other Lancer to advance, shocking the entire crowd with a 5-4 come-from-behind win over the third-seed Mitch Davidson of Jefferson. Davidson went into the locker room and broke two knuckles punching a wall. Ballinger sprained

175

Thomas' neck when he unexpectedly leaped into his coach's arms, creating a spontaneous pile-on next to the bleachers.

While the battle for the district crown was being waged by Flat River, Blakemore and North Winfield, the battle for ninth and last place was being waged by Timbrook and St. Agnes.

Tournament scoring is different in wrestling than dual meet scoring, with advancement to the next round counting as 2 points; additional points awarded for a major decision – 1 point, technical fall as 1 ½ points, pin as 2 points. So the 2 ½ points by which St. Agnes trailed Timbrook was not as close as the team thought. Yet, Thomas tried to explain and kept to his concept of wrestling being a team sport, although at this point in the season, Thomas would be the first to admit that it was every man for himself.

Thomas explained to Liam and Chris of the situation facing them. It was the school's first postseason, and St. Agnes would receive tremendous respect if it finished out of the cellar. Both wrestlers were guaranteed two more matches, a victory in the semis assured a spot in the finals and also a trip to the regional tournament. A loss and the consolation match provided one more opportunity to advance to the regions. Third place not only got a medal, but also an automatic bid to the next level, a rule change from two years back.

With the silence of the early morning testing the nerves of the participants, and the February sun filtering through the small windows high aloft the gymnasium walls beckoning for the two inexperienced Lancers to come outside and play, Thomas tried to keep the wrestlers' minds occupied.

Liam was extremely nervous, though, because he had to face the Number 1 seed. He wrestled sloppily in the first two periods of the school's first, big-time district match ever. Down 12-1 in the third, he was decked with a headlock. He left the mat, looking dazed, not quite sure what to think.

More than an hour later, Chris took to the mat against the Number 2 seed, but fared only marginally better. The sophomore simply was overwhelmed by the magnitude of the match. He survived the six minutes, barely, finishing on his back in a 17-6 loss.

Thomas told Chris to forget about the match as soon as he walked over to the side. "Let's focus on the next match. Technically, since you knocked off the third seed last night, that makes you the third seed – and that's how I want you to wrestle. Like a third seed who belongs in the regions." Thomas was taught not to look back during tournament play. Too much going on to think about disappointing losses.

Liam was first to compete in the afternoon session, and his career came to a quiet ending at the hands of the Blakemore 125 pounder. Tim Harris beat Liam 16-2 at one weight class heavier earlier in the season, but had trouble in the consolations. Liam kept moving and fought until the final second. He lost 4-1 but left the mat with a huge grin on his face.

"You'll always be a wrestler," Thomas said, receiving a handshake and a hug from Liam. "As long as you live, you'll never forget the winters of your junior and senior years."

And Chris Ballinger? Well, Chris Ballinger became the first St. Agnes Prancing Lancer to advance to the Region IX New Jersey State Interscholastic Athletic Association Championships, using a pancake and a pin in the second period. Thomas iced down his neck when he got home Friday night, but it didn't matter. Chris jumped onto his coach again, sending the pair falling to the mat. The crowd gave Ballinger a standing ovation when the public address announcer informed it of the sophomore's feat.

Following the consolations, Thomas sat with Liam and Chris, and Tony Kingery, Brien Cauldron, Mike Ennis, Jeff LeMone, Anil Nazif and Masterelli at the far end of the gym, at the far end of the bleachers. They watched the final 13 matches, Thomas pointing and teaching, noting different moves that would be better suited for each wrestler.

"This is where you guys want to be next season," their coach said. "You want to make it to four o'clock, Saturday afternoon. And I have a feeling some of you will be here."

Thomas was proud of the Lancer squad, last-place finishers in the district. They had grown a lot in the last two years, and so had Thomas. But he couldn't say the same for his colleague Mark Pierce, who had been milling around talking to all of the coaches, hanging out with the Covington wrestlers. A mark of high treason in the sporting world.

If Thomas could only avoid all contact with Mark. But realignment put Covington and St. Agnes in the same division next season and on each other's schedule.

And that was enough to motivate Thomas.

NINETEEN

Winters were never kind to the yard at 619 Garrett Avenue. Not that winters were harsher with stronger winds or that the storm clouds forever hovered above Thomas' house dumping immeasurable piles of snow on the property. The winters were harsh because the winds from the four corners of the globe gathered up all the nomadic debris and brought it to the Garrett Avenue yard, placing leaves, twigs, cups, candy and doughnut wrappers, aluminum cans and newspapers in the unkempt and ankle-high lawn.

Thomas didn't own a lawn mower, so about once a month he would call Cal to come over to have a beer – "and bring the lawn equipment." And Cal, who manicured other people's property six days a week would stop by, sit on the stoop, drink beer and watch Thomas mow the lawn.

Labor Day normally would signify the end of grass cutting season for Thomas and around that time, his oft-neglected lawn would be forgotten until the following May. After the second season at St. Agnes with a third season in promise, Thomas spent the off-season in a more productive fashion. In March, he joined a health club. In April, he bought a lawn mower.

And that's where he was during a beautiful spring Friday afternoon when the phone rang for the first time that day. At first he walked around and picked up debris in his yard, which was no more than 75 feet long by 150 feet deep yet yielded an entire tub of garbage. Then he worked with his bow saw, cutting dead limbs from a locust tree and trimming the privet hedges with hand shears. He dug up two azalea bushes, one on each side of the stoop, which had been dying for three winters. And then he started to mow the lawn, which, if it weren't matted down by the wind and snow, would have stood at least six inches high. He collected four large barrels of grass.

The sun disappeared, taking with it any remaining hints that it had been a warm April day, leaving behind a cool and moist dusk. Thomas put away the mower in his tool shed, which was actually a rickety old detached garage with a dirt floor at the southeast corner of the property. He heard the phone ringing as he locked the shed doors, but showed no signs of rushing to answer it.

Five, six, seven, eight, nine, ten, eleven, twelve rings, finally Thomas was coming through the rear sliding screen door. As he neared the table where the phone sat he decided to make a lunge – fifteen rings is about all a person can wait, he thought.

"Hello." But he heard nothing. "Next time I'll get in on 14, I guess."

Thomas grabbed a beer and sat on the couch, unlacing his boots. He found a New York Mets game on the television and sat back, nodding into sleep. He awoke with a jerk, his head snapping forward, the beer falling to the carpet.

The phone rang again, but he ignored it, opting instead to go to the kitchen for a towel. After throwing it to the spot where a puddle of beer recently flourished, he grabbed the receiver, said hello, and worked the towel with his socked feet.

"Tommy, where have you been?"

"I've been down in D.C. to give testimony in front of Congress on the problems of race relations. The vice president called late last night."

"You were not."

"I wasn't?"

"No."

"Okay, where was I?"

"You were probably at the Cornerstone."

"Nope. I was mowing the lawn. Who – may I ask – is so interested in my whereabouts?"

"It's Tammy!"

"Tamantha Jennings! Usually when a woman leaves my home, they never call back. It's only taken you . . ." Thomas counted the months on his fingers, ". . . five months. You saw something you liked, perhaps?"

"You're so funny," Tammy said. "As a matter of fact, I did see something I liked, my sister's old boyfriend."

"Mmmm. I am sorry, Tammy. I try to make it a rule not to date sisters, unless of course they're twins and it's one date."

Tammy laughed. Ever since she was in grade school, Thomas always joked around with her, except for the Halloween party the year before. Thomas liked to make her laugh. He found that it came easy. "Tommy, I'm not calling you for me. I'm calling you for Michelle."

"Ahh – you're still working on that angle. Well, you tell Michelle that I'm no longer available. I got married last week."

"Be serious, Thomas. Michelle's really hurting right now. She broke up with Todd."

Thomas stopped futzing with the towel and sat down. This was interesting news. Intriguing news. But he didn't want to speak so quickly, and he didn't want to remain silent. He didn't know what to think. "When? And why?"

"Michelle said that he was cheating on her, but she wasn't really sure. Things had changed, she said."

"Tammy, I really like your sister, you know that. But there's nothing I can do."

"Yes there is," Tammy said sternly. "I know you more than 'liked' my sister at one point. And now she's alone in Boston. She doesn't have any real close friends up there except for Todd, and obviously he's a schmuck. You gotta call her. I'd love to see you guys get back together, really, I think that would be great. But she needs to talk to a friend right now, and she won't talk to me, probably because I told her that I saw this coming. Please. Please!"

There was not much resistance Thomas could put up against a pleading sister. Tammy was ready to cry. The urgency in her voice gave Thomas no other choice but to call Michelle. "I doubt it will do any good."

"Yes, it will, Tommy. She'll be glad to hear from you. I know it."

Thomas began to dial three times, hanging up three times for the fear of not having the right thing to say. Honesty. Stick with honesty, he thought. She can't get upset at you for being honest.

He didn't know why he was so nervous. Michelle and he simply had grown apart, and Thomas accepted that. He just didn't want Michelle to get the wrong idea. Ultimately, he decided that point was the reason for his apprehension. He did not want to come across as some lonesome loser.

He dialed, and the phone rang three times before it was picked up and rudely slammed down. Thomas laughed. "That a girl. Give him hell," he said aloud and to himself. "This is going to be tough getting through."

He dialed. Three rings. She picked up the receiver and slammed it down.

Dial. Three rings. Slam.

Why won't she just take the receiver off the hook? Why won't she screen her calls through her answering machine? Maybe she just snapped.

Thomas dialed again. Three rings. "I don't want to talk to you," Michelle screamed, slamming down the phone. That was a breakthrough. At least she spoke. Now to keep her from hanging up.

Thomas dialed once again. Three rings and Michelle answered. She had answered the phone each time after three rings. There was some kind of pattern. "Fuck off," she yelled, and hung up.

Maybe Tammy had a system with her sister. So Thomas tried the basic, old-fashioned phone trick. One ring, hang up, call back. And that's what he did.

Waiting 10 minutes, he called back. One ring, hang up and redial. Michelle answered the phone after the second ring. "Tammy, he won't stop calling. I just don't want to talk to him."

"And why not?" Thomas asked.

Michelle did not hear Thomas' voice, only a male voice and assumed it was Todd. "I hate you. Don't call back." And mechanically, Michelle hung up the phone. But after she hung up, her muddled brain sensed a change. The last person was not Todd, but someone different. It searched for the bearer of the voice, and apprehensively concluded it was Thomas McCloskey.

A dark misery set in as she broke into an uncontrollable cry. She rocked back and forth while sitting on her bed, a pillow tucked between her drawn-in knees and her chin. "Please, let him call again," she cried into the pillow. "Please!"

Thomas found the entire scenario rather comical, as long as it was not he who was in the midst of a break-up. Hoping that Michelle heard his voice. Thomas waited a few extra moments to let her "think about what she had done."

He laughed. Then he dialed. On the third ring, Michelle answered. "Hello?" There was hope and an inquisitiveness in the tone.

"You sure do have an odd collection of telephone greetings."

"Tommy." Michelle was relieved. "I thought it was you. I'm sorry for hanging up on you."

"Now, did you know it was me before or after you screamed 'Fuck off' into the phone?"

Michelle smiled. "I didn't know it was you. I thought it was someone else."

"And if you thought it was me, you would have yelled, maybe something less harsh, like 'You stink' or 'You're an idiot'?"

"It's good to hear your voice," Michelle said, laughing, sniffling and crying all at the same time.

"Needless to say, your sister called and told me the news. Although, this time, I honestly believe that Tammy wanted me to call as a friend, not an old boyfriend." Thomas heard Michelle blow her nose. "Blowing your nose or giving me the Bronx cheer, Michelle? I'm getting an awful lot of mixed signals tonight."

Michelle sort of caught his jocularity and kind of thought it was funny, but she focused on the part of being a friend and not an ex-boyfriend, and she just unloaded.

"You know Tammy warned me about Todd. She told me he was the type that everything seemed just fine on the surface, but deep down there was this slimy, scummy creature lurking about."

Thomas chose his words carefully and proceeding with caution, asked Michelle if she was sure that Tad was screwing around, or if Michelle was unconsciously – or maybe consciously – following Tammy's lead.

"His name is Todd." Michelle knew that Thomas had deliberately butchered his name, and she played along. "And no, Tammy doesn't have that much influence over me. She just happens to be clairvoyant."

"So you're sure?"

"He had perfume all over him for Chrissakes!"

"Michelle, the last thing I'm going to do is stick up for Tad . . . ."

"Todd."

"Yeah, Todd." Thomas was glad to have Michelle play along. She was sounding better. "But perfume could mean that he was at a strip joint or a bachelor party or got sprayed in a department store by one of those annoying chicks, or annoying guys, which is a whole different set of problems. It could actually be . . . ."

"His pants were soiled."

What?

"His pants." Michelle backed up and decided that the full explanation, no matter how embarrassing it could be, was needed. "I was doing some work at his place, waiting for him. He mustn't have been expecting me, because he was drunker than hell. I usually stay at my apartment on Friday nights because I like to get work done before the weekend. Well, I tried to give him a kiss, but he shied away, I couldn't help but smell the perfume on his clothes. And I told him so."

"And his reaction to that?"

"The same type of crap that you just said. 'Oh it could've been anything,' he said," Michelle mimicked her fiance's voice, then continued in a whine. "'Marty's girlfriend gave me a hug. There were a lot of girls around the bar. The bar was crowded.' He just kept rattling off the excuses. I just said whatever. It's happened a few times before and I just wouldn't pursue it. I guess I was ready to believe him again, because I sat down and continued to read."

Thomas wanted to ask her if she was a martyr. Did she actually like getting stepped on like this? Was the prospect of marrying into the Boston lifestyle worth getting dumped on? But he asked nothing. Maybe he'd save it for a future Q & A. "Then what?"

Michelle's voice began to get shaky again, but she continued. "Well, then he went to the bedroom and got undressed. He usually says that he smells like a bar and wants to take a shower. God, I was such a fool."

Thomas let her cry for a piece. She would get to the point when she was ready.

"He was probably drinking scotch or gin because it was only 6:30 and he can't handle hard liquor like that. He was in the courtroom today, so he probably got out at 3 and headed straight to the bar. I mean, what the hell, did he fuck some girl in the

183

fuckin' ladies room. I mean, it was only 6:30." She began to cry again.

"Instead of getting into the shower, he passed out on the bed, and all of the lights were on and . . . I saw that his boxers were soiled."

Now soiled can mean a few things, but Thomas knew which definition Michelle meant. "Are you sure?"

"I'm positive. The bum has pissed in his pants before because he can't handle his liquor. A couple of times. I could tell the difference." Michelle did not cry this time. She was too mad to cry. But after a long silence on the phone, she began to sob. She said she wanted to close her eyes for a while.

"I really did love him so much, but it's over. It's got to be over."

"Why don't you call a friend to stay the night with you, then I'll give you a call in the morning," Thomas was extremely concerned. He had never seen nor heard Michelle this emotional. "I'm not calling anybody up here. I don't have any close friends up here, only colleagues, and this is the type of scandal that is great as office fodder. Todd was my closest friend."

"Does Tammy know where you live?"

Yes. Why?

"I'm going to call Tammy and pick her up. It's about a four-hour trip to Boston from here. We can be there by midnight."

No Thomas. Don't.

"Listen Michelle. I got nothing to do. Tammy's a senior in college, she's due for a spring road trip. You just straighten up your place and put the timer on the coffee. I'm going to call Tammy now, so don't try calling her. I'm serious."

Okay. Michelle did not mind the idea so much.

Four hours in the pick-up truck with a college senior was far from the scene Thomas imagined it would be. His memory of giggling females in the college dorms, the recollection of Tamantha as an adolescent, and her recent attempts to reunite him and Michelle gave him the idea that the trip would be more like babysitting. But the jaunt north on Interstate 95 proved to be an enlightening experience. Tamantha Catherine Jennings was quite grown up, much more sophisticated than he, Thomas decided. He could see striking similarities between Tammy and her sister.

The one difference, though, was glaring. Tammy was content with where she was at that very point in her life. If she were packed in a New York City subway in the sweltering heat of the summertime, well then, she would somehow enjoy the experience. Teaching a classroom full of brats is challenging, not trying. Reading a novel is relaxing. Sitting in a truck for four hours in the darkness of April is exciting.

Tammy loved to both talk and listen, and from this Thomas could tell that she was a great teacher. She talked about a range of topics, from working with preschoolers in North Jersey to her current student teacher course, where she had to teach four months of sixth-grade science. And while she talked about herself, she asked Thomas questions along the way, trying to get him to reveal more about himself. She talked as much as her sister did, but was more conservative in her thoughts.

Michelle was a "save the world" type of person. Starting in high school, she would lend a sympathetic ear to some of the more lonely girls. At lunch she sat with Amy Kausselbaum, nicknamed "frog" because of her bulging eyes due to a thyroid condition. In study hall, she befriended Mary Jo Weller. It was Michelle who brought it to the attention of the guidance department that Mary Jo was not a slow learner but had, in fact, a form of dyslexia.

From helping high school mates, Michelle branched out, working as a candy striper the summer after sophomore year in high school; at the local Red Cross and as a candy striper the following summer; and at the New Jersey mental institution in nearby Marlboro after graduation. That's when she decided that a career was more important than a boyfriend and told Thomas that a South Dakota girl might be better suited for him, anyway.

At Boston College, she joined all sorts of charitable organizations. She met Todd O'Malley Aldrich at a fund raiser for Tomorrow's Children Fund. Michelle was representing the psychology department; Todd was passing mandatory time for the Sigma Chi fraternity. Todd charmed Michelle with his Kennedy-like Boston charisma. It took her a long time to figure out that it was all an act.

And Tammy's resume? Even predating high school, Tammy was always pointed to being a teacher. She also wanted to save the world, but just in a more mundane manner.

For the greater portion of the trip to Boston, Tammy filled Thomas in on most of the details of the story of Todd and Michelle. Rather boring, Thomas thought, on both their parts. "Didn't they ever go to concerts or bars?"

"No," Tammy said glibly. "Michelle played soccer. Todd went to Patriot football games. That was the extent of their participation in pop culture. They went to black tie affairs mainly. Symphonies. Michelle has mentioned the opera. She said she did go to one concert on campus, but it was Doc Severenson and his band Xaxon or Xevron – or something like that. But that's not the type of concert you're talking about, is it?"

No.

"Now you see why she needs a little spice in her life and you need some stability. Like Donnie and Marie Osmond – a little bit country and a little bit rock and roll."

"First of all, don't ever compare me to any Osmond, and second, Michelle and I are never going to happen, Tammy. That was puppy love. We were a high school couple and we've both been searching and found different meanings to our lives. I consider your sister an old friend, but that's all."

"And you're saying that you have no feelings for her?"

"No. That's not what I'm saying," Thomas said. "I remember what it was like seeing Michelle for the first time and our first date and our first kiss. But that was a long time ago. I will never feel like that again because it was my first love. I've loved since then, but they were all different. And I will love again, but that will be different, too. Yes, I still love your sister, that's why I'm driving to Boston on a Friday night. But I've realized it's a different kind of feeling. And that's okay."

"You love her, only different?" Tammy asked in a way that a journalist or a lawyer would do in order to confirm answers.

"Yes." Thomas knew where she was going.

"Aha. Then there's still a chance!" Tammy was only being ornery. She understood what Thomas meant, although she did not have anything close to compare it to.

The cab of his truck seemed to be the forum for explanations and confessions, so Thomas pried cajolingly into Tammy's past. "Who was your first love?" Thomas felt that was the best place to start.

As far as true first loves, that would have to be John Fredericks. "It was only in the sixth grade but I loved spending time with him every day after school. I didn't care about homework, about Michelle or about mom, and I forgot about dad being gone, for awhile." Tammy stopped and felt badly about feeling that way so long ago. She had never forgotten about her father since that time.

"He was so cute. I called him Freddy." She let Freddy stay alone in the air before she continued to reminisce. "We went to the beach every day that spring, rain or shine. If it was raining, we'd find an awning or a porch to sit under and talk. My first kiss came on one of those rainy days, underneath the awning at the Yates Beach Store." Thomas could not see in the darkness of the interstate in Rhode Island, but Tammy actually blushed.

"Who was your first kiss?" Tammy felt embarrassed for blushing and talking so much, although she was pretty sure Thomas didn't notice either.

"My first kiss?" At one time, Thomas knew the answer, but that fact had long since been filed away in the deep recesses of his mind. He probed, first recalling the fact of nighttime, then the location of Whiting Beach, then a group of people and oh, yes, Mary Elizabeth Halstein. "She was a year older than me, and she had been drinking."

"And?"

"And she kissed me."

"She kissed you. That's all there is to the story!" Tammy acted extremely disappointed and demanded more. "Did she kiss you once or more than once? Was it a kiss, or you know, a *kiss*?"

"I was a freshman. She was a sophomore. And it was the second kind of kiss, and more than one."

"And did it develop any further?"

"I can't remember."

Tammy hassled Thomas but could get no more information with her questioning, so she stopped, folded her arms and pretended to pout. "That's just great. If you won't tell me any more, can I ask another question?"

Sure.

"Now I don't want details – well, not graphic ones anyway." Tammy hesitated in order to reword her question but decided that the original form was the best. "With whom did you lose your virginity?"

"Tammy!"

"What? That's not too personal, is it?"

"Nobody knows that, not even the other participant. So, yes, I would say that is rather personal."

"You've never told Michelle."

No.

Tammy thought that piece of information very interesting. Michelle said she had never seen Thomas naked, and now Thomas said Michelle never knew when he lost his virginity. Very interesting, indeed.

"I'll tell you about my first experience." Tammy was teasing, trying to entice.

Thomas turned up the music and began to sing along.

Now Tammy realized that she had embarrassed the driver. She couldn't see if he was blushing, but she could tell by his actions. Tammy looked at the outline of his face. He was handsome. Strong features. She wondered if her sister would notice that strength this weekend and understand the man she had once let go as a boy.

Tammy reached around and locked the door. She put the pillow that she had brought behind her head, half on the seat, half on the window of the door, announcing that she was going to take a nap. Tammy's eyelids pulled themselves slowly shut, bouncing open occasionally to catch a glimpse of the driver.

Thomas continued to sing off key.

Tammy had slept for the last third of the trip north. When Thomas neared the Boston city limits, he gently called her name. Upon the third call, Tammy awoke.

"I need to know where I'm going now," Thomas said.

"Okay. Umm. Where are we?" In the darkness, nothing looked familiar to Tammy.

Boston.

"Yes, I know it's Boston. But I need to know what part of Boston, Thomas."

"On Interstate 90 going through Boston."

Tammy told Thomas that he was impossible, and it would be better off if he would be quiet. She studied the names on the signs and told him to take Everett Street.

For the next 20 minutes, they were lost, and Tammy apologized between the corrective directions she gave to Thomas. "I'm sorry, Tommy," she said for the tenth time. "It was the right exit. I think we turned the wrong way at the light at Beacon Street."

"It's okay. We'll get there," Thomas said for the tenth time, each time more patiently than the previous.

Michelle had fallen asleep on the couch in her white terry cloth robe and white gym socks. When she opened the door, Tammy could see that she had been crying for most of the evening. Tammy hugged her sister for a long time at the door. When their embrace broke, Michelle gave Thomas a kiss on the cheek and told him "thank you."

Michelle looked at the clock. It read 11:50. She asked if they would like tea or coffee, something she could whip up to eat in a jiffy.

Before Tammy could answer, Thomas said he would like Michelle to put on jeans, an old sweatshirt and a ball cap. "Throw some water on your face and take us to the dark, neighborhood pub that I know has to be less than a couple of blocks away."

Michelle attempted a feeble resistance, starting with a 'headache,' then with 'I'm just not up for it,' then 'all the taverns have to be closed,' finishing with 'I look terrible.'

Tammy chimed in, teaming with Thomas, and by midnight, they were walking down from Michelle's third-floor apartment, three blocks to Flannigan's.

The bar was crowded and the three had to stand for the first round of drinks. Thomas and Tammy didn't mind standing, but Michelle shuffled back and forth on her feet, not quite having her normal reserve of energy. Just when Thomas was polishing off his second pint of beer and the ladies were finishing their first whiskey sours, Tammy spotted a table opening up against the wall. She scrambled over to get it.

Flannigan's was not the normal type of cocktail club atmosphere Michelle was accustomed to. She had not been in a pub since college, and she found herself saying 'what' too much at the start of the conversation. But Tammy felt comfortable and Thomas felt like he was in his living room. Slowly, Michelle adapted and into her second drink was feeling looser.

"Okay, ladies, how 'bout some music? Tammy, you're the youngest, so I'll let you choose first. Do you have a favorite band or album?"

"Yes, I have a favorite band and a favorite album. My favorite band is the Beatles, but my favorite album is *Hotel California* by the Eagles."

Michelle and Thomas started to look at one another but stopped. "I didn't know you like the Beatles and Eagles. Since when?" her sister asked.

"Oh, I don't know, since about freshman year of high school."

Michelle turned to Thomas. "Aren't the Beatles. . . ?"

But Thomas wouldn't allow that question, instead delving into Michelle's musical past. "And I believe that in high school you liked Earth, Wind and Fire and Supertramp, but I don't think I'm going to find any of their songs on this jukebox."

"I also like the Philadelphia and Boston philharmonics."

"Of course," Thomas said. "Well, I'm not so sure of the Philadelphia band, but I'm sure we can find the Boston Pops in this place."

Thomas disappeared, going past the jukebox and on to the men's room. When he returned to the table, the trio had become a quartet. A burly, bearded man in his 30s was sitting at the table, holding a pint of beer, trying to hold a conversation.

Thirty extra pounds, wide shoulders, jeans, boots, flannel shirt tucked in, no glasses, short hair. Thomas was slow to reclaim his chair, determined, as usual, to check out all aspects of a stranger, walking to his back, around the table, finally seeing his ruddy face as he sat down. Barroom fights should be avoided at all costs, because of the high probability of serious injury. That, Thomas had learned the hard way. He also learned, just in case, to be prepared. Every dragon has its weak spot. Some were more difficult to find than others. And most important, swing first, ask questions later.

"Hey," Thomas said to the stranger, then directed his attention to Michelle and Tammy. "I see you've found yourself some company."

"I was just wonderin' if I could buy the ladies a drink," the man answered defensively, with a slight slur.

Immediately, Thomas sensed no danger. The stranger did not speak in a belligerent tone, and he already felt out of place, not noticing the third glass sitting on the table when he approached. He was ready to depart when Thomas encouraged him to stay.

"I don't see any problem with buying the ladies a drink," Thomas said. He knew that if the three of them sat at the table alone, the topic would turn somber, speaking of lost loves and lonely futures. But the big, burly and apparently amiable stranger could help get the girls – in particular Michelle – drunk, for medicinal purposes of course. "But you needn't buy me a drink," he said to the stranger. "I might get the wrong idea."

The stranger laughed heartily. "It would be my honor to give you the wrong idea." The man called over to the bar for another round. His mannerisms indicated that he frequently visited the bar. "Now which one of these gals is attached to you?" Tammy blushed. Michelle smiled.

"Now slow down there, hoss," Thomas said in a friendly tone. Give this guy the green light to stay at the table and he wants to screw one of the gals right here. Thomas wanted to gently remind him that he was now a guest in his own bar. "First off, what's your name?"

Melvin.

"Nice to meet you Melvin," Thomas said, offering his hand. "I'm Thomas. This is Michelle. And this is Tammy." Melvin shook each hand, firmly taking Thomas,' gently holding the ladies.'

"Now your question was, 'which one of these beautiful ladies am I attached to?' Do you want the long or the short of it?"

Melvin opted for the short version.

"Well Mel, you've met Michelle. Michelle and I dated in high school. But that was some time ago. Tammy is the little sister, and Tammy and I never dated in high school. Now Michelle got engaged while she was in her fifth or sixth year of higher education at Boston College, but that didn't work out and very recently broke off the engagement. Tammy didn't get engaged in college but did fall in love with a chap named Freddy, whose first kiss sent shudders through her body, and if I remember the story correctly, actually caused it to rain, and they ran to the shelter of Yates Beach Store awning, where they continued to make it rain – or something like that." Thomas looked at Tammy. "Did I get that right?"

"Close," she said with a smile.

Melvin glugged at his stout beer. "So which one are you dating now?"

"Neither. But I'm always open for negotiations."

In the end, the four had some good laughs. Melvin realized that he would have no luck with either Michelle or Tammy, yet he stayed and tossed in some jokes along the way.

In turn, the trio found out that Melvin was a 34-year-old, divorced father of two. He grew up in Boston and now was a union pipe fitter. He loved his job. He loved the Celtics. He loved the Bruins. He loved his kids. And he hated his wife, but he was not ruling out future possibilities of marriage. After a couple more stouts, he asked Michelle and Tammy, twice each, if they'd be interested in a divorced pipe fitter from Malden. Michelle said it sounded rather kinky, and under normal circumstances each said they would, but with the way the Celtics and the Bruins had been playing lately, it just wouldn't work.

It was getting on to 1:30, and Thomas felt it necessary to whisk the girls off to the safety of the third-floor, brownstone apartment. He thanked Melvin for the hospitality and the drinks, and parted with a hardy handshake. The girls giggled as they bobbed and weaved down the foggy and damp street, happy to have met the divorced pipe-fitting sports fan from Boston.

At the apartment, Thomas asked if Michelle had dessert of any kind, but she didn't. "I'm dieting for the wedding." The sisters laughed uncontrollably.

"Would you mind if I look through your cupboard?" he asked.

"Why that's awful personal," Michelle said, still on the same laugh since leaving the pub. "First I get propositioned to be pipe-fitted and now you want to check out my cupboard. What? Is the moon full?"

"Aw – go ahead Tommy. Nobody'll be in her cupboard for a long time anyway."

Thomas was happy that the Jennings were having a good time, particularly Michelle. He knew it wouldn't last past the morning, but hopefully she'll understand that there are plenty of adventures out there. She only had to look.

The girls laughed, joked, giggled and joked some more as Thomas prepared tea and crackers with strawberry jam and grape jelly. "It's a specialty of mine."

It was 2:30 on Saturday morning when the Jennings girls began to run out of steam. "Why don't you two get ready for bed. I'm going to stay up and catch a movie. Maybe a western."

"No. No. No. No," Tammy said. "You two get ready for bed, I'll watch a movie." Tammy pushed Thomas toward the single bedroom, but he quickly spun around and was magically behind Tammy, gently pushing her.

"You're a nimble little guy." Tammy tried the maneuver Thomas just executed but got all tangled up.

"You are not too old to be put over my knee and have a switch put to your hindquarters," he said.

"Ooh. We'll go to the bedroom. You watch a movie," Tammy said to Michelle, taking Thomas by the hand.

Michelle continued her laughter the entire time.

After more shenanigans, Thomas got the two girls into the bathroom to brush their teeth, and eventually into their pajamas. He turned off their light. They were asleep in moments.

Thomas sat on the couch and found *Rio Lobo* on the Superstation.

Michelle woke up first with a headache and cramps. She went to the bathroom, took three Midol and then sat at the kitchen table, her head lying in her arms.

Tammy woke up at 10:30, about an hour after her sister. She had a slight headache and took only two regular aspirin. Her mouth was extremely dry, so she had a glass of chocolate milk while her sister had coffee and read the newspaper.

"Where's Tommy?" Tamantha asked.

"He went home."

"He did not."

Michelle looked over the top of the business section of *The Boston Globe*. "He went home."

"When?"

"At seven."

"Did you see him?"

"No. He left a note. It's on the counter."

Dear Michelle and Tamantha Jennings,

Thank you for a wonderful evening. It certainly was a fun adventure for me to jump in the truck and drive to Boston to share some time with some old friends. I hope our next meeting will follow more pleasant circumstances. I have to go now, for matters back home need some tending to.

To Tammy – you mentioned that you might stay until Sunday or even Monday, choosing to take the train back to North Jersey. "Blow off class," I believe was the term you used. Your backpack, which you left in the truck, is now sitting next to the couch. Make sure you get some schoolwork done young lady. If you don't, you'll be working alongside me at the Burke Gravel Pit.

To Michelle – A guy at work got a hold of a mimeographed saying and pinned it on the bulletin board. It read "Due to the increasingly heavy work load, the light at the end of the tunnel has temporarily been shut off." I think your light was just turned back on. You know my number if you need me.

Thomas Patrick

With the note was a 50-dollar bill with "For Train Use Only" penned over the picture of the United States' Capitol.

TWENTY

The year was distinctly being split into two seasons, just like it was back in high school. In November, with the sun disappearing in late afternoon and the mercury disappearing into its reservoir at the bottom of the thermometer, his world was engulfed in wrestling. At times, it could seem like a nightmare – dark, cold and painful. The season was never-ending. Up in the morning when it was still dark. Off to school to spend the day inside when the sun made its meek presence felt. To practice in the Covington cafeteria, large cathedral windows facing west, allowing the winter's sun to bid its farewell to the wrestlers who never got to enjoy it. By the end of practice, he could not distinguish the day from night.

That dreariness gave the season meaning. Keep fighting. Fight for the six agonizing minutes. Fight to keep the weight down. Fight those excruciating drills during the excruciating practice. Fight to forget about dad. Keep fighting until the days got longer. And the air warmer. Keep fighting until the nightmare was over. Until the arm was raised in victory.

When the season ended, the rest of the year began. Baseball teams were in spring training. Families were in the park. Squirrels and birds scrambled and flittered around, happy to be out. And the wrestlers gained weight.

The natural interest in an event, hobby, job, sport – whatever it may be – is better to entice than to prod. So Thomas left the St. Agnes wrestlers to themselves for March, April and the better part of May. After Chris Ballinger made his appearance in the regional tournament, getting pinned in 50 seconds, and after the team dropped off its wrestling gear on a Friday two days later, Thomas let them be. It had been a tough two years on the Lancer squad, and he thought it better to let the kids recharge their batteries than to dive right back into training and competition.

On May 17, Thomas made a lunchtime trip to see Terry Broughton. He received the schedule for the upcoming season and left a note announcing a wrestling meeting for May 19.

"There's one thing I need to apologize for, another I want to offer condolences and finally just some good news," Terry Broughton said.

"Which category does this Oak Hill Classic Christmas tournament fall into? We can't wrestle in this damn thing."

"That's what I need to apologize for," Mr. Broughton said. "All the local Christmas tournaments were booked, except the one at Oak Hill. Bishop Leary dropped out and Oak Hill was looking for a replacement."

"You know why Bishop Leary dropped out, don't you? Because they've finished last the past five years." Thomas was pissed, but the athletic director did the best he could, for someone who had no working knowledge of the sport. "Let's save the good news. What are your condolences?"

"Monroe Academy has moved north into District 41, along with Lancaster City and Hanstrom. Out are New Welsh, Carlysle and Fairview."

"Shit." It was all Thomas could say. The three schools that were bumped to the northwest district of 39 were good programs. Programs a tier above St. Agnes – measuring-stick schools. Of the three schools entering, Hanstrom was bad. Lancaster City was mediocre. And Monroe Academy was completely off the Shore map. In the last three seasons. Monroe Academy slowly climbed the state rankings, inching its way from sixth to fifth to fourth, challenging the western stronghold near the Pennsylvania border. With Monroe moving into District 41, the likely scenario meant that the number one seeds for its wrestlers would be taking on the bottom seeds of Timbrook, Hanstrom and St. Agnes in the first round.

"With Monroe, Flat River, Blakemore and Jefferson – 41 is now the dominant district in the Shore Conference," Thomas explained. "Condolences? You should be working on a friggin' eulogy."

Sorry.

"No need to apologize. Competition breeds competition. St. Agnes will either learn how to swim or it will sink. Now how 'bout the good news."

"A carpenter measured the mats, built three compartments in the cafeteria, stained the wood a dark brown, and all you have to do is get the kids to move the mats over here. And you also have three home matches next season."

That is good news. "Watch out Monroe Academy. Here we come." Thomas laughed all the way back to the dumpster.

It was discouraging to see only four boys waiting for Thomas at 3:45 in the St. Agnes cafeteria.

"You gotta be kidding me!" Thomas said loudly. "Where the hell is the rest of the team?"

Brien Cauldron, Tony Kingery and Chris Ballinger were sitting on the top of the newly built wrestling mat cabinets, taking turns fending off a scrappy Jeff LeMone, who was trying to get anybody to wrestle.

"Most of them said they have stuff to do," Chris said while applying nuggies to Jeff, who was stuck in a light headlock.

"How about Marc Cella?"

The wrestlers shrugged.

"Garrison?"

Suspended.

"Again?"

Yeah. For smoking in the bathroom.

"Anil?"

Math Club meeting. He said it was important.

"Masterelli?"

Babysitting.

"Ennis?"

Track. He's running the mile.

"Jesus Christ. At least he's doing something. I hope this isn't the beginning of a trend. Let's take you four and Mike Ennis – even if all five show up at a match and you deck – that's 30 points. That still wouldn't be good enough against eight forfeits. That's a 48-30 loss. A pretty good ass whuppin'. As a teammate, I wouldn't settle for shit like that."

Thomas did not want to do too much teaching on that spring day, just enough to let those four fellas know that their dedication was not enough. They needed to lean on their classmates, and lean heavy.

He did notice that all four students were from Evandale, a point he recognized during the first two seasons at St. Agnes.

Since it was a private parochial school, St. Agnes lured students from a 20-mile radius, which was a rather long commute in New Jersey. And the wrestling team exemplified that aspect. Other than the four wrestlers present at the May meeting, only two other freshmen were from Evandale. Chuck Garrison lived the farthest north at North Winfield and Mike Ennis lived a couple miles south of Blakemore. Having such a diverse geographical makeup made it difficult to conduct practice during foul weather in the wintertime. All schools with wrestling teams suffered if classes were canceled due to snow. On snow days kids stayed home and ate, and not having practice compounded the problem.

St. Agnes had it worse still.

The threat of snow any time during the day prompted parents to keep children home. Busses could get unexpectedly canceled and parents did not want to venture onto the cold winter roads.

Bitter weather also shut down St. Agnes. If temperatures dipped below 20 degrees Fahrenheit, school officials would automatically cancel classes simply because the ancient boiler could not produce enough heat. One time, 10 years ago, the pipes burst, leaving the cafeteria a frozen winter wonderland.

So Thomas planted a seed in these wrestlers' ears. "It's days like today and snow days in the wintertime that'll keep this team from winning. You guys have to let your teammates know that if I call a meeting, they better get their asses here. If the school is open and there's a forecast of snow, tell 'em to show up. Invite them to stay at your houses. Make arrangements with your parents. Because the more practices we miss, the shittier we become. And we can't afford that."

Thomas understood that his unorthodox teaching meant drilling information over and over again in the children's minds. So he let them know that they were the unfortunate ones to show up, because he was going to repeat himself until every last wrestler could recite his sermons.

"Well, since we're here, let's see what we can do. I guess there's three points – or matters – that I need to address. First, I could use some help getting the mats from the community pavilion and put them away in those closets you're sitting on. If each one of you guys could get one guy to show up tomorrow, then we'll be alright. Since we have to bring the three slabs through the courtyard door and down a flight of stairs, 10 guys is our minimum. If we can't get 10 guys, we have to stay at the pavilion. Won't that be fun?" Thomas asked the four boys if they could recruit anyone to help the next day. Everybody lazily nodded, which didn't excite Thomas.

"Next, the guys on this team need to lift, and the four of you need to take the lead." He turned to Tony. "It looks like you already started to lift."

Tony Kingery ended the season at 129 and by mid May he weighed 143. "Yeah. I joined a gym for only 50 bucks for six months for high school students."

"Fifty bucks! What? Do you have to bring your own weights?"

"No. It's on the beachfront in Evandale. It seems okay."

"Is anybody teaching you routines?"

"No. I'm just trying to teach myself some stuff."

"That's pretty good, Tony. Now my second point ties in with the weight training. We need someplace here where we can lift together – as a club, not as a team." Thomas explained the NJSIAA rule that allows a coach to meet only twice with the team during the school year outside of the designated season. In the winter sports' scenario, that constituted one meeting in the fall and one in the spring. "So we need a weight room."

"We got one, Coach," Chris Ballinger said.

"Where?"

"Right down the hallway, behind the cafeteria. Nobody uses it though. All the equipment in there is shit."

"Jeff, since you're the youngest and you were picking on everybody when I got here, you get to go and find a janitor. Get some keys so we can open up this room."

"I wasn't picking on anybody. I was beating the shit out of 'em."

Thomas let slide the use of profanity in the school cafeteria because no one was around and mainly because he liked the freshman's spunk. "Well, now you get to go because you're arguing with me."

LeMone jumped down from the cabinet, punched Ballinger in the leg and sprinted up the front stairs. Thomas called to him. "Hey! How much do you weigh?"

Out of sight, already at the top of the stairs and in front of the trophy case, Jeff yelled back. "Eighty-one and a half."

That's a long way to the minimum of 88 pounds. Thomas tried not to look concerned. "And the last thing we have to do," he said to the remaining three, "is wrestle. There are plenty of tournaments on the weekends around the state. There's a couple of programs, one up north past the Winfields. One down south past Toms River. They are like karate classes or judo classes – sort of. They're for the hardcore wrestler. Finally, there's camps – which are either good or bad, depending on the wrestler. I went to a few camps and learned a great deal, but some of my teammates from high school thought the camps were useless."

"Jeff's already been to three tournaments since the end of school," Chris said. "There's one this weekend in Cherry Hill, and I think I'm going."

"Good. What about you guys?"

Tony and Brien shrugged, which Thomas thought odd. Besides Jeff, Tony and Brien would be the first to wrestle if the opportunity presented itself. "Why not?"

"I'm supposed to look for a job," Brien said. "A friend of mine works at a sub shop and told me to stop by."

Thomas thought for a moment, but he had no solution. "Working is more important than wrestling," he said, quickly adding, "except during the season. If that's the case, maybe we can roll out the mats here a couple of times during the summer and work on some moves." He switched his attention to Tony. "What about you, Mr. Kingery?"

Tony shrugged again, but offered no explanation. Thomas sensed that something was wrong but chose not to pry. "Well, if you can get the chance, head down to Cherry Hill." And the coach left it at that.

Jeff LeMone returned with a ring of keys that was at least five percent of his body weight, twirling them in his hand, needing to stretch out his arm in order to keep the keys from hitting his biceps. Thomas held out his hand in order to receive the keys, but never got them. Jeff knotted up his face, his eyebrows curling inward, his mouth tightening. "Yeah, right," he said. And as Thomas gave a half-hearted lunge at the diminutive wrestler, the freshman took off running.

Thomas smiled. He really liked this kid. "C'mon," he said to the others.

Jeff was already trying a fifth key when Thomas arrived with the other three wrestlers. The coach grabbed the ring and said, "I can see that you're going to be a pain in the ass."

"I'm already a pain in the ass," Jeff said.

Thomas took a look at the lock – a Kwikset – and found the two keys that could match. The first key opened the door.

"I could've done that," Jeff said. Thomas nudged the freshman through the door and told him that he could find the lights instead.

The fluorescent lights flickered on, the ensuing sight making Thomas think that he should have left them off. The room was narrow and long, about 10-feet wide by 40-feet deep with a door at the rear. Back during World War II, it was the girls' and visiting teams' locker room. A plywood wall with a Dutch door was built at the back of the room, closing off the former shower area. That area now stored the equipment for all 12 freshman, junior varsity and varsity sports as well as the equipment for gym class.

In that front part, where lockers once lined the long walls and wooden benches were scattered about the middle, now stood a dusty, partially dismantled Universal weight unit, and a wobbly bench with about 250 pounds in metal weights. Thomas had more weights in his garage.

"Wow!" Thomas said.

"I told you it was shit."

Jeff beelined straight to the only seat attached to the Universal machine and sat down, placing his feet on the metal foot pads, pushing 15 pounds into the air continuously, working his hamstrings. Chris sat on the bench; Brien sat on the movable stool in front of the upright station and Tony took hold of the pull-down bar, slowly doing reverse military presses.

"You guys look at home," Thomas said. "More for lounging than for production."

"The room is open once in a while," Chris said. "Mainly when someone is in the trainer's room." Chris was referring to the equipment room which all the students referred to as the training room because that is where each team's medical kits are kept.

"And we come in here to get huge," Jeff said. "Look at my legs. They're pumped." His gray school uniform pants hung upon his spindly legs. The wiry freshman flashed his mischievous smile.

"This is pitiful," Thomas said. "Does anybody use it on a regular basis?"

"A couple of the gym teachers, but that's about it," Chris said.

"Getting yourselves and your teammates wrestling over the summer will be your responsibility. Getting this weight room in working order will be mine."

Thomas convinced Cal to blow off the last hour-and-a-half of Friday's lawn cutting to give him a hand with the mats in exchange for free labor on Saturday morning.

When Cal and Thomas arrived with Cal's trailer at the pavilion at 4 o'clock, the four Evandale wrestlers and two friends were waiting, and that's all the help that would arrive.

Thomas brought along paint drop cloths and laid them down in Cal's trailer, in order to keep the grease and oils and grass juice-and whatever else had accumulated over the past five years in a trailer that had escaped a thorough cleaning-off the mats. "This isn't going to be easy," Thomas said to Cal, trying to figure out the best way to get the mats out the door, down five steps and onto the trailer.

He had two sets of boys position themselves on each side of the two metal dollies, he and Cal up front preparing to take the bulk of the 500 pounds per slab as they would walk down the stairs at the pavilion and also at the school. And at the rear of the mat, he asked Jeff and Brien to work, the two smallest, about 60 pounds apart in weight. "Lock arms and keep the back of the mat from dragging on the ground. I don't know how much weight you'll be able to handle, but whatever you can will be a tremendous help."

Other than some lost balance, creases in their hands from the metal dollies and bruises on their hips from knocking into the door jamb at the pavilion and school entrances, there were no injuries, except that Thomas popped his neck again when bringing the second mat into the school. Only Cal knew something was wrong.

"What got you?" he asked as the two adults strolled back to the trailer, the youth already sprinting back, ready for more, ready to prove their manhood to their coach and his buddy.

"I keep poppin' the right side of my neck," Thomas said. "It happened last season, twice – right here," he pointed to the back of Cal's neck, at the nape of his neck, slightly to the right. "It feels like someone stuck me with a dagger."

When they got to the stairwell, Thomas sighed. "And the next year we got three home matches, which is great, considering St. Agnes has had none since the program started. But that means we gotta walk the mats up the bottom part of the stairwell, back 'em out the doors into the courtyard, set them down, turn around, relift 'em and walk 'em up there." He pointed up to the gym, where the second half of the stairs led. "I just hope we have enough kids. I hope we don't kill anybody."

"I'm busy," Cal said, offering no explanation.

When the sun went down, Thomas watched some television, then read in bed, then fell asleep. When the sun was up, he worked. First, putting in his time and gathering his check at Burkes', then going off and working toward prepping for St. Agnes' third season.

Thomas liked the Burke family and didn't mind working for them, but he would much rather work alone, making his own business decisions, setting his own schedule, setting his own pace. And that was the outlet wrestling was allowing him. Sure, he ultimately had to answer to the St. Agnes administration, but somewhere up the line everybody had to answer to somebody.

After work at the gravel pit, Thomas would shop around at the Kmarts and the Wal-Marts and the Sears of the world, checking for weight equipment. He knew the room would not be fully supplied overnight. Probably wouldn't be in 10 years, but nevertheless, he shopped.

The best deals he saw were in the newspapers, from homeowners who bought exercise equipment and used it for less than a week. To show a sign of good faith, the first piece of equipment he bought was an exercise bike, "practically brand new," for $150. Thomas thought that by purchasing an exercise bike, the other programs wouldn't bitch about the wrestling team's attempts to seize the room, which, actually, was the coach's ultimate plan. In the two years at St. Agnes, he heard snippets of back-biting among the other coaches, spiteful about what other teams had. Head coaches would go crying to the athletic director on a weekly, sometimes daily, schedule.

After buying the bicycle in late June, Thomas set out after control of the weight room. But instead of saying anything about the wrestling team's use of the room, he volunteered his assistance to attempt to furnish it and to monitor the room three days a week in the spring and fall for all students, not just for the athletes.

"Since I'm here, there's a couple things I need to ask."

The athletic director was becoming wary of Thomas, always "waiting for the other shoe to drop," something he really did not mind so much, welcoming the candor.

"I'd like to be in charge of the weight room – clean it up, set the rules, look for equipment."

No problem.

"And what's the chances for rolling out the mats a couple of times a week in July and August to let the kids roll around?"

The athletic director was hesitant on that request and told Thomas he would have to get back to him on that one. That night, the athletic director called Thomas with the excuses – insurance, other coaches wanting to open up the gym, parents wanting access since they were paying tuition – and the answer was an emphatic and resounding no.

"More back-biting," Thomas said to Terry Broughton. "Fuck it. I'll just find another way."

No matter where he was or how he felt or who he was with, on Sunday evenings ever since the end of the season in mid-February, Thomas headed over to Red Mike's at six o'clock to spend a couple of hours with Old Man Jack.

One Sunday night in the middle of the summer, Jack sensed a heaviness to his left, and asked Thomas if he wanted to talk. "Anything but politics. I'm in no mood for politics tonight."

Thomas started out slowly, but eventually unloaded, saying to Jack, "You don't need to hear my crap."

Jack looked at his Jack Daniel's on the rocks, grabbed the glass and twirled the contents, making the ice clink against the sides. "Tommy m'boy, I look forward, every Sunday, to listening to your crap." And he took a large swig of his drink.

"I'm afraid," Thomas said finally. "Afraid of failing – again. Failing again at wrestling. I didn't feel like I failed my junior and senior years in high school. Illness and injury sometimes just can't be overcome. But I failed in college. I failed miserably because my heart wasn't in it, anymore." His absent stare spoke more than his words that evening. Jack allowed the silence to be his transition.

"I've been watching you closely these last two years, Tommy. And you haven't failed. You've succeeded. You've succeeded in helping the wrestling program and you've succeeded in changing yourself. You left college with your tail between your legs, failing at wrestling and probably feeling like you failed also at life. And you wallowed in misery for a few years, but you've got strength kid. And you're showing it. People have noticed. I've noticed. Failing is one thing. Wallowing in self pity is another. You're not a wallower. And you're not a failure."

The words offered solace. But it dealt more with the success and failure of Thomas McCloskey, and he explained himself. "I understand that no man can be an island. I really do understand that. But when it comes to my personal success or failure, I really didn't give a fuck what other people felt these last few years."

"Ahh, Thomas, but you obviously do give a fuck what others have felt, otherwise this wouldn't be eating at you. It may be that you honestly don't give credence to the majority's opinion, but you have someone in mind – someone who counts. That is why you weren't taking any chances since leaving college," Jack said. "Going to work in a gravel pit – yeah, it's hard work, but you're not sticking your neck out there. Hiding in a bar. Hiding in a glass of beer, the only chance you take there is when you drive home. The ironic thing is that now you don't take that chance anymore. You nurse a beer all night long. That chance-taking part of your life is gone, because you've found meaning someplace else, and as much as I miss your company, the happier I am from your absence."

Thomas heard every word Jack said, but decided to move on, not acknowledging the feelings he expressed. "The problem being in the limelight is that now people out there will begin to measure me up. The problem is that this St. Agnes team doesn't have the resources other teams have. The number of students aren't there. Kids have to travel 10, 20 sometimes 30 miles to get to school everyday. They find it hard to get rides on the weekends. Hell, schools like Covington have two dozen wrestlers in walking distance from the school. And believe it or not, Covington's families have more money. I thought these kids at St. Agnes were rich brats. Hell, half of the team lives in split families, most of them with working moms. Of the six kids from Evandale, only one lives in a traditional type of family. Two live in apartments with their mother and one lives in a hovel with an alcoholic father. I asked this kid Kingery one time if he was going to wrestle in weekend tournaments this summer and he didn't answer. I come to find out he's got no money. As a matter of fact, his father's been stalling the school for $500 past due. And it doesn't look good. The kid is a freshman, just got a job and has made an arrangement with the school to help with payments. And I expect him to concentrate on wrestling? That makes my priorities all fucked up."

Thomas stopped. He had started to rattle on, and he realized it. Jack didn't say anything right away, but then spoke the words which were in both their heads.

"You're making excuses already, Tommy. You're stepping off that island of yours and the spotlight isn't even on you yet. You're hedging your bets, rationalizing failure even before you experience it. But what you just said about this kid who's got a bum for a father, that's what your focus should be. Winning doesn't come in titles. It comes in teaching. This kid is already learning, somehow – maybe from you, maybe from someone else – what winning is all about. He's starting to realize that it's not about the points on the board. It's about survival."

"You're right about the excuses, Jack," Thomas admitted. "It's just that ever since I can remember I've been responsible only for myself. I've called my own shots. You know, if I fucked up in wrestling, I couldn't blame anybody, so I made sure I didn't fuck up. If I did lose, I knew the burden belonged on me. But now it's not the physical part, it's the mental part. I'm not wrestling anymore. Now I'm teaching a couple of dozen kids and to fail now is to knock them as well as my intelligence. I don't know how to respond to attacks against young people I'm responsible for. And I definitely don't know how to take a hit on my intelligence. It's a completely different scenario. It's a different world."

"No it's not, kid. You have one job, and that's to prepare these kids to wrestle for the rest of their lives, and I mean wrestle in the ambiguous sense. And it's not how to win, it's how to wrestle with life. Winning and losing is a black-and-white world, and the world that most of us live in is gray, at best. You never achieved all of your goals, yet you've turned out fine – better than fine. If St. Agnes ends up being a shitty team, so what. The point is that they've learned the concept of wrestling, which you have described as the most rewarding experience of your life. Well, if it weren't for you, that program over there would already be disbanded and none of these kids would be doing much of anything."

Thomas sat silent while the words and advice seeped into his brain. Jack was right. Fuck the glamor or titles or accolades. Just teach the essence of the sport.

"Is that all?" Jack asked, trying to belittle the problem.

"I haven't gotten laid in awhile."

"Don't worry about that. Neither have I."

Thursday. August 13. 11:42 p.m.

The phone rang. And before he decided to answer it, Thomas wanted to figure out who it could be. His worst fears settled in on a couple of women, one ex-girlfriend from a few years back and one ex-fling from the year before. His decision – the ex-fling would be drunk and one night with her wouldn't be such a bad thing. One minute on the phone with the ex-girlfriend would be a nightmare.

Five rings. "Hello."

"You wouldn't happen to know of any big strong men who would want to help a damsel in distress, would you?"

"It depends on who that damsel may be. And what the payment shall be."

"You mean you would actually seek payment in lieu of your chivalrous duties? Which I know you hold in high honor."

"Ah, to joust very well, striking at a man's honor. May you be that damsel?"

"Yes. I am that damsel in dire distress."

"Well then, I must demand payment up front."

"Thomas Patrick!" Michelle acted flabbergasted, then relenting, "I'll buy you dinner."

"You certainly are a seasoned negotiator. A dinner for my services, it is."

"I thank you," she said. "The last time I saw you, I believe you had just finished serving tea and crumpets at an unusual hour, and then you sunk into my couch to watch a western."

"That was me," he affirmed. "How did everything work out with Todd?"

"Don't you mean Tad? Well, that is why I'm calling. Everything worked out just fine. I'm moving to New York City. To the Upper West Side. A one bedroom apartment in a brownstone."

"With a Flannigan's Pub just around the corner?"

"I don't know about a Flannigan's but certainly a Houlihan's." Michelle hesitated. Her formal question seemed to be such a terrible burden to ask of a friend. Especially one she had not spoken to in almost four months. And one who she had broken off a romantic affair with. "Thomas, I was wondering . . . .

"If I could drive up to Boston and help you move?"

Her answer was forthcoming, and it would be yes, but she didn't want to seem presumptuous. Michelle's apprehension alerted Thomas.

"I understand," he said. "I'm nearly 28 years old. I know the difference between friendship and romance. Calling me to help with your move falls under the friendship category. After we unload the last piece of furniture, I'll accept some romancin' as payment."

Michelle and Thomas laughed, and as adults, they both understood for the first time what it meant to be friends, and only friends.

And so, at the end of August, Michelle, Tamantha, Thomas and Mrs. Jennings departed from Boston, with a Ryder box truck packed with furniture and books, Thomas' pick-up with miscellaneous materials and Mrs. Jennings' Ford Taurus loaded with clothes. Tamantha drove the Taurus, accompanied by her mom. Michelle, who had sold her car because "New York City has plenty of ways to get around, plus the insurance would cost one month's salary," drove Thomas' truck, and Thomas drove the rental truck.

After they were all moved in, Michelle wanted to settle her account at that moment, but Thomas declined. It was time to get home and "tend to the chickens," he said. Michelle offered no argument and sent him on his way with a hug and a kiss.

"He's just like that sometimes, Mom," Michelle explained. "Sometimes he's full of energy and ready to take on the world, other times he just wants to go home, mill around the house, take a nap. He told me that I wasn't allowed to psychoanalyze him, but if I were allowed, I would say that he was a bit manic."

"Oh. I don't think so," Tamantha said as politely as possible but was boiling inside. "I just think that sometimes he expends so much physical and emotional energy that he just needs to relax someplace. If Mom weren't here, he would probably've gone out with us, had a couple of drinks and relaxed. But since Mom is here, it would've drained any energy he had left to act as properly as he could. Did you see his poor eyes? They were so droopy. The poor little guy needed beer, a ball game and a couch."

Michelle wanted to ask her sister how she knew so much about Thomas but suddenly realized that Tamantha had spent more time with Thomas in the last two years than Michelle had.

"I think he's just a bit lonely," Mrs. Jennings decided.

Junior

Thirty-five bodies bouncing up and down, all shapes and sizes and high school ages. The larger and older wrestlers led the jogging pack to the inlet, down to the Evandale beachfront, along the boardwalk, up along Logan Lake on the western border, and north along Main Street, back to St. Agnes. Never one to calculate the exact mileage or to time a running excursion, Thomas figured it was three miles or so. His philosophy was start out slow, master that level, then move on. Listen to your heart. Listen to your head. Move on.

Friday morning after Thanksgiving. Nine o'clock they began the run, and Mike Ennis came back first about 20 minutes later, followed by a few other cross-country runners who believed that if they could survive a grueling cross-country season, they certainly could survive a wrestling season. By Monday, four of those five runners decided to concentrate on academics.

If the first day of practice was any indication of where the St. Agnes program was heading, then Thomas was pleased. The returning upperclassmen looked comfortable running the three miles. And the 35 bodies were a good start. By mid-season Thomas figured the Lancers would be down to 20, which meant half a junior varsity squad. The new plan would be to let Mr. Kenneth Lawton recruit the entire season, sending as many delinquents as possible to spend detention in the cafeteria.

Into the school's refurbished weight room for the official early season weigh in. The room didn't have much more equipment, just the riding bicycle and a set of dumbbells from 10 to 65 pounds. The walls were painted with a new coat of white with Lancer blue and red as a border at the top. Exposed plumbing which dipped lower than the drop ceiling also was painted, randomly, with blue and red. The rug was steamed and vacuumed. The Universal chrome polished, its pulleys dusted and sprayed with silicone. And the front doors had shades covering the windows for a bit of privacy during weigh-ins.

Thomas had a legal pad and copied down weights next to each wrestler's name. The returning starters he kept separate:

Name	grade	last year	'93-94
Jeff LeMone	so.	79 lbs.	84.5
Pete McKane	jr.	112	118
George Galatin	jr.	119	128
Tony Kingery	so.	130	157
Brien Cauldron	jr.	135	141
Mike Ennis	jr.	140	152
Masterelli	so.	171	168
Chris Ballinger	jr.	189	193
Anil Nazif	jr.	215	215

Marc Cella and Chuck Garrison were no-shows.

Besides Cella and Garrison, a glaring early season gap was in the coaching position. Mr. Lawton simply had had enough the previous two seasons to ever consider taking on a third. But he had become enthralled with the sport, and although he never admitted it, thought Thomas McCloskey's abrasive coaching style was effective and embraced by the students. The boys liked the openness of the coach, and the respect was reciprocal. As Chris Ballinger put it, "Coach Tom doesn't treat us like babies." Ultimately that was why Kenneth Lawton did not return to the practices. He just could not relate to the students like Thomas did.

But the biology and chemistry teacher did recruit anybody who had good grades. And he monitored the wrestlers who had poor classroom marks or poor conduct. He even took a Commercial Driver's License test for a State of New Jersey Q endorsement, allowing him to drive the 16-passenger church bus. Occasionally, he drove to scrimmages, tournaments, special matches and to the districts and regions, helping the program save valuable dollars. And he attended every home match, for he became the official scorekeeper.

As for a true assistant coach. Thomas had no one. No St. Agnes teacher had any experience with wrestling, and Thomas did not want to take on anybody green. Old wrestling buddies who worked in private business either couldn't commit themselves to three hours every afternoon or didn't have the mandatory 60 hours of college credit. So Thomas decided to go it alone.

He experimented the first two weeks, trying, at first, to separate the returning wrestlers from the fresh troops. The seasoned upperclassmen were to follow the instructions he had left with them while he practiced moves with the freshmen and the first-year upperclassmen. After two days, the varsity members weren't getting in good workouts, so Thomas was forced to switch plans.

"God dammit," he screamed. "You do realize that right now, 39 other programs will be ready to wrestle by mid-December? Of this year. Not next. Hit the stairs."

The stairs. One of a number of punishing exercises, usually performed at the end of practice to finish off conditioning and to lose some of the extra weight. The Lancers had not yet had to endure this part of practice because the community pavilion did not have a set of stairs suitable. But behind the cafeteria, to the south side of the building, is a little-used stairwell, next to the ramp which leads to the dumpster next to which Thomas parks, without fail, on his visiting lunches.

"I want to see those windows steamed up," he said. "And hit every step."

But the drill was new. Even the upperclassmen didn't run the stairs properly, so Thomas would jump in and out of the line, demonstrating, forever trying to teach.

Touch every step.

And touch the wall.

Every step.

Every step.

Every step, Masterelli. If you can't run the stairs, then get the fuck off and let your teammates run them.

Masterelli was glad to get yelled at. He didn't want to run anymore, anyway.

The second experiment was to pair an upperclassman with a new body, but that failed miserably as well. Not having mastered the moves themselves, the varsity members had a rough time teaching the difficult body configurations. At one point, Thomas stood alongside the edge of the mat, staring at the team, switching his glare from one group to another. Soon, when the entire team realized he was not pleased with their efforts, they stopped.

"Might as well do some cals, because we're not getting anywhere with these damn drills."

With new drills, a new practice atmosphere, a new coaching "staff" and a few other kinks to become accustomed to, Thomas stuck to the bare essentials for the first 10 days of practice. He had the team stretching, doing excessive amounts of calisthenics, drilling, drilling and more drilling, with a minimal amount of live wrestling. "By the first match, I want you guys to be in shape for six minutes and I want you to execute the double-leg takedown, the stand-up and the sit-out in A-1 fashion."

Matters were progressing favorably, but Thomas wasn't about to let the boys know that. "Success – they'll have to learn on the mat," he told Old Man Jack. Dark times lie ahead, though, and none of those factors could Thomas control.

The first was Marc Cella, not surprisingly. Thomas beckoned him to practice once and received an abrupt 'no' from the junior. As he promised, the Lancer coach asked only once. Second was the absence of senior Chuck Garrison, and Thomas decided it was time for a lunchtime meeting with Terry Broughton.

"What do you mean he's on academic probation?" This was unfathomable. "When I saw him at the end of last year, he was pulling straight B's."

"That doesn't matter. He got a D in chemistry in the first quarter."

"One D – and that's considered academic probation?"

"Unlike public schools, parents pay a tuition and expect their children to display high scholastic achievement."

There was no point arguing. "When can he get back?"

Mr. Broughton thumbed through his desk calendar. "Reports are handed in on Thursday, January 20. Report cards are sent out the following Monday, the 24th.

"Shit. That's better than half the team's season. By the time he gets six practices in, we'll be near the February 9th cut-off."

"What February 9th cut-off?" The athletic director had been studying the wrestling schedule, program and sport in general. But he was not aware of any cut-off date.

"That's when teams qualify for postseason team championships."

Broughton thought Thomas was dreaming if he thought St. Agnes could wrestle for a state championship any time this century, but he didn't voice his opinion. "Ah. That cut-off. It's the same as in basketball."

"Except for one huge difference," Thomas said. "In basketball, all the small Catholic schools are battling it out for eight spots. And St. Agnes makes it every year with a 12-4 mark – or some record like that. Right?"

Broughton nodded. "Except in '84, the only time in the last 20 years when the team was 9-7."

"Nine and seven, and the team gets shut out of one of the eight spots. Well, in the last four years, only one Catholic team made the South Jersey Parochial B state tournament and that was St. Luke's, out of Mill City Bridge. Four-time, defending, unchallenged state champs. All we need is a .500 record by February 9th and we can challenge these guys."

"Why does only one school qualify?"

"Because it isn't a gentlemen's sport like basketball. All kids play hoops. Most kids study. So private and parochial schools get the pick of the top basketball players in the area with two criteria: they have money for tuition and they want a better education. But wrestling is a sport for rogues. The tougher a kid is, the more successful he's going to be in wrestling. Rogues aren't known for academics. St. Luke's is either in a weak division or it's built up a powerhouse over the course of time."

Terry Broughton was intrigued with the possibility of adding another state championship banner to the rafters in the new gym. "So if we have a .500 record by February 9, we get to wrestle one single match for the state championship?"

He made it sound so simple. All of the other sections – Parochial A, North Jersey, Central Jersey and South Jersey were divided into Sections I, II, III, and IV – always filled the entire quarterfinal bracket. "Sure. But it ain't gonna happen this year."

"Why?" The athletic director arrived at his own conclusion. "The team isn't good enough, huh?"

"St. Agnes could be good enough. We have an outside shot, if we have Garrison. The real problem is that our schedule is upside down. All of the tough matches are early, including the Oak Hill Classic. All of the gimmies are after February 9, and by that time I fear they won't be as automatic wins because these guys will be beat up physically and mentally by then, and they'll even question their worth against St. Peter's, Bishop Leary and Hanstrom."

"Is there anything we can do?"

"I doubt it. The schedule's set. That's your area of expertise. But . . ." Thomas appeared to be forming an idea, ". . . what if Garrison can get clearance to practice by the 14th? Lawton can help him with studying and his teachers can give him an early progress report. If his grades look good, he can suit up for January 22 against Fairview. It'll give a kick to the team for the stretch run. If they don't make the states, they'll at least be rolling into the districts."

Thomas checked his watch. "Listen, I'm running late. We'll talk more about the schedule when it's time to set it for next season. Get some Catholic schools – non-conference – up front and drop Oak Hill." And Thomas hurried from the athletic director's office.

Shortly after, Terry Broughton remembered about the Christmas concert schedule. McCloskey's not going to like that news.

The weight room was community, so Thomas could not claim providence over it, even during the wrestling season. But from 5:30 to 6 o'clock, Monday, Tuesday, Thursday and Friday, the entire wrestling squad descended upon and captured the room. If anybody was using the weights or was at the back to check out equipment, they soon left, for more than two dozen boys would strip down to just underwear.

Thomas would never announce the team's arrival. He simply would yell, "All right. Let's strip down." He instructed the team to wait a few minutes before disrobing, allowing stragglers to disappear. Once gone, the lightweights stepped onto the scale, followed by the middles, finally the disgruntled upperweights who were everyday complaining about going last.

From lightweight to heavyweight, Thomas would have a comment to every wrestler.

"Good job."

"An extra sweatshirt for you tomorrow."

"Good job."

"Only one lunch tomorrow."

"You gotta be fuckin' kidding."

"One at a time, Anil."

"Are you on the scale yet, Jeff?"

"Good job."

"Being last gives you more time to make weight."

"Good job."

Good job.

Good job.

It was mostly fun and games while weighing in at the weight room. Unless a wrestler was making absolutely no progress to his appointed goal, Thomas tried not to get serious. Only the night before a match would Thomas lay down the law.

Conversely, strict guidelines were set for the cafeteria, which sent a stream of complaints to the principal, vice principal and the athletic director, to the latter Thomas proclaimed, "For 2 ½ hours, for three months out of the year, I need to teach some discipline. And if I have cheerleaders skipping and giggling through the cafeteria, or some basketball player strutting through saying 'faggots' under his breath, or any other contingent of students able to interrupt practice and I can't say anything, then I lose a great deal of respect from the team."

"All right," the athletic director said, exhausted from creating a new set of rules for the wrestling team. "Please tone it down and try not to make the cheerleaders cry."

A couple of days into the new season in their new room, Thomas shut all of the doors. If anyone, other than teachers, administrators or nuns – especially the nuns – tried to use the cafeteria as a short cut to the rest of the building, Thomas would ask, "Excuse me, can I help you?"

The common responses: "I was just going to the library/ locker room/ weight room/ science lab/little theatre."

"Well," Thomas would say with the entire team looking on in complete silence, "you will just have to find another way for the next few weeks." He was very polite, as polite as Thomas could be.

If any resistance was apparent from a female co-ed, then Thomas asked one of the upperweights to escort her back to the door she had just emerged from. If it were a male student, the coach would lightly berate them. And if it were one of the arrogant basketball players, the use of profane language was not unusual. "Do you have shit in your ears? I don't think Coach Haskins would appreciate it if wrestlers strolled through basketball practice uninvited. Now turn your skinny ass around and get the hell out of my damn room!" The basketball player would retreat begrudgingly, mumbling 'faggots' as he shuffled through the exit. The wrestlers relished those situations, but no comments were permitted from the team.

With two practice days remaining before the Oak Hill Classic, Thomas had his hands tied. When he arrived at the cafeteria on Thursday at 3:45, the usual clamor of basketballs hitting the hardwood could be heard from above. But the wrestlers were not stretching. Unlike every day so far in the third season, they were not prepared for the beginning of practice at precisely the moment he walked through the southeastern doors. They were not even suited up. The mats were not washed, because the mats still were stowed away.

Twenty odd wrestlers sat atop the mat cabinets, watching the start of the choir's Christmas Concert rehearsal. Across the room, where the team usually lined up for wind sprints were 30 chairs in three rows, a piano, and "a gaggle of geeks," as Brien Cauldron phrased it.

Thomas could not form the question properly, not without including a few choice words, which undoubtedly would offend Sister Catherine. Quickly, Jeff LeMone, the courier for Mr. Broughton, sensed the urgency of the situation, and handed the note from the athletic director.

Mr. McCloskey-

Following your departure at our last midday meeting, I remembered the choir's use of the cafeteria on Thursday and Friday, 12/16 and 12/17 . The matter slipped my mind until this morning. I apologize for the inconvenience this may cause and for my memory loss. This is the only scheduled usage for the cafeteria.

TB

Thomas crumpled the note, slowly walked to the nearest garbage basket and dropped it in. He turned to the wrestling team, and with unnerving patience, said, "Go to the locker room, suit up, and get down here in five minutes." The team grabbed its bags and quickly disappeared.

Up on the third floor, in the carpeted hallway of the English department, the Lancer troops were assembled. It was 4 o'clock.

"As far as I'm concerned we have lost 30 valuable minutes of practice. Now let's stretch out as I map out a plan for today and tomorrow." The coach weaved in and out of the wrestlers, tiptoeing between knees and groins, shoulders and armpits, telling the varsity wrestlers that they must use these final days not to sharpen their wrestling skills, but to build upon conditioning and to skim off any excess weight. "That's all we can do. And we have to do it up here in the English department. How poetic."

The Lancers crowded at the end of the hallway and ran some light wind sprints in pairs. Then came some spinning drills, where one wrestler gets on all fours and the top man performing the exercise puts his chest on the down man's back, then spins, first in one direction, then another, placing hands in various spots, simulating moves, spinning, sweating, dripping, gasping and forever changing direction, until it was his time to rest on the bottom on all fours, as a base while his partner spun himself into hell.

Stand-ups. First alone, then with a partner. Then alone. Pyramiding, Thomas told them. Starting with 10 stand-ups, then 25, then 50, back to 25 and 10. Doing it until their young and recuperative hamstrings burned. Some would grunt. Some would yell. Others refused to show signs of weariness. Some merely stopped.

Thomas would give them a break, to rest and get some water. At a water fountain, down another corridor, some of the younger wrestlers complained, asking why they were getting punished for the choir being in the cafeteria.

"Just shut up and stop your bellyachin,'" Jeff LeMone said in a squeak. "If you can't take the sport, then just go home, you pussies."

A freshman 145 pounder, Pete Disling, took offense to the miniature sophomore yapping at them, and told him to "Stuff it, twirp."

Jeff remained quiet for a few seconds, nodding his head, his eyelids droopy, as if ready to fall to sleep. When Disling turned the knob to the ancient porcelin fountain and leaned forward for a drink of water, Jeff struck. "Yeah. I'll stuff it," he said, jabbing

Disling in the back of the head with an open palm, snapping the freshman's head forward, catching the bridge of his nose on the water spout.

Disling spun, and with a small gash producing a slight stream of brilliant red blood, yelled, "You asshole," and started at LeMone.

But at 84 pounds, Jeff was always ready. He had to be. First-strike capabilities were a must for a little fellow with a huge attitude. Immediately, Jeff had Disling on the ground with a double leg takedown, wailing away with roundhouse punches. Disling covered up his already bloody face, his forearms protecting his temples.

Mike Ennis pulled Jeff off the battered freshman. Chris Ballinger lifted up a stunned Disling. "You never talk back to an upperclassman when you're a freshman," were the only words of advice Chris could tell Disling before Thomas was on the scene.

He shook his head in the negative fashion. "Go get cleaned up," he told Disling. "And you go with him," he directed to LeMone. "And if there's the slightest indication that either of you can't act as teammates, neither of you will be around for the end of the season. Check that – for the end of practice."

Thomas was sorry to see blood on the bridge of the freshman's nose and was sure that he would receive a phone call from one of Disling's parents that evening. Upon closer inspection, the gash turned out to be a small cut, neither needing stitches nor in jeopardy of becoming a scar. Nevertheless, a call would be forthcoming, and a mom would inevitably ask, "Are you running wrestling practice or a boot camp?"

Phone calls were daily consequences of the fledgling program, but on this day the coach had succeeded in turning the distraction of not having access to the cafeteria into productive practice time, and he could live with one phone call. For the remainder of Thursday's practice, the team was eerily silent, working hard, executing drills and half drills, whatever the confined space allowed. The team was getting mad at Thomas. Mad because they were forced to improvise. Mad because the improvisation took them away from their comfortable routine. Mad because the last two days of practice before the start of St. Agnes' third season, despite being 30 minutes less than a normal practice, were excruciatingly painful.

If they could retain that ire into Saturday, then Thomas had succeeded in diverting attention from the real problem – the Oak Hill Classic.

Thomas was not nervous as he drove home in the December darkness. And he tried to understand why.

In all the big matches he competed in, and all the matches he was present at since he started coaching, Thomas always got the case of the jitters. He taught himself how to change those jitters into energy. It was strange how in a 10-minute period, the same nerves which would nearly send him to the bathroom to vomit were suddenly transformed into a dynamo of energy. And it was all done in his mind.

It wasn't until he almost got home that Thomas realized that the nervousness was absent because he knew this team was not ready for the start of the season. Terry Broughton was a nice guy and one hell of an athletic director, as long as he only had to focus on basketball. When it came to wrestling, Broughton was a functional idiot, either because he didn't care or because he didn't have the capacity to learn. How can a relatively new wrestling program start the season with the Oak Hill Classic Christmas tournament, followed by dual matches against Blakemore, Flat River and Covington?

The burden of fault could not be placed solely on the athletic director's shoulders. He did not have help from the previous brain trust of Mr. Kenneth Lawton and Mark Pierce, and Thomas had to shoulder some of the blame for not asking more questions concerning off-the-mat procedures. And so, as Thomas pulled into his driveway, he decided that due to the circumstances surrounding the St. Agnes program, he would have to postpone the idea of pushing for a state championship in his first season, thus cloaking from the world his sport ingenuity. He chuckled at his flippancy.

A Ford Taurus was parked outside his house and although it looked familiar, Thomas thought that it probably belonged to one of the neighbors. Methodical as he was after the truck comes to a halt – engage emergency brake, lights off, heat off, radio volume turned to low, kill the ignition, grab the empty coffee cups and newspaper, get the cigarettes off the dashboard, get out and lock the door, reach backwards into the bed for his gym bag – he failed to notice the figure sitting on his stoop, a muffled clapping from her hands gloved in hunter green cotton.

Thomas was stunned to see Michelle Jennings, knees up to her chest, gray overcoat wrapped tightly around her legs, a hunter green scarf bloused high around her neck, protecting her ears, spaced a few inches from her nose so her recycled breath acted as a heater.

"Hey." Other than her constant clapping, she did not move.

"Hey. That your Mom's Taurus out there, I 'spose?"

Yes.

"And you locked your keys in it?"

No.

"So you're sitting out here because you've changed after all of these years and you actually enjoy the wintertime?"

No.

"So you're sitting here because . . ." Thomas coaxed his last word into lingering, to let Michelle have the opportunity to finish his sentence.

"Because I know you, Thomas. If you see a strange car in front of your house, with someone sitting in that strange car, you'd head straight over, smash the window. Remember – 'Swing first, ask questions later.' Isn't that one of your commandments?"

"Yes, normally it is. But a Ford Taurus isn't a threatening type of vehicle. And you are not an imposing figure when sitting behind its wheel. I probably would go to the car, but with a cute girl like yourself – I wouldn't smash the window unless you declined my invitation for a date."

"Funny you say that, Tommy." Michelle stood and offered to take the newspaper and two 7-Eleven coffee cups as he opened up his front door. "I was wondering if you would like to go out to dinner tonight?"

"What is it with women of the '90s? I've been asked out more than I've done the asking." He dropped his bag as soon as he got in the door. "How about some tea?"

Michelle was about to address the '90s dating issue when she noticed how neat his house was. There were no newspapers strewn about. Or dishes on tables or in the kitchen sink. No empty pizza boxes or garbage piled in the corner, yearning for a trip to the landfill. It was neat. Not spotless, but neat. And suddenly she remembered why she was forced to wait on his stoop.

"Hey Mr. McCloskey – why didn't you ever mention that you've been coaching wrestling at St. Agnes. You afraid of being called a traitor?"

"You never asked," he said, as he filled up the kettle and placed it on a burner. "How'd you find out?"

"Mom called. It was in the newspaper. She was just skimming through – you know how mom is, checking out the local high school boxes to see if she recognized any names. And she saw your name as head coach of St. Agnes. She called me asking if this was 'our Thomas.' So I called you. You really need to get an answering machine."

Thomas grunted at the suggestion of an answering machine. "Sugar? Milk?"

"When I couldn't reach you I called Amanda Pierce and she said that Mark used to be head coach at St. Agnes, started the program, left it with you, and now he's at Covington." Michelle waited for a response, but received none. Thomas was used to the comments by Amanda, so it didn't surprise him.

"Well?" Michelle wanted the scoop.

"Well what?" Thomas told her that the tea was ready, grabbed the newspaper and sat at the kitchen table with his own cup of tea – cream and sugar.

"Well, I'm ecstatic that you're coaching. It's what you need to do." When Thomas looked over the top of the sports section at her, she quickly added that she was not being analytical. "You're a good teacher. A good wrestler. You'll be a great coach."

Thomas found the annual wrestling preview just as Michelle was finishing her inspirational speech. "We're picked to finish last in the division."

"It's your first year, Tommy."

"No, it's not. It's my third. And technically, Mark and some teacher did start the program at St. Agnes, but Mark had no intention of staying around. All he did was put on his wrestling shoes and horse around with the kids. After Coach Gibbons' wrestlers graduate in the next couple of years, Covington's going to take a nose dive. As a matter of fact, it could happen this year with Mark at the helm. He doesn't know his ass from his head."

"I thought you and Mark were friends."

"I'm a friend. He's an idiot. No – I'm an idiot, too." Thomas shook his head, he hated being petty. He read the "Outlook" in the newspaper's sketch of St. Agnes:

"A new Coach won't help St. Agnes. With only one district medalist returning to this year's squad, the future looks bleak. Nine starters return, most with losing records. On the bright side, things could only get better. Couldn't they?"

Thomas threw the paper onto the table. "Who writes this shit? You know, I try not to crack the whip in practice, not like some of the bigger schools with four or five coaches, anyway. But when high school kids read reports like this, they get embarrassed. And they want to do better. And I want to do better. So we'll work harder in practice and I'll scream and yell and treat them like young men instead of pampered babies that this generation's producing, and then I'll get a call from some parent saying, 'You're being mean to Johnny.' And I'll say, 'No. You know that kid from Flat River who just beat the shit out of your son. He's being mean to Johnny.'"

Michelle smiled, infecting Thomas, who also smiled. "There's some life left in you yet," she said.

"You know, I remember Coach Gibbons being a lot rougher on us than I am with these kids. Hell, he used to bring a paddle to practice and whack us in the ass if we weren't moving fast enough, and I'll tell you what, that paddle stung for more than a few minutes. With these St. Agnes kids, though, I have to coddle most of them because if I lean too much on them, they'll quit. And we don't have the numbers to afford any of them to quit. I'm stuck. I don't like to coddle, but I can't have 'em quit. So each kid I have to treat completely different. Sometimes I have to put my arm around some baby and nearly plead with him. And his buddy I may have to scream and curse at, at the top of my lungs – gives me damn laryngitis, I should get worker's comp." He sighed in order to break up his diatribe, the blood pressure lowering immediately. "Gibbons had enough kids that all he had to do was teach some moves and throw us into a pile. The best wrestlers got to go varsity." Thomas stopped and picked up the paper, looking at some of the other impressive school's summaries. "Sometimes I don't know if I'm confusing the kids or what. Is this one of those instances you hear in the news that a coach is emotionally scarring his players for the rest of their lives? Hell, they're scarring me." He attempted and failed at producing a smile.

Tamantha's words came back to Michelle – be a friend, not an analyst. But Michelle knew that at this moment, any advice coming from her would be taken as both a friend and a professional. Yet she sensed that Thomas was seeking a little bit of both, so she compromised within herself. "Do you have a singular purpose that you've defined as being a coach? A sort of mission statement."

"I just want to teach them how to be men. Half of them don't have fathers, the other half don't have fathers that ever learned the meaning of manhood. I don't know. The more I want them to learn how to be men, the more the world seems to be changing. My definition, the way I define myself as a man seems to be antiquated. I question myself constantly. Maybe this isn't the right way to coach."

"Tommy, you're doing the right thing. If these boys didn't want the discipline, they wouldn't show up every day. More boys today need a teacher like you."

Speaking the words removed the dreaded albatross that seemed to be hanging from his neck. But Michelle wasn't at his house to offer free clinical advice, and suddenly Thomas realized this. "What are you doing here anyway?"

Thomas and Michelle were a half an hour late in meeting Tamantha and her date for dinner at The Riptide, a classic, beach-style restaurant on Main Street in Evandale. It wasn't a far stretch how Thomas wound up dining out before the season opener in his first head-coaching experience, but he did put up a mild struggle to avoid it.

Mom, daughters and sisters. That's how he got there. Mom, daughters and sisters. Momma Jennings had made her call to daughter Michelle asking about Thomas McCloskey and St. Agnes. Daughter Tamantha called Mom Jennings to tell her she was coming to Evandale from Chesterton because she had a first date with Chad, whereas Mom Jennings told her about her phone call with daughter Michelle concerning Coach Thomas and St. Agnes. Then sister Tamantha called sister Michelle to find out more details and learned that sister Michelle was planning to take the 4:10 out of Penn Station to Evandale, pick up Mom's car and head to Thomas' house to say hello and force him to dinner for two reasons: the rain-ticket repayment and a celebratory coaching debut. Following in female order, sister Tamantha insisted that sister Michelle and coach Thomas create a table of four from a table of two at The Riptide.

So Thomas found himself walking into the restaurant at 8 o'clock despite his objections, citing a 5:30 a.m. wake-up call as the primary reason. Michelle proved to be the more stubborn.

It had been a while since Thomas had been in the restaurant side of The Riptide. Once in a while, he would frequent the bar area for a change of atmosphere, but he had not dined there since dating Michelle in high school. Being near her house, it was a convenient spot before he had a car and a comfortable stop after he bought his El Camino.

Nothing much had changed in The Riptide since high school. Some newer, colorful pictures interspersed with old black and white photos of championship lifeguard teams adorned the brown, plywood walls. Wooden crab and lobster traps hung in different corners where the walls met the ceilings. Wooden rowing oars with their championship years painted on the paddle hung gloriously in the midst of the main dining hall. And wooden nickels were still handed out by bartenders for free drinks.

Thomas and Michelle were late due to their conversation and his need to take a shower and spruce up – which entailed brushing his teeth and lacing up his construction boots. Tamantha smiled gleefully as they approached the table, but Thomas didn't notice. All he noticed was a thick leather appointment book lying closed, taking up a corner chunk of the table, and a cellular phone on top.

"Christ," Thomas said in a hushed breath. Michelle heard him and knew to what his remark concerned.

Tamantha got up and gave her sister a kiss on the cheek and gave Thomas a big 'ol hug. Chad remained seated for the introductions. Thomas pulled a chair out from the table to Chad's left and offered it to Michelle, then took the seat directly across from the young, spit-shined junior executive.

Chadwick Lewis. Twenty-four years old. Ambitious, upwardly mobile. Sat in a Prudential cubicle in Holmdel. Shared an apartment with two college roommates from Rutgers. Just bought a Grand Am, still had 58 payments left on it. And just took out a two-year contract on an Ameritech cellular phone, to impress the boss more than anything else. He also owned a beeper, a back-up to the cellular phone, just in case he was in the crapper and did not want anyone to hear him fart while on his phone.

Thomas could only attest to Chad's top half since he never rose to shake hands during the greeting. His brown hair was short, parted on the right side and had a high sheen to it. He had not much facial hair, maybe shaving with a razor twice a week – once on the weekends. A white shirt with a diagonal blue and gold tie, loosened at the knot, which hung between the two straps of his gray suspenders. Underneath the table, Thomas figured he wore gray pinstriped pants, gray socks, black wingtip shoes and had nothing hanging in his crotch.

"Hey, would you like a drink? It's on me," he said, immediately calling to the waitress. "I'll have a Tanqueray and tonic." It was his third. "And whatever they'll have. And put it on my tab."

Thomas wished Chad had not done that and wanted to explain a few things to the kid. But it was Tamantha's date and it was her night out, so Thomas refrained. He ordered a beer. Michelle a Tom Collins.

"Chad," Michelle felt obligated to start the dinner conversation off in pleasant fashion, "Tammy tells me that you're an underwriter at Prudential. That probably keeps you busy."

A perfect lead for Chad to give his dissertation of the dedication to work, starting at daybreak, going until sundown and into dinner meetings and cocktail parties. "If you want to succeed, you have to play the game." As if on cue, his phone rang and he answered, pushed his chair back from the table, angled his ass on the seat, turning his back to Michelle, crossed his legs and launched into a conversation as if the others were not present.

Thomas' left eye half closed itself and a nasty gimlet came from his right. Michelle noticed and quickly put her hand on his wrist and asked Tamantha a question about her upcoming student teaching in the spring semester. Tamantha was embarrassed about Chad's behavior but was glad to answer the question in order to divert attention.

"What's Chad short for?" Thomas asked.

"Chadwick." Tamantha suddenly noticed the pomposity in the name and the similarity in the character.

"How did you meet Chadwick Lewis?"

"At Homecoming at Chesterton. A childhood friend of his went to Chesterton and they showed up last month. I was sitting at the far end of the student section and . . . ."

"His phone rang?"

"Tommy!" Michelle thought it was funny, but didn't want to laugh. "What do you think you want for dinner?"

"Sorry about that." The apology was a programmed and gratuitious response as Chadwick returned his attention to the dinner group. "Waitress." He ordered another gin and tonic and another round for the two sisters and Thomas. "Put it on my tab."

If Thomas kept his mouth shut again, there would be no way of telling how Chadwick would commit the next etiquette faus paux. So Thomas told Chadwick he need not buy the drinks. "You see, normally I like paying for my own drinks and my date, but tonight is different because I promised Michelle she could take me out to dinner as repayment for a favor."

"A gigolo." Chad chuckled at his witticism.

Thomas remained pleasant. If he stepped across the line, he would ruin dinner in a best-case scenario. "So I would appreciate it if you let the waitress split the check." He pretended that he never heard that word gigolo.

"Whatever, chief." The gin and tonic was beginning to take effect.

The waitress came just in time with a beer, a madras, a Tom Collins and a T&T. She asked if they were ready to order and Chadwick took charge. "Yes, we are. And two tickets," he said, indicating the two dates and the recipients. Thomas felt a queasiness in his stomach.

"I'll have the 16-ounce Kansas City strip, medium rare – you know, juicy red – it most definitely has to be juicy red – with a baked spud and whatever rabbit food comes with it."

The waitress finished scribbling and looked at Tamantha. "The chicken Parmesan, please, with linguine." Her voice revealed the tenseness of the moment. She smiled forcibly.

Michelle ordered a burger with fries. Thomas, a cheeseburger with fries. Then Thomas excused himself and headed in the direction of the bathrooms.

When Thomas returned, Michelle deftly turned the conversation to wrestling just as dinner arrived. The combination of alcohol and steak kept Chadwick's mind and mouth occupied, so during dinner, Tamantha and Michelle were entertained by some of the stories of the St. Agnes wrestling team.

"At the start of every season, the freshmen want to know when I can teach them the sleeper hold, and then I have to explain to them that this isn't professional wrestling and that there are no turnbuckles or sleeper holds or flying Watusis or whatever the hell the other moves are called. And they always look so dejected, 'No sleeper holds. That sucks.' "

Thomas barely touched his cheeseburger, nibbling only at his fries, as he rolled along with the stories. Michelle asking questions, Tamantha listening intently.

"The two best excuses for quitting the team," Thomas reflected in order to properly answer Michelle's question, "have to be one kid saying that his mother didn't want him injuring his fingers because he played piano, and then this one kid, Joe, asking why he was suddenly getting dandruff and what he could do about it. I told him to shampoo with Head and Shoulders or quit the team. I never saw him again."

Chewing his last piece of gristle, Chad felt ready to re-enter the conversation. "Yeah, I wrestled for about a month my freshman year," he began but suddenly stopped as the waitress walked by the table. He grabbed her by the arm and told her to bring another gin and tonic. "But I quit," he continued, "because that sniglet or whatever you call those queer uniforms were suffocating my nuts." His cellular phone rang for the second and last time at The Riptide.

Hello.

"Hang it up," Thomas calmly said.

Excuse me?

"Hang up the fuckin' phone." Tamantha was scared. Michelle closed her eyes.

What?

"Either you hang up that fuckin' phone right now or I'm taking it and smashing it into a thousand fuckin' pieces." His voice was quivering but quiet, only the table to Thomas' left was within earshot of the exchange. "I don't know if Tammy will continue with this relationship, but if she does, and if I happen to run into you again, I'll start teaching you a few points of etiquette, you pretentious piece of shit."

With gin coursing through his veins, Chad normally may have thrust forward his chest and taken on the challenge. But with the conversation of wrestling and being a high school coach, but most of all the imposing granite-looking jaw in which these meancing words were formed, Chadwick thought better of any physical confrontation. He could not, though, give up without a bit of bravado. He said into the phone, "I'll call you back." And he pushed the end button. "You have some nerve. . . ."

"Shut the fuck up before I come across this table and break your fuckin' nose. You have pissed me off so much tonight that now I'm embarrassing myself in front of these two ladies. What I oughta do is take you outside and toss you across the fuckin' parking lot a few times."

Tamantha looked at Michelle who shook her head no. Chadwick looked down at his plate and played with his fork. Thomas didn't continue until the junior executive looked at him again.

"Now, before I go, I got a coupla simple pointers for you. Don't bring your fuckin' phone to the table – that's what your fuckin' beeper's for – and you can put that damn thing on vibrate and stick it down your shorts. You'll like that. Next, you let the ladies at the table order first. You sound like a schmuck when you order before everyone else. Finally – don't you ever buy me a fuckin' drink if you don't know me." Thomas' eyes locked with Chadwick's. They both knew there would be no need for violence.

"I apologize for my behavior, Tammy. I'll make it up to you." Thomas turned to Michelle. "Do you mind giving me a ride home now?"

Yes. "I have to get the check from the waitress."

"Dinner's already been paid for."

"She's in her room," Mrs. Jennings told Michelle as soon as as she stepped through the front door. "I tried talking to her but she wouldn't talk. Must have been some date." Mom's sarcastic tone did not phase Michelle at all. Mrs. Jennings reacquainted herself with Chapter 12 of Danielle Steele's *Daddy*. Michelle went into her sister's room.

Tamantha sat in the dark at her window, a bit to the right, staring into the road illuminated by a street lamp. She had been stroking Samson, who lay comfortably on her lap, but when the door opened, the cat disappeared, maybe for a bite to eat or a walk around the litter box.

Michelle sat on the bed. "How did things work out with Chad?"

When she eventually started to speak, there was so much mucus in her throat that Tamantha had to clear it before getting out any words. "It's over between me and Chad." Almost inaudible, Tamantha began to cry, keeping her eyes fixed on nothing in particular outside the window.

"There will be other guys. Nicer guys. Getting upset over someone like Chad is hardly worth the tears." Michelle tried the standard consoling procedure, not aware that she did not understand the impetus for the tears.

"Chad had a 50/50 shot going into tonight, anyway," Tamantha said, sniffling as she tried to explain. "I just don't know why Tommy acted like that."

"Do you mean you're more upset about Tommy than Chad."

"Yes and no. It's about the same."

"Well, don't be upset about Tommy, that's just the way he is. He was just looking out for you like a little sister."

"I don't want him to look after me like a little sister. I'm 22 years old. I'm a big girl now. I don't need to be treated like a child." The tears slowly rolled down Tamantha's cheeks, reflecting in the light coming from the street lamp. When she told Michelle that she was a big girl, she also reminded herself and stopped crying.

Previous thoughts returned to Michelle. She remembered the few times Tamantha had seen Thomas and how she spent more than just a few minutes with him. Again, Michelle wondered if Tamantha, knowingly or not, had developed amorous feelings for Thomas McCloskey.

"Don't be silly," Tamantha said. "You two were made for each other and you're both in denial." She got up and pulled some tissues from a box on her bureau. Tamantha wiped the scant makeup, which had smeared around the corners of her eyes. "I would never let myself fall in love with an ex-boyfriend of yours."

Michelle left it alone. "Then why are you upset with Tommy."

"I've never seen him like that before. He got so mad. I felt like he was even mad at me for dating someone like Chad. Chadwick." Tamantha thought about the name. "The Chadster." They both laughed.

Michelle began to explain Thomas, about his feelings of manhood and how he defined and rated himself within his gender. "He's not a chauvinist. He just understands that there is a biological difference between men and women, boys and girls. If anything, he's more bigoted of how men's roles should be defined than women's roles. And I think that goes back to seeing how hard his mother worked and seeing up close how Mom worked for us.

Tommy always said that the female population was the stronger of the two. He used to always tell me, 'Behind every good man is one damned outstanding woman.' "

Tamantha understood. "But it seemed he was also mad at me."

Michelle shook her head. "Tommy had two spots where he allows himself to display emotion, although he is getting better. Especially when we were in high school, at one end of the spectrum, where he normally stayed, he was friendly and pleasant and joking and smiling. But then if something upset him, he got eerily silent. And stayed silent. And he would simmer, and that would slowly grow to a boil. Finally, he would just blow up. It didn't happen often, but when it did, Tommy was dangerous. It happened when he wrestled. It happened one time at a party our junior year, and it happened a couple of times during wrestling practice and once during a match.

"That's what happened tonight. He kept his mouth shut for your benefit. But finally, the Chadmeister went too far for Tommy, and he had to let him know it. But like I said, Tommy's gotten much better, because the old Thomas Patrick McCloskey wouldn't have warned your little Chad darling."

Samson returned to Tamantha's lap, who had returned to her seat by the window. Tammy stroked Sam's coat as Michelle soothed Tammy's feelings.

The old stories hit a chord, bringing forth warm memories long ago buried. "We have a common history, but nothing in common anymore. Well, not the little things," Michelle said, exploring her mind, trying to recall what Thomas' ideals were. "And some of the big points, too. Tommy has absolutely no room in his world for the Todd Aldriches and Chadwick Lewises of the world. To him, they're bottom feeders, but a lot of those guys aren't. Someday, you and I will find a couple of real gentlemen who don't bring their cellular phones to the dinner table."

Tamantha smiled but could not help but quietly disagree with her sister. Thomas was the one fish you could not throw back. Maybe Michelle would get bitten by a few more of those bottom feeders and she would recognize Thomas for the man he was. Hopefully, it wouldn't be too late. Hopefully, he wouldn't be taken.

TWENTY-TWO

If the first match at the Oak Hill Classic was any indication of what the season held in store for St. Agnes, a betting man would not have liked the odds.

By the time the first weigh-ins sprung upon the Lancers, Jeff LeMone, the sophomore and only wrestler small enough to compete in the 103-pound weight class, was actually too small. During the final team weigh-in on the night before the tournament, Jeff was down to 80 pounds, eight pounds shy of the minimum weight for the first two weight classes. All Thomas could do was tell him to say a prayer and drink a lot of water in the morning.

At 5:45 a.m., Jeff got on the scale in the St. Agnes weight room and it topped off at 83 pounds. He got dressed and told Thomas, "I'm wrestling today," and produced two half gallon containers of distilled water from his gym bag. A smile that weighed more than his arm grew across his face. "Although I may end up pissing on the mat."

"It may not be your time yet," Thomas said. "We can just wait for midseason or even next year."

"I'm wrestling today," Jeff said, taking glug after glug down his throat. "That should be 84 pounds."

At Oak Hill High School in the boys' locker room, Jeff LeMone did not make weight his first time on the scale. He was a pound shy. So his teammates all weighed in and were cleared.

Two more schools undressed, stepped onto the scales and left before Jeff got a second chance. "Man, I don't know if I can fit anymore into me," he said. With his underwear and shirt on, the scale tipped to 87 ¾ pounds.

"Is that right?" Thomas asked the scale master, knowing it was but hoping that the man had a heart.

Yeah, it's right.

"How much time does he have left?"

Twenty minutes.

"I'll give it a shot Coach. But I don't know if I can do it." Tears began to well up in his eyes, and those tears portrayed two meanings: his love for the sport and dedication to his coach and team; and to prove that he's just not a little guy rolling around at practice for fun.

Thomas wanted to tell him to forget about it, but when he saw the determination of the 103 pounder, he let the kid go. So what if he looked like Paul Newman's character in *Cool Hand Luke* after consuming 50 hard-boiled eggs in one hour. A coach is supposed to provide the pragmatism for wrestlers that lose their heads when trying to lose weight. It's just rare that a wrestler is trying to gain weight instead of losing it. Thomas was in unfamiliar territory.

"You go ahead. It'll show the team a little something about heart and soul. Now, if you don't make it, I don't want you to think you've failed, because you haven't. You'll have succeeded in giving the team a backbone."

Jeff grinned, not his usual large grin, but one big enough to let the coach know he understood. The sophomore turned and walked away, much slower than his perky little self during the week. He was back in 10 minutes, weighing exactly 88 pounds.

Jeff LeMone won the battle but lost the war on that Saturday in December, giving Thomas an ignominious start to his head-coaching career. Overmatched against a senior from Camden's Martin Luther King Jr. High School, Jeff was pinned in the first period.

"I could have kicked his ass," he said to Thomas with tears welling up in his eyes again. "I just couldn't move out. . . ." Jeff never completed his sentence, barely making it to the garbage can in the corner of the gym, regurgitating much of the water he drank since waking that morning. With water and saliva dripping from his bottom lip and mucus running out of his nostrils, Jeff swore to his coach he would never throw up again.

Eight wrestling mats spread across the spacious Oak Hill gym floor, a rubberized mixture softer than St. Agnes' own used mat. In the afternoon, four mats would suffice for the quarterfinals. By Sunday morning, two mats would remain and by Sunday afternoon, with the stands packed and fans overflowing into the doorways, one mat would be left in the middle of the floor with the best preseason wrestlers in the state vying for a prestigious early season championship. The St. Agnes Lancers would be at home watching NFL football.

The team finished last. Chris Ballinger pinned his first round opponent, giving St. Agnes two tournament points. "It's better than being shut out," Thomas said, wishing to but not adding "than being laughed at, too." In the afternoon round, with 12 teammates eliminated and sitting bored in the bleachers wanting nothing more than to go home, Chris got pinned late in the third period.

With six juniors, three sophomores and four freshmen in the lineup, St. Agnes simply was outmanned and outclassed. Eleven of the Lancers wrestled tentatively, which included the normally vivacious Jeff LeMone, the reservoir of water contributing to his woes.

Only Ballinger and Tony Kingery wrestled aggressively. Tony went into the third period of his 152-pound match trailing 15-11, attempting not many other moves than standing headlocks. Thomas did not like the strategy and conveyed this to Tony when he walked off the mat. "Just because you lifted this summer and put on 25 pounds of muscle doesn't mean you have to prove it to everybody in the gym."

The hour-long bus ride back to Evandale was solemn. Thomas knew the likely outcome of the Oak Hill Classic, but in the back of his mind, like every other foolish rookie coach, he thought that maybe he had prepared the team enough to pull off a miracle. While he stared blankly at the newspaper as he bounced up and down on the yellow school bus, he tried to decide if he was a fool or a dreamer. Or if there was any difference at all.

"I thought about it all day yesterday, and there's no use avoiding the subject." Just as Thomas had explained to Mark Pierce in Red Mike's by writing down instructions on cocktail napkins, the current head coach addressed the team just after warm-ups during the first practice following the tournament. Despite the discouraging performances of the wrestlers at their first holiday tournament, Thomas spoke to a silent room, each student giving him undivided attention.

"This will not be an easy season. I know some of you guys are confident because St. Agnes finished strong the last two seasons, but we have to face one blatant factor. We are a slow-starting team. That fact, coupled with our youth, points to a very long and possibly dismal season." Most of the wrestlers sat on their asses, their knees pulled to their chests. Some lounged on their sides. Others lay on their backs. All listened. None liked what the coach was saying.

"I have to be honest boys. That February 9 date for qualifying for the states is looking bleak. But I do have a plan, and it involves everyone in this room sacrificing something – most likely free time and probably some television." Instead of pausing for dramatic purposes, Thomas laid out his idea in succinct fashion, "I've decided to split practices for at least a month. Maybe for the rest of the season."

The plan received no complaints from the wrestlers. With Christmas break coming up, wrestlers with experience would start practice at 8 a.m. and go for two and a half hours. At 10:30, freshmen and first-year wrestlers would go through two hours of moves, not as much conditioning. Any varsity member wishing to stay was invited and welcomed.

After the break, when school resumes, the freshmen and first-year wrestlers – "we will refer to this group as j.v." – will report at 3 p.m., roll out the mats and start running at 3:30.

"When I arrive at 3:35, I expect the j.v. squad to be warmed up and ready to go live. We'll run through moves and some conditioning until 5 p.m. Then it's the varsity's turn from 5 until a bit after 7."

Thomas expected the varsity members to go to the library and study during the early practice. "Don't think I'm stupid. I know you'll want to fuck around, but if you do and you get caught, I'm just going to tell Mr. Broughton that you had orders to use this time as study hall. If I have to, I'll require each and every one of you to sign in and out of the library."

For 20 minutes, Thomas talked and fielded questions and excuses, but in the end, his plan was set. Double sessions during Christmas break from 8 to 12:30 and after school starting in January from 3 to 7:15. Captains would serve as coaches for the j.v. practice.

"If there are any questions or complaints from your parents," Thomas said, knowing there would be, "just have them call me at home."

No sooner had Thomas stepped in the door that evening, the phone rang.

238

It was Diedre Douglass, nicknamed "DD" by her husband and "BB" by Thomas. This phone call would mark the fifth time Diedre called for her son Eric, a freshman 119 pounder, who got the start at Saturday's tournament by being the only wrestler near that weight.

"Well, Mrs. Douglass. . . ."

"Please call me 'DD' or Diedre. You always call me Mrs. and that makes me feel so old."

But you are – is what Thomas wanted to say but discretion prevailed once again. Diedre "DD" Douglass was a nice-enough woman, but it would not be advisable to turn one's back because she was liable to speak to anyone about anything. Thomas told Old Man Jack it was like playing the children's game Red Light, Green Light. That is how Thomas felt with DD. Turn your back and the gossip flows. In her presence, she's nothing but shits and grins. So Thomas spent as much time as humanly possible on the phone, explaining his philosophy and the reasoning behind his decisions. She would interrupt, interject and intercede with not much success other than constructive rambling. Her newest concern was that Eric was varsity, yet he was practicing with the junior varsity.

"Actually, it's the freshman team, but I opted to call them junior varsity for morale purposes," Thomas said bluntly, trying to remind Mrs. Douglass that her son was a freshman.

"But doesn't he need to learn varsity moves?"

"There is no such thing as varsity moves, Diedre. All the moves are the same, it's just that varsity has practiced more. The members are more seasoned and a little tougher."

"Well, how is he going to get tough wrestling with the freshmen?"

"If Eric continues to wrestle with the upperclassmen, he won't learn anything but how to get abused. If he wrestles with the freshmen and the rest of the first-year wrestlers, then he'll gain enough experience and confidence to move up eventually. Right now, St. Agnes needs a 119 pounder and Eric is the only person on the team in that weight class. Now, if either Eric, you or me decide that he shouldn't wrestle varsity, then he doesn't. The question for you is, how do you feel about your son wrestling varsity."

"I think it's tremendous. It will look great on his high school transcripts."

"Great," Thomas said, deciding not to allude to the high school transcript remark. "For the meantime, he'll remain in the varsity line-up."

"What about practicing with the varsity?" Some people just don't understand and others could not give a shit. Diedre was one who did not understand. Thomas didn't give a shit.

"I'll tell you what, Mrs. Douglass. I'll rename the early practice varsity and call the late practice junior varsity. Someone's trying to beep in, Mrs. Douglass. Give me a call tomorrow."

Thomas hung up and thought two things. One, it was time for a long talk with Eric Douglass and two, he should perhaps make an appearance at the Cornerstone tomorrow night, avoiding any more phone conversations with DD.

Just as his ass hit the couch, the phone rang again. He contemplated not answering, but relented. It could be Diedre, and she knew Thomas was there. Shit.

It was another mom. Lisa Cauldron. And she called not to complain, but to praise, and to seek some help.

"Are you busy?" Lisa Cauldron was pleasantly polite, always saying hello at the away matches, always with her shy little daughter at her side. "One thing I wanted to check with you was Brien's weight. All summer he kept saying, 'I'm going to gain weight,' and all he gained was six or seven pounds, now he's taken it right back off and I'm concerned about that."

"How is he eating?"

"He never eats breakfast, and the night before the tournament, he skipped dinner, but otherwise he has been sitting down and eating, passing up spaghetti and potatoes."

"That's my fault, Mrs. Cauldron. I usually tell the kids to stay away from sweets and carbohydrates and every day they ask about certain foods. During the season, spaghetti and potatoes always seemed to put on extra weight, so I steered clear of them. But I'm not a nutritionist and it seems with these daily news reports on nutrition and diet, they've proven it isn't an exact science yet."

"Did you miss many meals when you wrestled?"

Yes. "All the time. My mother hated the sport. I remember my first weigh-in junior year. I had to miss six straight meals."

"Why didn't you move up a weight class?"

It was legitimate question and if Thomas could answer it concisely, Lisa Cauldron would not call about her son's weight again. "Well, first of all, Mark Pierce occupied that weight class just above me in high school, although you'd never know by looking at us now. With me wrestling first and Mark behind me, it made our team stronger. It's the same thing with St. Agnes this year – and every other team in the Shore. Tony Kingery is at 152. Mike Ennis, who weighed 152, cut to 145. One guy pushes the other guy down and the team should get stronger.

"In Brien's case, well, it's the same reason why I decided to cut weight in high school instead of competing against Mark Pierce. I could have started in Mark's spot – excuse the candor – but my old high school coach and I talked and decided, one, our lineup would be stronger and, two, I could excel in the postseason individual tournaments. Brien chose 135 because he could be more competitive in the long run and second, we have a freshman 140 pounder who can't make it to 135 and nobody else but Brien can make that weight. Bottom line – he's working harder for the team."

Lisa Cauldron was apologetic for she sensed a bit of defensiveness in Thomas' voice. She claimed ignorance and said that she didn't want to be like some of the other parents who go to the wrestling matches. They seem so fanatical.

"Many parents and family members are," Thomas said. "The son out on the mat is the standard bearer for the family and usually dads are the most vocal on that front. Granted, they don't come right out and say, 'You're a Cauldron, damn it. You'd better win.' But if you listen closely, you can hear them mumble it. And moms – well, moms are moms. Motherly instinct takes precedence over manners, and that is why many sound like lionesses protecting their cubs."

"You have a very interesting way of putting things, Mr. McCloskey. And that's the second reason why I called. I just want to thank you for keeping Brien involved and his mind occupied. Between working and wrestling, it takes up most of the idle time he has, and I appreciate it. You are his role model, and that brings me to the last point."

Thomas snuck in a quick thank you before Lisa Cauldron could begin again, tacking on a slight warning, "You best explain what true role models are like, Mrs. Cauldron."

Anybody that would take personal time to sit down and answer difficult adolescent questions is a terrific role model, and

Lisa Cauldron asked Thomas to continue the frequent chat sessions he has had with Brien.

"On the bus. At practice. After practice. Brien says you'll answer any question he has."

"I must say that not all parents think that way. That's my guess anyway. I'm a commoner, Mrs. Cauldron, and I think like one. Some parents at St. Agnes are a bit more smothering and protective, and probably would not want me to give any sordid advice to their children. I'm just guessing on that point, but that's my gut feeling. But when a junior or a senior approaches me and asks me a serious question, I answer it as best I know how, and I imagine that will get me in trouble some day. Brien trusts my honesty, if not my intelligence, and I tell him to ask the same question of many people and then form his own opinion." Thomas switched to humor, wanting to take the heaviness away from the conversation. "Now, if a freshman or a sophomore asks me a question, I tell them to go ask their mom, then come back in a couple of years."

Lisa Cauldron thanked Thomas again. She told him about Brien's father, and how it was a shame that he had remarried and spent all of his time in North Jersey with his two other children, fruit of his present marriage. "Brien doesn't see his dad much, and I think he's grateful to have you. Thank you."

After Lisa hung up, Thomas unplugged his phone, sat back on the couch and tried to clear his mind. "Not even married and it feels like I have two dozen children."

Thomas desperately hoped that it was a case of things getting worse before they got better.

Just before Christmas, in an uncommon Friday morning match, St. Agnes opened up its dual season for a third consecutive year against Blakemore Preparatory. And for a third consecutive season, Blakemore smoked the Lancers.

"I took a vacation day for this shit," Thomas said in the locker room, following the 49-9 loss. "I thought maybe we were getting better. I thought maybe we could just close the points gap between us and Blakemore each year, so by the turn of the century we could be within 30 fuckin' points." He had more to say, much on the negative side of the ledger. Thomas regretted saying so much after the match but decided that if those thoughts were on his mind, then that is what should be said.

As the Covington match approached, Thomas could sense the pressure. No one said anything to him about the match. No one even mentioned the name Covington, except for Thomas, and the reminder of Mark Pierce jumping ship only added to the tension.

Mike Ennis and Chris Ballinger were the only winners at Blakemore, Ennis wrestling a complete six-minute match against a solid senior, and Ballinger becoming an automatic in the upperweights. But the rest of the squad just looked sloppy. Jeff LeMone simply couldn't make the weight; apparently all those high-profile water diets don't work. LeMone weighed in at 85 pounds. Brien Cauldron looked sluggish. And Tony Kingery was wrestling like he belonged in the World Wrestling Federation, trying all headlocks and muscle moves.

"I'm losing strength," Tony said to Thomas after getting pinned in the second period. "Everything I built up over the summer is gone. All of these guys are stronger than I am, pushing me around the mat." Tony sat on the practice mat behind the team's bench, his head bent in shame. "Is there some way I can get time to go lift during the season?"

Absolutely not. "Lifting and wrestling are polar opposites," Thomas said, trying to think of an analogy. "Do you remember those science magnets? The ones about six inches long? N – for north – was on one end. S – for south – on the other? When an N and an S are put together, they stick. Magnetize. Well that's the same with wrestling and conditioning. They belong to one another. They stick. They magnetize." Thomas paused to let Tony fully understand the meaning. "But when you attempt to put an N with an N or two S's together, their magnetic fields won't allow it. They repel one another. And that's lifting and wrestling. Weightlifting thickens the muscles, makes them more cumbersome and less flexible – exactly opposite what you want to be doing during the season.

"Sure, I admit that some of these guys are stronger than you are, but the style of wrestling you're attempting is playing right into their strengths. These two guys you've wrestled so far are thick-necked, muscle heads. Average wrestlers. But you're making them look good by wrestling their match. The answer is to adjust your style. Use speed when executing moves. Use strength in pinning combinations or countering moves. And always use your intelligence. Okay?"

Sometimes when Thomas conducted a lengthy sermon on behalf of his wrestlers, he was sure they fell asleep for blocks of time. His only hope, that with their selective teen-age hearing, they would pick out the important part. "Okay," he would ask a second time, which meant to each Lancer, 'Look up, look me in the eye and humor me by pretending you understand.'

"Okay," Tony said.

Tony did adjust in the only competition between Christmas and the new year, a Tuesday morning match against Flat River. He wrestled a quick first period, and with a lightening-quick, single-leg takedown, he quickly chopped his opponent's arm into a ball and chain – a painful move where the defensive wrestler has his own arm pulled back between his legs and wrenched against his own crotch. Tony finished the match with the ball and chain, pinning his man in a tilt.

The St. Agnes coach found himself saying good job to Ennis, Kingery and Ballinger and that was it. LeMone fell short, again, at 87 pounds, and Brien Cauldron ran out of gas midway through the third period and was decked for the third time in three matches.

Sensing something was wrong, Thomas began to pry, and not so gingerly either. If he could only get Cauldron and LeMone to come around, then matters could change. With a one-at-a-time attitude, Thomas finished his Q&A with Brien with nothing more than an excuse of being tired because of the weight loss.

"Bullshit, Brien. You know your mother's concerned and that she called me about that, and I have to smooth it over and talk about your eating habits, special diets, calorie counting and all that crap. But you and I both know that six pounds is a bucket of shit in wrestling. You can lose six pounds in one damn practice if you need to, so sell that fuckin' excuse to someone else." His voice was low but intense as he spoke to the junior behind the bench at Flat River. Brien never looked away, keeping eye contact the entire time.

"We both know," Thomas continued, "that you can cut to 130, but Momma Lisa would have a fuckin' aneurysm, so you have a nice easy cakewalk for 135. At the certification when the doctor checks weight and body fat and IQ and all that bullshit, you weighed 141 and got certified to wrestle 130. That was late October. One week into practice, you're at 135. One fuckin' week and you already make weight. Now either you search in your friggin' mind for what the fuck is going on or I send out the blood hounds and go snoopin' for the source of the problem. I will find out. It's either booze or pot or a chick, but any way, I'm gonna find out. I can see it in your eyes. I would just prefer to hear it from you. Now if you'll excuse me, I have to go help your teammate Ennis out. He's wrestling with some intensity."

Three wins and 10 losses at Flat River was not as good as Thomas expected, but he reminded himself as he sat alone up front on the yellow school bus that it was only the third year of the program. Teams like Flat River have a history and depth, which was synonymous to Thomas. Someday, St. Agnes will have its glory and with that glory, Thomas will have satisfaction. Closure. At last.

The team filed off the bus. Eleven members of the junior varsity bunched up in the middle weight classes, wrestling terribly at the beginning of their careers, but wrestling. They carried the team equipment: water jugs, medical kit, team bag with backup gear, scorer's book and paperwork. Following them came the 13 varsity wrestlers. St. Agnes might be 0-2 with a last-place finish in its only December tournament, but it's a different team. Wearing wrestling warm-ups and varsity jackets, gym bags in tow, cropped hair, black eyes and mat burns, the team walked disgustedly in single file through the dimly lit rear parking lot at St. Agnes. Some freshmen walked to a side door to wait for Thomas. They would need to use the pay phone. Others walked to cars and mini vans idling silently, emitting gray clouds of smoke into the damp, salty, wintry air. A couple of juniors had cars and offered rides to anyone heading in their direction.

St. Agnes was starting to look like a team.

One last body emerged from the darkness of the rear of the bus. He slowly walked and stopped as Thomas gathered his jacket and personal belongings.

"Coach," Brien said. "You got a minute?"

Thomas nodded.

"I've been going out on the nights mom works, with some of the guys."

Thomas remained silent. The bus driver sat stoically, listening to jazz toll from the single speaker of a small radio/cassette player propped on the dashboard. The engine hummed with a low, bubbling moan.

"And I've been having a few beers."

"What's a few?"

Brien shrugged.

"Awright then," Thomas altered his questioning, "when you say a few, does that mean you're catching a pretty good buzz?"

Brien nodded.

"You smokin' any dope?"

No!

"Any of your teammates know about this?"

"Ballinger does. He knows one of the guys I hang out with." Brien paused. "And one of the girls, too."

"You getting romantic with this girl?"

Brien shrugged. He wasn't quite sure how to answer to the word romantic. And Thomas knew.

"Are you having sex with her?"

No.

"Okay. We've located the problem to your shitty early season performances and now it's our job to find a solution. I don't want to be brash, so let's sleep on it and come up with a solution at tomorrow's practice." Thomas turned to get off the bus and received a wink from the driver. He stopped, tilted his head toward the driver and told Brien, "This gentleman will tell you. It takes a man to nut up and tell the truth, to admit his mistakes." Thomas walked down the three steps onto the slick sidewalk. "This is between you and me, Brien. I'll talk to Ballinger and let him know the situation. It's best if the team doesn't know you broke team rules, that way they won't try to take advantage of future situations."

As Thomas walked toward the school, the driver gave Brien an encouraging slap on the back. "Listen to your coach, kid. It sounds like he knows what he's talking about."

When the upperclassmen began to arrive at practice on Wednesday morning, Thomas called Chris and Brien to meet with him in the weight room. He left Jeff LeMone in charge of running the wind sprints, knowing that the Napoleonic lightweight would taunt the young wrestlers, raising their ire and eventually their desire. Thomas only hoped it wouldn't lead to bloodshed.

"Well Brien, what do you think?" Thomas started the session off as bluntly as possible as the three took up positions at opposing spots among the barbells and the dumbbells.

246

Brien shrugged. He was good at maintaining eye contact but terrible at communicating verbally. Chris was lost.

"Well then, I've got an idea," the coach said. "Chris, I've asked you in here because evidently you are the only silent witness to the affair, and being one of the team leaders, it's only proper that I include you." Thomas explained Brien's confession, which Chris did not know, and details of the confession which Chris was partially privy to. Then the coach asked if he had comments or questions.

No.

"Alright then, here's my proposal. Brien, you are now the starting 130 pounder. I thought about suspending you, but I didn't for two reasons. First, it isn't fair to this team. If we were someone like Blakemore or Flat River, then I might have opted for suspension, because any number of j.v. kids could jump in and help out. But on this team, any injury or illness or suspension demoralizes us, so you stay put – for the meantime. Second, idle time is the work of the devil, so they say. Suspending you from the team could blow up in my face. You may rebel and do worse things than you've recently done. So you wrestle with a penalty, and that's losing five pounds, for at least the Covington match. You give your mom whatever explanation you want, I leave that up to you, but I would suggest the truth. She's already frazzled about your weight. If you tell her the truth and explain the known effects to mind and body, then she'll understand. I expect that Momma Lisa will be calling me, and although I won't lie, I won't rat you out if she doesn't already know. I don't know if that's right or wrong, but it's my decision, and I'm going to live with it."

When asked if they had any questions, both shook their heads.

"That means Pete Disling can cut his three and a half pounds to 135. He's been getting beat up pretty good at 140, and anytime a freshman gets beat up too badly, it's a sure sign we won't see him as a sophomore. Another freshman will likely start at 140, either Pat Madison or Willie Sanderson. Or Mike Ennis can drop from 145, but I doubt that because he's already lost enough weight.

"So that's where we stand. You guys are big boys now, and I trust this conversation stays in this room. Are we all square?"

Thomas shook Brien's hand and ruffled Chris's hair. "I'll explain to the team our intentions. It'll be good to shuffle things up for Covington."

TWENTY-THREE

It just was not meant to be simple.

The forecast for late Friday night into Saturday morning was snow, and any time that the weatherman called for accumulation, Thomas became concerned. Confusion reigned, especially with parents, when school was canceled. The kids knew the drill, but parents always, without fail, were oblivious.

On ominous days, Leonard Burke would beckon Thomas to the office to give him messages and let him make phone calls from the office. Len would always comment on what a great thing it was to devote time to kids. And anytime he could lend assistance, within reason, the youngest Burke was available, or at least his phone was available.

So with two to four inches forecast by daybreak Saturday morning, Thomas wanted the Lancers' undivided attention as he first planned strategy and then contingency plans for the match and for the weather against Covington. As usual, the Lancers lined up in four groups at the end of the mat, just in front of the soda and candy machines. And as usual, the Lancers would finish off practice with wind sprints, fully suited with sweatshirts, thermals, gloves, knit caps and whatever clothing that would help produce sweat – except for a lightly dressed Jeff LeMone. At each whistle, a group of six or seven would sprint to the second set of pillars, back to the edge. Again to the second set, and back to the beginning. Then they would sprint to where Thomas stood at the third set of pillars, and finish off, back to the machines. That was considered one sprint. A suicide.

They would run and listen to a pep talk. Twenty seconds maximum to complete the full sprint. If one member of the group surpassed the 20-second time limit, the entire group went again, immediately, receiving an additional two seconds to complete the sprint. During this time Thomas would build up and tear down their confidences. Build up more. Tear down less. Build up until they had the fever to compete. Build up until they had the fever to win.

At the beginning of the sprints on the cloudy night prior to the Covington match, Thomas laid out the weather plans. If no snow was on the ground, the team was to meet at St. Agnes at 9 a.m. for the 10:30 j.v. match, 11:30 varsity match. Any accumulation from a dusting to one inch, either meet at St. Agnes or go straight to Covington, whichever is easier for the parents. More than one inch, stay home and wait for a phone call.

"Those of you who are close to or on weight, do not eat. Repeat – Do Not Eat Until You Hear From Me. Clear?" The team responded with a lackluster "clear." Louder, Thomas asked "Clear?" The entire team screamed a sarcastic "CLEAR," which brought a smile to Thomas' face.

Good. "Now line up and let's get ready to kick some Covington butt."

Six lightweights stepped to the line, including Jeff LeMone. "You're the key tomorrow," Thomas said to Jeff. "Covington's lightweights are uncharacteristically weak. That's why they're 0-2. They're going to be gunning for us early, so if you make weight, we'll be up six points guaranteed." Jeff stood poised. Nodding, knowing his role. Ready to sprint to show his worth.

"That's why I want you to come up here and sit down," Thomas said, pointing to the mat cabinets. "No more weight loss for you today." Jeff raised his hands in triumph, listening to his teammates boo in opposition.

"Now for the rest of you." Thomas blew the whistle and the team responded like fire spat from the belly of a dragon.

The sight of snow, yet untouched by man's machinery, was beautiful. The boughs of the maples, oaks, firs and sycamores succumbed slightly to the weight of the powder. In the yard, the billowy blanket remained virtually untouched, only the paw prints of a poor cat or a wayward rabbit disturbing the serenity of the surface. Snowflakes settling on roofs during the early morning were shifted about by sleepy gusts, the flakes swirling downward, coming to a resting place on a small tree, or perhaps a bush, only to be asked once again to pick up and settle, on the ground, adding to the weatherman's accumulation. Serving its purpose. Slowing down life.

Three inches in all by the time Thomas arose at 6:30. He walked into the kitchen, turned on the kettle, then the radio. The local station should confirm that the "St. Agnes wrestling match against Covington has been postponed." Every fifteen minutes the morning jockey would alphabetically run down any closings or cancellations. Most would be high school events scheduled for the morning. Some would be senior citizen events. Thomas figured he would only have to wait until the C's for assurance.

Precisely 45 minutes past six o'clock, the cancellations and postponements continued. Excluded were evening games and matches that were "expected to be held as scheduled." The A's finished. The B's finished. Catholic Youth Organization. Citizens for Political Correctness. Connor Center. Dansville Bowling League.

Thomas still was not awake, but he was sure that he was paying attention. Maybe it will be listed in the S's for St. Agnes. Otherwise he would just have to wait until the top of the hour for the next list of cancellations. There were many saints when S came around, but not the one he was looking for.

Another cup of instant coffee. He hated instant, but he had to be near the phone, just in case, so there was no 7-Eleven coffee in the immediate future. But the seven o'clock cancellations came and went without any Covington or St. Agnes reference.

Now Thomas was awake. And suspicious. Soon he would be livid.

"Mark?" he asked into the phone.

Yes.

"Tell me that you just haven't gotten around to calling the radio station yet."

"Oh, hey, Tommy," Mark said, either oblivious or a good actor at not having a conscience. "The roads are pretty clear. I told the athletic director that by weigh-ins, the sun would be out and the blacktop would be showing. He saw no problem with the kids getting there."

"So in other words, you two share the same fuckin' brain." Thomas tried to keep calm but was having a difficult time.

"What." The word wasn't inquisitive. Thomas could tell Mark was playing dumb by the way he said it.

"What," Thomas repeated, using the same inflection. "What about the St. Agnes kids who live all over two damn counties, Mark. You know damn well three fuckin' inches of snow

251

is too much to ask them to drive around in. It's too fuckin' dangerous."

"Tommy, the plows will have the roads cleared."

"You're a fuckin' putz. Fine. If the only way you see fit to win a fuckin' match is by deceit, then good. I'll be at Covington by weigh-ins. We'll wrestle with whatever we got." Thomas slammed down the receiver. If Mark were within arms' length, Thomas would have laid him out at that moment.

Immediately, Thomas began calling, explaining the situation to each parent, explaining Mark's decision and offering personal apologies to the parents. "I don't expect for anybody to come, but I'm showing up and I will offer a team forfeit under protest," is the statement with which he finished each of his 24 phone calls.

Thomas got showered and dressed, and drove the pick-up to 7-Eleven for an ungratifying cup of coffee. The roads were slick and rather dangerous, any vehicles other than plows and sanders out on the road were driving no faster than 20 miles an hour. He arrived at Covington High School at 8:45 and sat in the parking lot, reading the paper, not knowing whether to hope for the St. Agnes wrestlers' appearance.

At nine o'clock, Jeff LeMone and his father showed up and Thomas asked him if it was all right if they waited 15 minutes outside in their car. "I want to walk in as a team," he said. "And if that means me and Jeff, so be it."

"Do you think any others will show?" Mr. LeMone asked.

"Doubtful, but I wouldn't be disappointed at all."

By 9:15, Mike Masterelli arrived with his mom. "Now we got 'em worried," Thomas said to Mike, generating a grateful smile from the squirrely sophomore. Soon after, Pete McKane showed up with his neighbor, freshman Alan McCall, who wrestled behind another freshman on the j.v. squad at 160. Pete Disling showed up with his parents as Thomas got prepared to go inside for weigh-ins. Three starters: LeMone, McKane and Masterelli; one backup: Disling, who was to start his first varsity match at 140 against Covington; and one freshman not even on the j.v. squad.

A blue '84 Mustang came fishtailing into the parking lot, and slowed when the driver saw the coach standing with five wrestlers and a handful of parents. The Ford, suddenly cautious, parked next to the coach's pick-up truck, and out piled Tony Kingery, Brien Cauldron and the driver, Chris Ballinger.

"Sorry about the entrance, Coach. We thought we were late."

"Don't apologize to me. Apologize to these parents. And assure them that you didn't drive like that the entire way from Evandale."

Sorry. Sorry. Sorry. And the three took their places at the end of the abridged St. Agnes squad.

Thomas remained silent during the entire weigh-in process, simply nodding to each of the eight Lancers when it was his turn to step on the scale. At the end of the session, Mark Pierce tried to make idle conversation and the ancient athletic director, Harold Spiers, asked how Thomas liked the coaching profession.

"It's rewarding," Thomas said, shaking Spiers' hand, and he left the boys' locker room.

The scenario was bleak. Five forfeits amounted to 30 points, which meant that St. Agnes would have to get 39 of the possible remaining 48 points for a tie. But of the eight St. Agnes wrestlers, two were freshmen and one was Masterelli. Even if their five teammates could pin for a total of 30 points, it would take a minor miracle for St. Agnes to win.

As the team quietly prepared itself in the cold, pea-green, girls' locker room, Thomas sat on the floor mapping out strategies. With five gaping holes in the lineup, it gave him some latitude to move people around. Any wrestler can move up one weight class from his official match-day weigh-in. If Thomas so desired, he could bump up wrestlers, seeking out weak spots in the Covington lineup, maximizing team scoring.

"It really hasn't come into play," he told the team, "since we haven't had close match-ups with opposing teams the last two years. But when the captains go out for the coin flip prior to every match, it isn't just to shake hands with the ref and opposing captains."

The captains who win the coin flip were to choose odd, even or defer the choice to their opponents. Choosing odd meant the team was responsible for sending its wrestler onto the mat first during the odd-numbered matches. Choosing even meant responsibility during even matches. Once a wrestler stepped onto the mat, he is a representative for that weight class. If he is pulled back thereafter, it is considered a forfeit and his eligibility is expired for that dual match.

At the conclusion of his explanation, with blank looks on many of the younger faces, Thomas added, "So just be ready to wrestle at any weight today." Then Mike Ennis and Anil Nazif walked into the locker room.

"Sorry Coach," Ennis said. "My dad had a hard time getting the car out of the driveway, and then some of the roads weren't plowed on the way to Anil's house."

"I appreciate the effort." Thomas shook the wrestlers' hands and offered apologies for Covington. "My alma mater seems to have turned to chicanery, so I doubt that you'll be able to weigh in."

Weigh-ins started at 9:30 and the official rules allow 45 minutes for wrestlers to make weight. Mike and Anil walked into the locker room at 10:45, 15 minutes after the scheduled start of the canceled j.v. match.

Thomas walked over to the Covington locker room, where the referee was getting dressed, talking to Mark. Thomas stated his case briefly. The ref looked at Mark, "It's up to you Coach." If Mark displayed flexibility, the ref would also have been flexible.

"The weigh-in period's been over for 30 minutes," Mark said. "How do I know these kids haven't been using the extra time to make weight?"

"Because one of them is a heavyweight. You can at least let him weigh in."

"And then let more wrestlers weigh in as they show up?"

The ref said nothing. According to the rule, Mark was right. Ethically, he was wrong. The only reason why Covington had a ref for this match was because he lived four blocks west of town.

"Well, it was worth a try fellas." And for a second time, Thomas left without shaking hands with Mark.

Back in the girls' locker room, Thomas sat against the wall, reading the newspaper to the Lancers, waiting for the last half hour to elapse before the start of the varsity match. Thomas had already explained the situation to the St. Agnes parents and had already calmly spoken to each individual as to their responsibilities out on the mat. Not wanting to waste any of the wrestlers' nervous energy, Thomas was going over pieces of current events, flooring questions and answers, and cracking jokes. Now he was on to horoscopes.

"Alright. Who's a Libra?"

Alan McCall raised his hand.

"Good news, Alan. It says here that if you are starting your first varsity match, expect much excitement. You will raise your arms in triumph. A five-star day." Thomas looked up and smiled at Alan. "Hey. This is a good thing."

A knock at the door and Mark Pierce poked his head in. "Tommy, you got a second?"

Sure. C'mon in. "You're a Gemini, aren't you?"

Puzzled, Mark confirmed that he was born on June 4.

"Mmmm. Bad news. Bad news. A one-star day. It says to watch where you tread today. It's possible you could get lanced. I think that's double entendre for the sign of the twin."

Mark didn't understand the reference, but didn't know whether to inquire about the statement or to state his purpose for being in the girls' locker room. "Uh, Mr. Spiers was wondering if we could get started."

"A choice." Thomas had an opportunity to teach more than wrestling to his team, and afterwards he would tell them that the sport helped him stand up tall in deciding between good and bad. "A choice of saying, 'No, get the hell out of our locker room. You expect us to do you a favor after you have not shown one ounce of flexibility since daybreak.' Or 'Sure, we'll go out there because it's the right thing to do. Despite the fact that you won't let us wrestle with all of our available resources, we'll go out there, because it could snow again. And the roads could be dangerous. Again. And maybe we should have started 30 minutes before this moment in time.' "

Thomas turned his head back toward the team, flashed a smirk and a wink and said, "Sure, we'll go out. And we'll wrestle our asses off. But no matter what the score is at the end of the match, we know we've already won. Now if you'll excuse us, I'm gonna spit some fire into the air."

After Mark left, Thomas sent the Lancers out to the Covington mat to stretch quietly before bringing them back into the girls' locker room. While Covington warmed up in front of a sparse crowd, eight St. Agnes Lancers were behind closed doors in a confined space, doing sets of 15 push-ups, sit-ups and jumping jacks.

"It's a cold, dreary day. The gym is cold. The crowd is cold. Covington will be cold. Break a good sweat now, and upperweights, be sure to keep it going throughout the match. We have eight matches, and although I don't expect to make up those 30 points in forfeits, I expect to sweep the eight matches."

Thomas knew it was a lot to ask for. Before every match he asked for too much. "Set that bar high," he would say. "Go for the brass ring." Or "It's our window of opportunity." It took the underclassmen some time to figure out what the hell he was talking about.

That quiet Saturday morning snow crowd sounded like a fanatical mob going into the last two weight classes. Thomas and the Lancers put themselves into position to tie or win the match at 189 and heavyweight. Trailing 36-27, Thomas decided to forfeit 171. Covington had the responsibility of sending out the wrestler on odd matches, and was forced to send out Kelly Thompson, a sound 171 pounder.

That allowed Thomas to bump Masterelli to 189, against a weak and pitiful freshman wrestler and to bump Chris Ballinger to heavyweight, where Thomas was sure he would pick up six points. Everything hinged on Masterelli, who had never made it past the first period in his life.

With all the forfeits and quick pins, it didn't take long for the dual match to reach 189 pounds. Wrestling at 89 pounds and 13 pounds less than the Covington junior, Jeff LeMone surprised Thomas with his quickness and selection of moves. With his hands bouncing around like seismometer needles during an earthquake, LeMone hypnotized Matt Halsey. A takedown and a half nelson put Halsey on his back, but Jeff didn't like his own tentative balance, so he released and let a stunned Halsey back to his feet. Before he knew what hit him, Halsey was in a headlock, on his back and pinned in 43 seconds.

Pete McKane followed with a fireman's carry from his feet, straight into a body press. Pin – 36 seconds. Two forfeits at 119 and 125 tied the score at 12.

Brien Cauldron showed some signs of fatigue from cutting the extra five pounds. Thomas was satisfied with his 6-3 lead at the end of the first period, but sensed a great deal of momentum heading in the Lancers' direction. Wrestlers are required to remain in the middle of the mat between periods and during timeouts, only allowed to come to the side during injury timeouts. So

256

pantomiming moves without the other team's detection was an art form. Thomas pointed to his own head and then popped his right hip into the air. Brien understood. He chose the neutral position for the second period.

To the rest of the bench, Thomas explained, "These guys haven't gone over headlocks much this season. Now if you go out there head hunting, they'll get the idea and start countering. So wait awhile and if the time is right, I'll let you know."

Fifteen seconds into the second period, Cauldron had his guy tight on his back, pulling tight on an arm and the head, seeking submission. He got it, and St. Agnes led 18-12.

Covington received a forfeit at 135 and sent out junior 140-pounder Todd Machinicho, a district champ two years straight, to face freshman Pete Disling.

"Give 'em the forfeit," Thomas said to the ref, his hand on Pete's shoulder. Covington led 24-18. Mark Pierce was all smiles as he apparently thought he was sending out his freshman to accept a forfeit at 145.

"Go get him, Pete," Thomas whispered in his ear. "This one's going to put you on the map."

Covington's John Ferguson was shocked. He wasn't warmed up. He had no headgear with him. He simply wasn't prepared.

Mark called for a conference with the ref at the scorer's table. Thomas told Pete to stay warm, keep moving and stretching, 'jog in place if you have to.' John Ferguson started to walk off the mat to quickly warm up with teammate Todd Machinicho.

Thomas pointed to the mat and said to the ref. "He's gotta stay on the mat." The ref agreed and instructed both wrestlers to remain in the inner circle.

"Disling weighed in at 140," Mark said.

"Yeah. So." Thomas felt his was a strong-enough argument.

"So he can't wrestle at 145."

"Check your rule book." Thomas walked away.

The referee stayed behind to explain that each wrestler was eligible to wrestle at the weight class in which he weighed in as well as one weight class above. The minimum weight for 103 was 88 pounds, which Mark also did not know. And the minimum weight for heavyweight was 188. Mark wasn't aware of that either.

The coup helped Disling build up an early lead as he held on for a 7-3 decision, giving St. Agnes three points and a 24-21 deficit with Tony Kingery on deck.

"Double leg takedown. Let him up. Double leg takedown. Let him up. Arm-tie up, head lock. Come shake my hand." Those were the instructions in entirety to Tony.

One minute, eight seconds later, St. Agnes led 27-24.

There was not much to do with Alan McCall, except give him words of encouragement, send him out and let him be a part of this event. He returned in 27 seconds, apologetic. Covington recaptured the lead 30-27.

If Mark had weighed in his j.v. wrestlers, he could have countered some of the moves in the chess match Thomas was conducting. But Mark used only 13 wrestlers, and when St. Agnes forfeited 171 in order to send Masterelli out against Mike Handley, Mark became nervous. The Covington coach went to the scorer's table and checked Chris Ballinger's weight. One-eighty nine. He qualified for heavyweight.

The score was 36-27 in Covington's favor.

The battle at 189 was a one of attrition. Mistakes reigned. Masterelli was on his back twice in the first period; the second time he was saved by an illegal headlock. Handley led 7-2.

"Just keep moving. Keep standing. Sitting. Moving. The more you move, the more mistakes he'll make." Thomas spoke in an overly subdued manner, almost a whisper, as he looked into the crowd of 60 people, mainly parents, standing and screaming as loudly as any crowd he had heard in the last two years.

Period two of the battle of the Mikeys started with the Lancers' Mike in the down position; he was quickly awarded a point for Handley locking his hands when not in a pinning combination. 7-3. Twenty-seconds later he did it again, a third technical violation worth two points. 7-5. Handley rolled Masterelli to his back with a weak half nelson with 15 seconds remaining in the period. Thomas thought Masterelli looked decked, but the ref seemed to be having a good time and perhaps neglected to call the pin because of the Covington's coach earlier display – or lack thereof – of sportsmanship in the locker room.

At the end of two, Handley led 10-5.

"You win, we win." Thomas was furiously becoming more animated as he said this four times to Masterelli. It was all he could think of telling the sophomore. Anything else would confuse him.

At the beginning of the period, Masterelli illegally locked his hands, giving a point back to Handley. 11-5. But for the next 40 seconds, Handley locked his arms in place and became a boulder. Within a 10-second span, with Handley making no attempt to wrestle, the ref signaled a warning for stalling, followed by a stalling call. A fourth technical violation, good for another two points. 11-7.

Thomas knew there was no way for Masterelli to turn Handley to his back and then keep him there long enough for a pin. Since he recently had spent less time at the pubs and more time home reading material like the High School Federation Wrestling Rule Book, Thomas knew St. Agnes had one shot. It was not the proper thing to do, but in the locker room after the match, he told the team, "Sometimes you gotta do the things you gotta do."

Handley started flailing his arms, making it look as if he was busting his ass to get off the bottom. He made no progress, but it was a good enough acting job to keep the referee from calling another stalling call. "Let him up." Masterelli didn't hear Thomas. Thomas put his fingers in his mouth and let out his patented shrilled whistle. The Lancers knew what that meant.

Masterelli looked over. "Let him up." He didn't understand. "For Chrissakes, just let him up." Masterelli let him up with 45 seconds left. 12-7. Within five seconds, Handley barreled into Masterelli with a double leg tackle and had Masterelli in a body press a foot in bounds.

"Get out of bounds." The entire St. Agnes team screamed. And Masterelli bridged and slithered his way out of bounds. Two points for a takedown. Three points for back points. One point for purposely leaving the mat. 18-7.

Masterelli looked at Thomas. He couldn't understand. Just moments ago, he was on top, in control, wrestling better than he ever had. Now he was losing by 11 with 26 seconds left.

Except for going to his back and giving the coach a near coronary, everything was in place. "Trust me, Mike," Thomas said, his hands held outward, reassuring both the confused sophomore and the rookie head coach. "Trust me. Sit out and turn. Sit out and turn. Sit out and turn. If he locks his hands, you win."

Thomas said the last part loud enough for only Masterelli and the ref to hear.

Masterelli sat out, and Handley barely touched his hands together, but the ref gave the Covington wrestler the benefit of the doubt.

"Again!"

Masterelli sat out again, and again Handley's hands touched together on top of his opponent's stomach.

"Locking hands!" Thomas yelled for all to hear. The ref agreed and held his clenched hands above his head indicating the violation. He blew the whistle with 12 seconds left. He walked over to the scorer's table and checked the home statistical book.

Back in the middle of the mat, he instructed the wrestlers to stand up and shake hands. Then he raised Mike Masterelli's hand in triumph.

Mark Pierce went screaming and skipping and raving to the scorer's table. "Why? Why? Why?"

Five technical violations. The first two – illegal head lock and locking hands – one point a piece. The next two – stalling and locking hands – two points apiece. The fifth – locking hands – disqualification. St. Agnes received six points and trailed 36-33.

While the argument continued at the scorer's table, Thomas instructed Chris Ballinger to take his time and be smart. "We don't need a pin, so don't get anxious. A major decision will do. The only thing you got to worry about is this kid using his weight against you. He's about the same size as Anil but a little stronger. Be aware of that and watch your balance. Six strong minutes and we win. Now go out there, put your foot on the line and show everybody in this fuckin' place that we mean business."

Chris stood alone for two minutes while the ref convinced Mark the ruling was correct. Covington's 230-pound heavyweight strutted onto the mat, shaking hands and looking down at the St. Agnes 189 pounder.

The match was anti-climactic. Chris took the big bastard down with a double leg takedown and put him to his back with a half nelson. The match was over in 17 seconds.

With only eight wrestlers, St. Agnes defeated Covington, 39-36.

The teams and coaches shook hands. Thomas and Mark never uttered a word to each other.

TWENTY-FOUR

Momma always said she should've raised chickens.

Alan McCall, the only St. Agnes wrestler who lost on the mat at Covington, was half of a tandem that started a string of bad news for Thomas and the Lancer wrestling program. It was just not meant to be simple.

For the Monday and Tuesday practices following the Covington match, Alan was hard to corral. He was constantly joking around, talking and disrupting his iron-man groups. Because of the excitement in the practice room on Monday, Thomas let the behavior slide.

By Tuesday, Thomas had had enough. At mid-practice, he informed the entire j.v. squad that they were going to run sprints until every one of them was on the brink of puking. And Alan would sit on the side and watch. They ran until some heads hung and curses rained in Alan's direction, which was good enough for Thomas for the time being. If Alan continued the immature behavior, he would be excused from practice.

For the remainder of the j.v. practice, Alan pouted and refused to work hard, yet Thomas would let the behavior go unnoticed. It was better than disrupting the practice, and Alan had enough mental punishment for one day and more than likely would receive plenty of physical punishment from teammates in the ensuing practices.

But Alan had a spiteful streak, and while he pouted and moped around, in his mind he vowed to get even with his coach.

On Wednesday, the team was to assemble in the St. Agnes cafeteria at 4:30 for a 4:45 departure to North Winfield. Weigh-ins were at 5:30, junior varsity started at 6:15 with varsity kicking off immediately after – which would be approximately 7 o'clock.

Matches that were scheduled for Wednesday night gave Thomas just enough time to head home, grab a quick shower, find some clean clothes, gather the St. Agnes back-up gear and paperwork and drive back to the school. Some students did the same – went home and came back to St. Agnes. Others went downtown to the deli to purchase dinner. And others sat in the library studying, or stayed in the gym watching one of the basketball practices.

Alan McCall did none of these. At first, he sat in the cafeteria, waiting for most of his teammates to disperse. Once gone, he recruited fellow freshman Kurt Harris, a rotund 5-foot-1, 145 pounder, to wander around the school with him. "Let's see if any classrooms were left open," he told Kurt. "Maybe we can find some tests or something."

Alan tested lockers and doorways and chided Kurt to do the same. "Aw – no one's gonna be up here now," Alan said reassuringly. "And if someone does come, we'll just tell them we needed something from our lockers."

No doors were unlocked and no lockers accessible, except for one. But Alan had already known this. He had roamed the empty hallways of St. Agnes before, and never saw anyone. That's when he came up with his idea – alone, walking, forever scheming. And that Wednesday would be a perfect day to avenge the humiliation he received in practice after helping his coach and his team defeat Covington.

When Thomas arrived a few minutes before 4:30, cop cars and fire trucks had St. Agnes surrounded. He grabbed his gear and walked past a lieutenant in the fire department. "Wrestling coach," Thomas stated. "Is everything alright?"

"Dunno. Probably, though. Seems like the fire alarm was activated someplace on the second floor. Probably just a prank."

Thomas thought nothing more of the matter. His team was seated in the cafeteria, bundled up and waiting for the bus. Brien Cauldron had his varsity coat on, wearing gloves and a Washington Redskins knit cap, doing jumping jacks and chewing gum. Mike Masterelli was next to him, dressed the same, acting the same.

"I'm a pound over," Brien said.

"I'm a quarter," Mike said.

Thomas was going to tell Mike to quit exercising, that spitting into a cup would be good enough by the time the 171 pounders had to weigh in. But then the coach thought better of it. Masterelli needed all the exercising and warming up he could get.

All right, let's go. The team headed for the front of school where the fire trucks were leaving and the bus was arriving. "We're missing McCall," Jeff LeMone said.

"Where is he?"

"Up in the gym, we thinks."

"Go fetch him, would ya, Jeff? We'll meet you on the bus." As Jeff ran through the cafeteria to the rear stairwell, Thomas asked him his weight.

"Eighty-nine." The echo lingered as did the coach's smile.

Everything was going like clockwork at North Winfield. Everyone made weight the first time on the scale. The junior varsity nibbled on some food and got suited up. And nobody forgot shoes or uniforms or headgear. Just as Thomas gathered the j.v. in the locker room for a pre-match pep talk, a knock came at the door. It was Terry Broughton with an Evandale police officer.

"I was wondering if you could get all your wrestlers in here for a few minutes," Mr. Broughton said to Thomas.

The head coach wanted to object, but he saw the seriousness of the situation. He sent for the varsity members and turned the floor over to the athletic director.

"We had an incident at the high school this afternoon in which one of the fire alarm levers up in the hallway of the science department was pulled and activated. But more than that, a fire was set in a student locker. Only three lockers were damaged, thank goodness. Obviously, this is a serious offense and the police and school officials are quite determined to get to the bottom of this. As quickly as possible. Sergeant Wreggleman is prepared to interview each one of you, but I asked him to first allow anyone with any information to step forward. In this way, any punishment could be less severe. So if any of you fellows have knowledge of this incident, this would be the best time to share your thoughts." Mr. Broughton waited a few moments with no movement. "Good enough. The sergeant has agreed to wait until after the j.v. matches have concluded to interview those members, and during the j.v. matches he will conduct interviews with the varsity."

Any questions.

Mr. Broughton and Sgt. Wreggleman left without any objections from the wrestlers or their coach. No one moved. Nobody spoke.

Finally, Thomas told his team that he hoped nobody on this team perpetrated this offense. "If someone did, you'd better hope the good sergeant gets a hold of you first."

The interviews were a bit nerve-racking for most of the varsity members and posed a serious distraction. At the end of the night, North Winfield had a 47-14 victory.

And Sgt. Wreggleman had Alan McCall and Kurt Harris as the two firebugs.

The two freshmen were expelled from school the next day.

Kurt Harris wasn't a very good wrestler, but he was a good kid, and Thomas hated to lose anybody. You never know when an uncoordinated freshman could turn into a district champ. And Alan McCall had some talent. Now both were gone and the team's numbers were down to 22 on the active squad.

Every few days, early in practice, Thomas would tell the freshmen, "If you have any friends who want to wrestle, bring them to practice so I can talk to them. You bring 'em. I'll keep 'em." And every day he would announce to the team, "We need more big people. We need depth up top."

So with the daily reminder of the team's need for bodies, in the middle of January, Chris Myers came to the cafeteria to speak with Coach McCloskey. Sophomore. 125 pounds. Christine Myers.

And for the next 10 days, the team was thrown into turmoil, going 1-2 in dual matches, while the school's administration initially got involved, then the diocese, and "damn nearly the Vatican." Thomas spoke at length, trying to paint a vivid picture of the sport, hoping that the aggressive nature would dissuade Christine Myers from pursuing her quest. But she insisted on continuing.

After two days of deliberation, the administration and the diocese agreed to let Christine wrestle, wishing to avoid any possible litigation suits. "Coach McCloskey will handle the situation with utmost professionalism, I assure you." Mr. Broughton's opinion helped sway the school's decision.

Two long phone calls with Christine's mother enlightened Thomas on the matter, but did not resolve the situation. "Her father and I recently divorced," Mrs. Myers reiterated, "and this is her way of getting attention. I can't tell her that she can't wrestle after telling her since she was a child that she was capable of doing anything in this lifetime."

Thomas talked to Old Man Jack, Michelle, Tamantha, Coach Gibbons, Mrs. Jennings, school officials, an old high school chum who practiced real estate law, police officers, clergy and janitors. It was Michelle who gave him the definitive answer. "I've always heard you – since high school – describe a teammate or opponent as a 110 pounder or a 150 pounder. Well, you'll just have to think as this girl as another 125 pounder."

In the three years at St. Agnes, Thomas told Kenneth Lawton and Mark Pierce and any wrestler who joined the team, wrestling should have no cut sheets. Everybody gets to try out. They'll decide when they've had enough. This was no time to be a hypocrite.

Within three days of the second phone call, Christine Myers said she had enough. There was just enough of calculated aloofness from fellow Lancers and just enough razzing from opposing wrestlers from Decker High School to push Christine away from the sport.

Thomas admired her courage, but cursed her timing. Just when practices and procedures were beginning to run smoothly, everything changed. And the 33-26 loss to Decker hurt badly. It was a match that St. Agnes could have won, but instead lost, dropping its record to 2-5, with five matches left until the February 9th qualifying date. Thus, St. Agnes needed to go 4-1.

In the midst of the bad-luck run for St. Agnes, Thomas had the "luxury" of having two heavyweights on the squad at the same time. The trick was trying to squeeze wins out of the 13th weight class.

Anil Nazif was 1-6 after the Decker match. The one win a forfeit. The six losses he was pinned. But despite his inadequacies, he wasn't going anyplace. He told Coach McCloskey that he would wrestle until graduation.

Thomas wished he could get Anil to wrestle more productively, quicker. But the heavyweight was a major project. With most wrestlers, a coach can teach some moves and lead with a leash, slowly pulling them to their destination. With Anil, Thomas was in the pre-move period. The junior never exercised in the off-season, and most of practice time was spent working on basic balance and coordination.

Chuck Garrison was summoned to practice on January 20. "If you don't think you can get ready for the Fairview match, at least stick around and help me with Anil." It was a reasonable enough request for Chuck to have his father sign the permission slip.

Close victories over New Welsh and Ridgemont injected new life into the Lancers. With Central, Fairview and Winfield Heights – a sure loss, a probable win and a toss up – as the last three matches before the cut off, the team was in full click.

A 53-19 loss to Central didn't deter St. Agnes from working harder in practice. "We knew this was going to happen," Thomas reminded the Lancers. "Central's got championship qualities. Wrestling them will only prepare us – toughen us up – for Fairview and Winfield on the Hill."

Chuck Garrison was cleared to wrestle against Fairview, and Thomas thought that the way the teams matched up, Chuck may have to wrestle if the match were tight. But St. Agnes led by 10 points going into heavyweight and the coach decided to let Anil wrestle. "It'll keep you hungry," Thomas told the out-of-condition heavyweight. In reality, the coach knew a Garrison loss at Fairview could be devastating for his psyche.

Anil got pinned in 53 seconds, but St. Agnes won 34-30. The Lancers were 5-6 with one match before the cutoff.

<u>HS Wrestlers Grappling with Herpes Gladiatorium</u>. This was the glaring headline in the *Asbury Park Press* the day before Wednesday night's Winfield Heights match. Things come in threes. That's all Thomas could think about. Things come in threes.

The sport was accustomed to infections such as staph, ringworm and impetigo, and Herpes Gladiatorium had recently surfaced in pockets in wrestling communities around the state, but with the advent of AIDS came a heightened awareness of communicable diseases in all sports. Wrestling was most scrutinized. And Winfield Heights was the first casualty. St. Agnes became the second casualty by proxy.

The Press did not identify the specific wrestlers, but accurately reported that four Winfield Heights varsity wrestlers contracted Herpes Gladiatorium, "also known as herpes simplex Type I, a highly contagious form of viral infection that is most often spread by direct skin-to-skin contact – and even gets its name from its prevalence in wrestling. There is no cure for the virus, and it can recur at any time." The February 9th non-conference match against St. Agnes would be postponed.

Thomas was depressed. He checked with Terry Broughton. The match was definitely off. A team forfeit was out of the question because 24 hours was ample time to notify an opposing school of illness. Herpes Gladiatorium was classified as a disease and Winfield Heights was quarantined. An appeal to the state athletic board was quickly denied. "A match or game cannot be assumed to be an automatic victory."

And so St. Agnes missed qualifying for the Parochial B state championships.

Despite the monumental disappointment, St. Agnes kept rolling, entering the last third of its dual match season and the individual portion that followed – the Districts.

The Lancers lost one match to Carlysle Township down the stretch, but defeated Bishop Leary, St. Peters, Hanstrom and the rescheduling of Winfield Heights, 35-25, finishing the season at an outstanding 9-7. St. Agnes' success did not stop there.

Chris Ballinger captured the first district title at 189 and Brien Cauldron gave the school another medal, placing third and advancing to the Regions at 130. Tony Kingery, Jeff LeMone and Mike Ennis lost in the consolations and placed fourth, but their early-round successes helped St. Agnes to a fifth-place finish in the district.

It was the longest wrestling season Thomas had ever been a part of, and as he sat with Old Man Jack, tossing back beers and whiskey and tossing around stories, he could only dream of what could have been.

Monroe Academy took the team title in District 41, the No. 1 ranking in the state with a 22-0 Group IV championship season and a No. 7 ranking in the nation by *USA Today*. Bobby DeSimeon gained Coach-of-the-Year honors in the state, in the region and in his first year in District 41.

He was named on nine of the 10 ballots as the most outstanding coach in District 41. On the tenth, DeSimeon voted for "the guy from St. Agnes."

TWENTY-FIVE

It was a musty aroma mixed with a pungent fragrance of sweat and the lightly bitter taste of salt air that served as an enticement for a return visit.

Metal plates and dumbbells banging and clanging together created a disturbing symphony to the untrained ears; duct tape liberally used everywhere formed a sort of visual and artistic mosaic; mirrors strategically placed inviting egos and ethos to observe and admire – these all served as return invitations for further indoctrinations.

But it was simply the ultimate rush of lifting and the release of endorphines that kept him there. Tearing apart muscle fiber and letting it regenerate into larger and larger mass. Until massive. Tony Kingery had fallen in love.

While his coach and teammates broke free from wrestling to enjoy the spring, Tony was determined to be stronger than every opponent he would face his junior year. On the last day of the Districts in which he finished out of medal advancement, Tony vowed to his coach that he would be on the victor's stand next year. "I'm going to win the whole damn thing," he said. The next day he was at The Weight Station, paying his $50 student rate for six months and a key.

The Weight Station, located on Ocean Avenue and facing the sea on the north end of Evandale, looked as if it was ready to be razed. It had been a number of businesses in the last 35 years, the last as a one-man auto mechanic shop about 10 years back. About that time, Joe Castilone bought the place for almost nothing and moved all of his personal workout equipment into the shop and charged 10 bucks a month to lift. He kept the place open all day in the summertime, but once Labor Day rolled around, the door was locked and the remaining members who stayed around for the winter received a key and were allowed to lift whenever they wanted.

One wooden door with a padlock, a small four-paned window between it and an overhead garage door comprised the front. A custom wooden sign hung above the door – *The Weight Station* – the only piece of ornamental craft associated with the business. Memorial Day marked the official opening of The Weight Station, Castilone lifting the overhead door so he and his fellow musclemen could view the scenery of the boardwalk and the beach just on the other side of the avenue. The gym would unofficially be opened in April on the nice days, letting the room air out—the only form of advertising Castilone had other than word of mouth.

It was a warm, sunny day in April of his freshman year that Tony Kingery saw a handful of weightlifters diligently working out for the beach season. Tony stood on the boardwalk for almost an hour before he summoned enough nerve to go across and ask questions to the intimidating behemoths.

And so he began to lift for the first time anywhere other than the basement of his house, which consisted of a rusted bench and gold, concrete weights his father retrieved from a neighbor's curbside trash. Everyday after school Tony went to The Weight Station, wanting to gain weight, wishing to be an undefeated wrestler his sophomore season.

By March 1 following what he considered a disappointing season, Tony was back in full swing, lifting six times a week, taking Sundays off. With his own key, he could go to the Station before school, but most often he went right after St. Agnes' final bell.

Normally, he lifted alone in March. The summer was too far off for the older guys to be concentrating on shedding their winter coats. They would not be there until mid-April. Kyle Williams, a 25-year-old bartender, attended the gym sporadically at the tail end of winter, teaching Tony a few pointers. But most often, it was just Tony, lifting alone, thinking about a state championship.

The old mechanic shop was about 18 feet wide and a little more than 45 feet deep. Two heavy bags greeted visitors just inside the door, followed by a bastard combination of dumbbells along the south wall, three flat benches in the middle of the room and two incline benches on the north wall. A cross-over pulley machine, two squat racks and a rowing machine came next. At the back of the room was an assortment of curl bars, preacher seats, old stationary bicycles and a newer set of dumbbells.

Mirrors lined the entire length of the south-side wall from ceiling to floor. Some were newer. Some were scratched. Some stained. All had spots of slung sweat and droplets of spittle decorating various points where lifters would exercise and flex. Joe would only clean the mirrors once a month, twice in the summer.

In all, it was just enough to keep the avid weightlifter happy, but not enough to satisfy the dedicated body builder. A blue-collar type of place, Tony would relay to his coach.

With a regimented schedule that Kyle Williams taught Tony, the sophomore quickly added 15 pounds and was closing in on 170. On Monday, he would work on three exercises for his chest and three for his triceps. On Tuesday, the workout concentrated on biceps and all leg muscle groups. On Wednesday, he combined exercises for shoulders and back. On Thursday, Friday and Saturday, Tony repeated the schedule. On Sunday, he reluctantly rested.

By May 1, Tony's grades slipped a little to Bs and Cs, but at a price he thought was acceptable. He lifted from 3:15 to 5:30 every day and hightailed it downtown three days of the week to work at Carmine's Sub Shop until 9 p.m. On the weekends, he lifted on Saturday morning and worked at the sub shop both days from 12 to 5.

He was a busy kid. Working, lifting and eating his way to 183 pounds by mid May.

"I've stopped gaining weight," he said to Kyle one day. "And it's a bad spot. I'm right in the middle of the 189-pound weight class and that's where Chris Ballinger's wrestled the last two years, and he's been lifting a little, but he's only gained three pounds. The next weight down is 12 pounds away."

Kyle was looking in the mirror at his massive 250 pounds on his 5-foot-11 frame, easily curling 55-pound dumbbells in the standing position. "So. Just keep lifting. Get stronger and beat his ass."

Tony didn't like that choice. "Nah. Chris is a good friend. And he's gonna be a senior – a returning district champ. Even if I could beat him, it wouldn't be good for the team, and I don't think the coach would like it that much."

"Well then, stop building up and start losing weight. How much did you say you had to lose to get down to the next weight?"

Twelve pounds.

"That's a lot of weight. I guarantee you won't be as strong as you want."

Tony finished another set of dumbbell curls. "What about those protein pills? How much can I gain with them? Or maybe those protein shakes."

"Not much," Kyle said through a snicker. "You've been munching away as much as you can on salami, bologna and cheese. Protein pills won't do you squat."

Tony sat on the bench and stared at the poster of Arnold Schwarzenegger on the north wall. "Look at those guys. They're humongous. That's how big I want to be my senior year. How long did it take them?"

Kyle looked demoniacally at Tony through the mirror. "You wanna do it the way Arnold did, huh?"

TWENTY-SIX

Thomas opened his eyes when he heard the phone ring. Sprawled on the bed, he could see the receiver just beyond his arm's length. It rang a second and third time, then a fourth. A fifth. He thought about shifting his body around to better position himself to grab the receiver without moving, when suddenly the phone stopped. Good. And he went back to sleep.

Following St. Agnes' third season, it was two continuous weeks of old ways for Thomas. Trips to Murphy's Law, the SandSkrit and The Cornerstone Pub served as a form of reunion for Thomas. Almost every night, he would call a cab for a ride to a different bar. He wanted to slip in, find a stool at the corner of the bar, have some beer, talk to a familiar bartender and watch any sporting event on television. Inevitably, no matter where he went, an old friend or a drinking partner of recent winters would greet Thomas, asking questions of his disappearance. "What? You get married," was the most popular, followed by, "You been in jail?"

Some of the more informed people, the ones who actually read the newspapers, knew that Thomas had been coaching over at St. Agnes High School. Most often it was the bartenders who welcomed Thomas with free frosted mugs of beer and generally treated him as a celebrity, against adamant wishes. "Thomas McCloskey took a rag-tag bunch of kids from like 1-20 to 15-1, or something like that," said T.J. Oliver, the venerable bartender at the SandSkrit.

Thomas would correct the statistical errors, and soon found himself in detailed conversations about the sport of wrestling with barflies who had no real capacity for short-term memory. Realizing that many listened for only the sake of companionship, Thomas liked being out with the adults, although he did admit to himself that he had, by far, more meaningful conversations with St. Agnes juniors and seniors.

For the last 5 ½ months, Thomas was down to five Marlboro Light cigarettes a day, but as he delved back into his previous lifestyle, he returned to the red pack, and was smoking more than a pack a day during the week, almost two packs a day during the weekend.

Up at 6:30. Throw on a pair of jeans, a couple of shirts, two pairs of socks. Lace up the boots. Grab the wallet, money, keys, sunglasses and cigarettes. A cup of coffee at 7-Eleven. Off to work.

Work. Lunch. Work.

Back to his house. Fall asleep on the couch. Wake up, grab a beer, start the shower and steam up the bathroom. Turn on some Rolling Stones or Beatles – Eagles would have to wait until the summertime – do a quick make-over, call a cab, go to a local tavern.

Drink, sleep and repeat.

Except for Mondays and Tuesdays, this was Thomas' modus operandi. By the time the weekends would roll around, Thomas was in desperate need to let his mind sleep and his body recuperate.

Then the phone rang again.

Some substantial time must have elapsed since the previous interruption, for Thomas felt physically better, more able to move around. He sat on the edge of the bed, rubbed his scalp and answered the phone on the third ring.

"Tammy said you weren't home."

"Tammy who?"

"You went out drinking last night!" Michelle could tell by his tone.

"Ma!?"

"Tommy, that's not funny." Thomas' only response was to moan. "Have you been home the entire time?"

Yes.

"Then you did go out drinking last night. What time did you get in?"

Ma?

Michelle was frustrated and slammed down the phone.

Groggy, Thomas shuffled to the kitchen and turned the stove burner on, filled up the kettle with enough water for a platoon, found the package of Oreos and lounged on the couch. He

273

turned the television to ESPN SportsSunday and waited. He waited for the water to boil and for Michelle to stop simmering.

Five minutes later, the kettle whistled. Ten minutes later, the phone rang.

"Ma?"

"Thomas, that is not even remotely funny."

"Did you go out drinking last night?" Thomas sipped his instant coffee, which finally cooled. "Because if you did, you would think that I was hilarious."

"You've been out partying since the end of the season, haven't you?" Michelle found this to be astonishing. How weak can one person be? Take away a meaningful piece of life, and he reverts right back to drinking.

"Did you ever take a trip anywhere with Todd? To Niagara? To Bermuda? Anywhere?"

Yes. Of course.

"Did you drink some cocktails? Maybe the ones with the umbrellas?"

Yes, but . . . .

"Yes, but nothing. I don't travel anywhere, Michelle. This is my vacation. And I'm still working. I take my vacation days during the season, so I can concentrate on wrestling. Right now, this is my Niagara Falls."

Michelle tacitly accepted the rationalization, if only to move along with the conversation, and repeated that Tammy said that he was not home.

"I heard the phone ring. I just couldn't answer it." Thomas suddenly became curious. Why the hell was Tamantha calling his house on a Sunday morning?

"She also stopped by, but there was no answer," Michelle said.

"I can't hear the front door when I'm in my bedroom," Thomas said quickly, wanting to get to the point. "Why is there so much interest in me this morning?"

"You forgot, haven't you?"

Obviously, but Thomas already pissed off Michelle once and thought it better that he shouldn't do it again with sophomoric sarcasm. "Forgot what, Michelle?" He said it as pleasantly as the hangover allowed him.

"I called you on Thursday night. You were supposed to come with Tammy to the city. I got four tickets to the Rangers' game."

Oh yeah. "I'm sorry Michelle. I didn't write it down."

"And you didn't remember because you'd been out drinking." The fact that she brought up Thomas' recent drinking escapades and the tone of her voice did not sit well with Thomas. He was merely kidding before when he referred to her as 'ma,' but now she really was acting like a mother hen.

"Are you going to drop this temperance movement, Michelle?"

Michelle didn't respond verbally. She hung up the phone.

A few minutes later, Thomas was curious as to how long Michelle would let the phone ring before abandoning the cause. After 43 rings, Thomas decided she had won.

"I'm just upset because Tammy was looking forward to taking the train into the city with you and spending the day with both of us. I'm sorry."

No need to apologize. "Does the offer still stand for the game?"

Yes.

"I'll get in the shower right now." Thomas looked at the clock. Eleven a.m. "I can drive to MetroPark and be in Penn Station by . . ." he tried to calculate a safe time " . . . two."

Okay. "Where do you want to meet?"

"Let's meet under the tote board in Penn Station – right outside Houlahan's. If you two get hungry, grab a snack, but try to hold off on lunch. I want to treat you and Tammy for screwin' up."

Two o'clock?

Two o'clock. Sharp.

And so the three met beneath the tote board in Penn Station at two o'clock, and Tammy chose La Fondue on 55th as her choice for lunch.

They walked up Fifth Avenue and stopped at Saks. Then into Central Park just to look at people. When they passed by the carousel, both sisters pulled Thomas by his arms amidst mild protests. "I don't think going around in circles will be good for my stomach today." But the girls ignored him and for 90 cents apiece, they were on the ride. And for another $2.70, they rode again.

A pretzel for Michelle. Cotton candy for Tammy. A Pepsi and some antacid tablets for Thomas. They sat on park benches just inside Central Park South and along Fifth Avenue, and watched a man in a second-skin silver spacesuit with a painted silver face and hands, standing perfectly motionless on the opposite bench. A hat box sat on the ground to receive any earnings, his arm outstretched, inviting a pigeon.

It had been an overcast day in Manhattan, and with suppertime approaching, and spring not yet invited, the air was cooling quickly. The threesome walked back down Sixth Avenue, ducking into novelty shops along the way. Soon they were at Madison Square Garden, the crowd outside beginning to thicken just before game time.

"Kevin told me to meet him just outside Cosby's – wherever that is," Michelle said. "I told him you'd know where it is," she said to Thomas.

Kevin?

"He's the one who got the tickets."

A date?

"A pseudo date."

Thomas led the way to Cosby's and they met Kevin, a co-worker of Michelle's, who from the very start of the date was acting as if the pair were betrothed. Michelle smiled meekly at Thomas after introducing Kevin.

With Kevin fawning all over Michelle, Thomas held out his arm and requested Tamantha's. "It's only proper to ask if you would be so kind as to let me be your escort for the evening." Tamantha took hold, entwisting both of her arms with his right.

The Rangers lost that evening on the way to winning the Stanley Cup. But Thomas won. He finally realized the tremendous bond he shared with the two sisters, their companionship was rewarding and most welcome to a person such as Thomas. With his renewed vigor in wrestling and with reacquainting himself over the course of the spring and summer with the Jennings girls, the age-old thought of "there's more to life" began to spring into Thomas' head.

Events that sparked his interest, like wrestling, were abundant, he just rarely searched for them. And friendships – true friendships – you just stumble upon. Thomas had Old Man Jack and the Jennings girls. They all kept him happy. Now he had to search for more things to do besides sitting in a warm bar and getting cold.

"Alright, my vacation's over," he announced to Michelle in early April. On that first Sunday in April, Thomas picked up Tamantha and drove into the city, and the three went to the Guggenheim Museum.

Starting a trend, on Saturday mornings that spring, he would drive to Evandale, pick up some sticky buns or coffee rolls and sit down with Mrs. Jennings and talk current events. Tammy was still in school at Chesterton, completing her student teaching for her last semester at Garfield High School, so she was stuck in North Jersey. But when her mother mentioned that Thomas had twice stopped by, she became a wee bit jealous and invited herself to the Saturday morning roundtable.

Once a month and more frequently during the off-season, Thomas and Tammy would travel into the city on a Sunday to meet Michelle. "Culture me," Thomas would announce, and they would take him to a museum or an art festival or a Broadway show. "Teach me what fork to use." And they would stop in at Tennessee Mountain in Soho for some beer and some ribs. No forks necessary.

Other Sundays, the sisters would drag Thomas kicking and screaming to the beach. "You have a garbageman's tan," Tamantha told him. "You need more epidermis consistency." The first time they sat on the beach, Thomas refused to remove his shirt, telling Tamantha that he was proud of his garbageman's tan and insisted on working on the tan lines across his biceps.

Thomas also kept his dates with Old Man Jack, but on those Sundays that he went into the city, he traveled to Red Mike's on Wednesdays.

Saturday afternoons were reserved for wrestling tournaments. According to state rules, Thomas was not allowed to travel with or coach any of the St. Agnes wrestlers during the off-season while school was in session, so he would travel around the state and take notes, saving them for more appropriate and legal times. Tamantha even accompanied Thomas to two of the tournaments. Both Saturdays happened to be gloriously sunny, spring days, or so it appeared that way to Thomas.

Bills. Bills. Bills.
Electric. Mortgage. Phone.

Credit card bills. Cable bills.

One time Thomas received a letter from his brother in California, and at Christmas received cards from a few folks, but for the most part, the U.S. Postal worker trudged through the snow, ducked between the raindrops and got bonked on the head by hail to bring Thomas more corporate bills.

Then one day, a fancy letter arrived, addressed in Old English font to Mr. Thomas Patrick McCloskey. The envelope was firm, like a Christmas card, not flimsy like an "overdue reminder" notice. He opened it up, and it was an invitation to Graduation Ceremonies, at Chesterton State College, on the Chesterton State Grounds, Lake Vernon, New Jersey, on Saturday, May 21, Nineteen-Hundred and Ninety-Four. On the bottom, written in long hand, was a short note – Please find time to attend. It would mean a great deal. Tamantha Jennings.

He wore a tie. And he drove Mrs. Jennings to Lake Vernon in the Ford Taurus. He bought a gift and purposely left it at Mrs. Jennings' house. Thomas was stumped at what to get and thought about calling Michelle for advice, but decided on earrings. He was not sure of which birth stones belonged to which months, and didn't actually know Tamantha's favorite color, but in the end he chose a beautiful pair of ruby earrings with gold jackets. In the card he wrote:

> Dorothy clicked her ruby slippers
> and received her wish
> Maybe these will prove to be as lucky.

> Thomas

In September, when Thomas looked back at the past off-season, it was the most gratifying time of his life.

TWENTY-SEVEN

TEAM MEETING
SEPTEMBER 15
WEIGHT ROOM
3:45
ANYBODY WISHING TO WRESTLE, PLEASE ATTEND

When Thomas parked next to the dumpster in his customary spot at St. Agnes, he was prepared to see the usual suspects in an off-season wrestling meeting. Maybe double digits in attendees with a couple of newcomers, boastful of past accomplishments, armed with savior attitudes. As Thomas walked down the rear ramp and keyed into the back door, he did see LeMone, Cauldron, Kingery and Ballinger standing with a few others in the hallway just around the corner from the weight room.

"Hey Coach," Chris Ballinger said. "I think we'd like to start practice today."

Thomas turned the corner to open up the weight room door and saw that 27 pupils in all were being entertained by a priest, thin and young, who promptly stopped his teachings and introduced himself.

"Father James Patterson," he said. "I just arrived in the parish last month to aid Monsignor Grant. He had surgery in July and the diocese felt that he could use a little help. I'm expected to spend the entire school year, perhaps longer, if matters work out."

Father James was a tall fellow, about six-one, but thin as a rail. "I like to walk on the beach," he said of his thinness, which was partially true, but the weight loss in the last two years was due more to a bout with colitis. "Mr. Broughton asked me if I would have any interest in helping with any of the sports and I said 'Sure – who needs it the worst' and without hesitation, he said, 'Mr. McCloskey.'

"At first I thought that the wrestling team was pitiful and that it was in dire need of divine guidance," Father James put his palms together and looked skyward. "But Mr. Broughton was quick to note that you are an outstanding coach and divinity wasn't the problem. The lack of assistance was. So, if you wish, you can now have a lacking assistant."

The Father's laugh was infectious, and Thomas accepted his offer to help. How could there be refusal?

Thomas' normal ad-lib speeches for off-season meetings would not do for the start of the fourth year. With the tremendous turnout, he set a schedule to open up the weight room every day until the season started.

"Can we lay down the mats?" Father James asked.

Thomas explained the state rule forbidding coaches to practice with team members outside of the designated season. "Well, I am not a wrestling coach – yet," the Father said. "I can talk to Mr. Broughton and see what we can do."

Father James had "his troops" assembled on the mats by the following Tuesday, going through a new set of stretching exercises. It was an easy task to convince Mr. Broughton to let the Father practice with the wrestling team in the fall. "Intramural" and "for the kids" were the only terms Father James needed to use.

While the 20-odd members of the team were practicing a "sort of yoga," Father James spoke to them, very plainly, telling them stories of sports and religion. It is the same thing he had done with the youth in parishes throughout central New Jersey and Central America.

"I'm sort of like the mop-up pitcher when the baseball game gets out of control," he told Thomas in their first private meeting. "If a flock has become wayward, wandering off here and there and becoming mischievous, then I'm called in to tend to it. I'm a one-man Priest Patrol. And between you and me, the St. Agnes congregation has severe problems. Evidently, parishioners are choosing their own psalms and singing whatever and whenever they please during mass. And! – and the altar boys are going around and blowing out all of the candles!" Father James laughed and slapped Thomas hard upon the knee. "Can you believe that?"

In reality, other than knowing five languages and having traveled to four continents, Father James was an extraordinary accountant. For whatever reasons a local church may have become financially deficient, Father James was quietly put into place, never garnering much attention. He would scour over the numbers, suggest policy changes and implement fundraising events. Prior to his appointment to St. Agnes, he had spent six months in Costa Rica and a year in El Salvador. After his stay in Evandale, he had a gut feeling he would be sent to St. Dominic's in Trenton. "But that may just be my colitis acting up." He laughed as he patted his stomach.

It is true that Father James was at St. Agnes to temporarily replace Monsignor Grant, but it was not solely due to the fact that the Monsignor recently had his gall bladder removed. The surgery was just a convenient excuse to bring in the young Father.

At 36 years old, Father James represented something different, perhaps a breath of fresh air. Inspiration. Exuberance. Monsignor Grant simply was from "the old church" – a Father James expression. "The parish needed a new perspective and a good portfolio," he said.

Now in the dungeon cafeteria of the 65-year-old Catholic school in Evandale, Father James Patterson told of worldly stories and filled the boys' heads with adventures and possibilities, literature and legends. Thomas walked in during his rendition of the history of St. Agnes's Eve.

"How many of you young men know the story of St. Agnes's Eve?" Father James stood on one foot and leaned forward, his arms stretched outward like an eagle soaring, his left leg stretched rearward, all three limbs parallel to the ground. The wrestlers mimicked his posture which produced moans, but no answer to his question.

"Then I shall recite *The Eve of St. Agnes* by John Keats – all 42 stanzas. The last young man standing along with me will be excused from the next two exercises, a virabhadrasana and perhaps the setu bandha sarvangasana."

And Father James began, pivoting, ever-balanced on one foot, emphasizing words, imploring with his eyes that his students shall not fall.

> ...At length burst in the argent revelry,
> With plume, tiara, and all rich array,
> Numerous as shadows haunting fairily
> The brain, new stuff'd, in youth, with triumphs gay
> Of old romance. These let us wish away,

And turn, sole-thoughted, to one Lady there,
Whose heart had brooded, all that wintry day,
On love, and wing'd St. Agnes' saintly care,
As she had heard old dames full many times declare.

They told her how, upon St. Agnes' Eve,
Young virgins might have visions of delight,
And soft adorings from their loves receive
Upon the honey'd middle of the night,
If ceremonies due they did aright;
As, supperless to bed they must retire,
And couch supine their beauties, lily white;
Nor look behind, nor sideways, but require
Of heaven with upward eyes for all that they desire.

Full of this whim was thoughtful Madeline:
The music, yearning like a god in pain,
She scarcely heard: her maiden eyes divine,
Fix'd on the floor, saw many a sweeping train
Pass by – she heeded not at all: in vain
Came many a tiptoe, amorous cavalier,
And back retir'd, not cool'd by high disdain;
But she saw not: her heart was otherwhere:
She sigh'd for Agnes' dreams, the sweetest of the year....

Only Father James remained standing upon completion, save Thomas, who stood alongside the mat, the only member of the team truly mesmerized by the tale.

"So some of you lucky fellows may be in someone's dreams this January 20th, the night in which a woman is likely to dream of her future husband." Father James said, then directed a question to Coach Thomas. "Do we have a match that night, Coach?"

"The schedule isn't finalized yet, but I believe the 21st is a Saturday. Let's just hope no one will be dreaming of their opponent on St. Agnes's Eve." Upon that remark, some of the other wrestlers taunted one another, jibing and kidding.

"Oh that won't do at all," Father James laughed infectiously, as he always did.

282

"Father, did you ever dream of a woman on St. Agnes's Eve?" Jeff LeMone asked.

"No. I dreamt of God, and that's why I'm here," Father James said, nodding to Thomas. "Coach Tom has officially opened the weight room for this Tuesday. Mr. LeMone's presence is demanded."

Father James and Thomas McCloskey were the perfect fit for the St. Agnes wrestling program. Thomas was a dark angel, as Father James phrased it – using whatever means necessary to teach good and fight evil. "A tiny bit brash, which is fine. This is fine," Father James answered to Mr. Broughton one day.

And Father James was heaven on earth, always positive, always finding the silver lining.

In their first sit-down meeting with one another, before the mats were officially allowed to be rolled out for the season, the two coaches confessed their weaknesses to one another and quickly highlighted their strengths.

"I have a habit of cursing a lot in practice, once the doors are shut, obviously a lack of a stronger vocabulary," Thomas explained to the Father. "But actually, the language has abated in the last year, probably because the program has reached a spot where the students and I understand one another."

"And why do you think you have a habit of cursing?" Father James most definitely sounded like a member of the clergy. Thomas felt like he was back in Sunday school.

"You sound like an ex-girlfriend. Asking me a question in a certain tone and in that certain way to get me to analyze myself."

"Oh, is she a priest, too?" The Father laughed.

"She's a psychologist."

"Same thing."

Father James never coached wrestling in any capacity but was familiar with the sport. His specialty was conditioning and nutrition, which would prove highly beneficial, especially with the younger students.

With as competent a wrestling staff as could be assembled at St. Agnes, Thomas decided to combine practice once again, instead of running them back to back, the varsity previously going well past suppertime. Splitting the sessions into thirds, Father James could condition the upperclassmen while Thomas taught moves and strategy to the freshmen. Then the two groups would switch. And the last third of practice would be live wrestling with both groups.

"We can run practice like this until after Christmas break, then we can combine the squads. You can run them through conditioning drills while I take a nap. Then I'll take care of wrestling while you take a nap."

"Priests don't nap. We must keep one eye open at all times, especially with these wrestling types," Father James laughed infectiously.

In the interim, while the longing for the start of wrestling season was stronger in Thomas than it ever had been, he sat in the weight room, teaching technique and receiving daily reports on the Monday, Wednesday and Friday conditioning and Tuesday/Thursday wrestling with Father James.

The fall wrestling was a free-for-all. Once in a while, some serious matches or challenges would be accepted and performed, but mostly the kids taught Father James moves and horsed around with him. The participants on Tuesdays and Thursdays were mainly freshmen and sophomores, although the upperclassman such as Cauldron and Ballinger and Kingery would show up to please the coaches. LeMone was there every day.

The other three weekdays, weather permitting, were spent outside with Father James. "Bring some jackets, because the weather's getting cold and the wind at the beach will be blustery." Every day that he could, Father James brought more than 20 students to the beach. There they played touch football and had relay races. Beach volleyball. Tag. Rugby. Dog pile on the rabbit.

By the time the season rolled around, the wrestlers were conditioned, loose and hungry.

Millersburg, October 15

"Jesus Christ, Willie J. You're telling me that you're going to take 10 minutes to find a front-end loader, wait for the fuckin' air pressure to build up and come back here to move. . . ." Thomas counted ". . . . seven concrete parking slabs. Shit, I hope I never get old."

Willie J. and Thomas were teamed together on slow-day projects at the gravel pit. Willie, being 17 years older, had a host of nagging injuries, or so he claimed. Every day it was something different. And every day his close friend, Thomas, gave him hell.

"I'll move the fuckin' slabs myself," Thomas said. The concrete slabs, ones used in parking lots to impede the continued forward movement of vehicles, had become recessed in the gravel and knocked askew. Harry Burke wanted them raised, then secured in place with reinforcement bars knocked into the ground through the two cast holes. Busy-work.

Thomas walked to the first slab, picked up an end and tossed it away from the fence toward the center of the employee parking lot. The other end of the slab, he also tossed inward. Willie J. took a square point shovel and began to fill in the crevice and level off the ground.

Thomas moved the second one. The third. And fourth. On his second toss on the sixth slab, a shooting pain darted up his neck and into his head, directly behind his right ear. He dropped to his left knee.

"See, you young shit," Willie J. said. "Someday you'll be old, and it looks like you're starting already."

But Thomas did not move. With his knuckles planted firmly in the ground, he squeezed out, "I think you'd better take me to the doctor's."

Willie J. knew a Thomas McCloskey joke, and this was not one of them. Thomas never wanted a doctor.

"You want me to get an ambulance?"

"Shit, no! Go tell Harry that I popped my neck and that you're going to give me a ride. He won't care."

Thomas sat in the waiting room in some new satellite emergency hospital clinic in Whiting Beach. The overcrowding of Regional Hospital's Emergency Room with minor afflictions combined with the disappearance of general practitioners helped these small, roadside clinics spring up. Now Thomas sat and waited with a bunch of snot-nosed kids with the sniffles.

"Go home," he told Willie. "I can walk from here."

Willie J. looked around and saw each child with a parent. "I think I need to stay and hold my little Tommy's hand."

Thomas had to turn his entire body to shoot a dirty look at Willie J., but the Frankenstein movements only made Willie J. laugh harder. "Hee, hee, hee." A very distinctive laugh. "Hee, hee, hee."

"Just go. You're a pain in the ass."

Are you sure?

"Go! You're scarin' the kids."

Thomas waited another hour to be called, and another 15 minutes in a sterile room. Doctor Vandenburg walked in and asked, "How are we doing in here?"

"You need some magazines."

Excuse me.

"I don't mind waiting, but you should have a *Better Homes and Gardens* or *Highlights*, you know the one with the hidden-picture puzzle. Anything. Personally, I don't get much satisfaction out of reading the side of a bio-waste container."

Mmmm-hmmmm. "It says that you have numbness in the fingertips of your right hand."

Yes. "But it's starting to tingle."

"And how did this happen?"

Thomas explained the lifting and twisting motion, and then the pop.

"Okay. I think we'll run some x-rays." The doctor scribbled on the chart. "Someone will be right in."

He left, quietly closing the door behind him. Thomas spent another hour-and-a-half at the Whiting Beach Emergency Clinic getting x-rayed and poked and lectured on proper lifting procedures.

It was the first practice – weightlifting or wrestling – that Thomas had missed as a coach at St. Agnes.

Manhattan, October 15

Michelle sat at her desk in her 7th Street apartment, reviewing abstracts on a report she was working on concerning autism and the high rates of abuse in low-income housing.

Tamantha sat on the hardwood floor, her back against the couch, keeping an eye on a muted Clint Eastwood movie, red-marking second grade papers. Coming by a permanent teaching position that wasn't in the inner cities of Newark or Jersey City was tough enough, and Tamantha did not get such a position. But she did get her foot in the door by receiving a permanent substituting position. She would teach Mrs. Katzenbaum's second grade Englewood Cliffs class while Mrs. Katzenbaum took maternity leave. She moved in with her sister in a one-bedroom apartment in Manhattan so she could save up some money, but mostly, so she didn't have to live alone or with some stranger.

It was the first time the sisters lived together in eight years, but everything went smoothly. Their routines were set.

Michelle had Chopin playing on her compact disc stereo for more than an hour while the sisters finished off their work weeks by catching up on more work. It was now 8:30 and Chopin had been dragging on in Tamantha's ears forever. "I think it's my turn to pick out a CD," the younger sister said.

O.K. "But not too loud Tammy."

Tammy picked the Eagles' *Hotel California*. The music started and after 30 seconds, Michelle declared, "I guess I'm done for this evening."

Michelle went into the kitchenette and asked her sister if she wanted some tea. "I wanna try some coffee," she said.

Okay. Michelle put on a pot of coffee. "What are you watching anyway?"

"I'm not sure," Tamantha said. "I know it's Clint Eastwood – that's him there," she said pointing to the screen. "But I don't know the name of the movie. "A Handful of Gold" or something like that."

Why?

Tamantha was going to lie, but decided there was no need to lie to her sister. "I was flipping through the channels and I saw the western, and I wondered what Tommy saw in them."

"A western. Coffee." Michelle hesitated. "I know we've been over this before but – do you have feelings for Tommy?"

"Of course I do," Tamantha said bluntly. The answer surprised Michelle until Tamantha quickly clarified her position. "I've known Tommy since I was 10 years old, and recently we've spent a lot of time together. I mean, well, he's like a brother to me, at least."

Tamantha had stopped trying to reunite Michelle and Thomas, but she still thought it may happen. And that is why she did not elaborate on her feelings. As long as there was a chance Michelle and Thomas could get back together, Tamantha would never allow herself to fall in love with Tommy. Or at least admit to love.

She would be 22 soon and Tommy just turned 29. It didn't seem that she was so much younger than him anymore, not like when she was in grade school. Five years would be a perfect span for a mate, but Tamantha erased that thought from her mind as quickly as it entered.

287

The men that Tamantha was meeting were nowhere close to the ideal man. Maybe the problem lie in geography, Tammy thought, because all of the guys seemed to be like Chad Lewis. Ugh! She could use someone like Tommy. He was cute and funny and smart. Most of all, he was great company. Even Michelle found it easy to be around Thomas, walking about, not needing to speak all of the time.

"That's a mark of a great friend," Michelle would say when reminded of Thomas' company. Although the older sister always added, "but we're so different at our core. In our political views. And if we do end up talking about politics, it ends up in an argument." He's just so conservative.

Tamantha watched as Clint Eastwood hung a metal plate from his neck to protect his chest. She turned up the volume, finding herself interested as her sister brought into the living room two cups of coffee – cream and sugar already stirred in.

"And the coffee?"

"You and Tommy are always raving about how this shop or that has such a great cup of coffee, I figured I should try it." Tamantha blew on the rim and onto the surface of the chocolate-brown liquid. She took a sip and wrinkled her nose. "Eww."

Michelle laughed and reached for the phone. "Since we're talking about him so much we might as well give him a call. Maybe we can get him to do something this weekend." She dialed. The last time the sisters saw Thomas was on a Saturday, two weekends after Labor Day. Thomas was at the Jennings' house having tea with Mrs. Jennings, learning about art, when the two girls walked in.

Michelle was going to playfully quiz Thomas on his love life in general. She figured that he was on the couch wearing a pair of sweats, watching television. So getting him to talk would not be hard. He was probably bored anyway.

While the phone rang, Michelle decided that she felt the same way as her sister did toward Thomas, or at least what her sister was openly admitting to. She was not sure of her amorous feelings. What if Thomas still loved her? What would her reaction be then? Michelle was in a trance when Thomas eventually answered the phone.

It was a grunted hello.

"Thomas?"

A grunted yeah.

"Did you go out after work?" Michelle hated when he had been drinking alone.

No.

"Well, you don't sound so good."

Thomas sat rigidly upright on the right side of the couch, attempting not to make any sudden movements. Michelle never got to challenge the suspect.

"X-rays showed that the cartilage between the C-5 and C-6 discs in my neck has deteriorated. My neck is straight instead of curved. A nerve was pinched which caused my arm to go numb. A bunch of shit like that."

Michelle could tell that he wasn't himself and asked if they prescribed any type of medication.

Percocet. "That shit's better than whiskey."

Michelle thought about warning him of the addictive nature of prescribed pills, but didn't want to hear, 'Okay Ma.' Instead, she asked what the doctor said.

"It would be best if you stopped wrestling," Thomas said, imitating Doctor Vandenburg. "I asked him if there were any chance of breaking my neck or becoming paralyzed. He said slim at this point of my life, but with continued deterioration and calcium deposits building up, lateral mobility will greatly decrease, making it hard to do such activities as driving a car. Shit like that." Thomas spoke very slowly. He was getting sleepy. He didn't sound too concerned with the diagnosis.

"How about receiving some visitors tomorrow?"

"Hi, Tommy!" Tammy yelled cheerfully from the background, having a hard time following the conversation.

"Hey Tam," he said. "The doc told me to keep ice in that region. Even though I can't feel it, there is swelling. Then he gave me some exercises and a name of a specialist. I appreciate your offer, but I'm just going to relax and do some thinking tomorrow. Thanks anyway."

Okay. His last words were depressing to Michelle. She knew he didn't care about the injury, but she could tell that there was a possibility that he may have to give up wrestling. She was about to ask of his future intentions, but instead, again, just politely offered the Jennings' company on Saturday.

Thank you. No.

Thomas slipped the phone receiver onto its base, leaned his head back and fell asleep.

TWENTY-EIGHT

Nine days before the beginning of the winter sports season, students were wandering around, talking to coaches, slipping into the nurses office, talking to friends, wearing varsity jackets. It was the last informal meeting before the start of girls' and boys' basketball practices, indoor track and the "Friday after Thanksgiving" wrestling practice.

Some children affiliated with the basketball programs would practice a maximum of three days before coming into school on Monday, going to the Sports Bulletin Board, and running their fingers down the freshmen, j.v. and varsity lists, failing to find their names, anywhere. Cut.

But for nine days, those students could dream of becoming part of storied basketball traditions, working hard to climb to the top of the rosters. Starting and scoring. Becoming school heroes. The medical physicals nine days prior to the start of the basketball season were the seeds to dream of stardom.

There was indoor track, the winter version for individuals training for the spring season. The trips to the nurse's room for physical examinations were merely routine, giving clearance for them to run in the hallways during foul weather. Check for a heartbeat. Okay, go run.

Finally, the bastard wrestlers, already spitting into cups to lower weight. The more bodies present for the preseason check-ups, the merrier Thomas McCloskey was. There were no cut sheets. "You boys are signing up for service, and I expect you to stick."

More importantly than mere clearance to participate, the doctor's examination served as a state weight certification. The lighter a wrestler was at this time, the lower the weight the doctor would circle and thus legally allow.

With the Lancers lightly practicing with Father James in autumn, they were in better shape and the kids were lighter. "You don't mandate or even encourage children to lose weight," Thomas explained to Father James, trying to paint the various possibilities he had experienced and seen. "The doctors don't like to circle a weight that's more than one class away from a wrestler's weight during certification. The better shape a boy is in, the certification will be lower because doctors don't perform a fat percentage test. Not at this school anyway.

"During the first year, everything was so new, even the doctor was new. He didn't circle a weight class but instead wrote down a number. Just arbitrarily wrote a number. So during the season, kids would naturally shed and sweat off pounds, and be moving down weight classes. One kid got down to 124 without trying, but the doctor wrote 131, so he couldn't rightfully wrestle 125 or even 130. He had to wrestle up two weight classes at 135. Poor kid was always drinking water."

The fall practices Father James had been conducting helped tremendously. Most of the boys were in good shape and were lighter during weight certifications compared to the previous three seasons. "Every once in a while," Thomas explained to Father James while they sat through the lengthy certification process, "a wrestler needs a positive distraction to keep his mind off of a certain opponent or home or school. And it's good to have the lightest possible certifications. You tell a wrestler that he needs to drop five pounds so the team's line-up will become stronger, and his focus becomes sharper."

Thomas mainly was concerned with the middleweight certifications and the five-pound class increments. During the season, wrestlers will be all over the scale, and Thomas wanted to make sure every possible scenario was covered. Father James listened intently to all explanations and, when the wrestlers went in to see the physician, he would attend, assuring the doctor that the weight classes sought would be closely monitored.

Undoubtedly, Thomas would receive more than a dozen calls from parents inquiring about the certification. You see, there is an out clause on every permission slip – needed to be signed by a parent or guardian – that allowed the guardian to override the physician's recommendation. And Thomas would have to explain the natural weight-loss process. If that didn't work, he'd move to the son's desire to start on varsity and the lighter, unoccupied weight. As a last resort, the coach would explain the child's need to nut up, work hard and cut the umbilical cord. This he said solely to the fathers, who quickly signed the permission slips without any additional need of explanations.

The paperwork, already massive for a high school sport that required a minimal and inexpensive amount of equipment, mounted. The weight certifications also served as the continuing practice of skin checks. With wrestlers already stripped to their skivvies to check weight, the doctor then required each student to stand naked to be checked for any and all skin ailments. Individual sheets and team rosters were initialized, clearing a wrestler for competition. A dermatologist would come in every two weeks to check for Herpes Gladiatorium or ringworm. The diagnosis was only good for the following 48 hours, so a doctor would have to be paged for any emergency situations, which occasionally arose, but never to the detriment of the St. Agnes squad.

Thomas' neck stiffened toward the end of certifications, around 9:30. After the first medical visit following his neck injury, Thomas took the advice of someone at work, and went to see a chiropractor, who manipulated his spine so the pain went away and the mobility returned. Thomas practiced the required exercises and stretched his shoulders, but on long days such as this, his neck throbbed, usually casting a sleepless night.

A couple of Advil when he got home would do the trick, but that was some time away. He was ready to ask the school nurse for some generic aspirin, hoping she wouldn't ask for a note from home, when the appearance of a stout senior made the pain disappear.

The winds from students' mouths had brought to Thomas a rumor. A rumor that just one week ago, a transfer from the suburbs of Baltimore – a transfer with significant wrestling experience – enrolled at St. Agnes. When asked about his weight or even his name, Thomas received a plethora of accounts.

"He's huge," Jeff LeMone said. "His name is Hugo the Huge. I gave him that name." For seven days, Thomas asked his diminutive wrestler where Hugo was, only to receive, "He's coming."

Finally, he arrived. He was big. About 170. But he was smaller than the person he came with, Tony Kingery, who had been a no-show at practice for the past month-and-a-half, opting to lift during the weekdays, wrestling sporadically in weekend tournaments.

"Greg Shipley, Coach," the young man said, extending his hand. The hand shake was firm. His demeanor pleasant. When asked about his high school experience, he spouted off a tremendous record for the past two seasons – 54-6 – with a Maryland district second-place finish his sophomore year and a championship his junior year. Shipley looked like a wrestler and talked like a wrestler, but there was something in his voice that made Thomas skeptical.

"Why New Jersey? Why St. Agnes?"

"I was living with my dad in Maryland, and, well, I decided it was time to spend some time with my mother before I head to college. My mom lives in Evandale and she chose St. Agnes."

A reasonable explanation, but Thomas sensed there was more. "How do you like it so far?"

"I could live without wearing a uniform every day, but I think it'll be good to be a big fish in a little pond."

Mmhm. "Well, let's weigh you two in so I can get home and get some sleep."

Greg Shipley weighed in first. 171. Clean skin.

Then Tony. 197. Clean skin.

"What've you been doing? Eating the weights?" Thomas asked.

Tony smiled proudly. "I've been working out twice a day, before school and after school, taking protein supplements and shakes."

The coach gave Tony a bit of a stink eye. "First of all, watch those pills and drinks. Just eat steak and potatoes. Natural stuff. And second, you have to stop lifting and start stretching. Your muscles are going to be extremely tight and you need to be more flexible. Actually, you needed to stop lifting a good couple of weeks ago."

"I'll be alright."

"Well, if you can keep that weight up, I guess Anil will be backing you up this season."

Tony again smiled proudly. Thomas shook his hand and told him he had done a tremendous job, and he bid the last two wrestlers a good night.

Father James said that although he wasn't familiar with all of the intricacies of the sport, it looked like St. Agnes was in good shape.

Thomas found a piece of scrap paper and a pencil and started jabbering and scribbling. "Mr. Broughton got our schedule switched so we could have the easier matches earlier in the season." Thomas separated the 45 names at certification into four columns: varsity, junior varsity, freshman and quit. "And he also, thank God, got us out of the Oak Hill Classic and into the Eagle Christmas Tournament. It's a week later and a helluva lot easier. A helluva lot easier."

He produced a list and said, "This'll be a starting lineup." His body shivered momentarily. "Barring major injuries, this team is going to be tough."

Father James shook his head. "A good group of boys."

103	Jeff LeMone (jr.)
112	Quinton Barry (freshman with experience)
119	Pete McKane (sr.)
125	George Galatin (sr.) or Eric Douglass (so.)
130	George Galatin or Eric Douglass
135	Brien Cauldron (sr.)
140	Willie Sanderson (130 part-time starter as a freshman)
145	Pete Disling (so.)
152	Mike Ennis (sr.)
160	Greg Shipley (sr.) or Jacob Hester (so.) option to bump; Shipley to cover Masterelli at 171
171	Mike Masterelli (jr.) somehow finds an opening
189	Chris Ballinger (sr.) fourth year at 189 – from flubby to flabby to solid to muscular
Hwt.	Tony Kingery (jr.) 45 pounds more than junior wrestling wt. 27 pounds higher than off-season weight.
	Anil Nazif – may not wrestle, but will be alternate captain

* * *

Standing in front of the mirror, deciding the first outfit was not appropriate, switching to a second, back to the first, onto a third. Nothing felt comfortable.

It would be the first Thanksgiving dinner Thomas McCloskey celebrated since his sophomore year when he went to his college roommate's house. He was permitted to wear jeans that November. This time in New Jersey, he knew it would be more formal.

"Fuck it." He returned to the first ensemble, a pair of pleated black pants, a white button down shirt and a brown tweed jacket. "There ain't no way I'm wearin' a tie," he said to his reflection.

Despite the more formal setting, it did feel like family, with the three Jennings females, a pair of aunt and uncle sets, and three children – a 12-year-old girl, a 10-year-old boy and a seven-year-old girl. Thomas wasn't sure which set of aunts and uncles claimed which combination of children.

Thomas arrived at 12:30, and much to his surprise, the annual Detroit Lion football game was on the living room television. Uncle Ted and Uncle Eddie were entranced, holding cans of beer, smoking cigarettes. In the kitchen, Thomas exchanged pleasant greetings to all five women, said hellos with a crooked grin to the children, and attempted to remain in the living room with Ted and Eddie, unluckily being dragged back to the dining room by Michelle and Tamantha.

Michelle, Tamantha and Thomas shared cocktails at the dinner table before Tamantha excused herself to help her mother in the kitchen. When she rose, Thomas finally noticed her casual outfit, an ivory- and tan-flecked chenille sweater; brown wool pants; brown leather tie-shoes – a beautiful off-duty school teacher. Then, when he returned his attention to Michelle, he noticed her elegant attire – a white silk blouse embroidered in gold around the collar and cuffs, with matching gold-tone buttons; a black velveteen skirt, loosely pleated and tea length; black, brush suede pumps with gold accent. The Jennings girls had class with a capital K.

It was pleasant and comfortable to be included in the family gathering. The dinner of turkey, stuffing, cranberry sauce,

295

bourbon yams, cinnamon apple sauce and lumpy mashed potatoes kept his mind off the impending season. If it weren't for the Jennings' insistence, Thomas would be at home, watching football games and chomping at the bit, waiting for Friday morning.

Coffee and a choice of pumpkin, cherry or – Michelle's choice – Boston cream pies. After dinner, a choice of chocolates. Then some cocktails and after-dinner cordials. In all, it was a most memorable, perhaps the most memorable, Thanksgiving for Thomas.

Tamantha exclaimed that Michelle and Aunt Patty had agreed to dish duty. Thomas attempted to help but was thwarted by Momma Jennings and was told to stay at the table to entertain the remaining three women. The other men and children, she said, could stay or watch television. They chose TV.

The dessert wine did in the lady folk at the table. They were giggling and singing, having a grand ol' time. Thomas gracefully told them he had to get home to get some sleep and Mrs. Jennings allowed this, knowing the importance of his annual Friday.

Thomas Patrick McCloskey went to the kitchen to say goodbye to Michelle. With her hands full of suds, she pulled Thomas' chin to her, and gave him a long kiss on the cheek, leaving suds bubbling on his face.

"Thank you for coming," she said. "You're always welcome."

Tamantha said she would walk him to his truck. "It's a jungle out there, ya know."

Standing under the street lamp outside her bedroom window – the same light which she stared and cried at following a dubious double date – she now thanked Thomas for being there for Mom, Michelle and her. And unexpectedly, she kissed him, full, on the lips, for more than a fleeting moment.

Goodbye. And she skipped into the house.

The kiss gave Thomas something to think about other than his Friday after Thanksgiving.

Senior

There was no jog around town. The mats did not have to be taken from summer storage and stretched and flipped. Thomas did not have to take the first three days of practice to acquaint himself with new faces, nor for the returning wrestlers to reacquaint themselves with hell in the cafeteria.

Just as spring brings eternal hope to all baseball clubs, the first days of wrestling practice bring a curtain of dread to the unexpected grappler. The Friday morning practice room is cold and damp. So is Saturday. And Sunday. The boiler does not work as hard as it does on school days, so when the athletes assemble in the hallways and gyms and wrestling rooms, goose bumps and tight sacs are not hard to find.

But Thomas was ready. He convinced Mr. Broughton to have the custodian in early to fire up old Bertha. And when the wrestlers walked into the St. Agnes cafeteria, it was warm, like the tropics. And they started practicing as if it were mid-season.

For the first few days, Thomas excused the freshmen – except for Quinton Barry – and the first-year wrestlers from a number of drills and exercises. But the returning wrestlers were sweating and wrestling, listening to Thomas describe the difference of opening the season against Hanstrom and the Eagle tournament instead of the Oak Hill Classic and Blakemore.

"This year we start off strong and get stronger," Thomas yelled during wind sprints at the end of the first practice. "Down goes Hanstrom. Shoot for the top spot at the Eagle. Covington goes down. Timbrook – down. St. Peter's – down. Bishop Leary – down. Look ahead and dream. This team could be 5-0 when you meet Blakemore Prep –who we need to repay for a 75-0 initiation three years ago."

Father James used an arsenal of techniques to condition the wrestlers. They ran, they sprinted, they walked backward.

Push-ups, four different kinds of sit-ups, bridges and a bevy of exercises the normal athlete never heard of.

"This I got from a marine," he said one day. "This I got from a Navy Seal," he would say the next.

With no more split practices, Thomas and the team had more time to discuss the intricate details of sport, such as a song for warm-ups at home matches.

At the three home matches the year before, the gate revenue barely paid for the referees, clock attendant and the janitor. With small crowds, the Ozzy Osbourne song *Crazy Train* had little effect in pumping up the crowd. Jeff LeMone took care of the music the previous year, and it slipped by the scrutiny of his teammates and the coach.

A fiery debate ensued in the waning practices before the opening match. "I don't care what you guys decide, just make sure the upperclassmen agree that I would approve of the song."

With a full j.v. squad, the crowd started to shuffle in for opening night. The two-tiered bleachers occupied only one side of the gym. The bottom tier, with four rows that ran the length of the basketball court, is where the St. Agnes parents sat. Students sat in the upper bleachers, split into three sections. When full, it was nearly impossible to hear during basketball games.

Father James took a place in the bleachers near the St. Agnes bench, asking Thomas to allow him to monitor and learn from a safe distance. He offered many pleasant hellos and handshakes to parents and parishioners.

The Father noticed two young ladies walk in and wave to Thomas just before the start of the match. "Very interesting," he said quietly, and he repositioned himself a couple of rows back and more toward the center. Father James introduced himself and quickly sat between Michelle and Tamantha Jennings, to learn more about them and his head coach.

Just prior to the start of the j.v. 103-pound match, Thomas looked around. It was a nice crowd already, maybe a third full. Then he spotted the Jennings girls, sitting with the Father.

"Father James," he began, but got no further, for the priest knew of his intentions.

"I requested to learn the sport from the bleachers," he said. "Now, if you will go back to the bench, I have found myself two capable teachers."

Thomas shook his head and left.

Father James never fully focused on the proceedings of the junior varsity matches, opting to converse with the Jennings sisters, although afterwards, he would pay strict attention to the varsity match. Michelle and Tamantha took turns telling the story of Thomas Patrick McCloskey. Michelle was quite amazed at how much her little sister knew of his father leaving and the death of his mother. Michelle didn't think that Thomas talked much about those events, but Tamantha occasionally would add as a post script, "That, I just remember when they were dating."

Michelle spoke of his high school wrestling career, how she would go to every match, and he would glance over and wink before taking to the mat. "I was only a teen-ager, but I was as in love as you could get back then. He was just the ultimate warrior. No chicanery. No gimmicks. No excuses. Thomas acted valiantly whenever a situation warranted."

Then came the mononucleosis his junior year. "You think it would have devastated him," she said. "But it didn't. Covington won the conference title that year and that was his top priority. His next goal was the district championship. And he won that. He finished the year 22-0. I was dating a stud-muffin." A girlish grin snuck upon the face as Father James and Tammy were held in captivation.

Tommy's mother died that spring. "And he went into a shell. And that was the beginning of the end for us. It was gradual and the impetus for the breakup was on my part. He just didn't smile anymore. He used to say, 'I don't feel like smiling.' He just wanted to be left alone back then. Now he says, 'I'm smiling on the inside,' and I think that's true – he just doesn't want anyone to get close anymore."

Thomas worked construction for the Burkes and trained all that summer. "Sure, we went on dates and had a lot of fun, but he had one thing in mind – wrestling. He went 18-0 during the regular season with something like 15 or 16 pins, but Covington finished second. Tommy doesn't like to talk about it because Mark Pierce is – or was – his friend. I'm not sure why he won't talk about it, but I think because loyalty is very important to Thomas. Anyway, Mark was drinking and partying and missing weight, and it contributed to a couple of losses, which meant surrendering the team title. So Thomas went into the Districts with a vengeance. He was letting everything out on the mat, trying to avenge the team's loss and his – well, everything. The three district matches lasted a total of less than a minute and a half, if I remember correctly."

Michelle stopped her soliloquy and watched Thomas on the sideline, calmly teaching the young wrestler out on the mat, coaxing him into believing in himself. She saw him smile when he noticed confusion in the wrestler's eyes. It was good to see him smile again.

"Was that the end of the season?" Father James asked.

"No. Not at all." Michelle retraced the events in her mind. "He was undefeated going into the Regions. Three or four of his teammates advanced but were eliminated somewhere along the way, I forget the specifics. But Tommy was 23-0 going into the regional final. He'll never admit that winning the Regions was a goal of his, but I know it was. I know it was, because I was there. I saw the match."

His name was Marcellus Slaney and he, too, was undefeated, from Bridgewater Central. "He wasn't only mean-looking, he was out-and-out nasty," Michelle said. "Tommy was winning 4-0 halfway through the match when the boy – boy, he looked like he was 20 – from Bridgewater did some sort of move from the top. I don't know. Legs and an ankle pick? Tommy can tell you. Anyway, Tommy screamed. The kid had wrenched Tommy's ankle so bad that the doctor told him he tore ligaments. Coach Gibbons was going to stop the match but didn't. He couldn't. Tommy wasn't arguing or yelling or complaining. He just looked at Coach Gibbons and said, 'Please.' I was the in third row, 20, maybe 30 feet away, and I could see the tears in his eyes, and it wasn't because he was in pain. All of a sudden, ignoring coaches and trainers, he stood up, hobbling on one foot with a period and a half left.

"He sat on his ankle to protect it for the rest of the second period and lost a point for stalling. Then he chose top for the third period and used every move he knew to control Marcellus Slaney." Michelle stopped. After mentioning the name again, she was set back in time. Slowly, she continued. "It was kind of funny because Slaney was bucking like a bronco and Tommy looked like a cowboy. The match ended with the crowd on its feet."

The j.v. match against Hanstrom was wrapping up, Michelle decided to do the same so Father James could concentrate on the varsity match. "Tommy was 22-0 his junior year and 24-0 his senior year. I think he still holds some sort of record for most consecutive wins without a state title," melancholy creeped into her face as she continued. "We broke up that summer and he went to college in South Dakota. He spent two years on the wrestling team at college, but he never wrestled competitively after high school. His ankle took a while to heal, and maybe his heart, too." Her voice tapered off as her eyes looked toward the St. Agnes bench.

Father James understood a great deal after the conversations with the two sisters. He knew bits and pieces of the St. Agnes and Thomas McCloskey stories, but not enough to fully appreciate the short history of the program. He bid the sisters a good evening and thanked them for being a part of Thomas' family. "Our next home match is against Blakemore on the 21st, the night after St. Agnes's Eve. I'll tell you of the legend that shares this school's name, and perhaps you ladies can teach me more of our enigmatic coach." And off to the bench he ambled, laughing, because he was equipped with a multitude of questions just to annoy Thomas.

Meanwhile, the Hanstrom match went according to blueprint. Jeff LeMone came out and pinned in 37 seconds and the rout was on. Fifty-nine to 12 in front of a raucous, packed house.

But a crucial mistake was made prior to the actual wrestling that proved to be a punishable offense. The song the team came out to warm up to was the Rolling Stones' *Sympathy for the Devil*. In the locker room, Thomas had to feign anger despite the rout.

"Do you think that's an appropriate song to be representative of a Catholic school?" Thomas screamed, shocking the jubilant wrestlers. "Do you think Father James likes explaining to the principal and the diocese that the wrestling team is not a part of the occult, that they're just part of today's MTV ignorant mass?"

The team members showered and gathered their belongings as the j.v. team fought with getting the mats back downstairs to the cafeteria. The post-match atmosphere was as chaotic as the match itself. Thomas retreated to the coaches' room to remove himself from all areas. Father James joined him for a few moments.

"Great start to the season, Coach. Congratulations," the Father said.

"Thank you. But you get much of the credit, Father James. It has been your presence in the wrestling room that has given these kids focus. And the condition they're in – wow! They're in mid-season form. If it were me alone with this team again, hmm, we'd still be fighting and learning and kicking and screaming. You know, a normal, dysfunctional Jersey family."

Father James laughed, appreciated and thanked Thomas for the recognition, then addressed the song selection before he excused himself to "schmooze with the parents."

"You know that with the garbled words and the fact that the song is so old, I don't know if we'll get any complaints," he said. "And I actually like *Sympathy for the Devil*. It gives me perspective in my profession." He turned and adjourned to the gym, laughter trailing behind him.

December 27
Eagle Classic
Courtenshire, N.J.

Maybe Terry Broughton could become a wrestler's athletic director after all. The basketball-enthralled AD pulled off a tremendous coup in getting the Lancers into a tournament against unknown foes with which St. Agnes could compete. Suddenly, magically or even spiritually, St. Agnes' fans had another sport to pay close attention to.

Courtshire is 45 minutes due west of Evandale on the way to Princeton, in the remaining farm country of New Jersey. Thomas knew nothing of the teams in the area and did not care how his team fared. He was relaxed, and the team was relaxed. They all knew that this tournament was to sharpen their skills and had nothing to do with team standings.

Chris Ballinger got a top seed and won three matches, claiming a gold medal. Because he was the only district champ from St. Agnes, he was the only top seed. No other Lancer received higher than a fifth seed.

But that did not deter St. Agnes. Jeff LeMone won the tournament at 103. Brien Cauldron won at 135. Mike Ennis won at 152. Greg Shipley at 160. And Tony Kingery, weighing only 194, won the heavyweight division and received the tournament's Most Outstanding Wrestler award.

The successes did not stop there. Pete McKane took second at 119. And despite losing their first matches of the day,

George Galatin and Pete Disling used the double elimination tournament to wrestle back to third place finishes at 130 and 145, respectively.

The team finished first with 231 points. Nine wrestlers placed.

On the bus ride home, Thomas told the team not to use this to measure its worth. "This was an unknown. My guess is that we were paired with a bunch of Hanstroms and St. Pete's. We know we can compete with those teams. The big question is – how hard will we have to work to compete with the Blakemores and Centrals?"

With the help of the athletic director's reorganization of the schedule, St. Agnes became a juggernaut of the small school division.

Offering no explanation, Thomas asked Father James to conduct weigh-ins at Covington High School. Asking no questions, Father James obliged. In front of a packed house in Covington's gym, Thomas avoided talking to Mark Pierce, and Mark all but avoided coaching. St. Agnes won 11 matches. Covington 2.

The next to fall was Eddie Liddle and Timbrook. St. Agnes won nine of the 13 matches on the way to a 51-19 win, prompting Liddle to ask an assistant, "You think he's still mad?"

Then on January 11, a trip to St. Peter's bolstered the St. Agnes record to 4-0. The final, 61-3.

Three days later Bishop Leary fell, 45-10. St. Agnes stood tall at 5-0, heading back to the cozy confines of the little gym nicknamed "The Phone Booth" to face Blakemore Prep. The practice rally cry – "Remember the 75."

THIRTY

Tamantha arrived early the morning after St. Agnes's Eve, and Father James excused himself politely from an engaging conversation with Diedra Douglass. He sat with Tamantha and offered an early apology for eventually having to leave to coach the j.v. team. "They really need me," he said facetiously. "Sometimes I just don't think Thomas knows what he's doing."

Ever since the priest left the Jennings girls at their last talk with the prospect of hearing the story St. Agnes's Eve, Father James wanted to pick up immediately. Superstitious as he was, he wondered which one, if either of the girls, would become part of the legend. He tried to extract this from Thomas but got nothing more than, "Michelle's liberal and I'm conservative."

"And Tammy?"

"Tamantha's apolitical," he said, smiling. "She doesn't buy into anything unless it steps into the educational field. Then she takes a stand. Otherwise she's status quo for the status quo."

Tamantha arrived alone on Saturday just prior to the j.v. match against Blakemore. "Michelle needed to stay in the city last night," she said. "But she promised that she would be here before Brien Cauldron wrestled."

"Oh, never mind. I get royalties for the poem," Father James said, laughing, bringing Tamantha to laughter, also. "The legend still can come true." And he told the story of St. Agnes's Eve, reciting the passages of the lovers' escape:

> Beyond a mortal man impassion'd far
> At these voluptuous accents, he arose,
> Ethereal, flush'd, and like a throbbing star
> Seen mid the sapphire heaven's deep repose;
> Into her dream he melted, as the rose
> Blendeth its odour with the violet,
> Solution sweet: meantime the frost-wind blows

Like Loves' alarum pattering the sharp sleet
Against the window-panes; St. Agnes' moon hath set.

'Tis dark: quick pattereth the flaw-blown sleet:
"This is no dream, my bride, my Madeline!"
'Tis dark: the iced gusts still rave and beat:
"No dream, alas! alas! and woe is mine!
Porphyro will leave me here to fade and pine.
Cruel! what traitor could thee hither bring?
I curse not, for my heart is lost in thine,
Though thou forsakest a deceived thing;
A dove forlorn and lost with sick unpruned wing."

"My Madeline! sweet dreamer! lovely bride!
Say, may I be for aye thy vassal blest?
Thy beauty's shield, heart-shap'd and vermeil dyed?
Ah, silver shrine, here will I take my rest
After so many hours of toil and quest,
A famish'd pilgrim – saved by miracle.
Though I have found, I will not rob thy nest
Saving of thy sweet self; if though think'st well
To trust, fair Madeline, to no rude infidel.

"Hark! 'tis an elfin-storm from faery land,
Of haggard seeming, but a boon indeed:
Arise – arise! the morning is at hand;
The bloated wassaillers will never heed:
Let us away, my love, with happy speed;
There are no ears to hear, or eyes to see,
Drown'd all in Rhenish and the sleepy mead:
Awake! arise! my love, and fearless be,
For o'er the southern moors I have a home for thee."

She hurried at his words, beset with fears,
For there were sleeping dragons all around,
At glaring watch, perhaps, with ready spears
Down the wide stairs a darkling way they found.
In all the house was heard no human sound.
A chain-droop'd lamp was flickering by each door;
The arras, rich with horseman, hawk, and hound,
Flutter'd in the beseiging wind's uproar;
And the long carpets rose the gusty floor.

"And against great odds, they escaped with each other," Father James said. "Perhaps, if the odds are in your favor, you can dream of a soul mate."

"Rarely do I remember any of my dreams," Tamantha said. "And if I do, I try like the dickens to avoid analyzing them."

As predicted, Michelle missed only the first five matches of the dual match. Blakemore was winning 12-6 with Brien Cauldron leading 3-2 in his match. The battle raged for all 13 weight classes, the individual scores bouncing back and forth.

If Greg Shipley was a district champ down in Maryland, his results at St. Agnes were not reflective of that thus far. He was undefeated at 8-0, but he had no pins at 160 and had periods of extremely sloppy wrestling when he would end up on his back, inexplicably, in near-fall situations. Because of his sporadic style, Thomas rolled the dice at 160.

Blakemore's Art Whitney also was undefeated. But Whitney was 7-0 with seven pins and a championship at the Oak Hill Classic. Before the match, Thomas decided that if St. Agnes was trailing by nine points or more, he would send in a sophomore as a sacrificial six points and bump Shipley to the next weight class.

As scouted, St. Agnes trailed 24-15 going into 160 pounds. Thomas was positive Shipley would lose and might even get pinned by Whitney. Then Masterelli would get pinned. In the best case scenario with that line-up, the Lancers would trail 33-15 with only 12 possible team points left.

Instead, Matthew Bradford, a virgin sophomore was sent out to face Whitney and returned 17 seconds later. St. Agnes trailed 30-15.

"A decision and we can tie," Thomas told Shipley, who seemed to be pouting. "Anything above that, I'm confident Ballinger and Kingery can pin, and we win."

Johnny Loddiggs was a solid 171-pound wrestler for Blakemore. The junior was 3-3 with pins on each side of the column. He had yet to wrestle six minutes this season, and he wouldn't again. He decked Greg Shipley in 45 seconds, giving Blakemore an insurmountable 36-15 lead.

With Shipley failing to shake his opponent's hand and then firing his headgear past his teammates and finally hurling an obscenity back at the ref, St. Agnes was penalized two team points, readjusting the score to 36-13.

Chris Ballinger pinned and upped his record to 9-0. Tony Kingery pinned and was 8-1.

St. Agnes lost 36-25.

Michelle and Tamantha were sitting in the bleachers, waiting for Thomas to emerge from the locker room. Only a handful of people were left in the dimly lit gym, mostly parents, some siblings. Most were waiting for a Lancer wrestler.

Harriette Shipley was waiting for the head coach.

Thomas was the last one out of the locker room. First he shooed the stragglers from the showers, then he went downstairs to check the cafeteria and weight room for any extraneous equipment. Engrossed, he was surprised to see anyone waiting for him. He simply had forgotten about the Jennings girls.

"Hello Mr. McCloskey, I'm Harriette Shipley." Thomas shook her outstretched hand and looked nonchalantly past her, nodding acknowledgingly to Michelle and Tamantha. "I hope you really leaned into him tonight." The remark surprised the coach a bit.

"Actually – no. I was too mad to talk to him. I'd be lying if I told you I didn't mind losing. I accept losing as graciously as the moment will allow, and I never avoid shaking an opponent's or teammate's hand, but I despise poor sportsmanship, especially when it detracts from the team's performance." Thomas wasn't expecting to bluntly lay it on the line, but Mrs. Shipley presented him with the opportunity and, well, he took it.

"I was very embarrassed tonight," she said, choking back her emotions. "Then again, I've been embarrassed ever since Greg's father shipped him north. Like a change of scenery was simply going to change a wayward teenager's attitude. If his father couldn't control him, how the hell am I supposed to do it?"

Mrs. Shipley sat down on the first row of the lower bleachers, and Thomas felt obliged to do the same. He clandestinely motioned with his index finger to let the girls know he wouldn't be but a minute. Then Harriette Shipley began to sob.

"He's such a smart and talented boy. He was never like this, but since his father and I got divorced three years ago, he's slipped by. He's done what he's wanted to do – which means picking the wrong crowd, staying out late, getting into trouble without serving the consequences."

"That's not going to happen this time, Mrs. Shipley. I'll have to go home and think this one through. It might be a couple of days before I make my decision, but he'll pay the consequences this time."

"Will he be kicked off the team?"

It's a possibility.

"But you can't."

It depends on Gregory.

"But it will just give him the extra time to drift further away from me. I'm barely communicating with him now. If he doesn't have wrestling to get him through the winter, he may not make it to graduation."

Greg could always get a job.

"Are you always this callous, Mr. McCloskey? Does winning mean that much that you'd let one student lose his future?"

Thomas stood up. "My being callous has nothing to do with winning, Mrs. Shipley. If winning were so important, I wouldn't consider suspending Greg from even one practice because this team needs him so badly. The reason I'm being so damn blunt is that I want you to go home and tell Gregory exactly what I said, so he can sleep with the thought of not being able to wrestle and not being eligible for graduation and the prospect of having to go out and work for a living. I'm saying this to you now because this is exactly what I would've said to Greg if I weren't so damn peeved before."

He bowed his head and looked at his construction boots for an instant. "Four years ago, this Blakemore team shut St. Agnes out in the school's first match ever. Seventy-five to nothing. Since the start of this program, these kids have scraped and clawed their way to respectability. Slowly, tediously, these children, these wrestlers, these *men* have worked up some pride, so when someone asks them, 'Hey, who do you wrestle for?' they don't have to mumble –sainannes."

Thomas turned in place, completing a 360, perhaps hoping that by the time he returned his attention to Mrs. Shipley, the unfortunate circumstance would have been settled. "In one night, Greg attempted to wreck everything we worked for. And it's got nothing to do with winning. These guys didn't expect a Greg Shipley to turn up on their doorstep. They were willing to give it a go with guys like Mike Masterelli and Matt Bradford. They won

310

last year without Greg Shipley. And they can win this year. We also lost last year without Greg and we can do that again, too, without Greg, if necessary." A deep long breath helped center Thomas.

"My problem is this – Greg should be here talking to me right now, not you. He should be showing me his remorse, not you showing yours. And for his absence – I take that as a slap in the face. Now I don't know of a change in environment, or a poor upbringing or bad friends or bad drugs or a combination of all, but as long as I'm coach at St. Agnes, I will be the only one allowed to be penalized team points. And when that happens, I will immediately apologize to my teammates."

The words brought Mrs. Shipley to sobbing convulsions and suddenly Thomas regretted the words he had said. He waited for her to calm herself, then apologized. "I wish I had a handkerchief. . . ."

"I have tissues." She rummaged around her pocketbook.

"Tell Greg if he wants redemption, he gets me at the beginning of practice on Monday. If his attitude doesn't change drastically in the next week, he won't have a place on the squad."

Mrs. Shipley rose and thanked Thomas for his time. "I don't wish Greg to be a burden on you, Mr. McCloskey, but my son is at a crossroads and he needs someone to guide him. Have you ever been at a crossroads before, Mr. McCloskey?"

Every day, Mrs. Shipley. Every day.

Thomas watched a confused mother walk past the Jennings girls and out of the gymnasium door. He didn't know what to think.

No skin ailments. No girl wrestlers. No snow days, only a few delayed openings. Greg Shipley's outburst was the one early-season distraction that faced Thomas and the Lancers.

Greg showed up early January 23 just as Thomas had suggested, but was not nearly as remorseful as the coach had wanted. They sat in the weight room for an hour as Father James conducted practice. "We're not leaving this room until we have a solution to our problem," Thomas said. "Any suggestions?"

"You can acknowledge my presence more. Maybe send me out for the coin toss with Chris or Brien or Anil."

It was simple. Greg Shipley was starved for attention. He wanted to be recognized, for his gift as a pure wrestler, as a senior, as the new kid on the block. The big man on campus.

"No," Thomas said quickly. "I was thinking more like a two-match suspension. During that time, you have to help the freshmen roll out the mats, then it's your responsibility to put water in the bucket, add the disinfectant and thoroughly mop the mats."

Greg sprung to his feet and tossed his headgear against the white cinder block wall. "No fuckin' way."

"Then you don't fuckin' wrestle. And now the suspension is for three matches for throwing your headgear again."

Greg was surprised to hear his coach curse so vehemently in a private meeting. He thought it was a show in practice. Some of the older wrestlers told Shipley that Thomas was a great wrestler – the most recent rumor had the coach trying out for the Olympic team – but the senior transfer from Maryland didn't believe anyone. Since injuring his neck, Thomas had not wrestled live all season, just suiting up to conduct drills and instruct moves.

But when the coach rose to leave Greg alone in the weight room to ponder his high school wrestling future, Thomas looked mean and large and imposing. No nonsense. The fleeting moment that Greg imagined dropping his coach had disappeared. There would be no more challenging.

"Wait," Greg said as Thomas reached the door. "Why are you on me like this? Why are you treating me like a freshman?"

"Because last night you acted like a freshman. And now you have to be disciplined like a freshman, something that probably hasn't been done in four years." Thomas waited for a response, but the senior's silence was answer enough. "Winning on the mat does nothing for my respect. You're a natural wrestler. You have great balance and fly through moves that only LeMone knows. And that is part of the problem. You won't work hard to get any better. And because of the lack of desire and the lack of dedication, you don't have my respect. It's up to you – mop the mats and wrestle. Or mope and pout and join the chess club. Anil can give you a good reference."

Greg Shipley showed up the next day and halfheartedly rolled out the mats. He made a freshman prepare the water solution, which cost him five suicide sprints at the end of practice.

During the suspension, Thomas would walk over to Greg and whisper, "I'm going to lean on you until you get this right."

For the first few practices, Greg resisted, sloppily working with Mike Ennis. "Fine. Masterelli, partner up with Greg." Greg pouted. Thomas ignored.

St. Agnes won the next two matches without the senior transfer from Maryland, easily defeating Carlysle and Pope Pius, clinching a spot in the Parochial B state wrestling championships. "One goal completed, one banner yet to hang." It was stated by the coach every day.

The third match suspension, for Greg's outburst in the weight room, probably cost St. Agnes the match against high-powered North Winfield. Matt Bradford was no match for North Winfield district champ Brett Chambers; he was decked in the first period. If Shipley were in the line-up, a decision loss would have given St. Agnes the win. Instead, the Lancers fell 32-30, dropping their record to 7-2.

Greg's return to the line-up sparked St. Agnes to four consecutive wins and with them, an application, hand-delivered to Thomas McCloskey by Jeff LeMone from Terry Broughton. It was an invitation to the elite Shore Conference Tournament.

Coach –
The last three seasons I naturally filed this away.
But it seems that this year, the St. Agnes wrestling team has a chance to be in the 16-team field.
Please fill out the necessary blanks and return tomorrow.
Good Luck,
Terry Broughton

Thomas did not have to notify the team for Jeff LeMone had already taken care of that. Urged on by the team to complete the application right then, Thomas did so, and Jeff promptly ran it upstairs to Mr. Broughton's office.

Three days later, St. Agnes was accepted as the 14th seed. It's first match was against Number 3-seed Blakemore – at Blakemore.

These were unexpected headlines for the St. Agnes Lancers. A reporter from *The Star-Ledger* and another from a weekly out of Whiting Beach showed up to talk to Thomas, but he

313

deflected interviews to Father James, who had a knack for keeping the proceedings light-hearted. One at a time, the Father would summon varsity wrestlers to talk to reporters. Finally, Father James succeeded in wearing down the writers, and practice rose to another level.

"This will be practice for a state title run," Thomas said. "We know what Blakemore's got and they know us. Now we need to jockey some positions, bust our asses and pull a couple of rabbits from our hats."

Thursday, February 16, Blakemore Prep School

St. Agnes arrived at the 160-pound match in much better shape than in its first meeting with Blakemore that season. Instead of trailing by nine with Matthew Bradford on deck, the Lancers trailed by two, with a rejuvenated Greg Shipley to face Art Whitney.

"This is what you wanted last time, kid," Thomas lightly bumped his forehead with the senior's. "Six hard minutes and Whitney will be in the loss column."

Greg led 2-1 with 30 seconds left in the match, when Whitney hit a reversal and remained in control for a 3-2 win. Shipley was livid. "I'm not losing another fuckin' match," he said, both of the coach's arms wrapped around the wrestler's torso to prevent a similar scene earlier in the season. "I won't lose again."

"Listen Greg. I know you won't find comfort in this, but you may have just sent us to the quarterfinals. We most likely will be down 11 after this match. If Chris and Tony can finish off this match like they did last time, the Number 3 seed will go down."

That prospect did not ease the senior's pain.

"You haven't been around for many of my winning and losing lectures," Thomas said, releasing his hold. "By showing up today, you along with Douglass saved five crucial points. And the team may be grateful for that."

Chris Ballinger and Tony Kingery stuck with the coach's script, pinning the two Blakemore sophomores just as they did at St. Agnes. The crowd was stunned. Blakemore lost 31-30.

On Friday night, St. Agnes grabbed the headlines for a third time in a week, steamrolling sixth-seeded Webster 42-19. The emotions and the power, though, ran out of the St. Agnes

314

engine on the third consecutive day of the tournament in the semis against Central.

Simply due to a lack of depth, on Saturday afternoon against Central, only Jeff LeMone, Mike Ennis, Greg Shipley and Chris Ballinger won. St. Agnes never got to face the No. 7 team in the nation, Monroe Academy, in the Shore Conference Finals. "Thank God," Thomas said to Father James.

Monroe defeated Central, 52-6.

THIRTY-ONE

"Why is it that someone is always calling or ringing the friggin' doorbell or poundin' on my fucking window whenever I'm trying to friggin' sleep?"

Thomas was mumbling to himself as he stumbled to the front door wearing only pajama bottoms. As he neared the door, his question had reached a fevered pitch.

For the majority of Friday night, Thomas tossed and turned, nodding and waking throughout the night. Twice he walked to the refrigerator, opened the door, shut the door and returned to bed, hoping the excessive nocturnal exercise would create a deepened slumber.

Nothing. So he ran every possible scenario and match-up through his head. The junior varsity season was finished, so he had every eligible wrestler at the varsity's disposal. Unless something outlandish happened, it would be the regular 13 varsity wrestlers who would decide the fate of the St. Agnes season.

No gimmicks.

No tricks.

Twenty-six wrestlers to the mat. The best team takes home the South Jersey Parochial B championship.

Thomas had found an opening in the Lancer schedule to scout St. Luke's out of Mill City Bridge near the Delaware border. It was a solid squad top to bottom, so there was not much he could do to exploit weaknesses.

In his head in the wee hours of Saturday morning, though, he tried. After a while, he was just doing it to tire his mind, but nothing would work. Finally, sometime past 3 a.m., he fell asleep.

Now, at 8:30, someone was ringing the doorbell and knocking at the door. Maybe it was a boy scout. Or a Jehovah's Witness. Someone who wouldn't take up more than a few seconds, then he could shuffle back to his mattress.

Thomas opened the door, hoping to politely decline anything he would be offered. Instead he found himself inviting an old friend into his house, Steven Mullin, presently of the county sheriff's department.

"Shit, Stevie. Did I forget to pay a ticket?" Thomas was scratching his scalp, searching around for a shirt in the living room, finally finding a sweatshirt draped over a chair at the kitchen table.

"Nah," Steven said. "You checked out clean as the choir boy you always were."

Coffee? "All I got is instant."

Sure. The two high school acquaintances exchanged pleasantries, asking how family and friends were. "I see Michelle Jennings broke off her engagement," Steven said.

"Yeah. She's trying to get back into good graces, but you know me, never travel the same road twice." Thomas finished pouring the water into the mugs and pointed out where the milk and sugar were. "I know you're not here to ask me about Michelle, are you Steve?" Thomas was beginning to shake free from the grogginess that temporarily imprisoned his brain. Steven Mullin's presence could only mean haunting news for the St. Agnes wrestling program.

"I understand you have a match tonight," the deputy sheriff said. "We've all been following you in the papers. It's a miracle what you've done."

"Not really. You just point the kids in the right direction and they have enough energy and ignorance to move mountains. I wish you could come tonight. The match is down in South Jersey, though. We were so hot this season that we almost got the higher seed. If that happened we would have bumped the boys' basketball playoff game to Sunday afternoon. Now that's progress at St. Agnes." Thomas forced a smile as he took a sip of coffee. "Which one of the kids is in trouble, Steve?"

There was no sugarcoating it. "One of your kids is under investigation for the use and distribution of a controlled substance. He's been under surveillance for 10 days, and the sheriff's department feels it has enough to arrest, charge and prosecute."

Who is it? "Anthony Kingery and the controlled substance is. . . ."

"Anabolic steroids."

317

Steven shook his head affirmatively. "How long have you known?"

"I actually didn't know until now. I had my suspicions and even confronted him on it. The kids are always on the verge of doing something stupid, so if they're not asking me questions, I'm bugging them – girls, grades, sex, drugs." Thomas rolled his neck around. It was suddenly starting to stiffen up.

"What made you suspicious?" Steven asked.

Thomas heard the question but backtracked before choosing to answer it. "You weren't kidding when you said that I checked out clean, were you?"

No. "It's part of the job."

I understand. "Is your visit here part of the job, too?"

Steven was not offended at the question and welcomed its frankness. "I know how you were with wrestling in high school and how you are with this St. Agnes squad. My ass would be in a world of trouble if they knew what we were talking about."

"When is this all going down?"

"The investigation will wrap up in the next couple of days. Then the officers involved are going to get a warrant for his father's house and for a weightlifting place down on the Evandale beachfront. He should be charged Wednesday – at the latest." Deputy Sheriff Mullin repeated his question. "What made you suspicious?"

The usual stuff. A quick increase in muscle weight. The desire to constantly lift weights. Increased aggressiveness. "But I thought that those all could be just positive side effects from wrestling. So I sat down with him in December and asked him. He denied it and sounded sincere – obviously. I shook his hand – no bloating. He had no water retention. He's had acne since I met him four years ago. As a matter of fact, his skin has cleared up. Then in late January, he snapped at a teammate in practice and that was unusual, so I talked with him again."

Thomas stopped, sat back and reflected, trying to remember his own mindset during these conversations. He was so sure that Tony wasn't lying. There was no reason to lie to his coach. There was no reason to lie to Thomas.

"I'll tell you, Steve. Either that kid had the best poker face or he has ice in his veins or I'm just a sap for wanting to believe in the supposed innocence of youth."

"The area has changed," Steven said. "We're no longer the Jersey Shore, that sleepy resort area just south of the city. We're like Long Island now. We're just another suburb of New York. There's more people settling down. There's more people moving around. I've met more people in the last 10 years than my parents ever met in their entire lives. But Mom and Dad really knew the folks they met. Sometimes I'm not sure if I know anybody anymore. I mean, really know someone.

"And it's the same with the kids in schools. No one knows their neighborhood kids, because the neighbors' kids are always off doing something someplace else. The parents are never around. They're being raised by me and you and some immature parent a couple of miles away. They have no stability. No solid, responsible teachings, and parents don't give a fuck. You'd be amazed at how many of their little St. Agnes angels we actually deal with. St. Agnes is a great example of what I'm talking about. It's no longer a small, Catholic, neighborhood school. It's a regional private school who will accept anyone who is willing to pay the tuition and follow some lax rules."

Thomas and Steven continued the conversation of the disintegration of their little towns' values. Another cup of coffee and another hour passed, and Steven rose, saying it was time to go.

"I have to ask you to keep a lid on my showing up," Steven said. "I just figured I'd tell you to – well – you know. It'll probably be an embarrassing situation and this may help you in damage control."

"Nobody in the department knows you're here, right?"

Not a soul.

"I'll figure something out, but I'll never mention your name. You have my word."

They shook hands. "Good luck tonight."

Thomas made another cup of coffee and sat at the kitchen table and devoured the silence. The late February morning gave no reason to celebrate. The air was damp and cold, keeping all of the creatures hidden, and lethargic humans had not yet emerged from their warm hearths. The scene outside matched his mood inside.

Unmoving, except to sip from his St. Agnes athletic mug, Thomas tried to figure out a solution. He knew he could not let Tony Kingery wrestle, there was no question about that. Suspension without explanation? Have a doctor sideline him for a phantom skin ailment? Have Terry Broughton create an excuse to suspend him from school?

All of the thoughts had possibilities, but Thomas' mind would never let him follow though. As soon as he prepared details for a possible scheme, his mind would quickly take him to the Lancer line-up and Anil Nazif.

From the time Steven Mullin left to well past noon, Thomas sat in the same chair, never rising to eat or piss, only boiling water for instant coffee. His bladder was full from the three cups of Master's Choice, but he did not realize it.

Suddenly, he spoke out loud. His voice was coarse and barley audible. But he did speak. "Give me a hand on this one, Ma. Give me a hand."

He sat for 10 minutes more, trying to keep his mind clear, as if help would actually be sent from above. Nothing. Maybe a shower would help. And as he walked by the telephone, it rang.

It was Michelle. "Getting excited?"

Yeah. Sure.

"Have you eaten yet?"

No, but that sounds good.

"Well, Tammy drove Mom up to the mall and I was in desperate need of a lunch date. How about Tag's for a sub?"

Sure.

"I'll stop over in a little while."

Tag's is a little Italian sub shop in downtown Whiting Beach, so while Michelle spruced up and drove from Evandale, it gave Thomas time to take a shower. The hot water did not dislodge any provocative thoughts from the recesses of his mind, so when Michelle walked in, she immediately saw the heaviness in his face.

"What's wrong, Tommy?"

Nothing. "I didn't get much sleep last night."

"Nervous about tonight, are you?"

Yes.

It wasn't convincing enough, but Michelle fully understood that prying would not help him open up, it would only ensure his silence. So she quickly changed the subject. "So what are you hungry for. Maybe a meatball parm?"

No. "I think I'm going to get a chicken parm today." He attempted to sound spry, so as to be good company for Michelle.

Thomas got a whole chicken parmagiana, half for now, half to be stored in the refrigerator for later. Michelle ordered a hot pastrami, with swiss cheese, on black rye, with dijon mustard and two garlic pickle spears on the side. A bag of chips and a couple of Pepsis. "How about here?" Michelle asked, standing at a table near the door.

"If it's all the same, could we eat in the car. I'll try not to spill any sauce on your mom's seats."

They sat in the car and began unwrapping bags and wax paper and popping the tops of soda cans. After a burst of the crackling seltzer, the two sat quietly, nibbling at their meals.

"Something's wrong," Michelle said. "Can I help?"

Thomas knew, in some way, that she could help, but he didn't know how or where to start. He reached into his coat pocket and pulled a dollar bill of the change he just received from the counter clerk inside Tag's. "If I retain your services as a professional, everything I tell you is in confidence, isn't it?"

"You're my best friend, Tommy," Michelle blurted out, slightly offended by the mock offer of payment for services. Without thinking, she used the term 'best friend.' It felt as if she had said 'I love you' to someone for the first time, and quickly she tried to amend or even retract her statement – not that she didn't mean it – but because she noticed a peculiar look in Thomas' eyes. "Well, you and Tammy," Michelle said meekly, then she instantly sprung back to the topic. "Don't you dare offend me with money, even if you are kidding."

I'm not kidding. "Take the dollar. It makes it legal for what I'm about to say. That way if you're ever approached by some authority, you can claim doctor/patient privilege."

"You're being silly," Michelle said. "Who would ever approach me?" Thomas didn't pull back the dollar, and she realized that he wasn't being silly. "I don't need a dollar. If it ever came to a point that you are referring to, I would never violate our friendship."

Sorry. "I'm just a little squirrely this morning," he said. "My brain doesn't seem to be cooperating."

"Sometimes when something is traumatic or unexpected, it takes the synapse time to realign in order to get the process rolling again. In extreme cases, the human brain never gets straightened out and some people never regain normal thought processes." Thomas stared straight ahead. Michelle stared at

321

Thomas. "Most of the time, talking the problem out is all that is needed." Her technical humor was lost for the moment.

Good enough. "I got a visit from an old friend this morning. I told him that he had my word that I wouldn't mention his name to anyone. So if you figure it out, don't say it aloud."

Okay.

"It seems one of the wrestlers got himself in deep with steroids – buying, using, selling. The investigation is all but done. It's supposed to be wrapped up by Wednesday. This old friend stopped by to let me know so I can keep this kid out of tonight's line-up, because it will turn into an embarrassing situation by next week."

"Who is the wrestler?"

"The small heavyweight. Tony Kingery."

Michelle waited to see if Thomas began to speak, then asked, "Do you know what you're going to do?"

No. "I've got some thoughts. I can suspend him without an explanation, but too many questions will arise from all over the place. Plus, it would tip Tony off that something's up and he might take off, making matters worse. Or I could have the athletic director come up with some in-house excuse to suspend, but that's bogus, plus I'd rather not pass the buck. I was foolishly hoping to come up with some idea to avoid the bad press for Tony, but . . . I had a couple of other ideas, but they sucked, too."

There's only one thing you can do. "Tell him," Michelle said.

"Tell who what?"

"Thomas, you pride yourself on honesty. You're one of the most honest people I know. Honest to a fault sometimes, because you just happen to speak your mind at appropriate and inappropriate times. It's not time to change now. I've watched you closely this year. I've seen you with these kids. They trust you. They believe in you because you treat them like adults. You treat them like friends. Just because Tony made a wrong decision doesn't make him all bad. And it doesn't mean you've done him wrong. At this point, it's not a matter of right or wrong – it's a matter of consistency. Sit down and tell Tony the truth. Make a decision together, just like you would with him in any other situation."

He let her words sink into his mind. That was it. Michelle was right. Whether it would be right or wrong in the eyes of society or the law or Steve Mullin, Thomas needed to sit down with Anthony Kingery and continue to be a mentor, a friend. Figure out how to rectify the situation.

Thomas looked at Michelle and he smiled. "So, I'm your best friend?"

The yellow house paint was faded, looking almost white at points. Paint chips had long blown off into the neighbors' yards or the street, settling into the gutter or near a storm drain, waiting to be washed into a nearby lake. Screens, with faded white trim, remained in place winter after summer after winter, hanging from external hooks. The storm windows sat in a corner of a crowded and damp basement, unused for 11 years. Hinges hung loosely along the side of a door jam where a cheap aluminum screen door once resided, long blown away by a spring squall. An old brown door with two small windows high atop guarded the entrance from unwanted and unwelcomed visitors. The door was not the original, nor the replacement. Those doors were busted down in the heat of arguments back when Anthony Kingery was a baby. A ripped window screen flapped lightly in the afternoon breeze, brushing against half-empty cans of Miller Lite set on a sill. One rusty metal porch chair was placed in the far corner, representing the loneliness of the house.

It took a good five minutes for Tony to answer the door. He had been upstairs, listening to some music, preparing mentally for the evening's match.

"Hey Coach," he said, smiling proudly. "A little early for the match."

Shit. Thomas hated to do this to the kid, but he had to. Tony had cheated and cheaters were not allowed to play.

Tony saw the look in his coach's eyes and knew the jig was up. Thomas declined an invitation into the house, feeling better to take a ride in the truck. There would be less eyes watching the truck.

At the beachfront, Tony cried. He explained how he got involved using steroids. Then it was so easy to sell to the guys at the gym. Guys from the city who came down for the summer. The money came in handy around the house – little things like groceries and clothes. And he was still far behind in tuition. Something like three semesters.

It didn't make it right. And Thomas told him that the only way to succeed was through honest means. It was time to play honest.

"What can I do?" Tony asked.

"First, you can't wrestle." Tony fought back the tears. He didn't want to cry anymore in front of his coach.

"You don't suit up. There will be a lot of questions from parents and teammates, but the only thing you and I will tell them is that there was a violation of fundamental team policies, and we talked it over and the fair thing was to keep you out of the line-up. People will ask what the violation was and you just tell them to talk to me. Fundamental violation of the rules. Talk to the coach."

Tony understood. "What about the police?"

It would be a long, solemn bus ride to Mill City Bridge. Thomas made sure the majority of the team was occupied in the rear of the bus with conversation, sections of the newspaper – which would only be useful a short time longer in the sun's dusk – cassettes and CD headsets, and controversy. Pete Disling and Jeff LeMone were arguing about which was the better hockey team – the New Jersey Devils or the New York Rangers – when Thomas interjected with the Philadelphia Flyers. The argument became more heated and Thomas left the rear of the bus, satisfied, knowing that with the tumult he left behind, he now could have a private conversation at the front of the bus.

The coach's bag, first-aid kits, water bottles and water coolers occupied the large, three-person bench seat behind the driver. Across the aisle in the smaller bench seat, Tony Kingery sat, facing straight ahead.

Father James sat on the edge of the next large bench seat, his feet in the aisle, elbows on his knees, speaking covertly with Thomas who sat across from the priest. Thomas filled in Father James with as much of the details, leaving out the time, place and manner in which he received the information concerning Tony.

Father James sat pensively for many miles down the New Jersey Turnpike. The sun had long since cast its last rays on the late winter at the Jersey Shore. After much deliberation, the priest called Tony into the conversation. Thomas sat back.

"I know you and your teammates look at me as a young, skinny priest with a good sense of humor, full of hope and joy. And I want you boys to think that way, so I act that way every day of my life. It makes me happy, and it makes the people around me happy. The truth is that I was not always like this. I was bitter and cruel, a regular scoundrel and rogue. Just out of high school, back when the legal age to get into bars was 18, I got into a lot of trouble. Drinking, drugs, sex. I don't tell many people this, but it's something you need to hear. I ask that this conversation go no further."

Yes sir. Tony was his captive.

"The conscience is a strong weapon. While I poisoned a good portion of my mind with vices of adolescence, my conscience held its ground. For a few years, I wallowed in self-pity and anguish, until the poison in my mind didn't have its same effect upon me. It did not have the same strength. And my conscience finally fought back. And religion became my personal savior. Now it's important that there is not a misunderstanding. Becoming a priest was my destiny, and I would not imply that it be yours. My conscience brought me fully to God. And you must let your conscience seek the truth also, in whatever degree that may be. But you must do that now, before you sink as low as I did. Because the poisons both you and I have experienced work differently on everybody, and you do not – and should not – test the strength of your soul. Not if it isn't necessary. And this is not necessary."

The flashback had taken some energy from him, so Father James retreated a bit and breathed deeply. In a few moments, he continued. "You realize that this is more than a little sin. You can't rid yourself of this with a little 'Bless me father, for I have sinned,' and then you reciprocate with penance such as a couple of Hail Marys and Our Fathers."

Yes Father.

"Nevertheless, it's not too late to right the wrong. But since you thought you were acting like an adult and you trespassed into adulthood, you have to stay for awhile. Do you agree?"

Tony nodded.

"As an adult, what should you do?"

I dunno.

"Shrugging is an inappropriate response. We should try again."

Tony sat stoically, not wanting to do or say the wrong thing.

"Okay. Let's get more specific. What shall the team do about the heavyweight position tonight?"

"Anil should wrestle."

"And what should the coach tell the team?"

Nothing. "I should tell the team that I broke a major team rule." Tony was quite sure of what the coach wanted. "And I should apologize."

Welcome to the adult world. "Now what do we do about your illegal activity?"

"I wish it would just go away."

"It's not that easy," Father James said. "I wish it were for your sake, but it's not."

"I just want to get it over with. Go to the police and tell them I screwed up. But they'll want names, and there's no way I'm gonna squeal on anybody. One of the coach's rules is never rat on a friend."

"Are these people you're involved with your friends?"

Tony shrugged. Thomas leaned forward to help out the confused heavyweight. "I'd like to make an amendment to that rule, Father. Never rat on your friends and never rat on someone that could cause you or your family harm."

"That's reasonable," Father James said. "Then you go to the police and lay yourself on the mercy of the court. The punishment could be severe if you choose that direction."

There's no other choice.

Father James knew of the financial predicament Tony and his drunken father were in, so there was only one Christian thing to do. "I know some honorable lawyers who would do me a favor. I could ask one of them to go with you to the police station tomorrow. When all of this is behind you and you're raising a nice Catholic family, you can repay the service to me."

Okay. "Can the coach come along tomorrow?"

"That's up to you and the coach."

Tony looked at Thomas. "Sure," Thomas said.

As the crowd began to swell in the St. Luke's gym, Thomas gathered the 20 wrestlers who would suit up for the state championship match and ushered them to the home team's locker room. That excluded Tony Kingery, who sat despondently in the girls' locker room while his teammates weighed in.

If one boy did so, 10 asked about Tony's absence, most of the inquisitors upperweights, the lightweights oblivious as they meandered their way through the massive trunks of heavyweights. "Don't worry about Tony. Worry about yourselves. We'll meet up with Tony in a few minutes."

After the St. Agnes squad left the weigh-ins to return to the girls' locker room to prepare for the match, Father James told the Lancers to suit up "as quickly as humanly possible. We have a vital team meeting before warm-ups."

"Find yourself a seat," Thomas said to each wrestler as he walked into the middle aisle of a cramped locker room. "Grab a seat on a bench or on the floor someplace. No questions, this isn't a press conference."

When they were all settled, Thomas stuck his hands in his jeans and spoke. "We were lucky this year. Other than a couple of minor colds and Greg's outburst that cost him three matches, this team didn't lose a starter to major illnesses, injuries or disciplinary actions. As a matter of fact, I don't think one wrestler missed weight. And I'm proud of that."

Pete Disling raised his hand. "I missed weight against Pope Pius," the sophomore admitted.

"Shut up, Dis," Jeff LeMone said.

Thomas superficially admonished Jeff, then thanked Peter for the correction. "But in this program's first three years, in every match we were plagued by some misfortune, caused by ourselves or some outside force. Tonight, if we want to call ourselves state champions, we must call upon all of our knowledge and all of our power and every ounce of guts we have, because for the first time this season, we will be without the services of Mr. Kingery."

Dressed in street clothes, most of the team already had guessed that much when Tony was not present for the official weigh-ins. Their suspicions were confirmed when they saw the St. Agnes small heavyweight standing next to Thomas. Tony cleared his throat. "Coach Thomas doesn't want me to get into any details except to say that I screwed up and broke a team rule." He stopped. He wanted to simply apologize and get it over with, but his emotions were getting the better of him. Tony glanced at his coach. Thomas raised his chin, took a deep breath to expand his chest and nodded.

Tony imitated his coach and continued. "I want to apologize for letting you guys down." He paused. "This wasn't the

327

way it was supposed to end up. We were supposed to be state champs and I was supposed to be there celebrating, because I was the heavyweight. . . ." His head dipped and Thomas decided that was enough.

"Everybody line up for warm-ups. Father James will you lead them into the gym? I'll be out in a couple of minutes." The wrestlers started to head to the locker room door. Thomas called to Anil.

"For some reason, you stuck it out for this entire season without a spot to wrestle. And you've just showed up at practice every day and blended into the background. And I took advantage of that, because today I need you to fill a void that I wouldn't accept myself. You've wrestled against Tony and given him great matches in practice for the whole season. What I want from you today is to go out and wrestle like you have in practice." Thomas could see that no pep talk would inspire Anil. It was just the type of personality the boy had. Anil had a job to do, and he was going to do it.

"What I'm trying to say is – when you step out onto that mat tonight to wrestle, you do the same thing you've done every day this season. Try." Thomas patted Anil on the back and told him to go join his team.

THIRTY-TWO

The gym was dark and eerily quiet. Only a dome light hanging from the rafters gave any illuminance to the large blue wrestling mat with a formidable Celtic Cross painted in the middle. The Lancers had already completed their warm-ups and a dozen wrestlers nervously marched and paced behind their bench. Anil and the junior varsity wrestlers sat on the bench.

Most of the fans came to cheer on the St. Luke's Crusaders, but a healthy number came to see St. Agnes, including Michelle, Tammy and, for the first time, Mrs. Jennings. The crowd, more than three-fourths hometown partisan, was packed into the tiny gym and overflowing into the hallways. Seven Parochial B South championship banners hung along the north wall, out-numbering all other sports banners by six, the lone exception, a 1976 boys' basketball state title. On the south side, a large mural of a Christian soldier adorned the center of the wall. To its left was the scoreboard, and on each side of it was a tote board, listing the rosters of the home and visiting teams:

St. Luke's		St. Agnes	
103	Andrew Wetmore	Jeff LeMone	103
112	Jeremy Lobosco	Quinton Barry	112
119	Robert Anderson	Pete McKane	119
125	Bruce Hudson	Eric Douglass	125
130	Thomas Dixon	George Galatin	130
135	Preston Rennecke	Brien Cauldron	135
140	Ray LePage	W Sanderson	140
145	Kyle Russell	Pete Disling	145
152	Ted Griffith	Mike Ennis	152
160	Kevin Byrd	Greg Shipley	160
171	Andy Kinard	Mike Masterelli	171
189	John Bennet	Chris Ballinger	189
Hwt.	Willis Shields	Tony Kingery	Hwt.

Like thunder, the door to the boys' locker room bounced open against the inner hallway, 13 wrestlers bolted from the darkness, each purposely slamming the door against the wall.

Metallica's *Enter Sandman* blared over the sound system as the Crusaders sprinted around the mat, eventually matching up with a partner, performing upper-body throws, followed by jumping jacks and push-ups, each drill performed with precision.

Thomas was impressed by the warm-ups. It was enough to discourage any opponent. But not his Lancers. The St. Agnes wrestlers paced nervously in the background, feeding off the music, trusting the junior lightweight LeMone as he screamed at each of his teammates – "Follow my lead. Follow my lead."

The Lehigh Introductions.

Coin toss.

One-hundred-three-pound match. It took two minutes, 23 seconds for Jeff LeMone to post six team points.

It was just as Thomas expected. If the script held to form, the St. Agnes coach calculated a split in the first three weight classes. Strong showing for St. Luke's in the middles. Three out of four for the visitors in the uppers – that was with Tony Kingery in the line-up. To compensate for the loss of their heavyweight, the Lancers needed to steal a victory, and they got it from the freshman 112 pounder.

No sooner had Thomas mentioned to Father James, ". . . sometimes freshmen don't know the magnitude of the situation," Lancer Quinton Barry headlocked Jeremy Lobosco from the neutral position. It took the referee a lot longer to call the pin than Thomas did. As a matter of fact, from his sideline view, Thomas called 11 pins in the 1:41.

St. Agnes led 12-0.

Most of the scoring in the 119-pound match between Pete McKane and Robert Anderson occurred while the two wrestlers were on their feet. Takedown: St. Agnes. Escape: St. Luke's. Takedown: St. Agnes. Escape: St. Luke's. Takedown: St. Luke's. Escape: St. Agnes.

Thomas booted Jeff LeMone from the center aisle seat. "Good job, Jeff. Now go sit next to Anil. See if you can pump him up." Sitting was the only thing Thomas could do. Screaming moves was futile. The 119-pound match was going to be the case where the last man who shoots, wins.

Up 17-14 with 10 seconds left, Pete took that shot and converted it to another takedown. Nineteen to 14, good enough for a decision.

St. Agnes led, 15-0.

The Lancer bench and its fans were elated, while the St. Luke's fans were stunned. Everybody in the building was suddenly braced for an upset by an upstart squad, barely four years old, from Central Jersey. Everybody but the two head coaches.

St. Luke's was loaded for the next six weight classes while St. Agnes had gained a lot of respect during the last two seasons. St. Luke's, though, did not display any of that respect.

A 15-0 lead quickly disintegrated.

Bruce Hudson pinned Eric Douglass. 15-6

Thomas Dixon pinned George Galatin. 15-12.

Undefeated at 19-0, Preston Rennecke put a major decision, 12-2, on Brien Cauldron. St. Luke's took the lead, 16-15.

Ray LePage pinned Willie Sanderson. St. Luke's widened the lead 22-15.

Kyle Russell pinned Pete Disling. 28-18.

Finally, senior Mike Ennis stopped the bleeding. "You can always count on a senior," Thomas told Father James. It was but a mere 5-3 decision, cutting the Crusader lead to 28-21.

"It's a long shot, but there's still a chance. Say a prayer, would you Father?" Thomas said in a whisper.

"I will. But I think they have as much persuasion on the other side."

St. Agnes lined up in the tunnel formation. Thomas walked down the middle and met Greg Shipley nose to nose. "Now's the fuckin' time, Greg. Now's the time to shut this fuckin' crowd up and give us a state championship. Now, go kick the shit out of this kid."

Thomas had a strange confidence that something unusual and grand was going to happen. And it did.

Unexpectedly down 6-1 in the second period, while in a clench in neutral position, Greg Shipley bit Kevin Byrd between his neck and shoulder, right in the middle of his trapezius muscle.

The referee tooted his whistle obnoxiously and continuously, waving his arms, pointing first to the St. Luke's bench, then to the Lancer bench. Greg Shipley began to walk off the mat as the ref ran to the scorer's table.

"Get back out there," Thomas said. Greg obeyed, turning around and skulking back to the center of the mat.

Thomas still was not sure what the cause of the ref's gyrations were, but indicators were not in the Lancers' favor. As the ref started toward Thomas, the Lancer coach saw the trainer inspecting Byrd's shoulder. It was then he understood what had happened.

"Your wrestler bit the St. Luke's kid, the ref said, not quite believing the proceedings. "He's done. For the Districts, too!"

Thomas was too embarrassed to argue, saying only, "Are you sure?"

The ref was positive. And livid. "You want to come and look?"

No.

The referee went back to the center of the mat, forced the two wrestlers to shake hands, a gesture Kevin Byrd did not appreciate nor care to perform. Greg Shipley walked back to a wrestling bench for the last time in his career.

"I don't want to hear it," he said, knowing that his high school career had just come to an ignominious ending. He flipped his headgear lightly against the rear wall and lay on the practice mat.

Thomas bent his body to one knee, put one arm on each side of Greg's torso and leaned down so his nose was an inch away from the wrestler's nose. The coach's eyes squinted as he stared into his wrestler's mind.

"Get the fuck up and sit on that fuckin' bench. I won't cause a scene here, but I will kick the shit out your sorry pussy ass if you think you're going to show me up any more in this program. Now get the fuck up before I break your nose, right here. Right now."

"You're crazy," Greg said. But Thomas did not move, and he wasn't going to until Mr. Shipley either sat on the bench or lay bleeding in Mill City Bridge, N.J. "Alright, I'll sit on the bench." Like a spoiled kid, Greg got up and walked to the far end of the bench.

Thomas could hear Father James fruitlessly call ill-advised moves to Mike Masterelli as Greg chose the last seat on the St. Agnes bench.

Father James was proudly bellowing out moves he had learned during the course of the season. Crusader Coach Dave Insell screamed instructions from his side of the bench. Both sets of fans were screaming for a championship, neither side realizing that the match, for all intents and purposes, was over. Nobody noticed that Thomas was engaged in a battle for the respect of his 160 pounder. Nobody but Mrs. Jennings and her girls. "He's gonna blow, Mom," Michelle said.

With the crowd screaming for Andy Kinard to finish off Mike Masterelli for a 40-15 St. Luke's lead, Thomas topped the decibel charts. "Not there. Right here."

Most of the crowd continued to cheer, but many became interested in the development on the Lancer bench. Defeated once already, Greg Shipley was not about to test his luck. Hell, he had heard that Thomas won a silver medal in the '88 Olympics.

Trying to save face, Greg Shipley rose and strutted in front of the bench, arriving at the seat Thomas was pointing to. Greg slumped into the chair. "Don't fuckin' move," the coach said loud enough for the front few rows of fans to hear. Some were in shock. Some smiled. A few clapped.

And Mike Masterelli was decked.

"Line up." The coach called for his depressed gang. "This ain't over yet. We still have two teammates to cheer on."

Everybody but Greg Shipley lined up. Thomas walked back to Chris Ballinger and shook his hand. "You and a couple of your teammates have been through some of the most interesting times in wrestling I have ever witnessed. I thank you for sticking it out and for giving pride to this program. I'm going to ask you for one more favor. Will you shut this damn crowd up?"

Chris Ballinger smiled. He pinned John Bennet with a vicious cross-face cradle at the 1:37 mark of the first period. He shook hands with Bennett, then with Father James and finally coach Tom.

"Pussy," he said passing Shipley. Ballinger was 19-0. St. Agnes trailed 40-24.

There was no expression on Anil's face. There never was.

"Well Anil, you got more than just an activity to list on your college transcripts. You got to captain a state runner-up in wrestling. Now finish off your career in style." Thomas snapped the senior's headgear and patted the piece of equipment on both sides of his head. "Good luck."

Anil smiled. "Thank you, Coach."

As Anil lumbered out to the center of the mat to face Willis Shields, Thomas couldn't help but feel as if he had taken advantage of this heavyweight. Anil stuck it out for two seasons, taking a back seat, first to Chuck Garrison, then to Tony Kingery, never garnering much attention from the head coach.

Willis Shields snuck in two underhooks, and Anil was in quick trouble. At that exact time, Thomas thought maybe he used all of the wrestlers, not just Anil, to accomplish something he had long ago failed to do. Maybe it was the championship Thomas was after all along. Maybe the coach was fooling himself, telling himself that it was for the kids. Thomas stayed at St. Agnes for the kids, to teach them how to be men. That was how he always rationalized it.

No. That was bullshit. As Willis Shields turned the underhooks into a devastating bear hug, Thomas decided that he was the most selfish man in the sport.

Anil went crashing to his back.

St. Luke's won the state championship, 46-24.

OFFICIAL BOXSCORE

103 - Jeff LeMone (SA) p. Andrew Wetmore 2:23; 112 - Quinton Barry (SA) p. Jeremy Lobosco 1:41; 119 - Pete McKane (SA) d. Robert Anderson 19-14; 125 - Bruce Hudson (SL) p. Eric Douglass 1:04; 130 - Thomas Dixon (SL) p. George Galatin 5:34; 135 - Preston Rennecke (SL) md. Brien Cauldron 12 -2; Ray LePage (SL) p. Willie Sanderson 1:49; 145 - Kyle Russell (SL) p. Pete Disling 4:29; 152 - Mike Ennis (SA) d. Ted Griffith 5-3; 160 - Kevin Byrd (SL) by disqualification over Greg Shipley; 171 - Andy Kinard (SL) p. Mike Masterelli :25; 189 - Chris Ballinger (SA) p. John Bennet 1:37; Hwt. - Willis Shields (SL) p. Anil Nazif :18.

THIRTY-THREE

At the 9:30 mass on Sunday, Father James told the story of the St. Agnes wrestling team, how hopes and dreams could be worked for in such hard fashions and then could devastatingly crumble. "It is similar to being in the middle of a wondrous dream only to be awakened by a telephone call from your boss telling you that you're late for work. Which is exactly what the Monsignor had to do with me this morning. Watching those gallant young men wrestle sure did exhaust me."

Michelle laughed. If she had an avocation within her chosen field, it would be dream analysis. She had no formal training but occasionally read on the matter. She had a habit of jotting down dreams in the note section of her appointment calendar, if she could recall them. Once in awhile she would elaborate on dreams in her diary, but most often, like all others, she simply forgot about them before she awoke.

Mrs. Jennings stopped to talk to some friends while Michelle and Tamantha went to speak with Father James.

"Those were very nice things you said about the wrestling team and Thomas," Michelle said.

"But you didn't give yourself any credit," Tamantha added.

"I was just along for the ride. And it was some ride." Father James laughed infectiously. "I think I have whiplash." He rotated his neck counter-clockwise, grimacing animately.

"Well, maybe next year the dream won't get interrupted. Maybe it will turn out differently," Michelle said.

Perhaps. "Speaking of dreams, I've been meaning to ask you ladies if you ever dreamt of your future husband?"

Tamantha said no. Michelle did not understand.

"She arrived late that match, Father," Tamantha said.

Father James felt obligated to give his quickest version of St. Agnes's Eve. "Now be ready next year."

Michelle's heart quivered. She suddenly and desperately wanted to get home, but Tamantha kept the conversation going.

"Have you seen Thomas? We tried calling him all of last night after we got home, but he either wasn't home or didn't want to answer the phone.."

"I suspect he may have been out," Father James said. "That was not his envisioned ending. Losing would have been fine, but not the manner in which it happened. He did, though, have an appointment this morning, so he couldn't have stayed out too late."

Michelle was curious about where Thomas was. "An appointment?"

Yes. "But I'm not sure if I could speak about it just yet. I think it would be better for me to remain silent, which, as you both realize, is rather hard. Thomas should be home in a little while. Then he'll be able to tell you."

Tamantha began to form another question, but Michelle tugged at her elbow. "The Father has many more parishioners who want to bug him." Michelle winked at Father James. He smiled in return.

"Let's get Mom. I need to get home."

"What for?"

Goodbye Father.

Michelle went straight to her old room but could not find her appointment book. It wasn't there. To the living room and her valise. No.

"What are you looking for?"

"My address book. You know – the appointment binder."

"I saw it on the phone stand."

Michelle ran to the phone and nervously unbuttoned the leather bound book. She flipped back and forth past the NOTES page at the back of the book, finally finding what she wanted. January 7. January 10. January 12. January 18.

January 20. 'Dreamt that Thomas and I were knee deep in snow, building a snowman. We had moved far away and everything seemed so simple. Thomas seemed so happy.'

"Shit." Her heart pounded. Her back knocked against the wall and she slid to the floor.

"What is it, sweetheart?" Momma Jennings asked. "What's the matter?"

A tear rolled from her left eye and splashed onto the NOTES page. "I had a dream about Thomas on St. Agnes's Eve."

Tamantha smiled. "I told you so!" She was both elated and sad.

Up before the morning sun, Thomas drove to the oceanfront in Whiting Beach, then followed Ocean Avenue north through Galway and into Evandale. Three decades on this planet and he had never seen a sunrise over the ocean.

He stood with a cup of coffee on the Evandale boardwalk, amazed at how the sun first peaks over the line of the horizon, then slowly becomes more brazen, lifting itself higher and higher, sending forth pinks and purples and periwinkles into the cool winter air. He laughed at how all the old-time television cartoonists captured the scene so easily. He was waiting for the sun to yawn, zip back down past the horizon and sleep for another hour, just as the cartoonists played it to Thomas when he was young.

To Thomas, youth meant adventure. It meant curiosity. He empathized with Tony Kingery as far as understanding what it was like to explore. But in that 13-year difference between pupil and coach, times seemed to have changed. Teen-agers are growing up a lot quicker these days, Thomas thought. They take on adult personalities and adult problems much too quickly. It is as though life, today, was making kids skip a step.

After finishing his coffee, Thomas headed west toward Millersburg, found County Road 419, and slowly drove past the Burke Sand and Gravel Pit. The truck circled to the south back toward Thomas' house and then swept once more to the north, this time touring the business districts of Whiting Beach, Galway and Evandale. He could've closed his eyes for the sojourn. He knew every inch of the way.

He understood how somebody like Tony Kingery ended up in trouble. With no clear guidance and only minimal amounts of choices, exploring the wrong paths was inevitable. Young or old, whether it was steroids or recreational drugs or sex or gin mills, a person without choices will eventually linger at places they would rather not be.

As eight o'clock came upon Thomas, and as he came upon the battered house with chipping and faded yellow paint, he decided that everyone needs a challenge. Something that makes a person jump out of bed every morning to make sure that his sun doesn't yawn and dive back to the east.

Tony found that challenge. He had awoken and was out of bed, showered, dressed and on the porch more than 30 minutes before Thomas arrived. Sitting in the lonely chair on the dreary porch, Tony was ready to do the right thing. It would be his challenge forever again.

"Ready champ?" Thomas asked as he stood with one foot on the porch, one foot off.

"I'm scared, Coach."

"I know," Thomas said. He had been wandering, in his pick-up, trying to find the right answers and the right words, yet still, at this moment, he had none prepared. "You're only scared because you have to admit that you've done something wrong and, more importantly, of the impending consequences. After you get all of that out of the way, that fear will dissipate. Just do me a favor and try to always remember how you feel at this moment." Thomas watched as Tony gathered up a shoe box full of materials – paraphernalia and money – and walked to the truck.

"C'mon, Coach," he said. "I'm a wrestler. There's nothing tougher than walking onto a mat, half-naked, wearing a tutu. Right?"

They met Don Harvey, an attorney friend of Father James, at the parking lot of the Evandale police station. Don asked a host of questions with Tony answering them all.

"I have to advise against going into the station with a box full of vials and money," the attorney said.

Tony had been divinely advised. "I won't tell on anyone because that would put me in danger – not only from real people, but also knowing that if I could snitch once, I could snitch again. The police will want something. I want to give them me and this box, and I'm going to pray it will keep me out of jail."

Don Harvey looked at Thomas who, other than the formal introductions, had said nothing. He shrugged at the attorney's inquiring eyes. "Father James told Tony that he had ventured into the adult world, and he wasn't allowed to leave until he fixed his adult problem."

The attorney looked at the coach and surveyed the high school junior. "Good enough. Let's see what we can do."

In the second chair from the far corner of the bar, Thomas sat down, within sniffing distance of the ash tray that held Old Man Jack's cigar.

"Wish I could have been there, kid," Old Man Jack said.

"No you don't. And I'm glad you weren't there because I've seen your luck when you actually show up at the track, and we didn't need any more bad luck with us last night."

Jack called for Bobby. "How 'bout setting the champ up with a few rounds." Bobby drew a bright golden Budweiser from the tap and let a stream of Jack Daniel's flow into a shot glass.

"Old Number 7 and the King of Beers – for the King of Evandale. For tonight anyway." Bobby stuck out his right hand. "Congratulations, Tommy. It was a good run."

"And here." Old Man Jack pulled a Hemingway from his jacket. "It's not a Cuban, but then again, neither are we." The old man held his Jack Daniel's high aloft in the air. Bobby poured himself a quick one, and too, held it high in cheers. "Salud," the bartender said.

Thomas held his glass half as high. Salud. And he tossed back the shot.

"Maybe next year, kid." Jack turned from Monday's entries at the Meadowlands to the wrestling results. "I did have a couple of questions."

"Shoot." Thomas already knew what they were but allowed his friend to ask away. Then Thomas explained that Kingery got himself into a pickle with the law, but he did not elaborate, and that Shipley's disqualification was because of a biting incident which – no – was not permitted in the sport.

Against his initial desires, Thomas found himself entertaining Bobby and Jack on a slow February night at Red Mike's. Blow by blow, he gleamed as he spoke of the team's performance, even defending Shipley to a point. "Man, it was embarrassing, but the kid did say he wasn't going to lose for the rest of the season. I guess he didn't know that a disqualification counts as a loss."

He spoke of Chris Ballinger, who hadn't lost all season, and Anil Nazif, who had never won in high school. Yet, they both had the hearts of champions.

"How many kids are coming back next year?" Bobby asked.

The team was in good shape. Balanced, with a lot of young kids, although the upperweights will be a bit thin in their ranks. "I just don't think I'll be back."

"Aw, bullshit. You'll be back," Old Man Jack said.

About two, maybe three weeks remained in the season, the individual portion. "I'll finish it out, then I'm going to take a vacation. The time off may help change my mind, but I doubt it. I think I'm going to hang up my wrestling shoes for good this time, Jack."

Then what? "Back to the bar scene. Every night. Different gals. A couple packs of cigarettes. Tommy, you pulled yourself away from that crap. Don't slip back into it."

Thomas twisted his mouth around and took a sip of beer. He had been toying with the idea for some time, only a few things actually kept him from seriously considering it. One was Old Man Jack. "I was thinking of taking off – maybe going to California to see my brother. Or maybe go back to college. I don't know. A change."

"For how long, kid?" Old Man Jack suddenly felt lonely. "For good?"

Maybe. "I don't know. Maybe not," Thomas said. He hurt inside, but his home where he had grown up had nothing left to offer. Not now anyway. "Regardless, you'll just have to save some of your fuckin' winnings and fly out to see me – wherever it is. There's horse tracks and dog tracks all around the country. Hell, I may end up dealing cards in Vegas." Thomas was attempting to pick up the mood.

"Shit, I'll pay rent if you end up in Las Vegas." Old Man Jack also wished not to be sad.

The two friends sat and talked of all the places they wanted to visit. In the next hour they covered all seven continents.

Thomas loved the Sunday nights in February. It was too cold for most people to venture from their warm nooks. And most regulars were recharging after the exhausting Yuletide, New Year's and Super Bowl marathon season. At nine o'clock, only the bartender and the two patrons in the back corner of the bar remained.

"Hey, how about them gals – the two sisters that like you so much?" Old Man Jack asked.

340

Thomas was about to give his take on the matter, when the door opened, revealing a beautiful black-haired doll. She delicately pulled off the hunter green cotton gloves and put them in her overcoat. She walked with confidence, maturity and elegance, a sight that had long been seen in Red Mike's.

Vodka Collins, she said to the bartender. She sat three seats away from Thomas, past the elbow in the bar.

"Hello."

"Hello," Thomas and Old Man Jack said.

Bobby set down the Vodka Collins and looked at Thomas. Thomas motioned with a nod to the pile of money on the bar. "Could you get another round, Bobby?"

"It sure is frigid out."

"Sure is," Thomas said. Old Man Jack wanted to say 'much too cold for a lovely lady like yourself,' but he refrained, knowing that she was not there to see him.

Thomas sat quietly, nodding his head, not knowing what to say. "Oh – Jack," he said, gesturing to his right, remembering his manners.

"I've heard much about you."

"And this is Michelle Jennings."

"And I've heard a lot about you," Old Man Jack said, putting a lighter to his dead cigar.

"I've been looking for you everywhere," Michelle said to Thomas. "Four or five bars. Funny thing, every bartender knew you."

"They probably knew you, too. Most of them graduated from Covington. All of 'em had a crush on you." Thomas enjoyed kidding around with Michelle. He was going to miss her. "Why were you looking for me? Something dire?"

"We saw Father James following mass this morning. He was very tight-lipped about your whereabouts." Michelle took the straw from her Vodka Collins, laid it on the bar and took a sip from the drink. "I called your house all morning because I wanted to speak with you. It was past lunch when I finally called Father James. He reluctantly told me about Tony and the police. Then he gave me some pub names you like to visit."

Bobby stood a few feet down the bar lightly dunking some glasses in dishwater. Old Man Jack put his cigar into an ash-laden tray and stared – but saw nothing – at Monday's entries. Thomas searched his amber beer, not knowing how to reveal his nomadic intentions. And Michelle decided simply to continue.

It's a funny thing. "Evidently, Father James likes to tell the story of St. Agnes's Eve. And, well, I wasn't there when he told Tammy about the legend back in January."

Thomas didn't know what to think. What was going to be the next line from her lips? Who dreamt of whom? Did it really matter?

"Tammy always said we belonged together. I told you that." Michelle looked down at her drink. "Recently, I thought that Tammy had it all wrong. I started noticing things. The way she looked at you. The way she spoke about you. I began to think that it was you and Tammy who belonged together."

Thomas shook his head. "It's just a myth. St. Agnes's Eve is a legend. Tamantha and I will never. . . ."

Mysteriously flooding the air in the venerable Red Mike's bar were hopes and dreams and myths and legends. Michelle wanted them all. She so desperately yearned for Thomas, and she interrupted. "You are my best friend Thomas, and I love you. I have always loved you. It wasn't Tammy who dreamt about you that night. It was me. I wrote it down in my journal, but I just learned from Father James this morning about the legend. Maybe it isn't just a myth. And maybe it isn't just a legend. Maybe dreams do come true. And maybe for once in your life, Thomas, you're wrong."

Epilogue

The alarm began buzzing, but Thomas did not move. The house still smelled of Thanksgiving turkey and thick brown gravy. The lingering scent of pumpkin pie wafted through the air.

Thomas heard the beeping but chose to ignore it. His mind could turn it off, but his body chose not to. It was too cold for him to emerge from beneath the sheets. And if he did get up, all that waited for him was a fresh foot of snow outside.

Finally, movement, and an arm stretched out and ever so gently tapped the top of the alarm clock. Michelle found his arms and his legs and coiled herself around her husband. "Why did you set the alarm? You don't have class today."

Hmm. "Habit."

"What do you say we go outside later and build ourselves a snowman."

And sometimes you just step in it.